THE FAMILY TREE

A PSYCHOLOGICAL THRILLER

S.K. GRICE

Cover Design and Interior Format

© KILLION
THE
GROUP INC.

Author's Note

This is a work of fiction. Certain police and law procedures may or may not reflect true life processes. Even after research, they have been modified for dramatic effect.

For seekers of truth.

PROLOGUE

January 7, 2020

THE LETTER IN my hand was addressed to me, Jolene Parker, and postmarked from my hometown of Lighthouse Beach, Virginia. As with the others, the sender had used the same block-style handwriting and bogus return address.

I slit the envelope. Through the folded waxed paper, I saw the distinctive oblong shape of a red oak leaf. Chills rattled across my shoulders as dread pressed against my chest.

Darkness fell around me. I would never be free.

CHAPTER ONE

August 3, 2003

THE CICADAS IN the forest hissed like electricity on the night my life changed forever.

I parked my Camry in the driveway of the wood-sided farmhouse. This wasn't my place, but it was where I'd grown up. The home belonged to my best friend, Annette, and her mother Patsy—the closest thing I had to family. The only place where I got the love I craved.

But Annette had been avoiding me for the past two weeks. I'd meant to drive over and ask her what the hell was going on, but then she'd texted earlier today. Said her mom was down in the Outer Banks this weekend, and could I come over to chill tonight? Now, I'd find out what had been on her mind.

Bottle of Chardonnay in hand, I stepped into the humid night. Fireflies twinkled in the darkness over the freshly cut lawn.

A warm glow came through the screened front door, lighting the steps up to the verandah. The soothing voice of Nora Jones rolled outside. I walked into the living room where the comfort-

ing undertone of baking bread lingered in the
air. My muscles relaxed. Patsy's home did that to
me. Immediately put me at ease. The soft sofa and
armchairs in seafoam green were so fresh and airy
compared to the cramped home I shared with
my alcoholic father and his dimwitted girlfriend.

"Hello? Anyone home?" I set the bottle of wine
onto the pine coffee table and turned down the
CD player.

Annette pranced down the stairs in her fave
hip-hugging running shorts and sports bra, her
long brown hair pulled into a high ponytail. Her
tanned skin glistened like she'd just finished a
workout. "Damn, girl. It's about time you got
here."

I pointed to the wine. "I brought something to
celebrate our last week of summer."

"I have something better." She unfolded a piece
of aluminum foil and revealed two small squares
of paper, each with a purple dot.

LSD. I'd seen the stuff floating around our college campus. I crossed my arms. "What's this?
Back-to-the-sixties night? When did you start
doing acid?"

A rascal-grin spread on her face. "I've already
tried some. Last week with Nancy." She held out
the squares. "Come on. Let's have an adventure
before we head back to college next week."

Adventure. I'd worked my ass off all summer
and deserved some excitement. Blood surged
through my veins, then slowed. I licked my lips. I
wanted to live life to the fullest. Experience new
things. Was I game? No. Caution took over. "I

don't know. I had enough drugs when I was in the psych ward." I nudged past her and headed toward the bar cabinet on the other side of the room for two wine glasses.

"Don't be a baby." She huffed and followed me close. "This isn't that zone-you-out stuff they gave you in the hospital. I got this from Jackson. He's careful."

I rolled my eyes, then set the glasses on the coffee table. "Of course, we should trust the local drug dealer."

"I'm telling you—this batch is clean. Totally safe." She waved the foil in front of my face. "Come on. We'll see rainbows and butterflies. You'll never laugh harder in your life."

The spot on the paper looked so miniscule— just a tiny drop of ink. How much harm could it do? "I dunno. You're talking about the cool psychedelic trips. What about the bad ones? The kind that fuck people up for life? I'm not screwing up my mind."

"Too late for that, you wacko." She elbowed me. "Trust me. We'll have the best night ever."

A smile pushed on my lips. Annette was the only person who believed I wasn't looney. And she had a serious knack for making risky situations sound harmless. She'd encouraged me to jump back on the horse that bucked me off. Challenged me to surf big waves. Dared me to fuck the cute surfer dude in high school. Like an extroverted big sister, she'd pushed me out of my shell and given me the best times of my life. Taking acid wasn't any different.

"I'll make a deal with you." Annette's eyes twin-kled with her familiar infectious charm. "If you take this with me tonight, I'll go to one of those pretentious sorority parties with you this year."

I blew out a puff of air. An incentive. I'd tried all last year to get her to join me for one of the themed parties, but she'd detested the Greek life. And this was my chance to get her away from the slackers she'd been hanging out with at school. I straightened my shoulders. "And you'll stay for more than an hour?"

"I'll stay as long as you want." One hand went up in an oath. "I promise." She picked a blotter off the foil and popped it into her mouth, coax-ing me with her devilish grin.

I shrugged, then put the other piece on my tongue and swallowed. A granule of bitterness trickled down my throat. Flutters of anticipation rippled through me. I'd done it again—impul-sively followed Annette for the promise of excitement. Now I could add tripping on acid to my list of been-there-done-that experiences. I rubbed my hands together. "How long until it kicks in?"

Annette sat on the couch and poured the wine. "It took about forty-five minutes, maybe an hour, before Nancy and I started hallucinating. It's all laughs from there."

I plopped down next to her and held up my glass. "A toast to our last week of summer." We clinked glasses and I took a long sip of the cool, dry wine.

Creeeeak.

My heart slammed into my chest. The sound had come from the kitchen at the back of the house. "What the fuck was that?"

Annette jumped up and tip-toed toward the kitchen. "Hello?"

An eerie second of silence sliced through the room. My throat went dry. Willow Road was a dark and isolated rural backroad. Two miles long, it dead-ended at a loblolly pine-forest reserve. The nearest neighbor was at least a quarter of a mile down the road.

Slam. The back door.

Fear shot up my spine and I leaped from the couch. Annette grabbed my arm, yanking me toward the front door.

We were almost there when a powerful pull on my hair jerked me backwards so hard, I had to twist my body around to stay on my feet. I locked eyes with Mike Morton, the alcoholic beach rat who slummed around town. Hot rage pulsed through my blood, and I grabbed his wrist, trying to wrench free from his grasp. "Let go, you asshole!"

"Stop, Mike!" Annette shouted. "Let go of her. What do you want?"

He tightened his grip on my hair and twisted and pulled so hard that I felt my scalp pull away from my skull. My eyes watered as my mind scrambled for a defense. He aimed a long, serrated knife an inch from my cheek then glared at Annette with bloodshot eyes that nearly popped out of his face. "Give me all your money."

His hot breath drifted past my nose—whisky

and sewage. In my peripheral, Annette rummaged through my purse. The cold steel tip of
the knife touched my cheek, but I didn't flinch.
For a moment, I thought I might reason with
Mike, yet my slightest twitch might trigger him
to push the blade into my throat. My heartbeat
pounded in my ears.

"Here, Mike." Annette extended her arm with
my wallet in her hand. "Take this. You could've
just asked." Her voice was close to a whisper. "We
would have—"

Mike was as slight as Gumby. Still, he tossed me
aside with the strength of a linebacker. I slammed
into the ground, my elbow smashing onto the
hardwood floor. Sharp pain rammed deep into
my bone.

"Gimme that." Mike snatched the wallet from
Annette and scowled at the three twenties I'd just
withdrawn from the ATM. "This all you have, you
stupid slut?" He threw the wallet on the floor.

Tears had filled my eyes, each breath burning
my lungs. I had to get us out of this.

Annette held out her hands. "Yes. It's—"

"Fuck you." Mike slapped her hard. She stumbled backwards and grabbed the rail on the
staircase. He huddled over her, the knife raised
and pointed to her neck. "I know you rich-ass
bitches have money. Where is it?"

Annette whimpered and cowered against the
handrail, shielding her head with her arms.

I pushed myself up from the floor, my knees
shaking. A prism of light beamed into my vision.
On my right—lead crystal candlesticks on top of

the fireplace mantel. An easy reach.

Grab one. Hit him.

Adrenaline fired through my blood, igniting every impulse to act. My hands clenched then unclenched.

Hit him. Hit him.

I had only one chance.

Mike circled the knifepoint around Annette's ashen face. "I'm going to slice you up if you don't tell me where the money is."

My eyes stayed fixed on Mike's back as I lifted the heavy candlestick from the mantel. I held it tight, took three wide and calculated steps and then whacked the heavy square base into the back of his head. His skull cracked—the smashing-pumpkin sound so clear that it turned my stomach. Bitter bile surged up my throat.

Mike dropped the knife and turned to me. His eyes crossed, glazed in confusion. Blood dripped from his nose. He opened his mouth to speak. "Ggggh, gggh."

Fuck. What had I done? I backed up to the middle of the living room as Annette rushed to my side.

Mike reached for me and I held up the candlestick, ready to defend myself with another blow. Then his legs swayed…and he collapsed to his knees like a broken string-puppet.

I held Annette close, trembling and looking down at Mike. His arms twitched, and he rolled to his side, eyes fluttering.

I cupped my hand over my mouth to contain my scream. I'd never hurt anyone. Not even in a schoolyard fight or a mean-girls brawl. The only time I'd had the need to protect myself was when I'd been hospitalized and molested by my trusted therapist. But back then I'd been a defenseless, over-medicated minor, so that didn't count.

Annette dropped to her knees and brushed the scraggly hair from his eyes. "Poor Mike." Her tone was soft and deliberate. She smoothed her hand over his bloody face like she was soothing his injury.

I tossed the candlestick onto the couch and closed my eyes. What had I done? The darkness behind my eyelids dripped with blood and I covered my face with my hands, trying to block out the image. My breaths came shallow and fast. I heard Annette's voice. A whimper, a pleading. I didn't want to look.

A scuffing of scratchy feet came from the verandah. I opened my eyes, and the room spun. The rustling of shrubs. I pulled back the sheer curtain at the front living room window and looked outside. Pitch black. Most likely a raccoon.

The sickening sound of gurgling and gasping brought me back to the moment. Mike was alive. He could be saved.

Get help.

I dug my hand into my purse, searching for my phone. "I'll call an ambulance."

Annette jumped from the floor and grabbed my arm. "It's too late." Her skin whitened, and I saw my own fear reflected in her face. "He's dead." Her tone was as heavy and flat as a slab of marble.

Every hair on my body stiffened. Mike's lifeless body lay sideways on the floor, a trickle of blood seeped from his ear, and his plastic-looking doll eyes stared at nothing. Nausea rolled through me. I splayed my hands over my face, trying to register what I'd done.

I'd just killed a man. A man I knew only from his loser reputation.

But it had been an accident. He'd threatened my life. Annette's life. This was self-defense. "We have to call the police." Though I wasn't sure what I would say to the operator. *Hello, I'd like to report an accidental death.*

"No. No police." Her voice had turned deep, steady, and she stared me down. "We can't get the cops involved."

I'd never seen this side of Annette; even the angles on her face looked sharper. Neither of us were thinking clearly. "But we've done nothing wrong! He invaded your home—this was self-defense."

Annette's nostrils flared, and her blue eyes darkened. "The asshole deserved to die."

My skin tightened, pushing tiny hairs to the surface. Her guttural voice sounded like it had come from someone else. "What? Why—how can you say that?"

She blew out a breath. "I've been meaning to tell you something." She paced the floor in front of Mike's body. "Remember the party at Bulldog's beach house? The one you couldn't make?"

Bulldog's parties were legendary, and I'd been annoyed I couldn't get off work early that night.

"That was three weeks ago."

"Right. Well, I got wasted. Drank way too many shots. The house was packed. Somehow, I got separated from Denise and Nancy. I wound up having a few laughs with Mike." She sighed. "He was being nice, you know?" Her voice cracked, and she hung her head.

I recognized the tortured look of shame, but this wasn't the time for her to sort out feelings. "What happened, Annette?"

"The house got really hot and crowded, so Mike asked me if I wanted to go walk on the beach… get some fresh air." She moved to the staircase and sat on the bottom step, like telling the story was draining all her strength.

I slid into the space next to her on the step. "Make this quick."

She cupped her hands over her bent knees and looked to the floor. "As soon as Mike and I were on the trail to the beach, he surprised me with a punch to my face."

My hand went to my mouth, catching a gasp. "The bruise on your cheek…."

Her fingers traced the spot on her face where the cut had just healed. The same side he'd hit and made red again tonight. "That wasn't a door I ran into, but his fist. I tried to run away, but he was too strong. He dragged me to the dunes and… and he raped me." She put her face in her hands, hunched over, and rocked.

I patted her back, trying to stay calm instead of hurt that she hadn't told me sooner. I could have helped her somehow. But we had a bigger problem to deal with now. I needed to stay calm for Annette's sake.

She lifted her head, redness spreading across her face. "I tried to fight him off, but—"

"Okay. It's okay. I know his small frame is deceiving." My hand moved to my sore elbow. Nothing compared to the violence he'd inflicted on Annette.

With slumped shoulders, she looked straight ahead. "After he raped me, he just zipped up his pants and walked away. Not a word. I was dizzy and disoriented. Totally lost. It took a long time to find my way out of the dunes."

"This is why you've been acting so weird for the past couple of weeks." I swallowed my hurt. She knew about the molestation I'd experienced in the hospital and how no one had believed me. We'd always shared our deepest secrets. "Why didn't you tell me when it happened?"

"How could I tell anyone? Everyone at the party saw how drunk I was. People would've seen me happily go down to the beach with Mike. My lip was cut. I was a mess. I couldn't go back and face anyone, so I crawled into Nancy's car and slept. When Nancy and Denise got back to the car later, I told them I wasn't feeling well. Didn't say a word the whole ride home." Annette took a long breath.

"They dropped me off at my house and I drove straight to the police station and asked to speak to a female officer. I started telling my story, but once I realized I'd have to do a rape kit and that people would find out what happened... well, I retracted my statement."

"Does that mean they have the rape on record?"

Annette shook her head. "The police lady, I don't remember her name, but she told me that she was retiring in a couple of days, and that someone else was going to take over the case. That's when I started to panic. I didn't want the word to get out about what had happened to me, especially to my mom. So, I told her that I'd changed my mind—that I didn't want to press charges. That I was drunk and had gone with Mike willingly. She seemed disappointed with me withdrawing my statement, but promised that since no charges were filed, there would be no record of the rape."

"Did you ever tell your mom?"

Color drained from her face. "No. And you can't tell her. I don't want her to know. Especially now. After this. She couldn't handle this...I can't hurt her this way." Sweat dripped down the side of her face. She looked around the staircase rail at Mike's lifeless body. "Ever since that night, I wanted to kill him."

"He's dead. He can't hurt anyone. Not anymore."

"We're not calling the cops, Jolene." Her tone was as serious as the expression on her face. "That policewoman was nice, but she'd taken notes, you know. This could look like premeditated murder."

"Don't say that—"

"And think about it, do you really want to deal with glaring lights and police while we're tripping?"

Fuck. I'd forgotten we'd taken acid. Besides a bit of weed, the only drug I'd ever had in my body had been the mind-numbing injections at the hospital. Never had a hallucinogenic and had no idea what to expect. Heaviness pressed on my shoulders. It just didn't feel right to not report what happened. "It was self-defense. It's not hard to see what happened here."

Annette groaned. "Try explaining that to the police when they show up and you're busy talking to John Lennon in a Tibetan temple. 'Cause that's what's about to happen. And when they see you acting crazy, we'll both face a murder rap. Pre-meditated murder. You'll get sent back to the psych ward and I'll be shipped off to prison."

Murder. Psych ward. Prison. We didn't need more trouble. "Okay. Calling the police while we're high on acid isn't the best option. But we'll have to call in the morning."

"Don't be so naïve. Even if we report this tomorrow, do you think they'll believe anything we say?"

"We'll tell them it was self-defense. W-we were scared."

Annette glared at me. "And you really think they'll believe us?"

"There's a good chance they will."

"A better one they won't."

"Better to tell the truth."

"The truth could get us into trouble."

My throat constricted so tight that my words came out in a whisper. "So, what the hell are we supposed to do?"

She turned toward me. Our knees touching, she squeezed my hands. "We need to stick together. Like a family." Her voice was soft, but desperation undercut her every word. "You know the hole we have in the backyard… the one where Mom was going to put a koi pond?"

I remembered. Annette and I had helped dig the damn thing two summers ago. Patsy had wanted it exactly five feet deep so the fish could stay low and live during the cold winters. The pile of dirt we'd unearthed was still next to the hole. Another one of Patsy's many unfinished projects around the property. "What are you thinking…?"

"We bury him in the pit."

I dropped her hands. "You want to what?" I almost laughed, but she kept a straight face.

"We don't have time to think about this." She glanced at the clock on the fireplace mantel. "It's 9:35. Only twenty minutes since we took the blotter. We can get this over with, and then everything will be back to normal."

"There is nothing normal about burying Mike in your backyard. You need to calm down… think—"

"I am calm. I know exactly what I'm doing." Her words were stone hard, calculated. "We'll bury him right now. It'll be done in no time. Then, tomorrow morning, we'll go to the nursery and buy a small tree. We'll plant it on top of him. Mom's been talking about putting an oak tree there for the past six months. It's perfect."

I blinked several times and tried to make sense of what Annette was saying. She'd always had a risky and wild streak but never a violent or morbid one. She acted like there were no consequences to be considered. I glared at her. "What's happened to you? I've never seen you like this."

"I want to protect us. I don't trust the police in this small-minded town to believe two college girls high on acid."

An ache swelled in my throat. The authorities at the hospital hadn't believed me, either. And it'd taken years to get over the teasing I'd endured at our middle school after word had gotten out that I'd been in a psychiatric hospital. Psycho Girl, they'd called me. Now, at nineteen, I'd overcome that derisive label, and I'd do anything to keep from getting locked up again. I gritted my teeth. What an idiot I was for taking that acid. I couldn't change it now, but this—burying a body—it wasn't right. There had to be another way. I rubbed her arm. "Maybe we should tell your mom what happened. She can help."

Annette's eyes widened, and she pressed her hands together in a beggar's prayer. "No. Please. I want to keep my mom out of this. She'd tell the police. For certain." She grabbed my hands and squeezed and pulled like she was climbing a rope on a sheer wall, afraid of plunging to her death. "I'm protecting us. All of us. If Mom finds out what happened, she'll want to sell the house. We'll move out of state. I'm sure of it. Do you want to do that to her? To us?"

I breathed deeply. The strain in Annette's voice reminded me how desperate I'd been to get out of the psych hospital. How Patsy had come to my rescue. How Annette hadn't been embarrassed to be my best friend, even though the other kids had teased me. I owed her and her mother so much.

Being part of this family had always been important. Patsy, Annette, and me. The Three Musketeers. We'd been together for the past twelve years. My formative years. I was close to them—closer than to my own father, who preferred beer and football over anything to do with me.

If I betrayed Annette, our bond would be forever broken.

And there was vengeance. Annette deserved vengeance. I deserved vengeance. I couldn't blame her for backing out on pressing rape charges against Mike. Life had taught me to avoid situations where I might be shamed or humiliated. If I could help Annette avoid the pain as well, all the better. It was more important for me to support the closest person to me in the world than to take the moral high ground for the sake of someone like Mike.

Burying Mike was the simplest, most logical thing to do. The hole was there. Open and ready like the hand of a hungry child. Above all, I couldn't risk being locked up, and neither could Annette. This was about saving our skins.

"Please," Annette said. "Do this for me. I don't want anyone else to know. Just you and me."

My moral compass had lost direction, but I had to make a choice. Be loyal to my dearest friend or loyal to the law. I felt no obligation to authority, but Annette was different. We were like sisters. My only family. And if I helped her bury Mike, we'd be forever bound by our secret. "How are you going to live in this house knowing he's buried in the backyard?"

Annette jumped to her feet, her face beaming like she'd discovered a cancer vaccine. "I'm going to forget he ever existed. You can do the same."

I turned to Mike's lifeless body crumpled on the floor. Struggling to catch a breath, I wanted to cry out but had no voice. My heart raced. Could I make this happen without ever looking back?

This isn't real.

Annette stood over his body. "Please, Jolene. We need to do this. Now." Urgency threaded her words. She plucked the knife off the floor, then shoved it down the front of Mike's board shorts. She clutched onto one of his wrists. "Grab an arm. We'll drag him to the back."

A twist in my gut made me hesitate. Could I bear holding a dead body? I'd managed to block out unpleasantness before. I'd make sure I did it better this time. I took a deep breath. "I'm ready."

A tingling sensation rose from my core to my scalp, and my mind switched into a fixed gear. I mentally disconnected from what I was doing. Pretended this wasn't happening. *Bury the memory of this night along with the body.* I blocked any emotion which tried to invade my thoughts.

Swallowing what felt like my last drop of saliva, I stayed focused on what needed doing. I grabbed Mike's other wrist. The warmth of his skin shocked me, and I almost let go. But I'd made my decision, so I tightened my grip.

We dragged his deadweight through the kitchen, out the back door, and across the redwood deck. His sneaker-covered feet thumped down the two back stairs.

"One, two, three, four, five…" I counted each step under my breath as we dragged his body across the freshly cut lawn, deep into the darkness of the backyard. Counting had always been my way of coping with stress. After my mother had died, I'd used counting to soothe my fears. It was imperative to keep a precise beat and sequence in order to keep out the dark thoughts.

Thirty steps, I'd counted from the bottom of the deck to the edge of the pit. Twenty-nine, actually, but round numbers fit my mindset.

I dropped his arm.

Sweat rolled down the back of my neck. I lifted my long hair to cool off in the breeze. I took a moment to catch my breath and let my eyes adjust to the dark. Only a sliver of the moon and a sprinkle of stars gave us light.

"Let's roll him in." Annette dropped to her knees and pressed her hands into his back. "Come on! Help me!"

I kneeled next to her, hating what we were doing. Hating even more the risk of getting arrested for murder and going back to the looney bin. Not becoming a teacher. Not getting the hell out of this godforsaken provincial town.

Block it out.

I wrapped my hand around his waist then heaved him into the hole. Gravelly soil rolled over him, and his body hit the earth in a heap, like a crumpled bag of bones.

Feel nothing.

Annette hopped up and wiped her hands on her shorts. "I'm going to the shed for a couple of shovels."

I lifted the hem of my cotton tank top and wiped the sweat from my face. Silhouettes of the hundred-year-old pines surrounding the property swayed against the charcoal sky. My breath kept rhythm with the gentle movement of the forest, slow and steady. I floated outside my body.

"Here you go." Annette handed me a shovel.

My skin tingled as I took myself out of the moment. It was important to feel nothing, to see nothing. I jabbed the shovel downward and loosened a chunk of soil, sending an avalanche of dirt into the pit. Void of emotion, I went into robot mode, tossing shovelful after shovelful of dirt into the pit.

The breeze picked up, rustling the leaves in the overgrown forest surrounding the sides and back of the property. A symphony of sounds—wind and leaves, creaking old trees, the song of crickets and cicadas, each its own ensemble.

Then something else. I stopped shoveling.

Squish, squish, squish. A sound that wouldn't stop. *Squish, squish, squish.*

Running feet on the lawn. I gasped and peered deep into the darkness. Was someone there with us?

Random flickers of light came from the last of the evening's fireflies. In my side vision, a black figure ran from the forest behind us, across the lawn and toward the front of the house. My heart jumped, and the reality of what we were doing jerked me back into myself. "I just saw someone."

Annette jabbed her shovel in the soil and looked around. "No one's here." Her voice was low and raspy. "Come on. We're almost finished."

I shook my head hard, thinking the acid must have kicked in—that I must be hallucinating. Annette had said it would take forty-five minutes to an hour. Had that much time passed?

Didn't matter. I moved back into auto-mode, my head down, counting shovelfuls in sets of five. The numbers were all that mattered. Not the sweat dripping down my back.

The noise again. The squishing footsteps. *Something. Someone.*

I looked up. My equilibrium was off, my vision skewed. A black shadow along the forest's edge. Or was it a black mist? Air sucked out of my lungs. No. This figure was human-shaped, solid and swift.

Nothing seemed normal.

A strange weightiness came over me. My feet were like concrete blocks and my body grew heavy. The pile of dirt was almost gone now, but the earth became soft as a pillow. I sank down down down into the soft ground, the power of the drug being so unexpected that I lost focus.

Red-and-white tail lights of a passing car filtered through the trees. I marveled at the beauty of the streaming ribbons of lights, then remembered what we were doing. "Shit, look."

"Don't worry," Annette said, her tone full of assurance. "That's the Nichols. They go out every Saturday night. I recognize their old-fashioned tail-lights."

She'd know, having lived in this house her entire life. And we'd both known since childhood that this part of the backyard wasn't visible from the street. Especially at night. "This is good." Annette dropped her shovel. "Let's get cleaned up, and we'll deal with the final stage tomorrow."

I slapped my hands together. *Final stage.* She made it sound like we were building a clubhouse.

I walked across the lawn behind Annette who was headed for the hose at the deck. The breeze and the buzzing…the buzzing. I rubbed both my ears. What was that? Cicadas singing so loudly, I floated on the notes.

I stood next to Annette on the deck steps and reached for the spigot. She took my hand and squeezed. "Wait a minute, Joley."

Joley. A tingly rush of euphoria spread from my toes to my scalp, warming my body. My mom had called me Joley. Once in a while, Patsy called me Joley. But hearing Annette use my endearing name deepened my sense of our belonging and connection.

She looked me straight in the face. "What you did for me tonight…." She sighed deeply. "You're like the sister I've always wanted. We're bonded forever. You know that, right?"

A warm rush burst in my heart then spread out to my limbs. My bond with her was more than sisterly, because never had our connection been on a higher, more spiritual level than at this moment. "I've always felt that way."

She nodded an understanding and then turned on the spigot. "Time to get back to where we started an hour ago."

An hour ago? What had we been doing an hour ago? I used the hose to rinse off the dirt, the whoosh of warm water tickling my hands and feet.

I found myself back in the living room, holding a beach towel. I looked at myself, dry and clean except for some specks of dirt under my fingernails. What had I done to get so dirty in the first place? Had anything really happened?

"Now," Annette said in a chirpy tone, "time to get back to business." She picked up our wine glasses and handed me one.

I tossed the towel on an armchair and gleefully took my wine. My vision sharpened. Was it possible we'd never left the house?

Everything looked as it had before. Almost. The walls and furniture were distorted and out of proportion. Had time even passed? I looked at the clock on the mantel, melting like an image in a Salvador Dali painting.

Annette stacked CDs in the player and hummed a bebop tune. Betty Boop. Ha! Annette was Betty Boop in a red flapper dress and short black hair with pin curls. I burst out laughing.

Annette laughed too, like she was in on the joke.

Utter joy flowed through me, and I turned in a circle, enchanted by the dollhouse room with pink curtains and a leopard-print chair. Annette's living room—I knew that—but everything had changed into an animation. And the colors! A kaleidoscope of vibrant magenta, orange, and sunshine yellow.

The space around me luminated, my body becoming light as cotton candy. I swigged a mouthful of wine, and sweet bubblegum burst on my tongue.

Music. The Red Hot Chili Peppers sang "The Zepher Song." I floated a few feet in the air while Annette, now dressed in a white robe, danced a whirling dervish around the room.

Was this a dream?

A breeze brushed over me, and tiny hairs rose on my skin. I tasted the scent of sweet gardenias, and then suddenly, I wore a long, white, flowy dress, like the angels in storybooks my mother had once read to me.

I was so light that I could fly, and I leaped forward, away on the scented breeze, carried by a chorus of cicadas.

CHAPTER TWO

AT SEVEN FORTY-THREE the next morning, I sat in the passenger side of Annette's blue Ford pick-up. My head was as hazy as the mist hanging over the passing farmlands and oyster shacks on the way to the garden center. Though my feet were back on terra firma, my brain was still edging its way back to reality.

No more light and floaty body. Two hours ago, I'd fallen from my high hard and fast, like a drop off a cliff. Bam. Slammed back to reality. Now, just lifting an arm took effort.

Annette and I had spoken few words, each digesting what happened in our own way.

I looked at my hands. I'd scrubbed them hard this morning. Used a nail brush to get deep into the crevices. Still, grains of dirt stayed stuck under my nails. Remorse gnawed at my stomach in small, nagging bites.

Block it out.

The weight of my body sank into the seat. I'd forgotten so many details of last night, but not everything. The sweet, earthy smell of dirt. The hissing cicadas. Someone running across the lawn.

"Jolene." Annette's hard tone broke through

the silence. She stared straight ahead, eyes on the road. "We can't change what happened last night. We have to forget about it. Pretend it never happened."

My skin crawled. I wanted to believe last night wasn't real. But it was real. Real as the red mark on her cheek and the purple bruise on my elbow. Real as the cuts and scratches on our legs. "I don't understand what's happened to you. How can you be so blasé? I killed a man last night. We buried him in your backyard."

"That never happened." Her tone was dead-calm flat. "And I don't ever want to talk about this again. It's the only way."

"I'm worried someone might've seen us burying him."

"How? It was pitch black. *We* could barely see."

"I…I swear I saw someone running across the lawn."

"Who?" Annette tossed me a sharp look.

"I don't know, it was so dark. But I saw something… someone, running from the woods and across the front lawn."

"Girl, we were seeing unicorns and rainbows last night. Remember that part. Forget everything else. It only happened in our imagination." Annette's shoulders relaxed. "Get real. Don't you think if someone saw us burying Mike, they would've called the police by now?"

"My head's so cloudy, I'm not sure what to think anymore."

"No one can see the back of the house from the road. Especially at night. A car would have had to drive onto the lawn with its headlights on to see anything. And that didn't happen."

It was true that Annette's house was set back at least half an acre from the road. But I still felt uneasy. "But what if someone was out for a walk? They could've seen us."

"A walk at ten o'clock at night? Doubt it. If someone saw what we were doing, they would have already reported us to the police. But no one saw, so I'm not worried." She turned up the radio and sang along with the Eagles. "*Take it eeeeasy, take it eeeeasy....*"

I glanced at Annette, her cool face and mechanical movements. Did I really know her? We'd become best friends when we were seven years old and my parents moved to Lighthouse Beach. My mom had been best friends with Patsy for years. After Mom died, Patsy took me under her wing. Annette and I had bonded over our single-child status and had become like sisters. How could she act so calm, not show any feelings of guilt, remorse, or fear?

Annette turned into the parking lot of Old Dominion Nursery. "Okay, dear friend. Let's go buy a beautiful American Red Oak for my mom."

We weren't just buying a tree, though. We were buying a tombstone.

Fifteen minutes later, we drove back to Annette's house with a five-foot oak sapling in the flatbed of the truck, swaying in the wind. We had one thing left to do.

A tidal wave of nausea carried me back to last night. The crumbling crack of Mike's skull. His frozen eyes. Rolling him into the pit. I picked at the specks of dirt under my fingernails. Guilt was eating at me, and I needed to get a handle on what we were getting ready to do. But I remembered our mission. We both had big dreams. Graduate from college. Get the hell out of the backroads and move someplace more promising.

One day, I'd leave this narrow-minded town. All of this would be forgotten.

With effort, I could forget. I'd been forgetting for years. I'd built mental compartments specifically for storing unwanted memories.

My gut twisted. Loyalty versus social responsibility. I didn't want to compromise my loyalty to Patsy and Annette, but I hadn't been thinking clearly last night. Would I have reacted differently if I hadn't taken the acid?

Too late for regrets.

If the truth was discovered, I'd be doomed, sent to jail and ripped away from everyone I held dear. I hadn't intentionally killed Mike. It had been self-defense. But I'd become guilty of murder the moment we'd rolled him into the pit. There was no going back.

Annette turned into her driveway and my heart seized. A white-and-black police car. A grey-haired cop in mirrored aviator sunglasses standing on the verandah. He watched us through hidden eyes, hands on hips and a grin on his face.

Busted.

My heartbeat pounded in my ears. "Someone reported us," I said, trying not to move my mouth in case the cop could read lips.

"I'm not worried about Baker." She smiled and waved at the cop through the windshield. "He's just a hound in heat. Been trying to get a date with my mom ever since he found out she was getting a divorce."

I wiped my clammy hands on my denim shorts. Patsy was a sexy and flirtatious woman, so I had no reason to doubt he'd come by to see her. And perhaps this cop had taken a fatherly liking to Annette. But he was a law man, and he couldn't be trusted. "What's he going to think when he sees our bruises?"

Annette parked next to the police car. "Just act natural and let me do the talking."

Act natural. I wasn't sure how to do that anymore.

She hopped out of her truck and called out, "Good morning, Officer Baker." Her voice was all Southern belle and sing-song sweet. "You here to see my mama?"

Officer Baker moseyed along the walkway toward us. "Yeah. She around?"

I slipped out of the passenger side and kept my distance, afraid that if I got too close, he'd smell my guilt.

Baker stopped at the end of the walkway and shot me an indifferent glance. Then I recognized him. His son went to the same high school I'd gone to, though Noah was a high school senior this year, and I was going into my junior year at college. I doubted Noah's father recognized me.

"Mama's gonna be home later this afternoon." Annette stayed cool and relaxed. "Any message you want me to pass on?"

Officer Baker took a deep breath. "Just let her know I stopped by. I'll catch up with her another time." He took off his sunglasses and wiped the back of his hand across his brow. "Today's gonna be another scorcher."

My feet froze to the ground. I wished the fuck he'd leave, but he scanned the verdant landscape like he was taking in a painting, lingering over every detail and in no hurry to walk away.

Annette jingled her keys. "I'll be sure to let her know."

He slipped on his sunglasses. "Thanks. Have a good day, girls." Walking toward his police car on the other side of the truck, he hesitated at the truck bed. "You girls plantin' a tree in this heat?"

Annette tugged on her loose hair covering the red mark on her face. "It's a surprise for Mama. Always said she wanted an oak tree in the back-yard."

Baker turned his mirrored eyes to Annette. "Uh-huh. You tellin' me, with over twenty acres of forest land, your mama wants to plant another tree?"

Annette stood proud. "Not just any tree. A Southern Red Oak. One that reminds her of her grandma's house in North Carolina. She grew up there, you know?"

He ran his hand over the leafy branches. "Where you puttin' this?"

Sweat beaded on my forehead and I trembled from my core. What the hell was this guy doing?

"We have a spot in the back where she wants

it," Annette said.

"That's a long haul." Baker lowered the hatch on the truck bed and grabbed onto the pot. "Let me carry this for you."

A bolt of adrenaline sent me lunging to him. I gripped his arm. "No. No. Thanks. We've got this."

He looked down at my arm, dotted with bruises, and then two straight lines formed above the bridge of his nose. I yanked my arm away. I should've kept my mouth shut. Annette and I both had unmissable marks on our bodies.

Annette cut between us. "We want the exercise. Jolene and I are trying to get back into shape before we start school next week."

He lowered his glasses and considered us for a moment. "Okay." He laughed and pushed his sunglasses back up. "No sense in trying to argue with a couple of determined women now, is there?"

I laughed along with Annette, but the tension didn't leave my shoulders until he'd backed out of the driveway. "He showed too much interest in the tree," I said.

Annette shrugged then dragged the plastic pot to the edge of the flatbed. "So? What's suspicious about planting a tree?"

I wiped my sweaty face with the back of my hand. "Planting a shade tree isn't suspicious. But we are."

"You think too much." She dragged the potted tree to the edge. "Let's just get this done."

Block it out.

We each held a side of the pot and carried it around to the backyard, and all along I wished this was an ordinary summer day—Annette and I had gone to the beach and hung out with friends and met some cute guys. I'd covered my fair skin in sunscreen while Annette slathered suntan oil over her olive skin. A party was happening someplace at the beach. We were preparing to go. I wanted that. Go to a party. Could we go back to that innocence?

"Set it down here." Annette lowered the potted tree next to the filled-in hole.

I noticed the footprints on top of the soil. *My footprints. Annette's footprints.* Any fear that Mike had been alive and dug his way out disappeared.

Things would never be the same.

Less than thirty minutes later, the tree was planted, backfilled with fresh garden soil and mulched with fragrant pine straw. A sprinkler swished around the roots of the tree. We'd connected the sprinkler to the long garden hose from the house, making certain the sapling had excellent conditions for health and growth.

"It's done," Annette said, picking up the shovels. "And we will never speak about this again." She walked off to the shed in the corner of the yard.

Never speak. Exactly what I'd done after I'd lost my mother when I was nine. Trauma-induced PTSD was what the doctors had told my dad. Not uncommon in children who struggled to deal with grief and death. My silence had worried my weak father so much, he'd agreed to have me hospitalized.

But I was older now and had no choice but to keep quiet. Forget the past twelve hours of my life. Last night didn't count as something that had happened to me. It had happened outside of me, because I'd never been involved in such a horrendous offense. Someone else had buried Mike. I'd only been an observer, a holder of the secret.

I'd find a way to live with the buried secret. Somehow.

It never happened.

"Hello, my beautiful girls." Patsy's voice carried from the deck.

I startled and turned around. My neck ached like it had been stuck in one position too long.

"Mama!" Annette came out from the shed. "You're back early."

Patsy waltzed across the lawn, all sunny personality and golden tan. "I decided to get a head start and beat the traffic." She cupped her hand over her eyes, shielding them from the bright sun while the breeze flicked back her long, sunstreaked brown hair. She stopped at the tree and sighed. "What in heaven's name have ya'll done?"

Behind Patsy, Annette sent me a don't-say-anything-glare then sidled next to her mother. "We wanted to surprise you." She used her perkiest voice. "You've been talking about filling up the koi pond hole and planting a shade tree here since last year. So, we did it."

Patsy looked at the tree, hands on hips. Expressionless.

My knees weakened. Patsy and her flights of fancy. What if she didn't want the tree? Or wanted to move it?

"This is unexpected," Patsy finally said, a smile spreading across her face, "but I like it."

Relief washed over me, and I exhaled a pent-up breath.

"How's my second daughter?" Patsy hugged me, and my body softened in her arms. She smelled like coconuts and sunshine, and I didn't want to let go of her motherly warmth.

The first time she'd called me her second daughter had been after my mother had died. When my grief had spiraled into depression and my father had declared me mentally ill, it had been Patsy who'd taken me under her wing. She'd made me part of her family. How would she feel if she knew the truth about me? The truth about what we'd done? I held Patsy tighter, wishing I could make everything go away and not be the type of person who could do the things I'd done.

Patsy pulled back and looked at me. "Are you doing okay, Joley?" She brushed my bangs off my face. "You look peaked."

I gave a cheerful smile. "I'm just hot from the yard work."

Annette edged in, breathless and upbeat. "Hey, Mama."

Patsy gave her the same bear hug. "How's my baby doll?" She kissed her daughter's cheek. "I just can't believe you girls actually planted this tree on your own."

My hands tingled and I checked them for residual dirt. I'd rinsed them under the hose and picked the soil from under my nails, trying not to leave a speck. But it was there. The grime. The guilt. The urge to wash it all away.

"Look, Mom." Annette pointed to the back of the house. "The hose reaches all the way from the deck to here. You can turn the sprinkler on from the spigot at the house."

Patsy crossed her arms and stared at the tree with a rosy-cheeked smile. "I still can't get over you girls taking on a project like this."

I let the *whish whish whish* of the sprinkler fill a minute of silence. Water dripped off the young sapling's leaves and ran down the skinny tree trunk. I watched the water soak through the soil and imagined it reaching the roots. Roots which needed to flourish. An image flashed. Roots, like long, crooked fingers, clawing at the nutrient-rich corpse. My stomach churned.

Block it out.

Annette swooped in and wrapped an arm over Patsy's shoulder. "Admit it, Mama. The tree looks much better than that muddy hole and pile of dirt." She gave me a conspiratorial smile which clearly meant to assure me this was all over.

I nodded my acknowledgement. I'd promised to keep the secret, and I would stay loyal to Annette. Protect my family. Protect the tree.

Patsy laughed. "You're right. And putting a pond back here would only attract mosquitos, anyway. A shade tree makes a lot more sense."

Avoiding the sprinkler spray, I adjusted the fine green netting loosely covering the branches. "The branches need to stay covered for a few more weeks."

"Don't worry about that, sweetie." Patsy loosened the protective netting like she was adjusting a shirt on a child. "I'll keep those damn cicadas off the branches. God knows I'm ready for that noisy chatter to go away." She circled the tree with a satisfied smile. "This tree will be beautiful one day. Big and strong. I'll hang a swing over the sturdiest branch and watch my grandchildren run and play croquet on the lawn."

I had a different vision. Hopefully the surrounding woods would encroach on the lawn and the tree would blend into the forest. Become another one of Patsy's forgotten projects. "That's a nice dream."

"More than a dream." Patsy pulled me and Annette to her sides. "I'm so glad the divorce from David is over. No more marriages for me. All I need is you two girls. You're my family."

A deep contentment warmed my chest. Patsy deserved happiness. Her first husband was a rotten scoundrel who'd run off to France with a dancer once he'd learned she was pregnant. He hadn't even been around for Annette's birth. David, her second husband, had been a decent husband and good father to Annette, but Patsy was too flamboyant for simple-minded David, and they'd grown apart. But I had Patsy's love and acceptance and believed I could make this moment last forever.

"You know what?" Patsy looked lovingly at the tree. "I declare this our family tree." Her face lit up. "You'll both come here with your children. We'll make memories."

The three of us stood, looking at the tree.
We should have buried this secret deeper.

CHAPTER THREE

Seventeen years later

I SAT BEHIND THE wheel of my Jeep, closed my eyes, and snapped my fingers to the count. "One, two, three, four, five." Snapping out five more sets of five until I reached thirty. I had to do it perfectly or something bad would happen; I knew it would.

Finished with counting, I took a deep breath and opened my eyes.

The white-steepled church was cradled by a lush green forest showing sprinkles of pink camelia flowers. Bursts of magenta and white crepe myrtles lined the brick-paved walkway to the church steps. July in the rural backroads of Lighthouse Beach. Postcard perfect.

I needed to go inside, but the ache in my chest weighed me down. Only five months ago, I'd been here for Annette's funeral. She'd fought brain cancer for eighteen months and lost the battle at thirty-five years old. Today, it was Patsy's funeral, and I was as worn as a dried bone.

A piercing pain, like a string of barbed wire, tightened around my heart. I'd always thought that if I lost either Annette or Patsy, I'd crumble, like I had when my mother had died. But I was an adult now. I needed to stay present. If I didn't pull myself together, I'd lose the last family I had left—my children. I had to stay clearheaded if I wanted any chance of having my custody rights restored.

I looked down at my dry, cracked hands, at my nails trimmed and scrubbed free of dirt. To others, my hands might have looked clean, but I saw the filth. The need to wash away the dirt rose from deep in my core. *Scrub, scrub, scrub.*

No. The cracked skin had to heal. *Don't pick. Don't pick. Don't pick. Count.*

I took in deep breaths, slowly counting each inhale. "One, two, three, four, five." I picked at the raw skin under my fingernails. I could feel the dirt. Grimy. Guilty.

A knock on the driver's window jacked up my heartbeat. I shuddered. It was Melissa Harrington in a burgundy sleeveless shift, one size too big on her petite frame. A friend from back in our primary school days, and another person touched by Patsy's love.

She put her round face to the closed window. A breeze sent wisps of straw-like bleached hair over her suntanned skin. "Hey, girl." Her sing-song tone didn't match her grief-lined face.

I cracked a smile, then turned and grabbed my purse from the passenger seat, discreetly reciting my mantra. "Two, four, six, eight, now it's time to radiate." A pep cheer I'd created for when I needed encouragement. It worked, but I had to repeat it five times. Five perfect times.

Melissa tapped the window again. "Are you okay?"

My legs trembled, drained of strength, but I had to be strong. I had to trust nothing bad would happen if I didn't finish reciting my mantra. With the help of therapy and new medication, I'd gained a modicum of power over the compulsions. I could pretend I was sane, even if, deep inside, I was full of self-doubt.

I hopped out of the car and pressed the electronic lock. I could do this. "We have to stop meeting like this." My attempt at levity didn't hide the crack in my voice.

"This is all too much to take in." Melissa shook her head and pressed a tissue to her nose. "I didn't even know Patsy was sick."

"She died of a broken heart. I'm sure of it." I gulped the lump of regret lodged in my throat. I'd visited Patsy more often after Annette's death, did my best to be supportive. Instead, I'd been so consumed with my own grief that I hadn't noticed her declining health.

If I'd noticed her sooner, I could have taken her to the doctor—maybe saved her life.

Guilt urged me to pick at the slime under my nails. But I didn't.

We made our way to the chapel as haunting organ music became louder with each step. The ache in my chest deepened. My feet wanted to run, to go someplace where none of this was real, but I barely had the strength to walk.

Melissa linked her arm in mine. "It'll be over

soon," she whispered. Inside the church, she pointed to the pews on our left. "I'll be with the gang. We'll all catch up with you at Patsy's house after the service."

I waved at my old school friends, gawking at me with forced smiles and sad eyes. Back in high school, Annette and I had given them nicknames. The monikers had stuck. Demure Denise Voss looked serene in her navy twinset and pearls. Nasty Nancy Miller was here in a strapless black dress and accompanied by her quiet husband, Richard.

After my college years, I'd rarely seen the group. Our lives had taken different directions. Denise had married a naval officer, who I'd rarely seen around. Nancy and Richard had dated since high school and gotten married a few years after graduation. Two kids later and they're settled into suburbia. Melissa was divorced, renting someplace at the beach. A beach rat, Annette had called her—a local's term for an adult who still lived like a party-hard college kid in a rented beach shack. My marriage to Aaron had put me on the other side of town for the past twelve years. I hardly knew these people anymore.

Melissa slipped away into the pew, leaving me standing in the back of the church, reluctant to move forward. The vibration of organ pipes pulsed deep into my bones. Noise and crowds, my two least favorite things.

A hand pressed on my shoulder. "I'm sorry for your loss."

It was Noah Baker. His father, Officer Baker,

sat in a wheelchair, hiding under a ball cap and a baggy brown suit. The old man looked past me like he'd never seen me before. I'd heard he'd suffered a stroke and was showing early signs of Alzheimer's. Though, the red eyes and tears streaming down his cheeks told me he remembered Patsy.

I turned to the younger Baker. Athletically built, dark hair and eyes, and a clean-shaven face. He'd become a cop, too. Like father, like son. He looked at me as if he had more to say but remained silent. I understood. We all wished we could say something meaningful. "Thanks, Noah."

Making my way down the aisle, I spotted Jackson Howell, another member of the beach rat pack. He sat alone looking at his cell phone, his mop of brown hair flopping over his face. He'd been at Annette's funeral too. Lately I'd wondered how different my life would have turned out if Annette and I hadn't taken the blotter he'd sold her. Would I have reacted differently that night if I hadn't been afraid of the drug's unpredictable effects? I shuddered. I couldn't allow those memories to resurface.

This was no time for those thoughts. I took a deep breath and held my head high as I walked down the aisle searching for my family.

Familiar faces in the crowd blurred together, but I heard their chatterbox whispers as I passed.

Poor Jolene.

She was so close to Patsy and Annette.

Looks like she's hanging in there.

My heartbeat slowed. There he was. On the

right, second row from the front. The slicked-back dark hair of my ex-husband, Aaron. Our eight-year-old twins turned their smiling faces to me, and I swallowed the lump in my throat. My babies.

How I missed Jennifer's round brown eyes and eager smile. And Eric's new buzz haircut and the scrape on his face from a skateboarding mishap made me realize how much was going on without me. They'd inherited their father's olive skin and dark hair, while I stood out like the pale, red-headed stepchild. At least Aaron had had the decency not to bring his girlfriend. The funeral was bad enough. Seeing another woman with my children would have been a different kind of death.

I had no bitterness. All I wanted was to regain my shared custody rights. The past year had been a challenge. With the DUI had come the loss of my license, my children, and my dignity. I'd hit rock bottom but was crawling out of the dark hole.

I'd screwed up and needed to redeem myself. I'd do anything to make things right, to take away the pain my shattered mind had caused my children. Anything to reassure them Mommy wasn't sick anymore. I'd wracked my brain over this and decided the best thing to do was set a good example. Model kindness and tolerance.

I looked to the front row for Patsy's family. She'd stayed true to her word and never remarried. Devoted her life to hobbies, parties, me, and Annette. Patsy's only sibling, Lola, twisted around and gave me the stink eye, scowling as much as her Botoxed face allowed. I'd been in her sour company half-a-dozen times, the last time at Annette's funeral.

Lola would've flown in from her ranch in Texas, but she wasn't with her husband or two sons like at Annette's funeral. Instead, she was with a flat-faced man, fortyish, with dark hair and a suit. He nodded at me like I was supposed to know him. Did I? I took a deep breath. I forgot a lot of things these days.

Aaron stepped out into the aisle and touched my arm. "Hey." He wore a dark suit and smelled like he always had—of soap and deodorant. My heart didn't thump the same way it had when we'd met, two years after I'd graduated college. Back then, I'd managed to convince him I was levelheaded and loveable. We'd had several good years in our marriage.

Until the first leaf had arrived in the mail and twisted my head with obsessive thoughts and memories which I couldn't share with anyone.

Ten years married. One year separated. Three months divorced. I still found him attractive, though the romance was dead. The divorce had been amiable. We'd sold our house, split the prof-its and moved to separate homes. Shared custody fifty-fifty until I'd totally fucked up.

"Thanks for bringing the kids." I slid past him to my children, who scooted down the pew to make a space. Flutters rippled through me as I took my seat. I drew them close and kissed their soft cheeks. God, how I missed my babies. "I can't believe how fast you're both growing," I whispered.

Eric tugged the sleeve of my dark green dress, his voice not as quiet. "Can we come to your house next weekend?"

Jennifer looked at me with pleading eyes. Swallowing the lump in my throat, I stroked their shiny brown hair. "I'll talk to your father about it later, okay?" I sat back, hating that it was because of me my children were heartbroken.

Lola turned from the pew in front of us and shot me a glare hot enough to melt the stained-glass windows. She wagged a finger. "We need to talk when we get to Patsy's house."

I'd rather have poked out one of my eyes. What could the old biddy want to say to me? But I'd committed to attending the reception which Patsy's longtime friends and neighbors, the Nichols, had organized. I half-smiled. "Of course."

Keeping my head together. That was all that mattered. A clear mind and more time with my children so that I could prove to everyone I was a capable mother.

The organ music stopped. I tapped my finger on my thigh thirty times and blanked my mind from the service.

◆

After Patsy's coffin was lowered into the grave next to Annette in the church's cemetery, I followed the procession of cars through the winding rural roads for the five-minute drive from the church to Patsy's house. New houses had sprung up along Crab Creek Road, along with a corner Mini-mart convenience store and gas station. The cars turned left onto Willow Road. On my right was part of the McDougal family land. A forest of imposing pines with a thick underbrush of wax myrtles, holly, and woody vines—the woods where Annette and I had once picked wild blackberries. An acre of land had been cleared years ago for a house they'd never built.

On the left, Patsy's twenty-five acres looked the same as the day I'd first visited with my mom thirty years ago. The wood-sided country house faced the road and sat smack-dab in the middle of two acres of cleared and manicured lawn. The overgrown forest still surrounded all but the front of the house.

I soaked in the nostalgia one last time. This had been the place I'd always felt I belonged, and after today, I'd never come back. The end of an era. Another death.

I parked in the driveway as I'd always done. Patsy had told me long ago that this property would stay in the family. Lola's son would likely move in with his family immediately, and I would never park in this driveway again. Shame that he hadn't bothered showing up for his aunt's funeral, but part of me understood. He'd just seen his cousin buried five months ago. This much heartache was tough to handle.

Patsy's neighbors from down the road, Mr. and Mrs. Nichols, stood on the verandah at the front of the house, stone-faced and ordinary—doppelgängers for the middle-aged country couple in

Grant Wood's *American Gothic* painting, but missing the pitchfork. Mrs. Nichols waved.

I waved back but wasn't ready to go inside and mingle with the mourners where I'd have to face the pitiful looks of grief. My children came first.

I continued around the side of the house, to the backyard where I'd asked the twins to meet me. This was their favorite spot—under the gazebo next to the family tree, where they'd often played hide-and-seek or eaten snacks at the picnic table under the shady oak leaves.

The family tree was seventeen years old and at least thirty feet high. The long branches reached out in perfect symmetry, like a giant spade from a deck of cards. A beautiful work of nature feeding on a secret so deep that it didn't exist.

After Patsy had named the tree, life went on as usual. Annette and I had gone back to college. The tree had grown steadily through the years. Patsy had fertilized it religiously through the seasons, determined to help the tree grow tall and strong. She'd set up a canopy and picnic tables nearby for her annual Fourth of July parties. She'd put up a white gazebo. The same gazebo Aaron and I had exchanged wedding vows under, back when the family tree had been only ten feet tall.

I had a strange affinity with the tree. It had become a part of the landscape of my life and had grown to represent the familial love I'd shared with Patsy and Annette. With each passing year, I'd treated it more and more like a troubled sibling, torn between my love for it, and my hatred of its secret.

Usually, the tree looked beautiful, but in rare moments, like when a shard of buried memory flashed in my mind, the tree turned as hideous as an ogre.

But it was easy to forget, to live a lie when no one ever questioned me.

I inhaled and slowly released my breath. This was the end of a bygone era. The parties and celebrations. The love and laughter. Sadness squeezed my chest, and all I wanted was to be alone.

Goosebumps crept over my skin. I jerked my head around. Noah was on the deck looking at me. *No. Watching me.* We locked eyes, and he turned away.

My hand twitched, my pulse making a beeline to my brain and alerting all my senses. I couldn't shake the feeling that he'd read my mind.

"Mom!" Jennifer called from behind me. My heart missed a beat, and I switched off thoughts of Noah. I turned. My children ran across the lawn toward me with outstretched arms and bright faces. I stooped to one knee and embraced them. "Hey, guys."

Eric pressed his face against mine. "I miss you, Mommy."

The worry in my son's eyes only made me more determined to fight for my time with them. "I miss you more." I held them tight, never wanting to let go. How sad that the little time I had to spend with them was today at a funeral reception.

Aaron strolled casually across the lawn, lagging behind and giving me more time with the twins. Though, I'd given no him no reason not to agree to more access time. Over a year had passed since my DUI arrest. I had my compulsions under control. But it was important I prove I was mentally sound, too, because I needed the child custody court to agree I was capable of caring for my children.

Aaron waved. "Hey, nice service the Nichols put together for Patsy."

I stood, brushing cut grass off my bare knees. "They're good people."

Aaron hugged me like a friend. "How are things going for you, Jolene?" Compassion colored his tone.

I forced a smile. He already worried I teetered on the edge of crazy. If he thought I wasn't coping with the grief, I could kiss off any chance of getting my custody rights back. "As well as could be expected. Life goes on. Right?"

His gentle eyes looked past my calm façade. "This is a big loss. We all loved Patsy."

My shoulders tensed. Being with Aaron reminded me how much I missed the person I'd been only six years ago. Before the leaves had started coming. Back when my life had been complete. I'd lived a normal existence with family and friends who loved me unconditionally. I'd had control of my thoughts.

I used the counting and tapping to disassociate from the obsessive thoughts the stalker brought on. The more I counted, the more distance I put between me and the looming sense of dread. Counting and tapping. It was better than hand-scrubbing, and it calmed me. I needed these rituals to ensure the rest of my day would run smoothly.

I couldn't explain my obsessive thoughts and compulsions to Aaron. How could I explain something I didn't understand myself? The one time I'd mentioned the feeling of being followed, he'd turned cold on me. Said he'd hit his tipping point and I was losing my mind. After seeing his reaction to talk of the stalker, I didn't dare mention my paranoia about the mysterious letters with leaves I'd been getting in the mail.

Problem was, I wasn't sure what was going on in my obsessive brain. Wine had become a good friend. Too good. Fuck. If only the DUI arrest hadn't have happened with the children in the car, after I'd picked them up from school. That had been a new low, and the pain and shame had made my obsessions stronger.

The final blow had come on our tenth anniversary when Aaron had said he didn't want to live another day with my compulsions and drinking. He'd left me. Found a more stable woman, as he'd put it. Over time, I'd learned to stop obsessing over all of the mistakes I'd made in our marriage. I needed to stay present. To look to my children—my future, not my past.

I finally managed to speak. "Thanks. I appreciate all the support you've been giving me. I'll get through this."

The twins each pulled at an arm. I hated having to let go, but this conversation wasn't for their ears. "Guys, can you go wait for me at the gazebo for a few minutes? I need to speak with your father for a few minutes."

Eric took off for the gazebo. Jennifer waited, disappointment on her face.

Aaron sighed. "I have to leave in an hour. We have other plans this afternoon."

I stroked Jennifer's cheek. "This won't take long, sweetie, I promise."

Jennifer nodded and slinked away. I waited until the twins were out of earshot, and then met Aaron's eyes.

He narrowed his gaze. "Everything okay?"

"I want to talk about spending more time with the kids." I glanced at the twins tossing a ball in the gazebo then back at Aaron.

"It's not just up to me, Jolene. We need to get your therapist to agree. And you haven't really proven that you're ready."

"How can I prove I'm ready if I never have time alone with them?"

His eyes turned to my hands, then back to me. "What about the drinking? And all that counting and hand-scrubbing shit? You still doing that?"

"No, I'm not." My cracked cuticles itched, but I didn't flinch. At least I'd toned it down enough for no one to notice.

"I want you to spend more time with the kids. I do. It's just…when you get drunk and the kids see blood on your hands…." He shook his head. "They're too young to understand."

I shriveled inside but stood as tall as a sunflower. I hadn't fully forgiven myself for terrifying the twins, but I was moving ahead one day at a time. The new medication would help prevent a repeat performance. I was willing to do anything to prove I was ready to have my custody rights back. "It won't happen again. I have the drinking and OCD under control now. My therapist will back me up."

"Good. Then we'll work something out. India signed them up for surf camp and some swimming lessons...."

I tried to listen to what Aaron was saying, but my eyes darted to the redwood deck behind the house and the guests sitting under the umbrella-covered table and on the chaise lounges, drinks in hand. My attention zeroed in on Noah, talking to white-wine-swilling Nancy and Denise.

His crossed arms and hard-set jawline weren't signs of grief, but scrutiny. That made me uneasy. I sensed danger. But I was also learning how paranoia was just a symptom of my OCD. It made me sense danger at random times, so I'd been working to set the worries aside before they became obsessive thoughts.

Aaron's voice cut through my thinking. "How do you foresee this happening?"

"What...? Oh, the twins." I couldn't hide the jitters in my voice. I turned my back to Noah. "Since it's summertime, I hoped to have them for at least a few days."

Aaron's attention shifted toward the house. I followed his gaze. Lola came stomping across the lawn directly toward us.

"She's in her usual cheery mood," Aaron said under his breath.

Lola stopped inches from me and then looked

at Aaron. "Excuse me for interrupting." She cut to me. "I need to speak with you in private."

I gritted my teeth. Her arrogance and nicotine breath grated on my last nerve, but since she was Patsy's sister, I gave her some leeway. "Can it wait five minutes?"

"It's about the will." Lola's face pinched tighter than her tone. "You really need to come with me."

The will. Patsy must have left me something. Why else would Lola need me? Patsy had told me many times how she'd planned to leave everything to Annette and her nephews.

Aaron patted my shoulder. "Go ahead and do what you need to, but I do have to leave soon."

What I needed was to scrub my hands. Instead, I followed Lola across the deck and into the crowded country kitchen. Grief swelled in my chest.

I looked at everyone and no one, cringing under the prying eyes and sorry faces of people who knew how close I'd been to Patsy. Clear-wrapped platters of deviled eggs and rolled-up meats lined the countertops and dinette table. Nausea rolled through my empty stomach.

"We're set up in here, Jolene." Lola turned into the formal dining room off the kitchen.

Heavy white drapes covered the windows. The low-lit chandelier kept the room dim. Patsy had reserved dining in this room for special occasions like Christmas, Thanksgiving, birthdays, and other celebrations. This was my last time at this table. The flat-faced man from the funeral stood and politely nodded. A file sat on the table in front of him. Papers were stapled to light-blue legal stationery. He held out his hand. "Miss Parker, my name is Benjamin Clayborn. I'm the attorney and executor of the last will and testament of Patsy Farr. I'm sorry for your loss."

The attorney had addressed me like I was an important member of Patsy's family. "Thank you." I sat at the table across from him, anxious to get to the point.

Lola sat next to me, her eyes laser sharp and ready to burn through flesh.

Benjamin clicked his pen. Twice. "Now that everyone is here, as per Miss Farr's request, I will read out her last will and testament."

I squirmed in my chair, uneasy under Lola's glare as the attorney read.

"In the event of the death of my daughter, Annette Farr, I bequeath my entire estate to Jolene Parker, who has been like a daughter to me." He paused.

"What?" I choked on the word and looked at Lola. "Patsy always told me if something happened to Annette, the property was going to her family."

"That's what we all thought," Lola spat out. "And there's no way in hell I'm going to let an outsider take what belongs to our family."

I grabbed hold of the edge of the cherrywood table. I wasn't an outsider, but what would she know about my bond with Patsy and Annette? "When did you hear about this?"

"Yesterday, when I arrived. I went through

Patsy's files and found a copy of the will. I saw Benjamin was the executor, so I called his law firm."

"So, you've already read the will?"

"Ohhh, yes." Lola wagged a finger at me. "And something doesn't smell right. Patsy only left me token pieces of jewelry and a few worthless family heirlooms."

Benjamin cleared his throat. "This change was made soon after Annette was diagnosed with cancer. We have witnesses who can attest that Patsy was of sound mind and body when she made these revisions. She'd gone through lengths to have that verified."

Lola pounded a fist on the table. "But why?"

I looked at the attorney for an answer.

"Patsy had come to realize Jolene was like her own child," he said. "She wanted to make sure that, if something happened to her, Jolene and her children would inherit the property—"

"You!" Lola pointed a finger at me. Fiery red color rose on her neck. "You must have had some kind of magical hold on Patsy for her to make such a stupid ass decision."

Scooting my chair back, I put more distance between us. I wasn't prepared for this battle. "I didn't know. I swear—"

The attorney coughed. "Excuse me, ladies. I need to finish reading the will. There are some stipulations."

I sat back, but my restless legs wiggled, so I placed my palms flat on each thigh and pressed down. *One, two, three, four, five. Stay still.*

Benjamin continued reading. "Because I want to keep the property in the hands of the people I love, the transfer of title is subject to Jolene Parker taking up residence. The house may not be rented. The house is only transferable to Jolene's children and cannot be sold during the lifetime of Jolene Parker. It is my desire that the property will not languish and become abandoned. I do this because I know Jolene will love and care for this property the same as I did. To avoid any financial burden on the beneficiary, I have left funds in a trust account for the sole purpose of paying property taxes for the next twenty years. The house has no mortgage. The title is free and clear. Full transfer of title is to take place upon Jolene Parker's agreement to these terms, which I trust she will accept."

Lola leaned over the table, scowling at Benjamin. She raised her voice. "What if she doesn't accept?" Then she turned to me, her rigid face an inch from mine. "You need to do the right thing. The property belongs to my family."

I leaned back. I didn't want to take something which wasn't mine. "I didn't ask for this. It's what Patsy wanted. She made that clear."

The attorney lifted his eyes to Lola then back to the will. "In the unlikely event that Jolene Parker decides *not* to accept the estate, then the full title shall be transferred to the Church of All Saints under terms of non-development for fifty years."

Lola shook her finger at Benjamin. "I'm telling you Patsy wasn't in her right mind. I won't just walk away."

Benjamin clicked his pen twice, his expression stiff. "There is a request, a wish Patsy added into the will, which applies to anyone who inherits the property."

I blinked five times. It irked me that Benjamin clicked the pen two times instead of five. But I needed to listen to every word.

"The family tree shall not be cut down," he read, "but allowed to grow for generations like the tree at Patsy's grandmother's house in North Carolina."

"That damned tree!" Lola slammed her hand on the table. "Why was she always so obsessed with that fucking tree?"

I'd asked myself the same question many times over the years.

Benjamin took off his glasses and looked at me. "Miss Parker. You have forty-eight hours to decide if you will take ownership and residence of the property or donate it to the church." He slid a copy of the will and his business card to me across the table. "I'll wait to hear your decision."

My head spun. Ownership and residence. *Live in this house?* Benjamin kept talking, trying to convince Lola the will was ironclad.

"Excuse me, Benjamin." I stood and offered a handshake. "I need to go outside and see some people before they leave. I'll be in touch within forty-eight hours."

"Jolene," Lola said, "we're not finished talking."

I looked at Benjamin. "Do you need me for anything else?"

He stood and shook my hand. "We're finished

until I hear back from you."

"Have a great day, then." I left through the opening into the kitchen with my head swirling in a tornado of surprise and grief. *Patsy had bequeathed me her entire estate.*

"There you are."

I heard a familiar woman's voice, and my feet hesitated on the tiled kitchen floor. My vision slowly came to focus. Melissa, Nancy, and Denise stood at the kitchen counter wearing droopy smiles. I counted in my head. *One, two, three, four, five.* "Hi, guys."

Nancy poured white wine into glasses. "We've been looking for you."

Denise plucked another glass off the wine rack under the cupboard. "Come have a drink with us."

I rubbed my hands together and shuffled my feet toward the back door. "I'd love to, but I can't. My kids are here. I-I need to get back outside."

Melissa pulled me into the group. "Join us for a minute. I was just letting the gang know that I might have to move to Richmond."

"No kidding." Acting interested drained my energy, but I couldn't keep cutting people out of my life. "What's in Richmond?"

"My Aunt Kelly. My mom's older sister. She's had Parkinson's for a while, but it's getting worse. She needs someone living at the house with her." Melissa sighed. "I'm just hoping I don't have to permanently move away from the beach."

Nancy slung an arm over Melissa's shoulder, slurring her words. "Girrrl, I'm not letting you go. You belong here with us."

I'd heard enough. "Look, guys, I need to get back outside to my kids—"

"Wait just one minute." Denise snatched her cell phone off the counter. "Before we lose you again, I'm planning a girl's night out. You need to meet up with us." Her pink-polished fingertips slid over the phone screen. "Give me your number, and we'll stay in touch."

"Don't say no," Nancy grinned, the wrinkles around her eyes deepening.

Melissa gave me pleading, puppy dog eyes. "You've been through a lot these past months. We just don't think you should go through this all alone."

Warmth spread down my shoulders. I was grateful for their kindness. They'd tried to get me to meet up with everyone after Annette's funeral, too. I hadn't wanted to socialize back then, and I wanted to even less now, but I appreciated the thought. "Sounds great." I gave her my cell number, knowing I'd never go out.

Using tunnel vision, I made my getaway outside to the deck, ignoring the stares and murmurs of mourners. My head grew dizzy as I stepped down to the lawn. I paused at the bottom of the stairs, gripping the handrail. It was all too much to wrap my head around.

Patsy left me this house.

This inheritance annihilated any doubts I'd had about my place in Patsy's heart. She'd loved me like a daughter—loved me more than her own blood. She'd left me everything because she'd cared for me. Tears welled in my eyes and I pressed a hand against my chest, covering the gaping hole left by death when it ripped out my heart.

Lola's anger was understandable, but I couldn't let the guilt I felt that Patsy had left her sister so little diminish the huge amount of love she'd had for me.

I turned my focus to Jennifer picking wild-flowers along the tree line. Eric under the gazebo, tossing a baseball in the air and catching it over and over again. Aaron sat at the picnic table under the shady family tree, head down, pecking his finger on his phone. My family. Or what was left of it.

Aaron caught my gaze and jumped up, observing me with raised brows.

Keeping him out of my personal life had helped me move on from the divorce, but this news was too big to keep to myself.

Buck up, girl. My knees wobbled and my hands shook, but with the count of each step I gained a grain of strength. *One, two, three, four, five. One, two, three, four, five.* I continued counting in perfect sequence, warding off any bad luck.

CHAPTER FOUR

I SAT ON THE picnic table bench next to Aaron, bouncing my leg as I watched him absorb the news.

He shook his head, momentarily speechless. "Patsy left you this house?"

I glanced at the twins, distracted by a plate of cupcakes being passed around by Mrs. Nichols. Then I turned back to Aaron. "The land. Everything."

"I figured Lola wanted to see you because Patsy had left you a keepsake in the will. But this?" He waved his hand across the expanse of the house and land. "What about the mortgage? You can't—"

"There is none. Patsy owned the property free and clear. Just paid property taxes."

"That can't be cheap."

"Will be for me. She'd set up a trust specifically to pay taxes for the next twenty years."

"The fuck? You've just inherited a property worth over a million dollars, and you don't have to worry about paying taxes?" Aaron rose and turned in a slow circle, his eyes surveying the property. "This is huge. You could sell and make a fortune."

I shook my head. "Can't. The will stipulates I have to live in the house and keep this land in my family. I have to pass it down to Jennifer and Eric."

"What? Why can't you sell?"

"Patsy didn't want that. She wanted me to live here with my children. Carry on her legacy."

"Legacy?" Aaron laughed. "Sorry, but you're nothing like Patsy."

I was only half-offended. No one could replace Patsy and her *joie de vivre*. The annual Fourth of July parties. The endless backyard summer bar-beques with neighbors and friends. Spontaneous bonfires and oyster roasts on cool autumn nights. I didn't have the passion for hosting year-round parties. I preferred to keep my circle close and closed. Not because I was antisocial, but because I never knew when a trigger might set me off. If the wrong thought popped into my head, I'd need a safe place to satisfy my urge to count or tap or scrub. To cleanse my hands. I needed privacy.

"Patsy was one of a kind," I said. "But as far as actually inheriting this house, I'm not calling the moving company just yet. Lola is making noise about contesting the will even though the attorney said the will is ironclad."

"Lola?" Aaron smirked. "That stretched piece of leather doesn't have a leg to stand on. You'll get the property."

I'd seen that sparkle in his eyes before. Dollar signs. Like the rest of his investment-minded family. No doubt, Aaron saw this inheritance as an opportunity. I couldn't blame him, but I wanted to get back to our discussion. "We'll wait and see what happens." I sighed. "Let's get back to our conversation about me having more time with the twins."

He stuffed his hands in his pockets. "Why not? As long as you keep taking your medication, then I see no reason for you not to get shared custody back. I'll even recommend it to the court."

My muscles relaxed. The efforts at proving my stability and hiding my compulsions were paying off. "I appreciate all the support you've been giving me lately."

"At the end of the day, I want what's best for both you and the kids. They'll be better off if they can spend more time with their mother."

Filled with gratitude, I smiled. Regardless of our ups and downs, we both wanted the best for the other. "Thanks, Aaron."

He nodded. "And if you move into this house, all the better. Besides getting out of that cramped townhouse, the kids can finally get a dog."

A dog? Sure, the kids had begged for a dog plenty of times. Eric asked for a puppy every birthday. But Aaron was allergic to dog hair, so no matter how much they pleaded, he couldn't let them have a pet. After the separation, I'd promised the kids, once I found a house with a yard, we'd get a dog from the rescue shelter. I hadn't gotten around to that yet. "Yeah. A dog. Kids would like that."

"If it all goes well, and you're up to it, you can

have the kids for a week over the summer."

"A full week?" My tone went up a notch. "Are you serious?"

"As a trial. We can see how it goes for you."

"I'd really love that. So would the kids."

Jennifer and Eric ran toward us with cupcakes and cookies in hand. I had to pull it together for their sake. They needed to see I was better now—no longer jumpy, edgy, talking to myself or scrubbing my hands. And Aaron knew I wasn't drinking anymore. At least not around him or the twins.

Aaron rested his hand on my shoulder and exhaled through his nose. "Sorry about this, but we need to leave in twenty minutes. The kids have a birthday party this afternoon."

I nodded, but my insides hurt. I didn't like not being a daily part of my children's lives. Pasting on my best smile, I clapped my hands together and looked at the children. "Let's take a walk, guys. I want to hear about your plans for summer."

The three of us walked the grounds as the twins chattered about summer camp and piano lessons. Then, Old Man Baker caught my attention. He was in his wheelchair under the family tree. He lifted an arm and pointed a crooked finger at the trunk. His lips moved like he was speaking, but I was too far away to hear any words.

A chill brushed against my neck. My mind flashed back to the day Annette and I had come home from the nursery with the tree. Old Man Baker's voice played in my head. *You girls plantin' a tree in this heat?*

I picked at the sensation of grime under my fingernails as Noah circled the tree, running his fingers over the rough bark and talking to his father. What was he saying?

Jennifer's voice broke in. "When do we get to see you again, Mommy?"

I snapped back to the moment and wiped my sweaty hands on my dress. I was reading too much into what Noah and his father were discussing. My children were at my side, and I wouldn't waste time feeding paranoid thoughts. I stroked Jennifer's hair. "Soon, baby. Your father and I are working something out."

I led the children for a walk around the tree-lined perimeter of the property. A squirrel scampered across the lawn and ran up the trunk of a loblolly pine.

Eric pointed to a red-breasted robin with a worm in its mouth. "Mom, look." He tugged on my dress sleeve. "Do you think it's going to chew it up and regurgitate it to her babies?"

I chuckled. Eric shared my love of nature. It was my curiosity and joy for nature which inspired my work as a primary school life sciences teacher. I liked showing children how connected we all were to the Earth. "It's quite possible."

Jennifer dragged her feet along the plush lawn. I took her hand. "What's on your mind, sweetie?"

She sighed. "Daddy told us India is moving into the house with us this summer."

My neck straightened. Now it made sense. Aaron was ready for me to have the children because he wanted more private time with his girlfriend. I didn't blame him for moving on. "Oh? How are you feeling about that?"

Jennifer wrinkled her nose. "I don't know." She wiped a tear from her eye. "I want you to come home."

Home. The muscles in my chest twisted and I hugged my precious daughter. The four of us living in harmony. How could I explain to her we'd never be a family in that sense again? How my drinking, paranoia, and OCD had inflicted this change in their lives? How it ripped my spirit apart? "I know, sweetie. Things will get better. You'll see."

I looked over at Aaron. He stood under the tree talking to a solemn Mr. and Mrs. Nichols. The entire twenty minutes I'd had with Eric and Jennifer, he'd spent checking his watch. It hurt, but I got it. This wasn't Aaron's life anymore, and I couldn't blame him for wanting to make a quick exit. I was just grateful he'd brought the kids today.

Slowly, I led the children across the lawn toward Aaron's car where it was parked on the two-lane road. It wasn't unusual to see cars lined up on both sides of the road in front of Patsy's house for a celebration. Except today was her last party. I swallowed, then winced. My throat was raw from pushing down the grief.

"Sorry to break this up," Aaron said from behind us. An electronic beep unlocked the car door. "But we're already running late."

Eric wrapped his arms around my waist and looked up at me with his round brown eyes.

"When are we going to see you again, Mom?"

I stroked his hair, holding back my tears. My road to redemption was long and painful. "Soon, my love. As soon as I can."

Aaron opened the back car door. His cell phone screamed out AC/DC's "Back in Black" and he answered. "Hey. We're on our way right now."

India. A rock formed in my stomach. I hated knowing another woman was spending more time with my kids than I was, but I took a deep breath and hugged the twins. Blew kisses as they drove off, leaving me alone on the road.

Heartache spread across my chest and climbed up my sore throat with cleats. Pushing down the grief of losing my family was like holding a downward rolling car. Exhausting.

I wanted to call it a day. Go home. Sleep. Wake up from this dream.

A flock of black crows prattled in the pines, snapping me out of my self-pity. My eyes turned to an older woman several steps ahead wandering up and down the middle of the road. The woman stopped in front of Patsy's house then turned to the cleared land across the road. Her silvery blonde hair fell to her shoulders in a tangle of curls. She wore a baggy, purple velvet dress and black tights. Sensible Mary Janes on her feet. Overdressed for a hot July afternoon. Her hands stayed loosely clasped behind her back as she took in the surroundings, her nose in the air like she'd smelled something bad.

I kept walking on the road toward Patsy's driveway, getting closer to the odd woman. I didn't recognize her. Wasn't sure if she was lost or on a nature walk.

Once upon a time, I would have asked her if she needed help. But today my throat was tight, and it hurt just to breathe.

She looked my way and squinted. A chill ran over me, yet the sun was hot and the temperature in the high eighties. I ignored her and strolled up the driveway.

Noah rounded the corner of the house and pushed his grumpy-faced father's wheelchair onto the paved footpath toward the driveway. I groaned, wishing I could avoid them.

"Ah...there you are," Noah said. Old Man Baker looked up at me and scowled.

I flinched, because I couldn't forget how they'd been examining the family tree, like it had a shared meaning to them. *Stop overanalyzing. It's nostalgia*, I reminded myself. Patsy had thrown many a party in this backyard. I stopped at the footpath in front of the house. "Leaving already?"

"Dad is tired." Noah kept both his hands on the wheelchair handles. "But we'll talk again soon, eh?"

Again? My thoughts raced. Had I really talked to Noah recently? We'd never been chummy. But his tone had a sense of urgency, of unfinished business. Something I didn't like feeling around cops. I blinked hard and hoped my danger-sensing radar was off-kilter. Nothing made sense recently. "Sure. I'll see you around."

Melissa and Denise were on the front verandah waving me inside. I made my way toward them, resigned to dealing with the rest of the day. With Aaron and the twins gone, at least I could indulge in a strong drink. Just one. Until I got home.

Denise pointed to the road. "Look how many people are still coming to celebrate Patsy's life."

I turned and my eyes zoned in on Noah at the end of the driveway, shaking hands with the eccentric lady. A knot twisted in my belly. They laughed like they were in on some joke. A thousand needles prickled my skin, sweat beading at my hairline. Who was this woman? I hadn't seen her at the funeral, and I didn't recognize her as one of Patsy's friends. Noah waved the woman goodbye and rolled his father down the road with a satisfied smile on his face.

I wiped the sweat from my forehead. Damn, I needed a strong drink, but not until I got home, and not at the risk of another DUI. At least I had good meds to keep my chemically unbalanced brain under control until then.

More guests made the trek up the driveway to the house. Pressure built in my sinuses and I blinked away the moisture blurring my vision. Five deep breaths. I needed to do this. Talk to everyone who loved Patsy. Pretend I was doing just fine.

This day wasn't something I could block out.

CHAPTER FIVE

DAYLIGHT SEEPED THROUGH the shut-
tered windows in my living room. I rolled
onto my side on the linen sofa and hugged a
cushion to my chest. I didn't know the time—or
the day, for that matter. After Patsy's funeral reception, I'd gone home, swallowed two high-dosage
Xanax, chased them down with a bottle of wine,
and zonked out during a *Sopranos* marathon on
television.

I lifted my head from the cushion, but the
heaviness of grief weighed it back down. I didn't
want to move from my spot on the sofa.

My stomach growled. When had I last eaten?
I had to get up and take care of myself. Getting
healthy again was a crucial part of my recovery.
I heaved my feet onto the ground and looked at
my phone. Almost forty-eight hours had passed
since the funeral. I'd already given the attorney
my acceptance of Patsy's bequest before I'd left
the funeral reception. If Patsy wanted me to have
the property, then I had no choice but to accept.
She and Annette would want me to put aside the
grief and move forward.

The orange prescription bottle of Xanax on

the coffee table flashed like a beacon in a foggy sea. My fingers curled and uncurled. My doctor had prescribed half a tablet as needed. As if that could buffer this anxiety. I shuffled to the kitchen, brewed a pot of coffee, and made a grilled cheese sandwich. With sustenance in hand, I curled up on the sofa again and switched the television to the start of the six o'clock local news.

Channel 12 news anchors Becky and Don rattled off a few headlines: The schoolboard had requested more funds. A break in a main sewer line had caused water shut-offs in a midtown suburb. Yawn-worthy.

The camera turned to Don. "We'll start the news tonight with a special report." An image was displayed next to the newscaster—an enlarged photo of a smiling young man wearing a baseball cap.

I dropped the sandwich on my lap. My hands shook. *No.*

"Tonight police report they have new leads on missing person, Mike Morton," Don said, "a Lighthouse Beach resident who's been missing since August, 2003."

Mike Morton. His name crash-landed into the room like a boulder from the sky. It filled all of the space. I hadn't dared speak his name in years. Now, a news banner rolled across the bottom of the screen: *Exclusive News Report: Family of missing person, Mike Morton, put up a $50,000 reward for information leading to finding their son. The Morton family pleas with the public for help.*

I fell to my knees in front of the widescreen as

the photo of Mike stared back at me. My scalp tingled and every word the reporter spoke was like a megaphone in my ear.

The camera zoomed to Becky. "That's right, Don. Our opening story tonight is about the seventeen-year-old unsolved mystery of the disappearance of Mike Morton. Here for us live on the scene to tell us more is our investigative reporter, Candace Gailes."

The scene switched to Candace, a petite blonde reporter standing at the intersection of two rural roads. I swallowed. She was on Crab Creek Road, close to Patsy's house.

"Thank you, Becky." Candace walked alongside the busy road then stopped at the Willow Road street sign. "The mystery starts here. At this intersection of Crab Creek Road and Willow Road, where Mike Morton was last seen at approximately nine o'clock on the night of August 3rd, 2003. Theories about what happened to him next range from him running into foul play involving a drug deal to him moving out of town and changing his identity. The one thing authorities feel certain about is that Mike Morton was last seen on this corner. Then, he disappeared, never to be heard from again."

The television screen split with Don in the news studio on the left side and Candace live on location on the right. Don spoke. "Candace," Don said, "tell us about the leads in the investigation."

My breaths grew shallow, and my nerves reacted to every word with a twitch.

Candace nodded twice. "Investigators say they are analyzing the original reports for overlooked clues. Now, they're not releasing information which could jeopardize the investigation, but head investigators have indicated the new leads are encouraging."

New leads. Boom, boom, boom. Every vessel in my head pounded. No one knew anything. Did they? I recalled Noah and his father at Patsy's funeral reception—how Noah had pondered the tree as Old Man Baker pointed to the branches and trunk.

Bile rose to the back of my throat. I wished I could turn off the television and have this all go away.

"Candace," Don said, "can you tell us if the reward the Morton family is offering was instigated by any of these leads?"

Candace shook her head. "I can't confirm that, but with all the attention around the mystery, we hope the Morton family finds closure soon." She nodded at the camera. "Becky and Don, back to you at the station."

Don nodded. "Thank you, Candace. We look forward to hearing more from you about this investigation soon." The camera went back to full screen with Don looking into the camera. "Again, police are asking anyone with information to please contact the Lighthouse Beach Police Department at the number on the screen."

The screen flashed back to the news desk with Becky at Don's side. "We caught up with the parents of Mike Morton today outside police headquarters, where they made an emotional public plea to anyone with information about their son."

The screen switched to an elderly couple linked arm-in-arm as they left the police station. A younger horse-faced man and woman followed close behind them in a frenzy of flashes and news cameras. The Morton family. The parents looked frail and tired.

Guilt twisted around my heart and up to my throat. I didn't like being reminded that Mike had had a family who cared about him.

The foursome stopped outside the police building and faced the press. Mr. Morton took the mic and spoke to the camera. "We've waited seventeen years to find out what happened to our son. Seventeen years of not knowing," he said, raising his tone. "And we're certain someone knows. Someone knows what happened to our son."

Every muscle in my body tightened. *Someone knows.* Who? How?

Mrs. Morton stepped in front of the mic. "We plead to anyone with information to notify the police." Her voice cracked and she shoved the mic toward her daughter.

The daughter stood tall, proud, and stoic. The news banner read: Rebecca Morton, sister of missing man Mike Morton. "Our family is offering a $50,000 reward for any information which leads us to the whereabouts of Mike. Dead or alive."

I grabbed my throat. *No. No. No.*

Mike's sister continued, looking directly into

the camera. "Our family strongly believes someone knows where my brother is. Please. Please.
Anyone who has information, your call will be
kept confidential." She walked away, and the
nightly news duo came back on screen and seg-
ued into state political news.

I turned off the television, and the cold fist
of fear filled the silence, squeezed the air from
my lungs. I picked at my fingertips, at the dirt
embedded deep in the crevices of my skin.

I could've blamed what Annette and I had
done on the acid, but I knew better. Mike had
been dead and buried by the time the drug had
taken effect. I'd simply allowed myself to forget.

Seventeen years. That was how long I'd lived as if
that night had never really happened. As if it had
been a dream. Annette had been the great rein-
forcer of the lies we'd told ourselves. *It was only a
dream. Nothing happened.*

I'd taken for granted that Mike Morton would
remain just another face on a missing person's
poster, drifting in a sea of lost souls. That was my
theory, and I'd convinced myself it was univer-
sally accepted. If someone did know what we'd
done, the $50,000 reward would bring them out
in the open. But that wasn't possible—was it?

The thought scared me, because to this day, the
one memory of that night which I hadn't been
able to shake was the eerie image of someone
wearing dark clothes running across the lawn—
along with the feeling that someone had watched
us bury Mike.

The few times I'd brought it up to Annette,

she'd told me it was a hallucination from the acid and refused to discuss it any further. It had become easier over the years to convince myself that the memory was false. A false memory. Fake news. It had become a comfortable shell to cover the guilty secret. If no one knew, then it hadn't happened. I'd found a hazy comfort living this way—in that murky place where my secret stayed safe.

But now sharp images of that night played in my mind— the sky full of stars, singing cicadas, shoveling dirt over Mike, and a dark figure running across the lawn.

I shook the thoughts from my head. I'd shut that night out of my mind years ago. Only shards of memory remained.

Someone saw what happened. Someone knows. Someone knows.

Someone saw what happened. Someone knows. Someone knows.

No. The shadow had been a hallucination, like the thousands of cicadas flying around the house, the psychedelic rainbows, and the clownfish in the sky.

I crossed my arms and hugged myself. *Don't look back. Don't look back.*

Looking back triggered obsessive thoughts. Chalk it up to my Obsessive Compulsive Disorder. An overwhelming fear of impending doom was a classic OCD trademark. And once the floodgates of paranoia opened, the current was too strong for me to fight.

The feeling of being watched and stalked had

haunted me for years—ever since that night. I took a deep breath. I wouldn't allow my mind to wander to the past. I'd atoned for any sin. I was caring, giving, and compassionate. A teacher who went an extra mile with students who needed help. It was the small stuff which kept me on a path of redemption.

One might have thought I could find true redemption in confessing my crime. It might have seemed selfish that I hadn't called the police and given Mike's family the closure they deserved. But I'd been in a safe place for a long time. A place where the Morton family didn't exist.

But now I worried someone didn't want me to forget. The someone who was sending me oak leaves in the mail.

I went to the cupboard in the kitchen where I'd always kept my mail. Lifting the stack of paperwork, I pulled out the eight white envelopes bundled up with a rubber band.

The first envelope had come to my home with Aaron and the children, four years ago, at the zenith of my happiness. We'd just finished celebrating the twin's third birthday when I opened the letter addressed to me.

The bright red oak leaf inside the envelope was odd. I'd searched the Internet and postal areas to find out who'd sent it, but learned it was a bogus return address.

For the next four years, the leaves had kept coming at random times. Always the same. The handwriting, a generic block style. I'd had several students who loved the natural world as much as I did. The ones who liked to collect leaves or examine the geometric intricacy in a blade of glass. I wanted to believe that.

But I'd worried the leaves were more sinister. Something to do with what Annette and I had done.

I'd dared bringing up the letters with the leaves to Annette a few times. Each time, I'd been shut down with her stone-cold response: *You're having delusions.* Even on her deathbed, she'd refused to talk about what had happened. *Nothing happened, Jolene.*

But the thought had taken seed: The oak leaves were a message. A message relating to the only oak tree of significance in my life. The family tree.

After Annette had died, another leaf had come in. Then another envelope two months later. The last envelope and leaf had come to the townhouse last week, just before Patsy had died.

Overcome with the grief of losing Patsy and Annette, I'd put aside the leaf mystery. Now, I analyzed the envelopes once again. Eight pieces of a puzzle with no picture to follow.

Did the sender have anything to do with the investigation?

No.

It was the damned newscast about Mike which had sent my mind off in a tangent. Mike's disappearance. Oak leaves. I couldn't ignore the looming dread.

My children could never find out I was a killer. I'd lost the unconditional love I'd had with Patsy and Annette. All I had left was my children. And if I wanted to keep making progress, I'd have to make sure the secret about Mike stayed buried.

First, I wanted to know what leads the police had, and what I'd closed my mind to for all these years. I opened my laptop and logged into the Internet, eager to know what I was up against and arm myself with knowledge.

I typed 'mi' into the browser, then hesitated. My breath quickened. I was being paranoid, but what if something happened to cause the police to hack into my laptop, and if they saw I'd searched for information about Mike's disappearance? It was an illogical thought. Nothing should link me to Mike Morton in any way, but why invite suspicion?

Pacing the floor, I wiped the back of my hand along my cracked lip, painting a streak of blood on my thumb. What I needed immediately was a safe place to conduct a search.

A voice dug into the center of my brain and whispered. *Something bad is going to happen… something bad is going to happen… something bad is going to happen.*

My hands covered my face. *No. No. No.*

Something bad is going to happen… something bad is going to happen….

I grabbed the bottle of Xanax and tossed back two tablets with a mouthful of wine. Pacing the length of my small living room, I counted my steps. "One, two, three, four, five." I turned. *Again.* "One, two, three, four, five." I turned. *Again.* I did this thirty times without interruption, each step carefully controlled.

Something bad was going to happen.

CHAPTER SIX

ISLIPPED AWAY FROM the stampede of teachers charging toward the parking lot to return
home and resume their summer breaks. The
teachers' summer assembly in the auditorium at
Bayview Middle School had just finished, and I
only needed twenty minutes in the school library
to research everything I required. A week had
passed with no announcement of a reward, but
that didn't mean a damn thing. Investigations
could take time.

I crept around the corner to the next corridor.
The one-story school building was designed in
a maze of crisscrossed corridors. I stepped from
the B-wing into the main corridor—the double
wooden doors of the library were way down at
the other end.

Summer school classes were in session, and
right now, no one was in sight. Minimum staff
worked today, so it was easy to stay on the down-
low. But that didn't make me feel safe. Ever since
the news report last week about a new lead into
Mike's disappearance, and the investigation being
focused on the area around Patsy's house, I'd been
nervous and panicky, plagued by the feeling of

the shadow on my heels. A nervous ninja on my shoulder.

I headed down the long corridor lined with grey metal lockers on both sides. My sandals clacked on the shiny linoleum floor. I needed to research anything the media and police had reported about Mike's disappearance. What new lead had put news reporters on the corner of Willow Road?

A set of footsteps came up behind me. Squeaky sneakers.

My pulse quickened, and I picked up my pace with slow and steady breaths. I turned for a quick look. Someone dressed in loose black jeans and a black hoodie turned into a classroom. Doom pressed on my shoulders. *It was only a student.*

I kept moving forward, staying focused on the library entrance ahead.

News of the investigation had shot my paranoid thoughts to a new height.

Only a ritual could rid my mind from these thoughts. I could tap each foot thirty times, then do it again for five even sets. Timing and pacing were crucial. If I messed up, I had to start again. Sometimes, this routine would go on for hours before I could move on with my day.

I hesitated at the library door, looking up and down the desolate corridor. *No one is following me.* Releasing a breath, I went inside. It was empty except for Cheryl, the young librarian behind the book check-out counter, and a copper-haired student working one-on-one with Mr. Hadley, a relic of a math teacher.

Cheryl waved me over to the counter. "Hey, Jolene." Her tone was as peppy as her yellow floral dress. "How's your summer going?"

"Going by too fast, and my Internet went down." I pointed to the row of computers against the wall. "Mind if I pop onto one of these?"

"Take your time." She waved me on. "Hardly no one uses the library during summer break. It'll just be us."

Cheryl was one of my favorite staff at the school. She'd never snooped into my business. When I put in for a temporary medical leave from teaching for one semester to deal with my anxiety, she was one of the few staff who didn't give me pity looks or gossip about how tragic my life had been recently. I sat at the computer farthest from the door, logged in, and typed in my search: mike morton missing person investigation. A chill rippled through me. I'd rather forget my secret had a name.

Five references appeared. I hunched over the monitor and then looked around to make sure no one could see me. The only sound was my heartbeat.

I started at the top of the search page. The current local newspaper report. I'd already read the article in the *Lighthouse Beach Gazette*. A repeat of the television report, but enough to confirm this was happening.

Squeaky wheels dug into my thoughts. I looked up. Cheryl pulled an ancient book cart out from behind her desk. I went back to the search.

A blog page titled *'Where is Mike Morton?'*

appeared. It had been set up by Rebecca Morton, Mike's younger sister. If the purpose of the blog wasn't clear in the title, she made it clear on the opening page. Simply, the family wouldn't give up on trying to find her brother.

She'd been sixteen when her brother had gone missing and started the blog when she'd turned twenty. The posts were listed chronologically beginning with the most recent post:

June 29, 2020

Greetings fellow friends of Mike. I finally have some promising news. The police have some leads on the whereabouts of my brother. Our family is grateful for all your prayers.

Love to all,

Rebecca Morton

In another post, only a few years ago, Rebecca admitted her mother was suffering so much from worry she wanted to seek the advice of a psychic. My eyes were drawn to one particular response to the post.

I'm a local resident of Lighthouse Beach, and though I've never met your brother, I've visited Madame Celeste on several occasions to contact my brother who died in a motorcycle crash. She's the real deal. If your mother is serious about getting answers, I highly recommend she contact her.

I gulped a breath, but my throat was so tight that I couldn't swallow. Guilt seeped through my palms, and I picked at my fingertips to scrape off the filth. Mike's family was desperate to find him. They clung to the slightest chance of hope, and it hurt me to know that.

Squeaky wheels broke my trance. I looked up. Cheryl again, pulling the book cart down an aisle.

Going back to the blog, I scrolled through earlier posts. This wasn't an overly active site, but every year, on August 3rd, the anniversary of the last night Mike was sighted, Rebecca wrote a post titled, *Where is Mike Morton?* A reminder that she was still determined to find out what happened to her brother.

The heading of the next post caught my attention.

Possible sighting of Mike.

June 3, 2013

Hey all. I'm an old friend of Mike's, and I'm pretty sure I saw him walking around the streets at Cocoa Beach last winter. I used to live in Lighthouse Beach and knew Mike from way back in high school when all of us would cut classes and go surfing all day. Anyway, I live down in Cocoa Beach, Florida, now. Still surf lots. Then last year I saw this homeless guy always wandering around the beach area. He looked familiar, and I wasn't sure at first, but now when I think about it, I'm sure it was Mike Morton.

Anyway, after a few weeks, I didn't see him anymore. Then I went to Lighthouse Beach a few weeks ago for a visit. Conversation with friends turned to talk of old times, and they told me about how Mike disappeared ten years ago. That's what made me think of this homeless guy I'd seen wandering around. Not sure if this helps any in your search. If I ever see the guy again, I'll make sure to go ask if he's Mike.

Good luck in finding him. God bless.

Chuck Mankin

My throat tightened. This post would have kept the Morton family hopeful. I realized how detached I'd been from his disappearance. I'd convinced a big part of myself that I'd done nothing. It had become easier over the years. The tree had grown, and the parties had continued. As far as my life with Patsy and Annette, everything was grand.

True, I had detached myself from that night, but now I realized how detached from reality I'd been all these years. How I'd squeezed the memory into a pinhole-sized mental box, and believed it had no power.

Tapping the down arrow key, I kept scrolling through the posts. Some messages had come in from well-wishing friends and a couple from crime enthusiasts with theories involving drugs and bad people.

The loud tapping of my keyboard broke my thoughts and I stopped to glance around to check if anyone was watching me.

No one.

I took a deep breath. It was safe here.

Moving on, I closed out Rebecca's blog and searched the Lighthouse Beach Police Department List of Missing Persons. There was his photo. Mike, with a happy-go-lucky smile and a shaggy haircut. I logged out.

My fingers trembled as I searched for earlier newspaper reports in the *Lighthouse Beach Gazette*.

I stopped at the first newspaper report about Mike's disappearance. It had been published on October 17th, 2003, nine weeks after the night we buried Mike. The article was short, with a snap-shot photo, details about where he'd last been seen on Crab Creek Road, and a police request for anyone knowing anything to come forward with information.

My mind drifted back in time. Annette and I had been at college four hours away when the article was published. The police had questioned everyone who'd lived within a two-mile radius of the place Mike had last been seen. I knew that because Patsy had filled us in during one of our weekly phone calls. *"Officer Baker already knows I was in North Carolina that night, but he wants to ask you girls a few questions when you're back home for Thanksgiving break."*

Annette and I had corroborated and rehearsed this moment in the unlikely event someone cared that Mike had gone missing. One thing I'd learned early in life had been to count on unlikely events.

On the day Officer Baker had come by the house for the interview, Patsy had served sweet tea in the living room, and we'd calmly listened as he informed us how the Morton family had reported Mike missing after not hearing from him for a week. Police had put some feelers out, and a couple of witnesses had seen a man match-ing Mike's description on the corner of Crab Creek Road and Willow Road on the night of August 3rd.

"I noted in my logbook that I stopped by the house on the morning of August 4th." Officer Baker's attention had been focused on Annette.

"You girls just got back from the nursery."

Annette nodded. "Yup."

Baker's eyes shifted to me. "What did you do the night before?"

Keeping my cool, I'd given Baker our simple story. We'd stayed home listening to music and talking about our upcoming junior year at college. Gossiped about boys. Nothing more. "We never even left the house that night, and no one stopped by."

He'd been satisfied with the interview, and we were never questioned again.

In my day-to-day life, Mike's name had rarely been spoken. Not in public and not in private. I'd shut out what had happened that night for so long.

Until now.

Prickles covered my skin, as if I was being watched. I sat up straight and scanned my surroundings. Across the room, Cheryl strolled the aisles putting books back onto shelves. The teacher and student were putting away their pencils and worksheets.

No one's watching me. Don't be stupid. I closed my eyes and rolled my neck. If I expected to stay calm and sane through this, the paranoia had to stop.

The rustle of a backpack and low voices pricked my ears. I opened my eyes. The math teacher and student walked out of the library. The door clicked behind them.

Across the room, Cheryl waved me down and then pointed to the exit. "I'm making a quick run to the restroom. Be right back."

I lifted my hand in acknowledgement, then turned back to reading.

The door clicked shut.

Silence.

I was the only person in the room, but a heavy stillness made me feel I wasn't alone. Maybe someone was hiding, and I didn't see them. I hadn't scanned the entire library. There was a reference and periodical room in the back. There could have been another student back there. I suddenly wished I'd checked the entire library before sitting down to my search.

Stop the paranoia. You're almost finished. I turned my attention back to the screen.

Next was a short article in a neighborhood newspaper dated eight years ago. Another desperate but fruitless attempt. That was old news. I needed to know what the fuck was happening right now. What new leads did the police have?

Thinking I'd find out on the Internet had been naïve, but where else could I look?

The hum of cool air whirred from the vent over my head. Goosebumps rose on my skin, and I rubbed my arms. I smelled peppermint. Peppermint chewing gum.

A shadow passed over the monitor as a soft brush of a fingertip crossed my shoulder. Adrenaline shot down my legs—pushing me to my feet so fast that the chair fell over. I snapped my head around, searching the room.

No one.

Silence stretched for a mile-long minute. No

sound except the hum from the air vent over-head.

Stop it. No one is here.

I deleted my search history and logged out of the computer in two-seconds flat.

Flop. A book had dropped. "Cheryl?" My throat squeezed so tight that my voice squeaked.

No answer, but I wasn't alone. I snatched my tote bag up off the floor. The lights went out and the room turned dark. My eyes shot to the illuminated green exit sign over the closed double doors.

Swish, swish, swish.

The sound of nylon pants brushing together came from behind. I took off toward the exit, then a broad-shouldered man with a black hoodie pulled low over his face dashed past the front counter. He shoved the door's exit bar and bolted into the brightly lit corridor.

I froze, terror surging through me. My stalker. I'd seen him before. Sometimes in my dreams, but now, even in this shadowy room, he was clear as day.

Gasping for a breath, I ran out into the brightly lit corridor. The long hallway was empty except for the smell of disinfectant and sweaty sneakers. The clack of footsteps echoed, and Cheryl rounded the corner, wiping her hands on a paper towel. She stopped and narrowed her eyes. "Everything okay?"

By the worried look on her face, I must have looked horrified. "I just saw someone with a black hoodie run out of the library. Did you see him?"

Cheryl relaxed her shoulders and huffed like a frustrated mother. "The kids. They're running up and down the hallways again."

"S-someone turned the lights off in the library. Then, I saw this person—"

"We've got a couple of summer school students who've been pulling pranks since they got here." She shook her head and let out a frustrated sigh.

I pressed my hand against my head. Uncertain of what I'd actually seen—enough so that I questioned whether my paranoia was making me exaggerate the reality of what was going on. "I don't know. I don't think he was a kid."

Cheryl stroked my arm, her smile shifting to concern. "Should we call security?"

I didn't want to make a scene. Had I really seen a man in black acting suspicious? What if security did a CCTV check and found nothing? Then I would look like a fool. A crazy fool. "Of course. The kids." I laughed it off. "Have a great summer."

I left the building. Nope. I didn't want the attention.

Ever since that news report, I'd become sensitive to every sound around me. I saw suspicion and disdain in people's eyes. I couldn't end the incessant worry that someone had seen what I'd done and was watching me now.

I counted. *Five. Ten. Fifteen. Twenty.* I kept counting in five's until I felt safe from the darkness invading my mind. The more I counted, the higher the numbers, the further away I got from danger.

I hot footed it to the parking lot, knowing I had only twenty minutes to get to my therapy appointment. Bright sun stung my eyes and I put on my sunglasses. The heavy humidity begged for a cool breeze.

I looked around. Only a few cars were in the staff parking lot. As I got closer, I saw something on my windshield. A fresh green oak leaf under the wiper blade. My heart raced. I spun around. There were no oak trees on the school campus. Just pines and poplars. Not an oak in sight.

Then, I saw the back of the broad-shouldered man, jogging away from the parking lot and toward the wooded running trails behind the school.

He was not a shadow. He wanted me to know he was real.

CHAPTER SEVEN

THE ATMOSPHERE IN my therapist's waiting room was intended to put me at ease. Posters with positive and encouraging quotes lined the walls. A candle burned, and the subtle scent of lavender lingered. But the stalker and oak leaf had my senses on high alert.

Too much was happening at once and my brain couldn't find a spot to settle. The stalker. The leaf. The investigation. The determined Morton family. The reward.

I was fucked.

I'd once been able to turn away from any word about Mike, but now I had to face the truth every day. People hadn't forgotten.

After seeing the hooded man again today, it was harder to convince myself the stalker wasn't real. Then, the oak leaf? Were the stalker and the leaf related? Why would anyone follow me, or leave me a leaf?

Pity I couldn't talk to my shrink about the stalker and the leaves, but I'd worked too hard at convincing her I was rational and stable. Getting my kids back was too important. Part of me wanted to open up to Katie, but my stint in the psych ward when I'd been nine had taught me not to trust therapists. Showing vulnerability was dangerous.

The only thing I needed from Katie was a coping strategy. I'd talk about my grief and the stress I'd soon have to face. The stress of moving into the house which held so many nostalgic memories. About how difficult it was going to be for me to adjust. I had to find a way to live without getting stuck reminiscing about the family I'd once had. I'd stay focused on that goal.

The stalker, I'd deal with in my own time.

I was here today because it helped if I played along. It was part of the condition of regaining shared custody of Jennifer and Eric that I attend therapy twice a month. And I was determined to reverse the damage I'd done to our family. Get my shit together.

I'd even given my therapist my dysfunctional life story to dissect.

My happy childhood as a doted-on single child. The tragic moment when my mother had been killed in a car accident. My falling into a grief so deep that I'd quit talking. How my father had sent me to a psych ward in his cowardly effort to help me. How I'd been drugged by the nurses and molested by my therapist. How the doctor hadn't believed me. The humiliation. The confusion. The pain of betrayal.

The therapist knew all of that, and it gave her plenty to work with.

She didn't need to know I had killed a man and buried him under a tree. Those twelve hours of my life story were best kept buried in the sound of silence.

Katie walked into the reception area. "Sorry to keep you waiting, Jolene. Come on back."

I followed Katie down the narrow hallway to her back office. I pegged Katie's age at somewhere in her forties. Bobbed hair with streaks of grey. A bit dowdy, with a kind face and compassionate voice. Easy for me to tolerate.

Katie sat in a high-backed cushioned chair and I sat on the soft sofa.

"I heard about Patsy Farr's passing." Katie's sad eyes searched my face. "I know this is hard for you. How have you been doing?"

My cracked red hands had healed, and I made a point of keeping them on my lap in full view. I'd started sessions with Katie soon after Annette had died, so she was familiar with the people close to me. "Grieving," I said in a croaky voice. "It's still a shock."

Katie watched me, like she expected me to say more.

The tingles under my fingernails urged me to scrape and pick off the sensation of grimy dirt. I clasped my hands and squeezed hard. "I inherited Patsy's house."

Katie's chin dropped. "Huh." Her calm voice didn't waver. "Were you expecting to receive an inheritance?"

I told her about the will. How I had to move in to take ownership. How Aaron had agreed to recommend I regain my custody rights and have the kids for a week over the summer.

"That's a lot to have happen so fast." Katie raised her brows. "It sounds like you're feeling overwhelmed."

If only I could tell her about the stalker. The oak leaf. "Yes. Overwhelmed is a good way of putting it."

"Any unwanted thoughts?"

My fingertips itched, but I resisted the need to dig the dirt out from under my nails. *The stalker.* "No. I mean, nothing I can't handle. The Anafranil is working, you know, keeping random thoughts at bay. What I'm worried about is... how can I live in Patsy's house and not get stuck in grief? I have so many memories, and while they're good memories, it's all too..." I shook my head, not wanting to drone on like a pathetic loser struggling with her good fortune.

"Let's talk about that. Tell me what memories worry you the most about living in the house."

The family tree. My stomach tightened. Some things were unspeakable. "That I'll miss Patsy and Annette even more. The house will be a constant reminder. I'm worried I'll slip into obsessing again."

"Understandable. When do you move into the house?"

Lola still hadn't legally contested the will, as she'd threatened to do. "In two weeks."

"Do you have to move in right away?"

"No. But my lease is up in a couple of months, so there's no sense in delaying. Besides, I really want to beat the fears and obsessions. I want to focus on getting better. Getting stronger."

Katie smiled. "You have an incentive to get better. A strong determination. I see that."

"I do. I want to live in the house. Focus on the positive and be normal."

"You are normal, Jolene. You're just going through a tough time. But let's talk about moving into Patsy and Annette's house. If you're as intent on living there as you say, then we can discuss Exposure Response Prevention Therapy. Like we did with your hand washing. You can expose yourself to being inside the house in small steps."

Shivers ran down my spine. I recalled doing ERPT and having to get my hands dirty. I'd hated those exercises. Brushing my fingertips over the dirt, with that musty smell, and plunging my arm into bags of soil. It had helped me gain some power over the fear, but at times, I'd felt earthworms crawling through dirt beneath my skin. "I think you're right. The exposure therapy is a good place to start."

"Once you have the house keys, give me a call and I'll meet you there for a session. In the meantime, we can prepare for what you might confront on the first visit."

I nodded. Katie could help me learn how to control my fear of grieving alone in the house before the fear morphed into an illogical obsessive thought. She'd helped me so much with my compulsive handwashing. She could help me again. She had to. My future depended on it. "I'll do whatever it takes."

"And what about other friends? Is there someone who can stay with you for a while as you settle into the house?"

The few friends I'd made with the mothers at the twins' school had drifted away. Truth was, I'd inadvertently pushed them away. Hiding my anxiety and paranoia had become difficult. It was easier to isolate myself. I'd separated from all society except my children and my work. Unaware it was happening, it seemed that one day I'd been getting invited to all of the mommy-and-kid events, and the next day, I hadn't been. Simply ousted. I'd never bothered to figure out why. I didn't mind fading off into the background. "That's another setback I have to contend with. I've lost contact with my friends over the past couple of years."

"It would do you some good to get out and socialize with people who have similar interests and a positive mindset. People you work with, maybe?"

"Right now, I prefer to stick to myself." I didn't like the idea of people I worked with knowing about my personal life.

Katie gave me the hard look of a caring friend. "In the long run, that's not going to help you get any better."

Yes. I did want to get better. I had to prove to everyone I was a functioning human being. Normal humans interacted and socialized.

Then it hit. *Denise.* I inhaled a breath. I remembered the text from her urging me to meet up for a girl's night out. "I suppose I do know some people I could catch up with."

"Oh?" She tilted her head. "Tell me more about

that."

"Old friends. I went to school with them from third grade through college. We've recently reconnected because—" my breath hitched. "Because of Annette and Patsy's funerals."

"I see. Sounds like you were all close at one time."

My chest squeezed, and tears welled in my sinuses. "It was Patsy who brought everyone together." I smiled at the memories playing in my mind. "She was a real social butterfly, you know? All through school and college, she'd throw parties for any reason and invite all her friends and neighbors. Her impromptu backyard barbeques were famous. I guess that was one reason Patsy did all that entertaining, to keep Annette and me close to home for as long as she could. My old friends—we all moved in the same crowd."

"They could be an excellent support system for you."

I looked to the ground. She was right to encourage me to get out of my headspace and my generic rental. Back into the real world. I took a deep breath. If only the past hadn't reared its head.

Katie observed me for a moment. "How has your anxiety level been?"

My leg twitched and my eyes shifted to the flickering candle. I teetered between spilling everything to Katie and keeping my trap shut. I needed to release the pent-up guilt and remorse, but I could only dream of confiding what I'd done to Mike to someone who cared. Someone who would keep my secret and still love me even after what I'd done.

But I wouldn't risk losing what little I had left. My secret belonged in a tight compartment in my mind. I'd never open that headspace to anyone. Besides, I was overreacting and being paranoid. No one had harmed or threatened me. Wearing a black hoodie was not an offense and leaves got stuck on windshields every day.

Cheryl was right. The hooded person had been a prankster. I'd obviously overreacted.

I smiled at Katie. "I'll make an effort, Katie. I really will."

I'd move into the house and pretend everything was fine. I was good at pretending. Besides, soon the investigation would fizzle into a big nothing-burger.

One day at a time.

CHAPTER EIGHT

STEPPING INTO OCEAN Joe's Bar and Grill was like entering a time warp. Not much had changed since my college days when Annette and I had been regulars. Jimmy Buffett sang "Wasted Away Again in Margaritaville…" through the speakers. Behind the indoor tiki bar, strings of colored Christmas lights hung on the wall. Never mind that it was late July.

Denise had invited me to join her and Nancy tonight to watch Jackson fill in as drummer for the local band, The Creed Brothers. I hoped getting out of the townhouse would take the investigation off my mind. Someone bumped into me from behind, and I stepped out of the way, searching the long and narrow bar for Nancy and Denise.

"Hey, girl!" Melissa called out from behind the bar, filling a pitcher of beer. "Everyone's waiting for you at the back. What d'ya want to drink?"

Her chirpiness put me at ease. "I'll have a vodka martini." Tonight, I needed something strong to help take my mind off the investigation. I'd taken a Zoomer to the bar, so driving wasn't a concern. *If someone knew what had happened, they would have gone for the reward by now.*

Melissa shooed me. "Go on. I'll bring the drink to the table."

I walked along the row of booths lined in front of open windows overlooking the Atlantic Ocean. Floodlights lit the waves crashing on the shore.

I was doing this. Taking my first step into a social life. The last week had been calm. No stalker. No leaves. No paranoia. Upping my meds another half a dose had helped keep random thoughts at bay. Unfortunately, the higher dose sometimes made me dizzy and disoriented, but I'd found that easier to cope with than obsessive thoughts and paranoia.

The exposure therapy recommendations from Katie were helping. I only had to remember how I'd once easily socialized at school functions, mom's night outs, Aaron's work parties, and Patsy's ongoing festivities. Until the leaves came and started triggering obsessive thoughts and hand-washing rituals which could take up to an hour. Keeping secrets was never easy.

Any discomfort or stress associated with the evening would be worth the benefit in the end. Catching up with old friends felt like a fresh start. Sure, they knew about my stint in the psych hospital, but it hadn't been them who'd taunted me and called me 'Psycho Girl.' The schoolyard nickname had long worn off.

Tonight, I would put my best foot forward.

Jackson caught my eye and stood, waving me to a window booth straight ahead. Tall, with thick, shaggy brown hair and a round friendly face. If he killed the goofy grin, he might have been half-handsome.

They all looked at me from the booth—Nancy, Denise, and Jackson—stretching their necks like a trio of meerkats. I'd moved in different social circles for the past fifteen years. Rarely seen people from this part of town. Never considered any of them a close friend. Now, they were my only friends, and I was grateful. But they didn't know me. Didn't see me. Didn't notice I wasn't as even keeled as I acted.

Exactly the way I liked it.

Jackson sat on the outside of the booth with Nancy next to the window, and Denise across from them. Denise patted the space next to her and scooted in. "Have a seat, sweetie."

I slid into the spot. Across the table, Jackson slung his arm over the back of the booth, almost touching Nancy's shoulders. She smiled and inched closer to him. Anyone passing by would think they were a couple. But Nancy was married to Richard and had two boys. I turned a blind eye. What others did was none of my business.

Denise cupped a strawberry daiquiri and made an animated I'm-so-sorry-for-you face. "How are things going for you, sweetie?"

Here we go again. I hated when I felt the need to convince someone I was doing fine. Especially Denise. True, she'd been kinder to me recently, but we'd never formed a close bond the way I had with Nancy and Melissa. Didn't help that she'd tattled to my PE teacher when I'd once cut a class.

I put on my bravest face. "Really good. I mean—I miss Patsy and Annette horribly. Sometimes, it doesn't feel real that they're both gone." I paused, realizing that all three had their attention squared on me. Why not? I'd lost a lot when Annette and Patsy had died. "I have my good and bad days, and lately my good days far outweigh the bad ones."

Denise squeezed my hand. "That's my girl."

Jackson unslung his arm from around Nancy, leaned into the table and looked at me with a grin. "I heard you've inherited Patsy and Annette's house," he said.

Hearing their names sent a wave of grief through me, leaving an aching hole in my chest. But I stayed in control. "Yeah. That was an unexpected surprise."

Nancy cleared her throat. "A very nice surprise. That's a beautiful property."

"Probably worth two million dollars," Jackson said, widening his eyes. "So, what… you plan on selling the place?"

"Uh, no. I'll be moving in."

"No kidding?" Jackson's eyes lit up and he slammed his hand on the table. "We'll be neighbors. I live on Cardinal Street. Only a couple of miles from you."-

Nancy shot Jackson a glare which could have leveled a barn. Then she turned to me and her expression shifted to that of a know-it-all. "Hell, if I owned that property, I'd sell it."

I rubbed my lips. I'd already disclosed more than I'd wanted about the inheritance. "Patsy requested that I live in the house, so that's what I'm going to do."

"That's a big house to live in by yourself," Denise said. "Have you thought about a room-mate?"

"Live with someone? I don't really know any-one—"

"Melissa," Denise said. "She just got notice from her landlord that she either needs to renew her lease for another year or move out in thirty days."

I didn't find the idea completely off-base. Even Katie had asked if I knew someone who could stay with me for a while. And I liked Melissa. "But I thought she was moving to Richmond."

Denise stirred her pink drink with the straw. "Not if she can help it. She's kind of in limbo right now. You should talk to her."

"That's a good idea," Nancy said. "You won't find anyone more trustworthy or easier to get along with. And she works all the time, so it wouldn't be like you'd be stepping on each oth-er's toes."

Jackson drummed his fingers on the table and stared at me with a smirk. I turned to Nancy. "It's something to consider."

"She stayed at our house for a few weeks after she and Mark divorced," Denise said. "She was an emotional wreck, but very respectful of our space."

Melissa had friends to support her during the

downtimes. How nice. I needed some of that karma. "That's not a bad idea. It would be nice to have another person in the house."

Melissa came over with my drink on a tray. She wore jeans and a tight, white Ocean Joe's T-shirt. "It's so nice to have us all back together." She set my drink in front of me.

"Jolene's looking for a roommate," Jackson blurted out.

"No kidding." Melissa rested her empty tray on her hip and smiled at me.

My cheeks burned. I had to get comfortable talking about the inheritance at some point. "Guess you've heard I've inherited Patsy's house, and well, I'm moving into the house soon and Denise suggested you might need a temporary place to stay."

Melissa's eyes widened. "Patsy's house? I'd love to. But I can't commit for long. My aunt's situation is iffy."

A buzz of excitement warmed my skin. "That's fine. I don't need a commitment. I'm planning on my children moving into the house in another couple of months."

Melissa lifted the tray into the air. "This might just work. Let's catch up later this week and talk about it some more."

"You got it." I was doing it. Socializing. Moving on. It helped that I'd known these people for years. Our lives had changed since we'd been kids. Melissa had been smart in school. I'd always thought she'd become a doctor, or a lawyer. But she seemed happy enough working as a waitress and taking bartender shifts.

A beach rat, some might have called her. I wasn't one to judge. Melissa had been good to me since Annette and Patsy had died, and I valued her friendship.

Jackson lifted his glass to me in a toast. "I'm happy you're moving back to this part of town. You're back with your own tribe now."

My own tribe. I wasn't sure where I belonged anymore. But I tapped my glass to his and he winked. A flirty wink, and that made me uncomfortable. So did the glare I was getting from Nancy. I'd have to let her know I had no interest in Jackson.

"Ohhh," Denise said. "What about the annual Fourth of July party? You going to keep the tradition?" She sighed. "Patsy threw some great parties."

I lowered my head, twisting the stem of my martini glass between my fingers. "Nah. Patsy's parties belong to the ages."

"Totally understandable," Denise said. "It would feel strange to have a party without Annette and Patsy around."

"To Patsy's parties." I lifted my glass and we toasted. Taking a long drink, I pretended not to notice how Jackson watched my every move.

Jackson leaned forward and hunched his shoulders over the table, his eyes darting to each of us. "Hey, you guys been following the Mike Morton missing person investigation that's been in the news?"

My skin prickled. Just hearing his name could

set off my anxiety, but the topic wasn't unavoidable, and I'd been curious about what the locals where saying. I sat an inch taller. "I read about it."

"That happened so long ago." Denise said, stirring her pink drink.

Nancy eyes were wide with interest. "What about it?"

He took a swig of his beer then wiped his mouth. "I heard the reason the police have reopened the case is because the family put pressure on them. Mrs. Morton has an uncle who's a senator or something high up like that."

Panic seized my chest and I struggled for a breath. If that was true, the family had no intention of stopping. "How did you hear that?" I asked.

He leaned his elbows on the table. "I have a few friends at the police department. They talk."

A drug dealer with police connections. It didn't surprise me. "And? Any clues to what happened?"

"Well, here's the kicker." Jackson sat back and clasped his hands together. "Word is that Carol Morton, Mike's mom—she hired a psychic."

A knot twisted in my belly. I didn't believe in psychics, per se, but the family's desperation gave me no comfort. "Guess they'll try anything to find him."

Nancy looked at me. "Jackson's one of those conspiracy theorists. Thinks man never landed on the moon."

Jackson laughed. "I don't go that far. But you have to admit, there's some strange shit going on."

I shifted in my seat. *Strange shit.* "Like what?"

Jackson looked back at me. "Apparently, both the police and the private investigator are taking what the psychic lady says seriously. She's pretty well-known here at the beach." He rubbed his nose. "She's convinced Mike's mom that he's buried in the woods somewhere around Crab Creek Road and Willow Road."

Jackson narrowed his eyes and looked closer at me. "What's your theory?"

A vein in my neck pulsed. "About what?" I raised my brows and took a sip of my drink.

"About what happened to Mike Morton," Nancy said, as if I'd been living under a rock. "Everyone has a theory."

I smiled, like this was a fun game. "Oh, uh… let's see… I bet he's living someplace down south where it's warm year-round."

"Is that what you really think?" Jackson asked.

His question ruffled my calm. Did Jackson know something more? Or was paranoia distorting my rational thought? I'd used ERPT before coming tonight. Breathed enough air to blow up a Macy's Thanksgiving Day Parade balloon. "Well, I don't believe in psychics," I said, "so I'm thinking of other possibilities."

"Lots of psychics have solved crimes," Nancy said, her tone taking a turn toward sarcastic.

It was true, but the conversation made me uneasy. I ran my fingertip around the rim of my glass but said nothing.

"This psychic is supposed to be the real deal," Jackson said. "She's helped police in other crimes."

I twisted the cocktail napkin, picking at the

corners and nearly shitting myself. Was I about to get caught? So many questions came to my mind, but I was afraid to ask. Afraid of the truth coming out. *Nah. Police station gossip.* But even gossip could include a shred of truth. What else did Jackson know?

A bearded man in shorts and T-shirt knocked on the wooden table and pointed to Jackson. "We're up, dude."

Jackson downed the last of his beer and then rubbed his hands together. "Time to hit the drums."

A moan of disappointment stuck in my throat. I didn't want Jackson to leave us yet, not until I knew everything he knew about the investigation.

He slid out of the booth and put his meaty hand on my shoulder. "Now that you're back into the neighborhood," he said in a fun and flirty tone, "we should hang out sometime."

I wanted to do that, to see Jackson again. I had so many more questions. But his come-hither grin told me he had other motivations. Nancy watched us with tight lips. I wasn't there to start drama, so I brushed his hand off my shoulder. "Yeah. See you round the 'hood.'"

Jackson took off toward the stage, seemingly unaware of Nancy's forlorn face.

The curiosity was killing me, so I asked Nancy a direct question. "Something going on between you and Jackson?"

She half-shrugged and scrunched her face. "He's just a friend. Besides—" she lifted her hand

and wiggled the flashy diamond, "I'm married. Remember?"

Richard had always been a low-key guy who blended into the background. Easy to forget. "How is Richard these days?"

"Old and boring." She glared at me. "But you're single now. So, you and Jackson are both free to see each other anytime you want."

"I don't want. Jackson's a nice guy and all. Just not my type."

Nancy's lip twitched. "Why's that?"

I had plenty of reasons to list, starting with conflict of values. But Nancy was ready to defend him to the death. "I guess he's too nerdy."

Nancy's face softened, and she laughed. "True that."

I threw back the last of my martini. The only thing I wanted from Jackson was more information about the police investigation. I couldn't shake the thought of cops banging down my door. I never wanted to be under police scrutiny again.

"Welcome to Ocean Joe's, folks!" the long-haired lead singer screamed into the microphone. The crowd cheered then the band ripped into "Sweet Home Alabama" by Lynyrd Skynyrd.

My leg bounced, not to the beat of the music, but to the thump of my rapid pulse. Why was the psychic focused on Willow Road? What did she know? This information was too close to home on so many levels. I crossed and uncrossed my legs.

Socializing had opened my eyes and made me

realize how detached I'd been from the rest of the world. Staying locked up in my mole-hole had dimmed my vision, and I had no intention of staying in the dark.

"Guys," I rubbed my temples. "I'm sorry to do this, but… I feel a migraine coming on. It's been happening a lot lately. I have some medication back at my place."

"Oh, you do look pale," Denise said, patting my back. "And listening to Jackson on the drums isn't going to help. Do you need a ride home?"

"No, thanks. I took a Zoomer here." I gave her a quick hug and scooted out of the seat, looking as queasy as I could. "I'll book a driver and wait outside. The fresh air might help."

Nancy didn't stand but waved and said, "Stay in touch, girl." A shadow of a sneer was on her lips.

Pushing my way through the crowd, a guitar riff cut through the air, shredding everything but the image of Mike Morton's bones under the oak tree.

Relieved to be outside, I booked a Zoomer on my phone app and made my way off the pier to join the tourists strolling along the esplanade lined with mid-rise hotels. The balmy night air was filled with the familiar smell of fried donuts, cotton candy, and saltwater.

Come winter, when the beaches turned cold and windy, this place would become deserted, and businesses boarded up, but tonight every hotel was full and live music spilled from ocean-front bars and restaurants.

I took the landscaped path between two hotels

which led to Ocean Avenue, the main drag bustling with souvenir shops, a small amusement park, and a few haunted houses. A Honda with a Zoomer placard on the back window idled in a No Parking zone next to the Seabreeze Hotel. I hopped into the backseat.

"Hot night," the middle-aged woman driver said, turning around with a smile.

I rubbed my head and sighed. "Yes." I wasn't in the mood for conversation and felt relieved when she quickly tuned into a local pop radio station. Who the hell was the psychic Mike's mother had talked to?

The driver turned left off Ocean Avenue and onto Lighthouse Beach Boulevard, the main road running a straight-line east to west through the town.

Heading west, the lights of the resort area gave way to the dim back streets where the low-rent homes and apartments spread out for the next ten blocks. We passed an Applebee's, Dairy Queen, and a Popeye's Chicken. American cuisine. The driver merged into the right turn lane as we approached the town's main intersection and commercial hub. She stopped at the red light.

The turn signal clicked to the beat of Nicki Minaj on the radio. Besides the oceanfront resort, there wasn't much to see in town. Straight ahead was the town's shopping mall and car sales lots. If we turned left, we'd head toward the rural part of town, to the farmlands and into the wooded zone, to my new home. The light turned green, and the driver turned right, toward the bayside of town with hospitals and banks and leafy middle-to upper-class neighborhoods. My townhouse was here, on the fringe of this side of town.

Five minutes later, I was at home sitting cross-legged on the floor with my laptop on the coffee table and my back against the sofa. Jackson's news about the psychic might've kept me awake all night agonizing and analyzing, but the double dose of Xanax I'd taken a few minutes ago would soon take care of that.

I typed 'lighthouse beach psychics' into my browser. I wasn't as worried about the police finding my search for local psychics on my laptop. I'd lost two significant people in my life recently. Three, if I wanted to include my father. A lot of people hired psychics to help heal their grief. Why would I be any different?

The search yielded seven names—three doing business near the oceanfront. Top rated of the three was Madame Celeste. I visited the website and blinked at the image on the screen. It took a moment, but I recognized the silvery-blonde hair with corkscrew curls. The woman I'd seen wandering back and forth past the house on the day of Patsy's funeral. "Bingo."

Then I remembered how Noah and his dad had greeted the psychic like they'd known one another. My heartbeat pounded at my temples. *What did they discuss?*

I clicked through the psychic's site pages. World-renowned. Spiritual Advisor. Intuitive Readings. Mediumship. The testimonials spoke of warm and insightful experiences.

One-hundred-fifty dollars for one hour. A long-distance call to the dead wasn't cheap, but even at extortion level prices, I wanted to talk to her. If I had any balls, I'd go in pretending I was a news reporter and interview her about Mike's disappearance.

It wouldn't take a psychic to see I was a twisted ball of anxiety. What if she saw deeper into my being? Intuitive people worked that way. The last thing I needed was a psychic reading my spiritual aura. Worse yet, what if she found out I lived on Willow Road? Surely, she'd report her suspicions to the police.

I wasn't game to test the waters. I snapped the laptop shut.

My eyelids grew heavy, and I lifted myself onto the sofa. The fuzzy warmth of Xanax rolled through me.

I'd have to wait for more public news about the investigation, just like everyone else.

CHAPTER NINE

THE TRANSFER OF Patsy's property into my name took place one hot August afternoon and without interruption. The attorney handed me the keys, and I headed straight to the house for my one o'clock appointment with Katie.

I arrived thirty minutes early because I wanted to face my grief head-on and alone.

I was already familiar with the warm-up for ERPT. Desensitizing started with a moment of meditation. I stood on the verandah and kept focused on the present moment. Cotton-ball clouds floated high in the clear blue sky as a symphony of cicadas and crickets filled the silence.

This was a chance to become a person unencumbered by unwanted thoughts and compulsions. Free of disturbing memories. Someone who people didn't know was crazy.

A true fresh start.

Stepping inside, I felt mold and dust weighing heavy in the stale air. Muddy footprints tracked through the living room. I huffed. Patsy wouldn't have liked that. She'd always kept the house clean.

I hung my purse on the staircase rail and looked around. It was still sinking in. This land, house, and all its contents now belonged to me.

A layer of dust covered every surface. The room had a hazy hue from muted sunlight.

The place was dated. Ethan Allen country furniture from the 1990s. 1980s sponge-washed walls. Patsy had had good taste, with a lean toward the eclectic and trendy. Pure Patsy. But the fuzzy pink chair shaped like a hand had to go.

I walked around downstairs. When I had been a child, this house had seemed like a mansion. At thirty-six years old, I saw it for what it was. A tired, two-story farmhouse. Four bedrooms and two bathrooms upstairs. A formal living and dining room, and a large kitchen with enough space for the dinette and family television area. The huge deck off the kitchen.

The house was quiet. Everything exactly as Patsy had left it.

I went upstairs. On my right was the master bedroom, Patsy's room. The location at the top of the stairs had made it hard to sneak in late when we'd stayed out after curfew. I looked inside. The comforter was pulled over the pillows in a half-effort to make the bed. The curtains were open, and the window framed the family tree. My stomach hardened. A lump grew in my throat. I closed the door. It made sense to make this my room, but I wasn't ready to sleep in the room where she'd died.

The two bedrooms at the end of the hall had been used as guest rooms, though one was more of a storage room. These would become Jennifer and Eric's bedrooms.

Annette's childhood bedroom door was open. It had remained untouched, exactly the way she'd kept it during our college years, before she'd moved out on her own. A bedroom frozen in time. Snapshots of friends and fun times pinned to a corkboard. The canopy bed with its rumpled bedspread and a dent in the pillow. I sat on the edge of the mattress. A pile of crumpled tissues was next to the pillow. Tissues filled with the dried tears of a mother who'd lost a child. I thought of Patsy being alone in this room, this house, crying herself to sleep each night. My heart grew heavy.

Slam.

A vein across my temple pounded against my brain. The noise had come from downstairs. Like the front screen door.

Katie.

I bounced up from the bed and smoothed my hair. Katie would be pleased to see how I'd coped with being here in the house. So far, so good.

At the top of the stairs, I froze. The heavy, red front door was wide open, as I'd left it, with the transparent screened door closed. My purse still hung on the rail. No one was at the entry. "Katie?"

No answer.

My heartbeat pounded against my head as I tip-toed halfway down the staircase. A quick eye scan showed no one in the living room.

Rap, rap, rap. The screen door hit against the jamb. I took a relieved breath and hurried down the steps. I mustn't have closed the door all the way. I checked the driveway. Only my car was there.

"Damn wind." I clicked the door tight and headed toward the kitchen. A flash of green caught my eye. An oak leaf lying on the pine-wood floor in front of the fireplace. I froze. My pulse pumped a few hard beats. I didn't remember seeing it when I'd come inside. I picked it up—fresh and tender to my touch.

I whipped my head around, searching every corner of the room. Had this leaf come from the family tree? Or had it blown in when I'd come into the house?

I'd never believed in ghosts but thought maybe I should've.

Was this leaf a message, like the leaves I'd been getting in the mail from some weirdo?

No. No. No. No. I couldn't have thoughts start up now. I inhaled deep, in and out. *Focus on the breathing.* Leaves blew into houses all the time; there was no need to obsess.

I crept into the kitchen. A drip of water plunked into the stainless-steel sink. The smell of stale spices and cooking grease hung in the air. The round dinette table, and the two-seater sofa and small flat-screen television she'd set up in a cozy corner. Nothing had changed. The remnants of Patsy's presence in the house still lingered.

I bolted out the kitchen door and onto the deck. The hissing and rattling of the cicadas drowned out all sound as I walked into the back-yard. I counted aloud in sets of five. "One, two, three, four, five." *Again.* "One, two, three, four, five." *Again.* I repeated the process until I stood before the majestic family tree full of green summer leaves.

The leaves on specific tree species could vary; they could be as distinct as an ethnic group of people. People fit into different groups and families. So did trees. The forest surrounding the house had grown into a community of loblolly pines, birch, holly, maple, and the common white oak. The leaves on forest oaks had rounded tips on their lobes.

The family tree was different. It was a Southern Red Oak. The leaves on this tree were oblong with eight slender and pointy lobes. Exactly like the leaf in my hand.

Ice cold shivers ran down my scalp, my spine, and to every limb in my body. My knees shook. *Someone had been in the house. Someone had intentionally put the leaf on the floor.*

The hiss of cicadas grew louder. Males screeching for mates. I tossed the leaf aside and it landed with the cicada exoskeleton shells littering the ground. The relentless insects crawled all over the branches, and I quivered as a slow growing prickling sensation spread across my skin. It was late into the season for so many cicadas to be around.

For seventeen years, the insects had lived deep in the ground under the family tree, feeding on the juicy roots. The same roots which fed on soil soaked in the blood of Mike Morton. Roots which carried human DNA through every limb on the tree.

A cicada jumped on my bare arm and I flinched, brushing it off. "Get off me, you bastard." Another cicada flew at me and hooked itself onto my long hair. Chills pushed through my body with the force of an icy shower.

I swung my head back and forth as the cicada dug deeper into the tangle—*bzzz, bzzz,* buzzing toward my scalp like an electric razor on a mission. My fingers desperately threaded through the mass of hair, separating strands to free the bug.

"Jolene?" A man's voice called out.

I turned my head. It was Noah, walking toward me from the side of the house. "Fucking great," I mumbled with my head upside down. I wasn't in the mood to talk with a cop.

"You doing okay there?" He drew closer.

"Damn cicada flew into my hair. Can't get it out." The buzzing moved closer to my scalp, and I pulled through my hair even harder. Noah was a couple years younger than me, but probably remembered my 'Psycho Girl' days, so if he'd ever doubted my sanity, this moment would have confirmed it.

Noah gently grasped a handful of hair, with the bug now so close to my scalp that I could feel the prickle of its legs. "Stay still for a second," he said. "I'll get it out."

Goosebumps covered my warm skin. I held my breath. I could feel him gently pulling apart the long strands. I really needed a haircut.

"Here it is." He flicked his hand, and the buzzing stopped.

I stood straight and watched the cicada fly away, wishing I could do the same. I smoothed my knotted hair and looked at him. His face was warm, kind, inquisitive. "You're my hero for the day. Thank you."

"I was driving by and saw your car out front. Thought I'd see how you're doing."

Passing clouds blocked the sun. I shivered. "As well as could be expected."

"It's been a tough year for you. I know how close you were to Patsy and Annette. The three of you had a long history together."

I hesitated. He was trying so hard to be cool, but I knew he wasn't here to console me. "Yeah. We were close."

"Visited my dad at the nursing home today," he said.

"How's he doing?" I squirmed and brushed my arms because I still felt cicadas clawing.

He laughed. "Alzheimer's is a funny thing."

"Funny how?"

He eyed the tree, from the base of the trunk to the leafy crown, and then turned to me. "Dad can't remember what happened yesterday but can remember every detail of what happened seventeen years ago."

"I'd call that tragic. Not funny."

He smiled, considering my face for an awkward moment. "I got a promotion, by the way."

I crossed my arms. "Oh, yeah?"

He opened his jacket and revealed a shiny silver and gold badge. "Homicide detective."

"Congratulations." My knees wavered, but I'd kept my voice steady.

He put his hands on his hips and looked around the property. "Dad won't stop talking about the

Mike Morton missing person's case."

Heat rose to my face, causing sweat on my forehead. My instincts were right. This was no friendly visit. Keeping a straight face wasn't easy, but I had to act like we were just two friends shootin' the shit. "Oh, yeah. I remember he was involved in trying to find out what happened to him."

"His dementia symptoms come and go, but he's still obsessed with the mystery of what happened to Mike."

Every muscle in my throat constricted, muting my voice. "Uh, huh."

"Dad remembers a lot of details about the time Mike was last seen. And it's the details that gnaw on him. For example, he remembers he'd stopped by to visit Patsy." Noah chuckled, then shook his head. "He had a crush on that woman. Not that she'd ever give him the time of day."

I glanced down at my hands. The vein in my wrist throbbed, and I counted each beat in my head. *Five, ten, fifteen. Stop.* "We all miss Patsy. Is that what's gnawing at him?"

"Oh, he's mourning her, that's for sure. But it's what happened on that day when he came here—August 4th, 2003, to be exact—the morning after Mike was last seen. Dad said Patsy wasn't home. Just you and Annette."

My stomach clenched. "That's right. Patsy was down in North Carolina celebrating her divorce. Annette and I were just hanging out, listening to music, talking about college." *Taking acid and burying a dead man.*

"You were both up early that Sunday morning. Went straight to Old Dominion Nursery and bought this tree." He pulled on a branch and plucked off a few leaves.

My tongue stuck to the roof of my mouth, but I needed to speak if I had any intention of figuring out what the hell was happening. "We went to McDonald's for breakfast first. Hash browns and coffee." My tone blurred the line between naïve and sarcastic. Now I was certain Old Man Baker had given Noah an earful of something.

He looked at the oak. "This is the tree you two bought."

Sweat dripped down my spine. What had Annette and I done to make Old Man Baker suspicious? An image of that day flashed in my mind. The bruises on our arms and legs. The red mark on Annette's face. I cracked a smile. "That's right. Is it a crime to buy a tree?"

He laughed then play-punched my arm. "Lighten up, Parker. I'm just curious."

Part of his friendliness felt genuine. If I'd lived a normal existence, Noah would have been the type of guy I would have made a play for. Handsome and hardworking. Rough edges under his pressed shirts. I had the feeling he wasn't as clean-cut and all-American as he liked people to think. Probably secretly surfed kinky porn sites on the Internet.

But homicide detective was the role he played now, and he was here to dig up information about Mike's disappearance. "Why's your dad so interested in this tree?"

"Not many people plant trees in the dead heat of summer." He put his hands on his hips, exposing the shiny badge hooked onto his belt. "That's one thing that's been itching my Dad's intuition for years. It's made him come up with some outlandish theories."

I kept my expression blank, like I had no idea what he was talking about. And I didn't. Changing tack, I shifted my tone from curious to nostalgic. "Patsy wanted to plant an American Red Oak right in this spot. Annette and I decided to plant it before we went away for college the next week." I laughed for a second. "If we'd left it up to Patsy, it never would've gotten done."

A rumble of thunder filled a few moments of silence. Cumulus clouds expanded to cover half of the blue sky.

"Convenient," Noah said. "I mean, how the deep hole had already been dug."

My heart thumped. How would he have known the hole was already there unless his father had told him? What else had his father said? Was Old Man Baker the person I'd seen running across the lawn that night?

I laughed, like Noah had triggered a happy memory. "That damn hole had been there for two years. Patsy changed her mind about the pond and decided a tree would be better." I smiled and looked lovingly at the surrounds of the tree. "She was so excited that Annette and I had planted it for her. This was her favorite place to sit, you know. Right here at this picnic table."

Noah considered me for a moment. "You have

a strong connection to this tree."

"For the whole property. Sounds like you do, too."

"I do feel connected. And now I'm interested." He kicked the tree trunk.

I winced at the thud, and my stomach tightened like he'd punched me in the gut. Was he playing games, toying with my mind? I stayed blank-faced, but fear clawed at my skin. "Interested in what?"

Noah rubbed his leather-soled shoes against a frayed ground root. *Scuff, scuff, scuff.* "We have a new police chief. He's shaking things up at the department and we've been looking into some unsolved mysteries."

"Oh?" I cringed at the grating sound of shoes against the fibrous root. Like sandpaper scraping on skin. I wanted to tell him to stop.

"Wants to get closure on cases which have gone cold. As it happens, the chief is good friends with the Morton family. He's determined to help them."

A cool wind came in a rush, and an avalanche dark clouds moved in, throwing shadows on the forest. I shivered. "I heard about the re-opening of the investigation on the news."

"I promised Dad I'd find Mike." Noah sighed. "His parents are still alive and healthy. They've always refused to believe Mike just disappeared. Mike's mom is convinced he's dead and buried somewhere."

"That's an awful thought. I would have figured they had hope of finding him alive. Living on skid row somewhere."

"I'll get to the point." Noah sighed. "The police have reason to believe Annette and Patsy knew something about Mike's disappearance."

His blunt words jabbed my gut. "What? Why?" I glared at him. What the hell was he talking about? Patsy had known nothing about what happened to Mike. I was sure of it. Her warm and kind heart wouldn't have been able to handle the truth.

"We're re-interviewing people who lived within two miles of the spot Mike was last seen. Retracing his footsteps. Checking all angles." Noah rubbed his nose. "I can't disclose our reasons, but since you were a close friend with Annette, and you were at her house around the time Mike was last seen, I thought you could help give us some insight into the case."

Nerves scrambled in my stomach. Noah had most likely learned about Annette's retracted rape charges against Mike, either through Old Man Baker or police records. Inspector Gadget could've seen the motivation, but I wouldn't bring it up. "I-I mean, your dad questioned me and Annette years ago. He talked to Patsy, too. But if it helps, I'll go over it again. I arrived at here around 9:00 p.m. We stayed home all night, listening to music and talking about going back to college the next week."

Noah pursed his lips. "Yeah. I read the police reports."

Thunder pounded the air sending birds screeching from their forest perches. I rubbed my bare arms to smooth out the goosebumps. My name was in police reports. I'd stored away the memory of the day Old Man Baker had showed up at Patsy's house to question whether we'd seen Mike Morton. Another buried blip. "Maybe he was hitch-hiking and someone with bad intentions picked him up."

Noah ignored my comment. "How was Annette feeling when you arrived that night? Did she appear anxious?"

"Anxious? No. We were both in good moods."

The air crackled. Noah looked to the darkening sky and then the surrounding forest. "Something happened on these backroads. And someone knows exactly what."

I looked at him, nodding. If only he knew he stood over Mike's body. "I heard about the reward. Anything come of that?"

His jaw twitched. "I can't comment on an ongoing investigation."

"Oh. I thought that was what we were doing."

Noah glanced over my shoulder. "I think you have company."

I turned. Katie stood at the side of the house waving. "I'll wait for you on the verandah!" she called out.

"Go ahead inside," I called out. "The front door is open—I'll be right there." The raindrops increased and I smoothed back my hair. I'd prepared for this therapy meeting with Katie and left my house that morning full of confidence. Noah's visit had changed that.

Thunder boomed and birds shrieked in the forest. Chills ran over my skin and I hugged myself, shivering in my rain specked dress. "Time for me to head inside."

"Sure thing." He tapped his forehead and gave a goodbye salute. "Glad we had a chance to talk. If you remember anything you think might be helpful with the investigation, let me know. Any little detail."

"You'll be the first to know." I forced a friendly smile. "Bye now." The raindrops increased to a shower, and I took off toward the back deck while Noah ran toward his car in the driveway.

I had more than a stalker and random leaves to worry about. Now I had the heat on my ass. I couldn't lie to myself any longer. The investigation was in full force and showed no sign of fading away.

CHAPTER TEN

THUNDER POUNDED THE sky and the ground shook as I charged through the rain, up the back deck, and through to the kitchen. I ripped a handful of paper towels from the roll on the countertop and blotted my face. *Fucking Noah.* Wasn't hard to figure by his interrogating questions that he'd linked Mike's disappearance with the family tree.

"Everything all right back there?" Katie called out from the living room.

I pushed my damp hair off my face and the thoughts from my head then I walked into the living room, still dabbing my arms with a paper towel. My bones rattled, but I steadied my voice. "Uh, sure. I'm fine. Just got a bit wet."

Katie narrowed her eyes. "You sure everything's okay?"

"Of course. Why?"

"It's just, I noticed the police decal on the license plate." She looked at me as if she'd just asked a question.

The police are looking for the body I buried under the oak tree in the back yard. Chills crawled across my skin. I wished that thought hadn't snuck in.

"Noah's an acquaintance. Just stopped by to see how I'm doing."

"That was nice." Her tone was soothing, but her expression was pure I-don't-believe-you.

Heat flushed up my neck and face as the thoughts came through unbidden. *Noah is onto me. Onto the secret.* I tossed the paper towels on the coffee table and fanned myself with my hand. "Whew. It's quite stuffy. I think we need to get some air in here." I slid open the front window, and the humid summer air hit my face.

Katie tilted her head and examined me for a moment. "You look anxious. Anything to do with your friend who was here?"

"No, no. Definitely not." I fidgeted with my hands. "It's the house, I think. The memories. I mean—I came here about half-an-hour ago by myself. Already walked around a bit."

Katie touched my shoulder with one hand and gestured to the armchair with her other. "Let's sit down and go through this together. We can talk about some strategies for moving past the grief and make living here on your own easier."

I plonked down into the armchair. "I won't be living here alone. A friend is moving in and renting for a while."

"A renter?" Katie looked pleasantly surprised. "How did this come about?"

Relieved to get off the subject of Noah, I talked about Melissa moving in and the rekindled friendships with Nancy and Denise. "And I've hired an estate sales company to sell everything. With some paint and new furniture, I can make this my home."

"Starting fresh is a good idea." She smiled, tilting her head. "How's the medication working? Is it still helping control the thoughts?"

My eyes drifted to the spot on the floor where I'd found the leaf. *Stop overthinking.* Leaves flew around everywhere on this property. It was the intense investigation which stood between me coping and falling apart. I turned to Katie. "I'm not having crazy thoughts anymore. It's been easier to control my crazy."

Katie looked at me disapprovingly. "You're not crazy. We've discussed this before."

Few people ever thought I was sane. Annette. Patsy. And now Katie, if I wanted to believe a therapist.

She gave me a warm smile. "Soon, you'll be living in the house and enjoying the life you want."

I admired her optimism, but I had a bigger problem than how to cope with living in the house. That wasn't even on my radar at the moment. It was the damned investigation looming over me that had my nerves on edge. I didn't like any kind of attention. Especially homicide detective attention. Not when I was so close to getting my children back.

But with my name linked to Mike's missing person case, laying low and waiting for the investigation to fade away wasn't an option anymore.

Thunder pounded and the raindrops popped against the roof.

Katie placed a notepad and pen on the coffee table. "Shall we get started with the exposure therapy?"

Figuring out how to block police interest in me and the tree was foremost on my mind, and I would have deal with that, but now wasn't the time. I straightened my spine and stood. "Let's begin with the grand tour."

———◆———

Wandering the rooms of the house alone, surrounded by the accumulation of Patsy's material life on display, I could still feel her presence. But today, I would finally let go. After a month of ERPT sessions with Katie, I was finally ready to begin the process of moving into the house.

Nothing new had been reported about Mike's missing person investigation, or maybe I hadn't been paying attention. But I figured the leads the police had claimed to have had fizzled out or else they would have already hunted me down.

Instead, I'd enjoyed a full week with the children as Aaron had promised, along with random trips to the beach and the new house so they could pick out their bedrooms. It had all passed quickly and uneventfully.

Since the twins had gone back to school a week ago, I'd kept myself busy packing up the townhouse and getting quotes for some cosmetic updates to the new house.

The crew from Beloved Keepsake Estate Sales had come the day before and taken inventory of everything down to the smallest bric-a-brac, then staged the house into a vintage 90s shop.

I was obsessed with planning for a more positive future, and soon the old reminders of the past would go, and I could make this place my own home. Peeking through the curtains in the living room, I saw that cars were already lining up on the street. I expected the estate sale crew any minute.

Ring, ring. Ring, ring.

The landline. I turned toward the kitchen. Patsy had stayed old-school and kept the same handset and message recorder for thirty years. I remembered how Patsy had set the machine to pick up on the sixth ring in order to give herself enough time to pick up a call.

Ring, ring. Ring, ring.

I would have preferred to get rid of the machine and line, but Mrs. Nichols had told me that old friends of Patsy's were still calling this number and leaving messages. Over the years, I'd seen a string of long-time friends stop and visit or call out of the blue, so it wouldn't surprise me.

Ring, ring. Ring, ring.

I hesitated. I wasn't good at delivering bad news.

Ring, ring. Ring, ring.

Exhaling a breath, I picked up the phone. "Hello?"

Someone was breathing, but not talking.

"Hello?" *Did we have a bad connection?*

"Mmmm." A moan. More breathing.

My temperature rose. I didn't have time for pranksters. I plonked the handset back in its cradle. I actually wanted to take the phone out. I didn't need a landline. But Patsy would've wanted me to keep it for a little while just in case an out-of-town friend called.

Ding dong. Ding dong. Ding dong.

"Knock, knock. It's the Beloved Keepsake crew here."

I shook off the weirdness of the phone call and went into the living room where two other estate sale staff wasted no time in setting up sales stations.

Time to get this day started and done.

"Good morning." Melissa's chirpy voice filled the room. She came inside and handed me a takeaway coffee from the Espresso Bean Café. "A double-latte for you."

I curled my hands around the warm cup. "I really appreciate you being here for me through all this."

She gave me a half-hug. "You shouldn't have to go through this on your own."

"You loved Patsy, too. I'd really like you to have something of Patsy's. I already told Denise and Nancy, if you guys see anything here that you want—you know, for sentiment, or whatever reason—it's yours. Take it. They're already roaming around upstairs looking for something."

"What about the estate people?" Melissa whispered.

"I've already informed them I was donating some of the stuff. Just let them know what you're taking so they can mark it off the inventory."

I wandered around the living room as buyers walked up the driveway.

"These are gorgeous," Nancy called out from the dining room. She came to me holding out a rectangular red velvet case.

The box wasn't familiar to me. "What's in it?"

Nancy lifted the lid. "Aren't they pretty?"

My knees weakened. Crystal candlesticks. The crunch of Mike's skull exploded in my eardrums and drowned out all sound. I grabbed hold of the side chair and clutched my T-shirt at my chest.

"Are you okay?" Nancy put her hand on my shoulder.

The room spun, but I didn't want anyone to see me like this. Moving into this house was going to be a challenge; I was putting myself in danger of triggers, in the firing line of triggers for obsessive thoughts. My medication had been working, though, and the thoughts came and went fast instead of clawing into my mind. I was determined to get what I wanted: a stable home for me and my children. To be a sane mommy. I took a deep breath. "No. I'm fine. I-I just remember those, too. Patsy had meant to get rid of them after finding the chip. She was superstitious about things like cracked glassware." I grabbed the box from her. "You don't want these. They're bad luck."

Nancy took the box back from me. "I don't believe in that stuff."

"I'd hate for you to be cursed. Like Patsy. Like Annette." I pressed my clasped hands to my chest. Desperation clipped my tone. "Let's sell them. Better yet, let's throw them in the trash."

Nancy's face twisted. "I don't think they're cursed. These will bring back memories of Patsy's parties and the holidays." She took out the cracked candlestick and held it up to the light coming through the front window. A rainbow prism reflected on the wall. "It's just a small nick. No one will notice."

I snatched the candlestick out of her hand. "Please, Nancy. Take anything else. It's just... if I see these candlesticks at your house... all the bad luck, I-I—"

Nancy's expression shifted from bitch-you-just-told-us-to-take-what-we-want to flat-faced confusion. She shoved the chipped candlestick at me. "Okay, then. Take them."

My face burned with embarrassment as I put the candlestick back in the box and closed it. But this was one item that had to disappear. "Sorry, Nancy. I don't mean to overreact. But this is so hard for me."

She shrugged and looked away. "Don't worry about it. There's nothing else I really want anyway."

"Everything going okay in here?" Melissa held a Tiffany-style lamp. Her face wrinkled into worry.

I didn't know how long Melissa had been standing there, but the concerned look on her face told me it had been long enough.

Nancy tilted her head toward me. "All is good."

Melissa nodded at Nancy and then pointed to the velvet box. "What's that?"

"Just candlesticks." I held the box tight. "Something Patsy thought was cursed. I-I'm surprised she kept these."

Melissa looked at me with wide-eyed curiosity.

"Well, show me."

I opened the box but didn't look inside.

Melissa's face brightened. "Oh, I remember those. Patsy used them all the time." She looked at them longingly.

Nancy wrinkled her nose. "She's worried they'll make her sad and bring bad luck." Her tone didn't hold back on sarcasm.

Melissa set down the lead lamp. "We don't want to take anything that'll make you feel sad."

I was acting odd, off-balance, and I didn't want Melissa and Nancy to notice. It was important I appeared sane, capable. I was getting closer to my goal of having my children back, closer to fitting back into the world, and closer to developing friendships. I didn't need to start acting bizarre now. "No… I'm okay," I said.

Denise walked into the room and gave me a look of pity. "Hey, I couldn't help but overhear. I don't need to take anything either. I mean, that's what you're trying to do anyway. Get rid of everything."

I blinked hard. It hadn't been my intention to come across as grudging. "All of you, please. Take anything you want. Anything but these candlesticks." I laughed it off. "Leave the bad luck for someone else."

All three women looked at me like I'd lost a screw. My vision blurred. It had happened again. I'd disappointed people. My erratic behavior was damaging new friendships before they even got started. I couldn't risk that. Having friends was part of my overall plan to blend into the world again.

At that moment, I needed to get away. "Excuse me, guys. I'm going to check in with the sales staff and make sure everything is okay." I flew out the front door, holding the box close to my chest. *Run. Run. Run.* It was how I'd dealt with shame. Turn my head and run.

At the bottom of the verandah steps, I took a deep breath of fresh air.

Estate sale lookie-loos drove slowly past the house. A car door slammed nearby, and I blinked. Bargain-seekers ambled up the driveway. People. I didn't want to talk to people. I only wanted to get rid of these damn candlesticks.

A sales attendant was in the driveway greeting and directing people into the house. I slipped into the open garage for a moment to regain my calm. A disarray of shoes and handbags spread out over three tables triggered my need for organization. I set the candlesticks on a table displaying old bottles and books found in the attic, and then went to work organizing. I separated the shoes by color and arranged them in rows of five. "One, two, three, four, five."

"Excuse me," a man said.

The voice startled me, and I blinked a few times, easing my mind from my ritual. A man in khaki pants and a white button-down shirt smiled at me. He was too preppy for a typical garage and estate sale buyer. I didn't trust men who wore long pants and button-downs on a Saturday. "Can I help you with something?"

"I think you can." He laughed like we were

friends. "I understand you're the owner of this property."

I rolled my eyes. Whatever he was selling, I didn't want it. "That's me. But all sales are being handled by the attendants wearing name badges."

He held out a business card. "Name's Shep Black. I'm a local developer and—"

I waved my hand at the card. "Oh, I'm not interested in selling."

"You know the McDougal property across the street sold?"

A muscle in my neck twitched. I hadn't even known it was on the market. "Hadn't heard."

"Sold for one-and-a-half million dollars."

I bit my lip. Damn, what I could've done with that money. "That land's been vacant for a long time. Are the new owners building a home there?"

"Not a home." He lifted an eyebrow. "Twenty homes."

"What the—you mean the city has approved a subdivision?"

"Plans are in the final phase of approvals." He looked around the house. "Are you planning to develop the property?"

"Look, I'm not going to waste your time. I'm bound by contract not to sell or develop this property in my lifetime. I couldn't sell it even if I wanted to."

"Contracts have loopholes."

"Not this one." I pictured a developer razing the oak tree and finding Mike's decomposed body. I shivered. *Never.*

A middle-aged woman in Bermuda shorts came

inside the garage and rummaged through Patsy's collection of antiquated soda and medicine bottles. Shep jabbered on about other properties in the area that were up for sale. Interesting, but selling wasn't an option.

Then, I noticed the woman in shorts holding the candlestick box. My stomach knotted as she removed each candlestick and examined every detail.

"I'll let you get back to your sale." Shep held out his hand. "Thanks for your time."

I shook his hand, but my eyes were on the woman as she removed each candlestick and examined every detail.

"I'll go ahead and take these," the woman said. She closed the box and looked at me. "Now, where do I pay?"

Just then, Nancy came into the garage from the front of the house. "Hey, you. There you are. The lady running the estate sale is looking for you inside the house." She looked at the woman holding the candlesticks, and her expression shifted from perky to deflated.

My skin burned under Nancy's glare. "Uh… thanks, Nancy." I turned to the woman. "You'll find someone inside to help you."

The lady walked away with the candlesticks, taking the memory while leaving the tension.

The muscles in Nancy's jaw tightened. "I need to head home now. Richard and I are going to the garden center."

Guilt and shame squeezed my throat. Nancy had been so supportive, and all she'd wanted was the candlesticks. I'd hurt people who cared about me, and if I didn't watch my step, no one would want to be my friend. I'd make up this candlestick debacle to her somehow. I rushed to hug her. "Thanks for coming by this morning."

Nancy walked off, leaving me alone with my misfit personality.

CHAPTER ELEVEN

I PACED THE LIVING room floor of my new home. It had taken another three weeks after the estate sale to finish the painting and update the place. The old-fashioned curtains had been replaced with white shutters. My slate-colored linen sofa and armchairs fit easily into the room. The country dinette and a cozy corner and comfy two-seater were similar to how Patsy had liked her large kitchen arranged, but I'd made the house feel like my own. Still, the emptiness and shadows played games with my mind.

I'd been living in the house for four days now. Melissa had moved into Patsy's old bed-room upstairs and we'd spent the past few nights together eating take-out and drinking wine. I'd grown used to her chirpy chatter. But tonight, she was working the late shift at Ocean Joe's, and I was alone with nothing but my thoughts for company.

Ring, ring. Ring, ring.

My heart jumped a beat. It was the damned landline again. As I walked into the kitchen, I considered letting the answering machine pick up.

Ring, ring. Ring, ring.

I stared at the phone on the countertop. None of Patsy's old friends had called or left a message on the answering machine like Mrs. Nichols had assumed would happen. So far as I knew, the last time the phone had rung, it had been that creepy heavy breather.

Ring, ring. Ring, ring.

I picked up the phone. "Hello?"

No response, but I heard a shuffling noise and murmurs, like someone talking at a distance. Shivers crawled across my shoulders and down my arms. This was no prank. "Who the hell is this?" I yelled into the phone.

The rustle of paper sounded, and then a mouth close to the receiver, breathing like the person had just run up a flight of stairs.

My heart stopped. "Who is this?"

Click. The hum of a dial tone.

I pressed *69 on the keypad to retrieve the phone number. *Blocked.* Fear crawled up my spine like a line of centipedes. I slammed down the receiver.

Someone wanted to scare me. Why else would I have gotten a second call?

No. I was overreacting.

What I really needed was to flush out the paranoid thoughts. Nothing a Xanax and a bottle of wine couldn't cure. I shook a pill out of the orange bottle and reached into the refrigerator for a bottle of wine. Finding the fridge empty of alcohol, I remembered that Melissa and I had been enjoying drinking a bottle, or two, every night since she'd moved in.

I realized knocking myself out every night with wine and Xanax wasn't going to help, but I planned to hop off this merry-go-round of zoning myself out very soon. Just not tonight.

Thank goodness a Mini-mart had recently opened on the corner of Crab Creek Road and Marshland Drive. It had become the busiest corner in this rural suburb. Handy for an emergency alcohol run. I put the pill in my front jeans pocket and left the house.

Five minutes later, I plonked a bottle of cheap Shiraz on the Mini-mart cashier counter and handed the clerk a twenty. Twangy country music played on a radio.

"Hey, kiddo." A man's deep voice from behind. "We meet again."

I turned. It was Jackson, a goofy grin stretched so wide across his face that I couldn't help but smile back. I pointed my chin at the carton of milk and bag of BBQ potato chips in his hands. "Planning a big night?"

"Just me and Netflix." His eyes shot to my bottle of wine. "I've got something better back at the house. I'm only around the corner. Wanna join me?"

"Uh—" I couldn't form an answer. On one hand, this was a chance to find out if Jackson knew anything more about Mike's investigation. But socialize at someone else's house? It'd been a while since I'd done something that simple without feeling the need to run back to the safety of my own home.

"Anything else I can get you, miss?" the clerk's quick words cut into my thoughts.

"No, thanks." I picked up the wine and put the change in the children's charity box on the counter. I looked at Jackson and nodded to the door. "Let's talk outside."

Standing by my car, I contemplated whether or not to go to his house. His subtle flirting at Ocean Joe's had made me uneasy, but he'd always been playful and harmless. I needed to drop the paranoia and lighten up if I expected to have a normal conversation with Jackson and get more information.

Jackson whistled as he pushed through the storefront's glass double doors. He was safe enough, and I had pepper spray in my bag, should I need it.

His lit-up eyes met mine. "S'up?"

"If I can pick the movie, it's a deal."

"If it's not a RomCom, you're on."

"I'm more of an action kind of girl."

"Niiice. Let's do this." He pointed to his blue pick-up truck. "I'm just up the road."

I followed his truck about a mile down Crab Creek Road, in the other direction from my new house. He turned left onto Cardinal Street and then another quick left at a rickety grey mailbox on a post. The long, narrow driveway cut a swath through loblolly pines and a forest thicket until we reached a clearing.

An outdoor sensor light went on and I saw an ordinary and unassuming brick ranch home. Complete with a welcoming red door. Jackson parked in front of the house, killed his headlights, and walked the short path to the front door.

Parked next to him, I didn't turn off my car yet. A chill ran through my bones. This place was dark and isolated.

"Come on," Jackson called out. He gestured for me to get out of my car.

Seeing Jackson wait for me at the front door with his carton of milk, bag of chips, and boyish smile struck me as innocent. I shoved aside my negative thoughts, switched off the engine and went inside.

Jackson shut the front door behind me and turned the security bolt. "My house is my castle."

His house was a shit box. It smelled like old socks and stale pot smoke. A gaming station was set up in front of the mega flat screen mounted on the wall. Bachelor pad. A golden retriever met us with a wagging tail, and I softened.

Jackson tossed his keys on top of a stack of gaming magazines on a sideboard then patted the dog. "Hey, Buddy."

Buddy's wet nose sniffed my hand and legs as he circled me, his soft tail whipping against my jeans. Patting his head, my muscles melted. I wanted a dog. For the kids and my own company. I could take Jennifer and Eric to the pound to pick one out soon. Giving love to an unwanted pet was something I could do.

"Check this out." Jackson lit a spotlight. "What d'ya think?"

I turned to my right. A display of swords and sabers fanned out across an entire wall. The handles joined together in a semicircle and the tips pointed outward in a starburst. Prickles spread over my scalp. Shit, what had I gotten myself into?

The sharp-edged steel gleamed in the light. An icy chill ran through my blood. Knives and swords. "Civil war?"

"Yup. Confederate and Union." He stepped closer to the display and ran his fingertip along the blade of one of the longer swords. "This one is still razor-sharp." His eyes glazed and the corner of his lip curled. "Sometimes I wonder how many people died by these swords."

His trance-like admiration as he touched each piece struck me as disturbing and unsettled my stomach. "That's a strange thought."

His eyes cleared like he'd snapped back to the present. "Nah. I'm just obsessed with American history."

Obsessions. That, I understood. *He's a collector. That simple.* This was not the time to overthink. I turned away from the display, ignoring the uneasiness rolling through me. "Cozy place you have here."

He turned off the spotlight and pointed to the worn brown leather sofa. "Make yourself comfortable. You ready for a glass of red?"

I wanted a tumbler full of wine, but I was only two days away from the high possibility of getting my child custody rights reinstated. No way I'd risk another DUI. But he'd invited me there for a drink, and half a glass wouldn't even register on a police breath test. My full bottle of Shiraz and Xanax in my pocket would have to wait. "Sounds good."

"Drinks coming right up." He disappeared through the archway into the kitchen.

I sat on one side of the couch. The house was small and typical of the older homes in the area. The difference being this two-bedroom, one-bath house was filled with thousands of dollars' worth of antique collectible swords and sophisticated computer equipment.

"So how do you like being back in this part of town?" Jackson said as he walked back into the room. He handed me a glass of ruby colored wine. "Remind you of the old days?"

I took the wine and snickered. Jackson himself reminded me of the old days more than he realized. "Speaking of the old times, I don't know if you remember seventeen years ago—"

He fell back into the space next to me on the sofa with a beer can in hand. "Oh, man. Seventeen years? I was a wild kid back then."

"Do you remember selling Annette some acid one summer? Back when we were in college?"

"The purple haze?" His eyes brightened. "Hell yeah, I remember. There was a big supply of it going around for a couple of years. I sold about a dozen sheets. Made some ridiculous cash."

"Did you ever try any yourself?"

"Damn right I did. Acid like that only comes around once in a lifetime." He put his hands up. "Not that I'm doing that shit anymore."

"So, that was a rare batch? I only ever did acid that one time. I have nothing to compare it to."

"That acid, my friend, was some potent shit.

Like, each blotter had an extra milligram in it. And the high…." He flicked his hand in the air. "Whoosh. It took me away to different worlds."

"Do you remember everything that happened while you were on it—I mean, tripping? What did you remember afterwards?"

Jackson rubbed the stubble along his jaw then nodded. "I remember hanging out with Johnny Fasio and Richard Miller one time—"

"Wait. Nancy's Richard?" I didn't recall him being part of the crowd from this part of town back then.

"Yeah. Anyway, we'd each taken a blotter. After a half hour, we got impatient. So, we each took another half. Then, it hit us hard. Boom!" He made an exploding hand gesture next to his head. "We laughed our asses off all day. Everything was beautiful. I loved that shit."

"So, the acid you guys took was from the same batch that you sold Annette?"

"Absolutely." He moved closer and casually ran his fingertip along my arm. His eyes met mine, and he grinned like we shared a secret. "You said you did some. What was it like for you?"

Cringing at his touch, I set my wine glass on the coffee table and scooted away a few inches, hoping he'd get the message that I wasn't interested. "It was surreal. The hallucinations…incredible. I can still remember the crazy colors and images Annette and I saw."

Jackson sat back and sighed with a smile. "Ahhh, Annette. All the dudes at school had it bad for her at some point."

"Did you?"

"Nah." He winked at me. "I had a thing for you."

I picked up my wine glass and laughed, like I didn't notice his flirting. "See—my thing back then was to get the hell out of this town. And look where I am. Still here."

He raised his beer in a toast. "Cheers to that. It's great having you here."

Matching his toast, I took a big gulp of wine. "Hey, speaking of the old stuff, heard anything new on Mike Morton's disappearance?"

He raked a hand through his hair. "Not much. I know his family is really hurting and getting desperate to find him."

My gut twisted. I didn't like being reminded that Mike had family who cared, but I needed to press on for information. "So, what about the psychic you were talking about last time I saw you? Is she giving the police any useful information?"

"I dunno. You'd think the $50,000 reward would have brought something out."

I sank into the sofa. "No kidding. I wonder if police have been getting any calls."

"Who knows?" Jackson said. "Probably from a bunch of crazies hopin' for an easy buck. Turning sideways to face me, he rested his bent knee on the sofa and leaned closer. "You know…" his voice had lowered, like he was telling me a secret, "Mike went missing around the same time I was dealing that acid I sold Annette. I even sold him some."

My heart jumped. The acid. Mike's disappearance. Had Jackson put two and two together? "What do you mean?"

His smile faded. "It's just—I sold it to him a few days before he went missing. I hope he didn't overdose and get into trouble. I mean, the guy was an asshole, but... I do wonder what the hell happened to him. It's like the earth just swallowed him up."

I flinched. "A lot of people are wondering the same thing."

Jackson looked to the ceiling. "You know what I remember about that summer? The cicadas. Never heard 'em hiss so fucking loud." He lowered his gaze to me. "Remember that?"

"Yeah. I do." But my ears were tuned into something else at the moment. Crunching noises outside the window behind me. Footsteps. I caught my breath and turned. Thick dark curtains covered the windows. Rustling of leaves. Buddy lifted his head and looked at the door. The dog whimpered.

The hair on the back of my neck rose. "Is someone here?"

Jackson rolled onto his knees on the sofa and pulled aside the curtain. Floodlights lit up the overgrown shrubbery and leaf-littered lawn. My car sat in the driveway.

He opened the curtain wider and scanned the front of the house. "I don't see nothin'. You probably heard a raccoon or a fox." He shut the curtains and sat back.

"I guess I've been living in suburbia too long,"

I said. I forgot about the animal noises in the forest."

He patted my shoulder. "You can relax. You're safe with me."

I picked at my nails and my senses pumped into overdrive. The stale smells, the worn leather sofa, the unorganized mess—it swirled around me, making me nauseous. I considered calling off the movie and going home. "I'll get used to the sounds again."

"Hey. If you need to chillax, I've got some killer kush."

I shook my head. Pot and paranoia didn't mix with my biochemistry. "I'll pass. Thanks for the offer."

"How about a foot rub?" He nudged me. "I'm told I'm the best."

"Let's stop with the touchy-feely stuff, okay?" He wasn't forcing anything, but he needed to know flirting with me was a dead-end street.

He shrugged then picked up the remote. "*Fast and Furious?*"

"Sure." He played the movie and my mind wandered to the reward. Fifty thousand dollars. Fuck. I remembered what Noah had said to me. *Someone knows what happened.*

It was 10:37 p.m. when I got home from Jackson's house. Melissa was stretched out on the sofa in the living room, reading the latest Nora Roberts paperback. Grateful to have her back, I felt tension I hadn't known I'd held melting off my shoulders and back. "Hey, you're home early. Quiet night at Ocean Joe's?"

Melissa sat up and tossed the book on the coffee table. "The new manager put too many people on the roster. I decided to take the night off and keep you company. Been home over an hour. Where've you been?"

I fell back into the armchair. "I ran into Jackson at the Mini-mart and he invited me to his place to kick back and watch a movie."

"Oh, yeah? How's the good ol' boy doing?"

"I'd say he's doing fine. This was the first time I really sat down and talked with him in years."

"What about his sword collection? Kind of creepy, huh?"

"You've seen it?"

"Who hasn't? He loves showing it off."

"It's confronting. I'll say that."

"Was Nancy there?"

"What? No. Wouldn't she be home with her husband and their boys?"

"Doubt it." Melissa stood with a grunt. "Never can tell with Nancy."

She held up her empty wine glass. "I'm getting a refill. Get you one?"

The Xanax in my pocket came to mind. "Sure."

"Don't get up." Melissa patted my shoulder. "I really appreciate you letting me stay here and giving me a deal on the rent. The least I can do is get you a glass of wine."

"Thanks for that." I fell back into the armchair. I'd forgotten the cheapo bottle of Shiraz from the

Mini-mart in my car. I'd have to share that with Melissa tomorrow. Contentment settled on my shoulders, and I rolled my neck. I had a home. Friends.

"Here we go." Melissa handed me a wine glass filled to the rim. "It's a Sauvignon Blanc I found on sale up at the BiLo."

I popped the pill into my mouth and gulped it down with the crisp wine. "Delish."

"Did Jackson mention anything about Nancy?" Melissa sat back on the sofa and put her feet up on the whitewashed coffee table.

I curled my legs under me. "No. Why?"

"I think Jackson and Nancy are having an affair," Melissa said in a low voice, as if someone might hear.

"Seriously? Why do you think that?"

"She spends a lot of time with him. Does that sound like something a married woman does?"

"They've known each other for a long time. Could it be they're just friends?"

Melissa giggled. "Nancy is obsessed with Jackson. They've been hooking up off and on for years."

I'd seen Nancy act protective and attentive toward Jackson on that night at Ocean Joe's. Flirting. She definitely hadn't liked Jackson giving me any attention. "And Richard… is he aware of all this?"

"He's an idiot, but he ain't that stupid. He'd have to know something."

"I always thought Richard and Jackson were friends."

"Oh, hell no. Richard had a falling out with Jackson a long time ago. Before he and Nancy got married. Something about a girl they both liked. Back before Richard and Nancy got married. Richard can't stand Jackson. He'd be crushed if he ever found out Nancy was seeing him behind his back."

I took another drink of wine. Gossiping about Nancy's personal life felt uncomfortable. How could I know if what Melissa had said was true? Besides, I had more exciting things happening. "Guess what—I have my child custody hearing in a couple of days." I held up crossed fingers. "I'm hoping to get my rights back."

Melissa's eyes lit up. "Oh, that's right." She pressed her hands into a praying pose. "Tell me all about that."

"I have a good feeling." Getting my children back was one of the few situations I did feel good about.

"I hope it works out for you." She sat back and sighed. "I always hoped to have children."

I saw the longing in her face. Soon after high school, Melissa had married a rat-faced guy from Kentucky. It had lasted a few years—until he'd up and left her for 'no damn good reason,' as she'd put it. She'd stayed single all these years since then, and with the free-spirited lifestyle she liked to live, I'd thought that was exactly how she liked it. "You still have time."

"I need a man first. A responsible man. If you can tell me where to find one of those…." She groaned then took a swig of her wine.

Her cell phone lit up and pinged on the coffee table. She picked it up and read the screen. "Shit. This isn't good."

"What?"

"My Aunt Kelly in Richmond. Every time she calls me, there's a problem. I need to give her a call." She stood and went into the kitchen.

I laid my head back on the headrest, grateful that I had a friend like Melissa. I knew she'd had a rough upbringing with her alcoholic mom and no dad. But even at school when we'd been growing up, she'd always been upbeat, a go-with-the flow kind of person. I hoped she'd find someone to settle down with one day. Someone who appreciated her.

Melissa returned to the living room. "Looks like my aunt needs someone to stay with her for a couple of days, so I'm going to head out to Richmond early in the morning." She narrowed her eyes. "You going to be okay while I'm gone?"

My muscles tensed and I picked at the grime I felt under my nails. Alone in the house? It had to happen eventually. "Of course. Your aunt—is she going to be all right?"

"Yeah." Her tone turned melancholy. "Her Parkinson's is getting worse. Nothing anyone can do about that."

Tightness gripped my chest. My own mother. If she were alive, she'd be close to sixty years old. Though Melissa's aunt was pushing eighty, I realized at this moment how I'd never have an older family member who needed my care.

I didn't want to be alone, but Melissa had her

own problems. I'd made progress and was ready to put my ability to live in this house alone to the test. I'd be fine. "You don't need to worry about me. Go take care of your aunt."

I emptied my wine glass and let the warmth of alcohol and Xanax soothe my worries.

Everything would turn out fine.

CHAPTER TWELVE

THE HARD-FACED CHILD custody arbitrator sitting at the head of the long conference table reminded me of an over-worked schoolmarm, haggard and stern. I sat on the other end of the table with Aaron at my side. For the past five minutes, the old bitty had flipped through the psychologist's report without saying a word.

My hands trembled, but I kept them clasped and under the table so my shaky anticipation couldn't be construed as neurosis. Aaron alternated between tapping his foot and drumming his fingers on his thigh. I exhaled through my nose. He had no rhythm, no beat to count.

"You've made progress." The arbitrator's sharp tone cut through the silence. Her eyes stayed on the report as she flipped another page.

I straightened my spine. "Yes. The therapy sessions have helped immensely." *Lie. Lie. Lie.* Thank goodness I'd taken the time off during the school semester and I could keep myself numb on Xanax every day. Well, every day but today. Today I was stone-cold sober, and I'd promised to wean myself entirely off the mind-numbing drug.

The expressionless woman looked down on

the report and pursed her lips.

Every muscle in my body contracted. I was so close to having my rights reinstated, I could feel the children's warm breath on my cheek. Katie had provided plenty of proof that I was capable of caring for the twins. Only minutes ago, Aaron had given the arbitrator his statement of faith in my abilities. The court had no reason to deny the request.

"You've moved into a new home." The arbitrator peered at me over the reading glasses almost falling off her nose. "Tell me about that—how are you coping with the change?"

Aaron stopped drumming and shifted his weight in his seat.

"Losing another person in my life hasn't been easy. But the responsibility of caring for my children motivates me to stay strong and take care of my mental state. Besides, the children know and love the house and property I've inherited. I see a positive future." I sat up straighter and plastered on a face of serenity. The past few days without Melissa at the house had worked out surprising well—with a little help from my friend in the orange bottle.

"I can vouch for that," Aaron said. "The kids are excited about their mom moving into the house. Patsy was like a grandmother to them. They grew up around that house."

My heart warmed, and I gave Aaron a grateful smile.

The arbitrator nodded. "Good. Then, I concur with the therapist." She closed the file and looked into my eyes. Her face and tone softened. "Jolene, you've made great strides in getting your life back together. I see no reason for you not to have your custody reinstated."

Tightness in my shoulders melted, and I released a long breath. Finally, I had what I wanted. Relief swept over me for the first time in what seemed like forever. I'd done it. I'd convinced Aaron, Katie, and the court that I was mentally stable. Pretending sanity had become my forte.

Walking through the lobby of the colonial courthouse with Aaron, I laughed, unable to contain my joy. The hearing had ended so suddenly that I hadn't adjusted to the good news. Now, I understood the expression 'over the moon' because my feet were so light that I could have leaped into the exosphere.

Aaron chuckled. "It's really nice to see you doing better."

"Having the kids again is going to help even more." I couldn't erase my smile. My efforts at convincing everyone I was stable had worked. Katie, the arbitrator, Aaron. Maybe Nancy and the others didn't see me that way, but the important people in my life had noticed how stable and sane I'd become, and that was all that mattered.

"It'll be good for the kids too," Aaron said. "And I'm glad you have a good friendship with Melissa. Seems like she's been a real support to you. Good friends are hard to find."

"Yes. Melissa and I go way back." My weird behavior had caused me to lose friends in the past. I'd always believed only Patsy and Annette had ever really cared. Maybe it was time to rethink my perspective.

"That's great." Aaron rubbed his hands together. "Once India and I get back from London with the kids, I'll drop them off at your house."

"I'll be ready." I'd known months ago about the two-week vacation Aaron and India had planned with the kids. I could live with that. It wouldn't be long now before the children would be mine for a week. For the first time in almost three months.

We went our separate ways. The sun was high in the sky, and I drove home with my windows down and the cool October air whipping around my face. The exhilaration gave me a new perspective. I was truly on the road to getting my life back in order, excited about exploring new horizons.

I walked into my empty house through the garage and dropped my purse on the kitchen counter. Everything was still, quiet. The clock on the wall ticked a steady pace forward, each second an empty echo. Though I'd been fine on my own for two nights, I wished someone was with me now to share the joy.

The furniture was mine, and the dishes, silverware, coffee pot, and every other damn thing a house needed. Not a single remnant of Patsy and Annette's life remained in the house. I'd thought getting rid of the reminders would make moving forward easier, but the truth was, I missed them both too much.

I longed for the old days—when Patsy, Annette,

and I would sit around the kitchen table, laughing and planning the next house party. Whether for Christmas, the Fourth of July, or an oyster roast on a cool autumn night, Patsy had always enjoyed opening her home to good friends and neighbors. It had been hard to fall on the wrong side of the fence with Patsy—she'd accepted everyone.

I rubbed my arms and paced the living room floor. Soon, my children would share this place with me. Though, at the moment, I could've used the company of an adult to join me in celebrating my victory.

It wasn't even noon, and I was ready to numb my loneliness and grief with wine. I opened the refrigerator and reached for the chilled bottle of Pinot Gris, but hesitated, closed my eyes and remembered the innocent faces of Jennifer and Eric. My shoulders slumped, guilt wrapping so tight around my chest that I had to catch a breath.

The wine was too tempting, and I knew one glass wouldn't be enough to quench this thirst for love and acceptance. I closed the refrigerator door. I didn't need to anesthetize myself anymore. My children were coming back to me. Soon, I'd have everything I needed.

Keys jingled and I heard the front door open.

"Jolene?" Melissa called out in a strained voice.

My breath released and I moved into the living room. I hadn't expected her back from Richmond until tonight. I hesitated in front of the fireplace—a heavy weight of dread landing on my shoulders. Melissa was guiding a shaking and frazzled Nancy to the sofa. Something was horribly wrong. I rushed closer. "What's happened?"

Melissa's normally tanned face had been stripped of color. "I've been trying to call you for the past hour." Her voice cracked. "Something awful has happened."

"I'm sorry... I was at my child custody hearing. My phone's been off all morning." I looked down at Nancy on the sofa, unnerved by her bulging eyes staring off into space. She'd clearly been traumatized. I sat next to her on the sofa and kept my voice calm. "What happened?"

Nancy turned to me. Her weathered face had aged twenty years. "Jackson...he's, he's... dead. He's been murdered." She bent over and sobbed into her hands.

Murdered. The word sucked air from the room. I clutched at my throat and stumbled for words, but I had no voice—only images of a vibrant and alive Jackson parading across my mind with his hearty laugh, his larger-than-life presence. I shook my head. "No—it can't be. I just saw him the other night."

"I know." Melissa looked down at me. Her forehead wrinkled. "And I'm sorry, Jolene, but I had to tell the police you were at his house."

"W-why did you do that?" My eyes darted between Nancy and Melissa. Their looks turned cold and chilling, like those of two ghosts.

They think I had something to do with Jackson's murder.

Chapter Thirteen

MELISSA WALKED IN circles around the living room, patting her chest. Nancy sat next to me on the sofa and bawled into her hands. This didn't seem real. *Jackson. Dead.* I'd just been at his house. "Melissa, tell me—what the fuck is going on?"

Melissa stopped in front of the fireplace and took a deep breath. "I'll tell you exactly what happened. Nancy called me this morning from the police station. Told me she'd found Jackson dead." She paused. Lines deepened on her forehead. "I drove straight to the station from Richmond. When I got there, the detectives asked if they could talk to me—you know, because I'm a friend of Jackson, too."

"Of course. But how did my name come up?"

"They asked me if I'd seen Jackson and if I knew who he'd associated with in the past few days. I mean—I saw him at Ocean Joe's on Friday, and I told them that." Her face twisted into agony. "I'm sorry, Jolene. I wish I didn't have to mention it, but I couldn't avoid telling them I knew you went to his house on Saturday night. They would've found out eventually, and I had no reason to lie."

My shoulders slumped. "It's okay. You don't need to apologize. The police are just doing their job. Besides, I have nothing to hide. He was alive and well when I left." I turned to Nancy. "But why were you at the police station?"

Nancy scooted a few inches away from me and dabbed her puffy eyes with the back of her hand.

Melissa sat on the sofa on the other side of Nancy and patted her back. "Go ahead," she said in a motherly tone. "Tell Jolene what happened."

"I found his body," Nancy said, clasping her hands to her chest and rocking. "I found his body. I called the police."

A ball of grief and tension filled my chest. "Found him... how?"

Nancy wiped the mascara dripping down her cheeks. "We planned to meet at the target shooting range yesterday afternoon. When he didn't show, I called him, and, well, he always returns my calls. Always." She dabbed a tissue under each eye and then wiped her nose. "So, I decided to stop by his house this morning. I left early for work so I could catch him before he went to his job site."

Tingles ran down my neck and my blood ran cold. I remembered the noises I'd heard outside Jackson's window. Was Nancy in the habit of randomly showing up at his house? I couldn't rule out the possibility that it had been her I'd heard.

Nancy blew her nose then took a deep breath. "So, this morning, when I got there, Buddy was in the backyard, running the length of the chain fence, barking like mad. I rang the doorbell and noticed the front door was cracked open. Jackson never leaves his front door unlocked, so I figured he was just inside." She paused and her face contorted.

Melissa stroked her back. "It's okay. It's okay. Go on."

"No one was in the house. Everything looked normal." Nancy took another breath and her shoulders shuddered. "Buddy was still barking, so I thought Jackson was in the backyard. I went back there—didn't see anyone, but Buddy nudged my hand and ran to the fire pit at the far end of the yard." She bowed her head, her shoulders shuddering as she sobbed.

I rubbed my hands on my thighs. I didn't want to pressure her, but if the cops had my name, I wanted to know exactly what had happened. Using my quiet voice, I pressed on. "What did you see, Nancy?"

She looked to the floor and spoke in a monotone. "The fire pit—it was filled in with a mound of dirt, and a small tree was planted in the middle."

The ground dropped and my chest fell like a collapsed soufflé, sucking all the oxygen out of my lungs. *Someone saw us.* "D-did you say a tree?"

Nancy nodded. "Buddy pawed at the soil around it." She made a scratching motion, imitating the dog. "He sniffed and barked at the ground. I-I took a closer look." Her breath hitched. "At first, I wasn't sure—then I saw it. A hand sticking out of the ground—Buddy was licking the fingers." She wiped her eyes. "I knew it was Jackson when

I saw his silver ring."

A chill stabbed my core, and I pressed a fist to my stomach. *The tree. The tree.* I wanted it to be a coincidence. "What kind of tree was it?"

Nancy's eyes narrowed, her voice flattening. "Why does it matter? Someone killed Jackson and tried to hide his body."

"They didn't do a good job," Melissa said.

I pressed my fists against my temples. Dark terror spread from the crown of my head to the pit of my stomach. The tree had been intentional. *Someone knows. I've been right all along.* Small stars burst in my vision, growing larger, brighter, and multiplying until I was blind and all I could see was Mike's rotting body under the tree.

Shit. Now wasn't the time for a panic attack.

"Jolene," Nancy's graveled voice cut into my thoughts, "what were you doing at Jackson's house on Saturday night?"

I put my hands on my lap and stared into a dark space of my mind's making. Nancy was talking—I heard her muffled voice—but a vision dragged me way back. Back to someone running across the lawn on that dark night long ago. *Someone knows.*

"Jolene." Melissa's sharp tone sliced into my thoughts. "Nancy asked you something. What are you going to tell the police when they ask what you and Jackson did on Saturday night?"

It took a moment for my eyesight to adjust. "Sorry. I'm still in shock."

Nancy squared her jaw and pointed a finger at me. "Why were you at Jackson's house?"

Heat rose up my neck and a primordial urge to attack swirled through my blood. Nancy's accusatory tone had worn thin. I mourned Jackson, too. But I'd seen her jealous and protective streak, and now wasn't the time to rile her any further. I kept my voice gentle, but firm. "I ran into him at the Mini-mart, and he invited me over to watch a movie. That's all."

Nancy's scowl said she wasn't convinced. "How long did you stay there?"

"A couple hours. We watched *Fast and Furious*. Then, I went home." *Poor Jackson. Dead.*

"That's right," Melissa said to Nancy. "That's exactly what I told the detectives. She got home around 10:30 that night."

The tree. The tree. I needed to redirect the conversation. Find a connection. "Was Jackson robbed? He has that huge sword collection...all the expensive computer and gaming equipment."

"Nothing was stolen that I noticed." Nancy lowered her head.

For all we knew Jackson had kept a secret cache of drugs and money which could have been taken, but I'd keep that thought to myself. "Jackson was such a nice guy. I hope the police quickly find the killer."

"It doesn't matter anymore." Nancy dabbed her eyes. "I'm fucked any way you look at it. The police said they might have more questions. How am I going to explain to Richard what I was doing at Jackson's house at six o'clock in the morning? And the police... they might want to question Richard, too." Her body slumped.

"Fuck. My marriage is over."

Melissa stroked Nancy's back and whispered, "It'll be okay. Take deep breaths."

I stood and paced the floor. The initial shock had drained from my veins, but my heart pounded with fear. Nancy had every right to be worried, but so did I. The police knew I was one of the last people to see Jackson alive, and they wouldn't waste any time tracking me down for questioning.

My alibi was flimsy, but the clerk at the Minimart had seen me Saturday night with Jackson before I'd gone to his house, and Melissa had made a statement about the time I'd come home. I wasn't too concerned about proving my innocence. But if this story blew up and my name appeared in the press, Aaron would read things the wrong way, thinking I'd been hanging out with a rough druggie crowd and making bad choices again. He'd worry for the safety of the children, and I could kiss my custody rights goodbye.

But I had two weeks before Aaron and the twins returned from London. My best hope was that the police would find the killer and wipe my name off the radar before then.

Breathe. I grabbed the corner of the fireplace mantel, lowered my head and slowed my thoughts.

The tree.

Jackson's murder.

My steps stayed even, from one side of the room to the other. This foreboding sense of danger wasn't paranoia. I couldn't lay low and carry on with my days as if what had happened to Jackson wasn't somehow connected to what Annette and I had done to Mike. I needed to figure out the connection.

Something bad is going to happen.

I whispered and counted in sets of five. "One, two, three, four, five. One, two, three, four, five. One, two, three, four, five." I repeated the process I didn't know how many times until I heard my name. I stopped mid-count.

"Jolene." Melissa's face read 'what the fuck,' but her tone was all concern. "Are you doing okay?"

A banging in my chest muffled my hearing. This couldn't happen. I couldn't slide backwards. Melissa and Nancy stared at me with confused expressions, waiting for me to answer. "It's my nerves." I wrung my hands. "This whole situation has me shook up."

"I know." Melissa rubbed her forehead. "We're all shocked."

"I can't put this off any longer." Nancy lifted herself up from the sofa. Her thin legs trembled in her skinny jeans and black, over-the-knee boots. "Richard's left two messages. I need to go home and tell him everything."

Melissa rose from the sofa and jingled her keys. "Let's do this. I need to get back here to get ready for work. Joe said I could work double shifts the next few days to make up for the time I had to take off to care for my aunt."

A spasm gripped my gut. Melissa wouldn't be home much the next few days. If the detectives came by to interview me, chances were that I'd be alone to deal with them. Then, I saw Nancy looking into the small mirror next to the front door, wiping mascara off her cheeks. My chest joined my gut and squeezed my entire core. I was being selfish to worry about myself when Jackson had just been murdered. I got up and gave Nancy a hug. "Take care of yourself. Be sure to let me know if you need anything." Her body stiffened at my touch and she pushed away from me.

"I just want to get home." She turned and walked out the door.

Ouch. Her tone held no kindness and that hurt. I hugged myself, realizing Nancy didn't trust me.

Melissa wrapped an arm around me. "She's not always like this. She's just stressed out right now."

"Of course. She's been through a lot."

With everyone gone, I released a pent-up breath. It didn't soothe my nerves. Adrenaline pumped through my veins and every nerve in my body snapped to attention. If I wanted to understand what was happening now, I had to allow my mind to wander back to that night. Every detail was crucial.

The tree. Answers lay with the family tree.

I bolted out the back door and across the yard, and then stopped. The tree was magnificent—a crimson explosion against the blue October sky. My breathing slowed and warmth filled my chest. I remembered how Patsy had loved the tree in autumn.

How, in the early days of its life, she'd planted a flower bed around the trunk—water-sucking impatiens which she'd cared for each day. That had been Patsy's jam: making things beautiful.

The tree had flourished, growing fast and strong; its bulging roots had long ago choked out the flower garden. In summer, it had given us a shady spot for the picnic table; in autumn, it exploded with color; in winter, Patsy had hung LED Christmas bulbs on the bare branches; and in spring, when the green buds reminded everyone of new beginnings, she'd hid colored Easter eggs in the cradle of forked boughs for the twins to find.

This tree was part of the happiest seasons in my life. Part of my family. It felt natural to forget Mike was buried underneath its thick trunk.

I stood there breathing slowly, helpless and yet desperate to get us out of danger.

For the first time in a long time, I took a close look at the tree. The alligator skin bark and two knots high on the trunk which Jennifer had once said reminded her of a pair of eyes looking at the house. At least thirty-five feet high, its bulky, bare branches reached out like the arms of a giant Mandrake with hundreds of leaves as tiny red hands.

A cool breeze brushed across my face. I pulled my cardigan tight across my chest and hugged myself as I gazed over the manicured two acres. Autumn color blazed through the surrounding forest of evergreens. Splashes of magenta, gold, orange, and red. But nothing compared to the crimson color of the family tree.

Through the thinning trees near the road, I caught a quick glimpse of a car driving toward the end of the road. An image from that night slammed into my mind—the trailing ribbon of colored tail lights through the trees as we'd buried Mike. The Nichols' car. I'd never asked Patsy or Annette what the Nichols had reported to the police all those years ago. Never had a reason.

My head pounded, and the palms of my cold hands sweated. Looking back triggered obsessive thoughts. Thoughts which clawed into me like blood-sucking ticks.

I wouldn't jump to conclusions. Not yet. As long as Aaron and the twins were still in London, I had time to dig deeper and figure out who killed Jackson. I took a deep breath. It was time to face my demons.

CHAPTER FOURTEEN

IT DRIZZLED RAIN on the morning Jackson was buried at the Lighthouse Beach Cemetery. The seats under the canopy for the graveside service were full of family and close friends.

I sat in the aisle seat in the back row next to Melissa and Denise, dabbing my eyes and nose as Sarah McLachlan sang "In the Arms of an Angel" through the speakers behind the pulpit. My watery eyes glossed over the photo of Jackson with his happy-go-lucky smile on the cover of the funeral program. He hadn't deserved to die.

"Guess what?" Denise held up her cell phone and spoke low. "Nancy just texted. She and Richard won't be coming to the funeral."

Melissa curled her lip and spoke even lower. "Jerk."

When Melissa had suggested we make an appearance as a show of support and comfort to Jackson's family, I'd agreed. I had other reasons for coming, of course. For the past two days, I'd stayed locked up at home, on edge and hoping the police had found the killer or had been too busy following stronger leads than to come and question me.

The earthy smell of freshly turned soil permeated the air, clogging my lungs. I picked at the phantom filth beneath my nails.

The tree. The tree.

Dirt. Decay. Death.

The music stopped and a young pastor stepped up to the pulpit and began the service with a prayer.

Jackson's mother hunched in the front row while his white-haired father sat straight with his hand on her back. Grief twisted up my chest and into my throat. His parents were suffering the agonizing pain of losing a child. Like Patsy had. Like no one ever should. But I needed to stick to my mission, not get lost in grief.

It was said that most murders were committed by someone close to the victim, so while the pastor led a prayer, my eyes scanned the crowd, and I played a game of spot-the-killer. I stretched my neck for a better view of the crowd. At least a dozen people stood outside the canopy and beneath umbrellas. My two biggest suspects weren't here, though.

The way I broke it down, Richard could have killed Jackson out of jealousy, and Nancy was covering up for Richard. Considering his wife had been having an affair with Jackson, Richard had the motivation. Jealousy had been the cause of many murders. And how well did I really know him or Nancy?

We'd all gone to primary school together. I'd attended Richard and Nancy's wedding fifteen years ago and seen him half a dozen times since then, lurking and bored at Patsy's parties—which Nancy had dragged him to—and more recently when he'd showed up at both Annette and Patsy's funerals. A man of few words, we'd rarely spoken.

But how did that explain the oak sapling planted over Jackson? Could Richard be Jackson's killer and the person who saw us bury Mike? No. He was the type who would've taken the reward by now. And Nancy. I'd only seen her treat Jackson with adoration, but I'd seen her jealous streak, and who could know people's twisted minds? I couldn't rule her out as the killer.

Who else?

A family member? Jackson's older brother and sister sat next to their parents. Sibling rivalry could be motivation for murder, but I didn't know them well enough to make any assumptions. His bandmates sat with their wives and girlfriends. Creative rivalry? Maybe. I turned to the people closest to me. Melissa and Denise.

Nah. Melissa loved Jackson like a brother. Besides lacking motivation, she'd been in Richmond in the hours he'd been killed. Her whereabouts had been verified by the police. And Denise? A woman who didn't go to the beach because she didn't like getting sand on her? Nope.

My gaze caught two poker-faced men in dark suits holding umbrellas who were walking toward the canopy. A tall, grey-haired man with a low brow, steely blue eyes, and square jaw that looked strong enough to crack walnuts—a direct descendent of Neanderthal Man. His slick-haired, younger companion hid behind dark sunglasses.

The older man caught my eye. He acknowledged me with a nod and held my gaze until I looked away. I had a sick feeling they weren't here to pay their respects.

I elbowed Melissa. "Take a look at the men in black walking this way."

Melissa glanced toward the walkway. "Shit." She leaned toward me, covered her mouth. "Those are the detectives who questioned me and Nancy about Jackson."

I crossed my legs and shifted in my seat. I'd figured they were cops.

Denise leaned forward in a cloud of Chanel perfume. "What's going on?"

Aware of the detectives watching us, I patted my nose with a tissue, concealing my lips. "The detectives investigating Jackson's murder are here," I whispered to her. "We'll talk about it later."

Denise's mouth opened then she sank back in the chair, shooting a sideways glance at the detectives.

I watched the two men from the corner of my eye. They hadn't moved. But here they were, surveying the guests at Jackson's funeral and searching for the same person I was—the murderer.

The service continued with a few of Jackson's close friends giving brief eulogies that included heart-warming stories and funny anecdotes.

I wanted to leave right after the tributes, but the detectives had their eyes glued to me and I didn't need to draw any attention to myself. While the pastor wrapped up the service, I blotted my mind with mindless images of ocean waves and drifting clouds. But other pictures intruded. *Blood. Bones. Bodies under trees.*

The minister's voice boomed over my head like a cue from above. "Let us bow our heads in prayer."

With my head bowed, my mind wandered to ways I might find out what was happening with the investigation. What leads were the detectives working on? For all I knew, they'd already stopped by to question me as a person of interest. The doorbell had rung a couple of times in the past two days, but I'd weakened and kept myself numbed with wine and Xanax, and besides a brief Facetime conversation with the twins in London, I'd avoided human contact.

At the end of the service, I turned to Melissa and Denise. "I'll catch up with you two later."

Melissa waved. "I should be home from work by six."

Denise blew us both kisses. "Bye, my lovelies."

Making my way to the parking lot, I peeked over my shoulder. The two detectives followed in the distance. No slipping under their radar.

A ray of sun peeked through the grey sky. My damp hair stuck to my neck, and I pulled it back. Then, I saw him in the distance. Noah.

He struck an eerie pose standing alone among marble headstones adorned with crosses and angels. He wore jeans and a casual blue jacket with the hood pulled low over his head, but not so low that I couldn't see his somber face.

I almost waved, but he looked sheepish, like he didn't want to be noticed. Then he turned and walked away.

I hopped into my car and drove off with Noah on my mind. As far as I knew, he'd never been close to Jackson, so why was he hanging out on the sidelines of the man's funeral and not in a suit and tie like the other detectives? The Lighthouse Beach Homicide Department wasn't huge, and I couldn't imagine they had a surplus of homicide detectives on staff. Something was off, but I couldn't put my finger on it.

A glare of afternoon sun caught my eye, and I checked my rearview mirror. There was the white sedan I'd noticed on my tail when I'd left the cemetery parking lot. The tinted windows made it hard to see who was in the car, but I recognized the familiar silhouette of a massive head in the driver's seat. The detectives from the funeral.

Taking deep breaths, I figured they had other reasons to drive in this direction. Nancy and Richard, along with some of Jackson's friends, all lived out this way. They could've been on their way to see any of them.

I turned onto Willow Road, and the sedan turned too. Tightness pulled across my shoulders. I wasn't too surprised. I couldn't fake a flu forever.

I pulled into my driveway, pressed the garage door remote, and drove inside.

Car wheels rolled on the asphalt driveway.

My eyes closed and I tapped a finger on my thigh. "Two, four, six, eight, now it's time to radiate." I repeated my stock-standard mantra five times.

A car door slammed. Then another.

I opened my eyes and filled my lungs with air. *I had nothing to do with Jackson's death. I have nothing to hide.* All I needed was to tell the truth. Then I'd be cleared in the investigation.

Releasing a breath, I hopped out of my car with all the moxie I could manage. The two deadpan detectives stood in the driveway. I pasted on my best confused-and-concerned expression and walked toward them. "Can I help you?"

The Neanderthal held up his badge. "I'm Detective Warren and this is my partner Detective Larson. We're with homicide. We're looking for Miss Jo-leene Parker."

His baritone pressed against my composure, squeezing out my tiny reservoir of confidence. I eked out a polite smile, hating that my lips trembled. "You found her."

Detective Warren put his badge away, but he kept his eyes drilled on me. "We've just returned from Jackson Howell's funeral. I'm sorry for your loss."

I sniffled. "Thank you. And, yes, I did notice you there."

"May we come inside and ask you a few questions about Jackson?" Detective Warren asked.

"Of course. Come on in." Dabbing my nose with the back of my hand, I led the detectives through the front door and repeated the truth in my head.

I have nothing to hide. I have nothing to hide. I have nothing to hide.

"Please, have a seat." I gestured to the living room sofa. "Can I get you both something to drink? A glass of water?"

Detective Larson sat on the sofa and straightened his tie. "No, thanks," he said. "We're fine."

Warren didn't sit, but he wandered across the room while scanning every corner like a nosy kid looking for a candy bowl. He turned to me. "You've been busy these past few days?"

A vein in my neck twitched. I knew when I was being baited. I wanted to ask why he wasn't out looking for the murderer, but I simply sat myself into the armchair. "I had a terrible flu. A temperature of one-hundred-and-four degrees. Could barely get out of bed for the past two days." I ripped a tissue out of the tissue box on the table and wiped my nose. "I'm still recovering. Probably shouldn't have been at the funeral."

Warren rubbed his chin. "Uh-huh. Is that why you're not attending the family's funeral reception?"

"No, it's not. See, I've lost two of the dearest people in my life this past year. Jackson is another loss, and frankly, I've hit my quota on wakes, funerals, and receptions."

Larson rested his elbows on his knees. "We're sorry for all your loss. Right now, we're trying to get some answers on what happened to Jackson. Can you help us with that?"

I sat back. "Of course. What do you need to know?"

"When was the last time you saw Jackson?" Larson asked.

"Five nights ago. I believe Melissa Harrington told the police that. She's my roommate and was here when I came back from Jackson's place."

"Can you tell us more about that evening?" Detective Warren's attention was on the framed photo on top of the fireplace mantel—me with the twins at the beach last summer.

"I ran into him at the Mini-mart," I said. "Jackson, he's—*was* an old friend. We reconnected when I moved back to this part of town recently."

"Did you arrange to meet Jackson at the Mini-mart?" Detective Warren asked.

"No. I did not." If I had come across any more adamant, I would have sounded defensive.

Warren adjusted the photo on the mantel. "You said you've just moved back to this part of town... where did you live before?"

"On the bay side of town. I recently inherited this house." His non-reaction gave me the feeling he'd already known that.

Larson pulled a small spiral notebook and pen from inside of his suit jacket. "Go ahead. What happened at the Mini-mart?"

"Jackson... he invited me to his place to watch a movie."

Detective Warren took slow steps toward the sofa. "How long did you stay at his house?"

"Less than two hours. We watched *Fast and Furious*, and I left around ten-thirty. Came straight home. Jackson was fine when I left his house."

Detective Larson eyeballed me. "Do you know of anyone who had a grudge against Jackson? Someone who might've been threatening him?"

Nancy's husband, Richard, came to mind. But I had no evidence and was reluctant to point a finger. "No. He'd always seemed easy-going. I don't know anyone who'd have wanted to hurt him."

"Uh-huh." Detective Warren sat on the other side of the sofa and then rested his gaze on me. "And how was Jackson's mood that night you were with him? Did he seem edgy? Upset?"

Jackson's cheerful face flashed in my mind, and I swallowed back the pain rising in my throat. "No. He was happy and laid-back. Typical Jackson."

"Did anyone call or stop by while you were there?" Larson poised his pen on the pad.

The rustling shrubs outside the window came to mind. "No. But we'd heard some noises outside. Buddy barked at the front door like someone was there."

"And?"

I shrugged. "Jackson turned on a bright outdoor light. We looked out the window but didn't see anyone. Figured it was a raccoon or a fox."

"Uh-huh." Larson jotted a note on his pad and shot another question. "What time was it when you heard the noise?"

"Not long after I got there. Before we started watching the movie."

He raised an eyebrow. "Anything else?"

"The movie ended, and I went home. Melissa Harrington confirmed that." I didn't like repeating the obvious, but I also didn't like how they'd minimized my alibi.

Larson clicked his pen twice. "And did you and

Melissa go anywhere after that?"

"We watched some TV and then went to bed."

"You were both home all night?" Larson asked.

The wine and Xanax had hit particularly hard that night. I'd slept like a rock. "Yeah. I woke up around seven the next morning. Melissa got up about half an hour later. She was upset that she'd overslept because she'd wanted to beat the traffic to Richmond."

The detectives nodded at each other like they were in agreement over something.

"And you?" Detective Warren asked. "What did you do on Sunday?"

I clasped my hands on my lap, ignoring the need to pick at the dirty guilt and grime under my fingernails. I wanted to tell them how I'd gone grocery shopping, baked an apple pie, and had coffee with a neighbor. Truth was, that Sunday had been my last hurrah with mixing a double dose of Xanax and a bottle of wine. I'd promised myself that if the court reinstated my custody rights, I'd stop using the drugs and wine as a crutch. "I stuck around the house. Did laundry. Caught up on paperwork."

Detective Warren stared me in the eye. "Did you leave the house?"

"No."

He leaned forward and rested his elbows on his knees. "Did anyone stop by?"

"No. Melissa was in Richmond. I was alone."

Larson spoke. "How well do you know Nancy Miller?"

I shifted in my seat. This had started to feel like

an interrogation. "About as long as I've known Jackson."

"And Richard Miller," Larson said. "How well do you know him?"

"Nancy's husband? I mean, he's from the area. We've all known each other since primary school."

"Nancy and Jackson," Detective Warren said, his tone so deep it would have made Johnny Cash jealous. "What can you tell us about the nature of their relationship?"

My mouth dried, and I wanted a drink of water. "They were good friends. We've all known each other since primary school." I didn't want to believe she'd killed Jackson. She loved him too much.

"Oak trees," Larson said. "Tell us what you know about oak trees?"

Blood drained my face, and my hands went cold. "Oak trees?" My voice barely cracked out the words.

"That's what I said." Larson kept his eyes on me. "What d'ya know about them?"

My bones rattled so hard that my teeth chattered. I spoke with my mouth slightly open, avoiding teeth-to-teeth contact. "I-I don't understand."

"The killer placed an oak sapling over Jackson's body," Detective Warren said matter-of-factly.

I hesitated, worried I'd stutter. My danger radar detected a strange vibe. No matter how hard they tried to act like this was a casual conversation, I could sense their true motivation. They suspected me. "Yes, well… Nancy told me about the tree."

"Why do you think the killer would've put an oak tree on top of his shallow grave?" Larson asked.

Oak. Oak. Oak. Why did he keep saying *oak*? "I have no idea."

The detectives looked back at me, unconvinced. "Uh-huh. Right," Detective Warren said. "If we have any more questions, would you mind coming to the station next time?"

I almost asked if I needed a lawyer, but I already knew the answer. I pressed my heels to the floor to stop my legs from shaking and then rose from the armchair. "I'll do whatever I can to help you find who did this."

Detective Warren smirked. "We're sure you will."

The detectives left the house, and I collapsed to the sofa. Blinding sparks popped in my brain. The police were suspicious of me. I could feel it. That meant the detectives weren't any closer to finding Jackson's killer.

They knew something more, though. Something they weren't telling me. Why else would they have asked me about the oak tree?

I believed I knew the answer. Someone had set me up for Jackson's murder. Someone who knew what I'd done to Mike. But why?

Terror ripped through me, lighting every impulse to run for cover. But who was I running from, and where would I go?

I remembered the Xanax in the kitchen cupboard. Three pills would put me to sleep for a long, long time.

No.

I did things differently now. No matter how uncomfortable, I had to allow my mind to drift back to the details of that night.

What was missing in my memory?

CHAPTER FIFTEEN

IT TOOK TWO hours to gather my resolve after the detectives left. I locked the front door and made my way toward the Nichols' house about a quarter of a mile up the road, toward the pine reserve. The late afternoon sun was low on the western horizon, a golden glow on the clear blue sky.

Looking back at what happened to Mike was scary, but I'd never get answers until I faced my demons—the random thoughts about that night, the guilt, remorse, the dark figure on the lawn. What other details were missing?

The ominous figure was my sharpest memory. Now, it was a vision which refused to die. The colorful tail lights of the Nichols' car, though— that was no vision. I'd never given the odd old couple much thought. Annette and I had been certain they'd seen nothing, because if they had, they would've immediately reported it to the police. No, the Nichols didn't know what we'd done, but Mrs. Nichols had made it her business to know other people's business, which made her a good place to start. Patsy had found her snoop-iness annoying, but the woman was as loyal as an old dog when it came to being a friend and neighbor, and Patsy had valued that.

Within minutes of heading out, I arrived at the red brick ranch home—plain and traditional with no pretense, just like the owners. The place looked the same now as it had when Annette and I had been children feeding apples to their Palomino horses.

"Jolene? Is that you?" Mrs. Nichols stood behind a hedge, a floppy straw hat on her head and a rake in her hand.

I waved. "Sorry for just dropping by unannounced—"

"My goodness, no. It's been so long since we've seen you." She dropped the rake, took off her gardening gloves, and walked toward me with open arms.

We hugged, and then I pulled back. "I never got a chance to thank you and Mr. Nichols for arranging the gathering at Patsy's house after the funeral." My hand went to my throat as if that could stop my voice from cracking. "It's hard to believe three months have passed since Patsy died. The shock still feels new."

"I miss her, too." Mrs. Nichols took my hand and squeezed. "Come on, dear. Let's go inside."

The austere décor of her pristine house was early colonial American. Seventeenth-century early with no soft seating. Nothing about the cold, hard furniture welcomed me to stay.

Mrs. Nichols hung her hat on a hook at the doorway and smoothed stray hairs from her low bun. "We loved Patsy. Poor dear. Her last months were full of heartache." Her lined jowls lifted into a smile. "Please come sit. We rarely get company these days." She gestured to a bare wooden bench which was meant to be the sofa.

Cough. Cough. Agggkkk.

I turned toward the sound. Someone in the back of the house was having a coughing fit.

"Dear Mr. Nichols has been sick and in bed for the past two weeks. The doctor said it would be a slow recovery, but I just hope he's better before winter hits. We're too old and fragile to deal with illness." She sat on the bench and patted the space next to her. "It's nice to have a visitor. Tell me, how are you adjusting to living in the house?"

I sat next to her. "So far, so good. But about the landline… you'd said Patsy was getting calls from old friends?"

"Well, she'd had a couple of messages from friends back in July. Why? Has anyone else called?"

"Just someone who hangs up whenever I answer. It's probably just kids, but I'm thinking about getting rid of the line. Do you really think any of Patsy's old friends from home haven't heard that she's died?"

"Hmm. I suppose most would have. But she only died a few months ago," she said, raising a brow. "And with the holidays coming up, I'm sure an old friend or two will try to contact her."

Patsy's phone had rung non-stop during Christmas and New Year's. I did remember that. Calls from her childhood friend who now lived in California, or a distant cousin in Italy. Once from a long-ago lover in Costa Rica. Patsy had friends everywhere. "I suppose I can keep it until after New Year's Day. After that, the phone is gone, though."

"I think keeping it a little longer is a good idea," she said. "So, how's everything else going at the house?"

"Without Patsy and Annette around, it can get lonely at times."

"Can't be too lonely." She looked at my left hand. "I've noticed another car in the driveway."

My thumb went to my bare ring finger. "I guess you hadn't heard that Aaron and I divorced."

"I did, dear. And I'm so sorry—"

"Don't be. The red Volvo you see in my driveway belongs to my friend, Melissa Harrington. She's staying with me for a short time and helping me get settled in. You might remember her from when we were all kids."

A wide smile crossed her face. "Melissa. Of course. I remember all you girls. Riding your bikes up and down the street all day long. Always picking my apples."

"We thought you'd never notice."

She narrowed her eyes. "I see everything."

Did you see us bury Mike Morton? Shivers spread over my skin.

"Tell me," Mrs. Nichols said as she clasped her hands on her lap. "Are your children living with you?"

"They will be. The lucky ducks are in London with their dad right now. A trip of a lifetime. We have shared custody, so you'll see them around soon." I hoped I wasn't being blindly optimistic. But it was time to change topics and get to the point. "You probably heard the police have re-opened the investigation into the disappearance of that guy who went missing all those years ago—Mike Morton."

Her back straightened. "Oh, yes. The young Baker boy is the detective handling the case now."

"Noah."

"Yes, Noah. Nice young man. He came by about a week ago and asked me and Harry some more questions." She paused, frowning. "I feel for the Morton family. They've even put up a big reward if I'm not mistaken."

"That's right. Fifty grand."

"Tsk, tsk." She shook her head slowly. "I hope for the family's sake that something pans out and they find the boy."

Boy? A sour taste came to my mouth. Mike had been twenty-two, not a child. More like a fully grown, violent criminal man. But now wasn't the time to argue semantics. "If someone knew what happened to Mike, don't you think it would've been reported by now?"

A troubled smile grew on Mrs. Nichols' lips. "We can only wonder what's going on in other people's minds or what the police know that we don't."

A random thought popped into my mind. The last person I'd talked to about Mike had wound up dead. I shook my head, and the paranoid thought flew away. A lot of people in town were talking about the reward. No need to read into things. I continued with what I'd come for. "Well,

I know they believe he disappeared somewhere near Willow Road. But no one reported actually seeing him on this road."

A twinkle flashed in her light grey eyes. "Oh, I saw someone."

My stomach hit the floor so hard that my head spun. Had I heard right? "You saw Mike Morton?"

"Well, I saw someone." She rolled her eyes and sighed. "I told the police all of this seventeen years ago. Told the young Baker boy about it again when we talked last week. But in all honesty, I can't tell you if it was that Mike Morton fellow. The person I saw was dressed in all black and running along Willow Road."

My hands grabbed hold of the edge of my hard seat. I had to make sure this was true. "You saw someone dressed in black. On Willow Road."

Mrs. Nichols tapped her forefinger on her lips for an excruciating second. "Yes. It was a long time ago, but I remember exactly what happened. I told Harry to slow down—you know, it seemed strange seeing someone in a black hoodie on a hot summer night."

I squeezed the bench tighter. Why had I never heard this? "Did Harry—Mr. Nichols—did he see this person, too?"

"No." She pointed to her squinty face. "I'm the one with the eagle eyes."

My jaw slackened and my vision blurred. Only, the truth was clear. The dark figure I'd seen running across the lawn that night hadn't been a hallucination. It had been a real person.

The weight of doubt slipped away, and my vision cleared. All these years, my paranoia hadn't been delusional.

I'm not insane.

But I wasn't blind to the other side to the truth. Someone had seen what Annette and I had done. My blood chilled, and I choked on a staggered breath. My stalker for all these years and the runner dressed in all black. They had to be one and the same.

Mrs. Nichols put her hand on top of mine and wrinkled her brow. "Jolene, are you all right?"

I loosened my white-knuckled grip on the seat. Nothing was right. The clearer my thoughts, the more questions came shooting into my head. I put my hands on my lap and rubbed them together. "Where exactly did you see this person…the one dressed in black?"

"Saw him right after we turned onto Willow Road. He was jogging toward Crab Creek Road."

My heart pounded, reverberating up my throat. "The police…did they investigate? Did you tell Patsy about what you'd seen?"

"Well, yes." She clasped her hands on her lap. "It's been so many years it doesn't matter anymore."

I rubbed my forehead. "Patsy was notoriously overprotective. She would've wanted us to know if a lone man was lurking in the woods."

"Ha—that's what I thought. But no. Patsy sided with the police." Her face sagged. "She didn't believe in what I'd seen, either."

"Hmm." I understood the pain and frustration

of not being believed. And though Patsy had told us on more than one occasion how Mrs. Nichols had a habit of embellishing stories, this was one story I believed.

"But things were different back then, and Patsy didn't want you girls getting worked up about a non-existent boogey man living in the reserve." She pressed her lips together and shook her head. "No siree, Bob. Patsy wouldn't want you two all scared for no reason."

Typical Patsy. Protecting us like we were babies even though Annette and I were nineteen years old at the time.

I looked Mrs. Nichols in the eye. "Did anyone else report seeing this person running?"

"Ha." She flicked her hand like she was shooing away a fly. "Nobody. See, the police didn't take what I'd seen seriously. Said the Morton boy was tall and skinny, wearing a light-colored T-shirt and those surfing shorts all the young people wear."

An image jarred my mind: Mike in his shorts and a beige Rip Rider Surf Shop T-shirt smeared with blood. My stomach turned and twisted into a knot. "Board shorts," I whispered.

"Anyway, when I told the police what I'd seen—you know, the person dressed in black— well, I recalled that person being shorter."

I'd never been close enough to get a read on the person's height. "They dismissed you that easily?"

"Didn't completely dismiss it. Officer Baker showed the most interest."

Tingles needled up my spine, spreading over my

scalp. Old Man Baker. My danger radar was right on target. Baker did know something. "Officer Baker, huh? Why was he more interested than the other cops?"

"He knows the Morton family pretty well. I suppose he didn't want to miss any detail. I remember he checked the area for footprints and interviewed all the residents on Willow Road. No one had seen either Mike or the person dressed in all black. But I don't know. The cops could've been right." She'd changed her tone to that of a Doubting Debbie. "I mean—there were a lot more deer on the roads back then."

It wasn't a deer. It was a person. I saw him, too. The words were on my lips—the need to share my truth, my secret, to someone, to anyone—welling in my chest like an overfilled water tank.

"I guess the police still don't have any clues," Mrs. Nichols said.

"Oh, they have clues. They're just not telling us what they are."

"And why are you asking so many questions?" She tapped me with her elbow, a sly smile on her lips. "Looking at that fat reward?"

I forced a laugh. "Nah. Just an interesting story to talk about."

She tilted her head, like she was considering what I'd said. "I suppose you heard about the murder of Jackson Howell over on Cardinal Street."

"Yes." My curiosity kicked up a notch. What else could this old lady know? "You remember him? He went to a lot of Patsy's parties."

"Of course. He was always a happy boy." Her eyes widened. "Have you heard anything about what happened?"

Woman, you tell me. "Nothing. What about everyone else in the neighborhood? Heard anything from them?"

"Pfft." She waved a hand. "People around here tend to keep to themselves these days. Like I said, we don't get many visitors."

The loud coughing and hacking started up again. She turned to the noise and wrinkled her nose.

"I should go... it sounds like Mr. Nichols may need you." I scooted forward on the cool, slick seat. I had to get out. Had to find out who the hell both Mrs. Nichols and I had seen that night.

She squeezed my hand, pleading in her eyes. "Please. Don't go yet. These are strange times, and it's nice to have someone to talk with."

Mrs. Nichols seemed needy for company, and I understood. I was her closest link to Patsy. But her desperation felt borderline creepy. Then again, I wasn't used to being smothered.

"Maggie!" The hoarse call of Mr. Nichols.

Mrs. Nichols rubbed her nose and sat up straighter. "I suppose I should check on Harry. He's been unwell for some time now, you know?"

"Maaaggie!"

Mr. Nichols' voice scratched against my raw nerves and I stood, wiping my hands on my jeans. "I'll let myself out. We'll catch up again soon. In the meantime, if you need anything, make sure to call me. You have my number."

I gave her a hug and made a quick exit.

The orange glow of sunset framed the tree-tops, and I zipped my lightweight jacket up to my neck, shivering against the chilly autumn air. Willow Road was quiet with no traffic. I walked on the asphalt road back toward my house with my head in a tailspin. All these years, I'd believed I was crazy, looney, on the verge of insanity. I'd questioned why I'd always believed I was loco and numbed myself with pills and alcohol because I'd found no answers.

But I had no time for regrets. It was time to think straight.

My stalker was real. But who was this person, why where they after me, and why hadn't they turned me in and taken the reward?

Maybe that was the reason Noah had taken an interest in the tree.

Noah? What did he know?

On my left, I passed the horse paddock with its heady smell of hay and manure. The outer edge of my forested property to my right; the entrance to my driveway was visible ahead. The pines groaned in the soft breeze, every sound amplified, the earth talking, warning me.

Danger. Danger. Danger.

My pulse beat faster, and I counted my steps in sets of five. "One, two, three, four, five. One, two, three—"

An engine sounded from behind me, breaking my perfect sequence. I moved aside to the road's gravel edge and focused on taking even steps on the uneven ground. The engine slowed. Tires rolled closer behind. I picked up my pace, the vein on my forehead throbbing.

I looked back, then released a breath. A white postal service truck. The mailman waved and drove past, sending a flurry of leaves twirling around my feet.

My muscles loosened. I'd overreacted, but I couldn't let my guard down and pretend all the drama unfolding around me was going to fade away. Not now that I felt certain someone else had been on Willow Road when we'd buried Mike.

The mailman stopped at my driveway, stuck mail in my letterbox, then drove off. I filled my lungs with crisp October air, tinged with the musky sweetness of fallen leaves. My mind slowly refocused. I was getting custody of my children back, and I couldn't let myself fall apart.

I opened my letterbox. A white envelope. I pulled it out and noticed the familiar block–style handwriting. A slam to my chest threw me back. The postmark from the main post office was two days ago. I tore open the envelope just enough to see the red oak leaf. The last leaf had come in June, right before Patsy had died.

My pulse quickened and thoughts bloomed like images in a word cloud. *Danger. Run. Hide.* Bolder words appeared. *Kill. Murder. Stab.*

A flock of clattering crows broke my thoughts, and I looked around. The sun had dipped behind the treetops, dropping the temperature to what felt ten degrees cooler.

I ran into the house, bolted the door, switched

on the alarm, closed all the window shutters—slam, slam, slam. The banging in my chest made me dizzy, and I fell back into the armchair, panting.

Looking at the envelope in my hand, I considered all the pieces of the puzzle. The person on the lawn. My stalker. The leaves. Jackson's murder. The family tree. All were connected but drew no clear picture.

A primal burn grew in my core, firing my survival instinct. I couldn't take this torment anymore. It was time to get ten steps ahead of the problem, not stay ten steps behind. First, I had to know who I was up against. I realized the day may come when I might have to face more police questioning. When that time came, I'd need credible evidence that my terrorizer was Jackson's killer. Only then could I truly protect myself from the law and this demented murderer.

Whoever was tormenting me wasn't after the reward, but me. What did they want?

Grey lines of fading daylight seeped through the closed shutters. The living room grew dimmer with each passing moment. My hands turned cold, and for the first time since moving into the house, I was afraid. Really afraid. But I didn't know of who or why.

The first thing I'd do the next morning was call the security company and arrange for a thorough inspection of the security system. I'd do everything I could to stay safe while I figured out a way to discover who I was dealing with.

I tossed the envelope onto the coffee table,

jumped to my feet, and turned on the floor lamp. If it was police protection I wanted, I only needed to confess. I might even help solve two murders all in one phone call to the police.

Pacing the floor, I thought about it. Telling the police how we'd killed and buried Mike, my theory about how the murder and oak tree planted over Jackson was a message to me and had been done by the same person. How Mrs. Nichols and I had both seen someone on the road all those years ago. How that person had stalked me to this day. Sent oak leaves to me in the mail.

"Ha!" I couldn't stop myself from laughing out loud. Just like the police would as they dragged me away to jail.

Honesty wouldn't exonerate me from jail or Jackson's murder. If anything, I'd look even crazier than most people already thought I was.

I had to find a way out of this.

This was about my future and justice for Jackson.

Mike's parents wanted that for their son, too, but while I hated being cold and harsh, I had no control over the injustices in life. I was sorry for the Morton family, but justice for Mike had been served, and the suffering of his family was collateral damage. My teeth grinded and heat flushed to my head. Mike had deserved to die. He'd raped Annette. Threatened to kill both of us. He'd ruined our lives. But not Jackson; he'd never hurt anyone.

It wasn't an easy choice, but even with the guilt and remorse, I wasn't ready to turn myself into the police. I'd lived with the secret this long, and I'd live with it for the rest of my life if I had too. The problem was that someone else couldn't.

My task wasn't easy. I needed to figure out how I was going to find Jackson's killer and stay safe while not allowing my OCD to confuse my logic. To lose control was paramount to giving in and letting the terrorizer win. I wouldn't allow that to happen.

I pulled my phone out of my back pocket and pressed the number of the person I'd been afraid to call for too long.

CHAPTER SIXTEEN

THE HOUSE OF Celeste wasn't hard to miss. A wood-shingle beach house painted aqua with a pink neon sign in the window: *Psychic.* I'd called yesterday, and her male assistant had been able to book an appointment for me today, under the fake name of Jolene Denton.

A sun-bleached shingle hung on the door: *Please Come In.*

My hands trembled, but even after learning that Mrs. Nichols had seen someone on the road the night we'd buried Mike, I'd coped without the Xanax. I had to stay focused and learn what the psychic knew about Mike. What she could foresee about Jackson.

Inside, the front room was arranged with a pillow-adorned sofa and two mismatched side chairs. I sat in a red velvet high-back. The sound of crashing waves came from a speaker hidden somewhere. On a coffee table was a fresh bunch of blue irises.

I picked up a magazine. *Celestial Connections.* I didn't believe in talking to the dead but did believe in the possibility of something more than just this life, and that some people were truly more intuitive than others. If this psychic really could tap into the spirit world, what could she see? The face of Mike Morton? An electrical jolt touched my nerves. I twitched and tossed the magazine back onto the table.

This was scary shit, but I'd come prepared to deal with anything. I had to find out if this psychic was the real deal, or one of many frauds.

"Jolene?" Madame Celeste waltzed into the room wearing a flowing green kaftan with the eye of a peacock feather design on the front.

I stood, not certain how to address her. 'Madame' sounded so phony. "Hello."

"I'm sorry to keep you waiting." Madame's voice was as soothing as a lullaby. "Please. Come in." She stepped aside and gestured toward the dark hallway leading to the back of the house.

A white light streamed through an open door. Light at the end of a dark tunnel. Was this an intentional metaphor? I took a deep breath and proceeded down the hallway smelling of musk and patchouli oils. Burning sage. I passed two closed doors and had an itch to leave, but I went into the purple-hued room and sat at the round table for two. Stones and crystals lined the surrounding bookshelves.

Madame put her hands on the table, palms up. "Miss Jolene, please give me your hands. I'd like to feel your energy."

I put my rough palms against hers, all soft and smooth. She clutched me harder and closed her eyes, then took a few deep and even breaths. Was she conjuring long-lost ghosts or a bullshit scheme? I stayed on high alert for either.

She flattened my palms on the table and placed her hands atop mine. "You're nervous." Compassion colored her tone. "Have you seen a psychic before?"

Her palms were warm and mushy against my skin. I wanted to slide my hands back to my lap but kept still to let her do her thing. "No. You're my first."

"Mmm." Her eyes squinted. "You're holding in a great deal of pain."

Who wasn't? "It's been a tough year."

"You've lost someone close to you...." Her eyes glazed over, and she continued in her monotone. "A woman. Older. Maybe your mother. Pam... Patty."

My pulse ticked, and I knew she could feel the imperceptible change on my skin. I probably should have let her figure it out, but I wanted to cut to the chase. If she could talk to the dead, then I wanted a warning from beyond. "Patsy."

"Ahhh." Madame smiled and her shoulders relaxed. "She wasn't your biological mother, though."

My heart lurched, but I kept a straight face and let her continue.

Madame patted my hand. "She was happy in life and is happy in spirit—I can feel that." She tilted her head like someone was talking into her ear. "She's showing me someone next to her. A younger woman."

Had she really made contact with Patsy and Annette? My stomach fluttered with hope, but I said nothing.

Madame shook her head, her face tightening. "I don't know. The younger spirit is fading. All I hear is Patty repeating that they are both safe."

"Patsy."

"I feel another presence." Celeste was writing on a notepad now. "A darkness from beyond. Something looming." She looked into my eyes. "Does this make sense to you?"

My body stiffened. My stalker. The leaves. I could tell her all about what was happening, but it was her job to reveal something to me. "Uh, I'm facing some challenging situations right now."

She wagged the glittery pen at me. "There is darkness looming over you."

"Oh-kay. Can you illuminate?" If I came across as a smartass, she didn't seem to notice.

"I have a special mix of herbs which I put into a sachet for the purpose of warding off the negativity." She turned in her chair and reached into a small drawer, then handed me what looked like a basket full of bouquet garni—a mix of herbs wrapped in fabric and tied with twine for use in cooking—except these bundles weren't made with white cheese cloth, but brightly colored fabrics. "If you carry one with you at all times, and repeat daily positive affirmations, the negativity will soon leave. You may purchase one at the end of our session."

I wanted to scream into her face: *CHARLA-TAN*. Instead, I smiled. "I'm feeling a sense of peace. Maybe it's because now I know Patsy and—" I hesitated because I didn't want to give

away too much information. "Anyway. I'm feeling better and I have a busy day ahead." I stood.

Madame's face wrinkled with disappointment.
"But we've just gotten started."

"Thank you for your time." I walked out of
her room and down the hallway. The glare of a
computer screen through a cracked door caught
my eye. A pot-bellied old man with long stringy
hair and wearing headphones sat at the keyboard
with his back to the door.

This psychic received her messages the same
way the rest of us did, from the holder of almost
all human knowledge: the Internet.

The psychic was a dead-end, but she wasn't my
only lead.

CHAPTER SEVENTEEN

L ATER THAT DAY, I sat in my car three houses down from Nancy and Richard's ranch home. I was desperate for any information or clue that would lead me to Jackson's killer. Desperate enough to confront a possible murderer. Melissa had said that Jackson and Richard were not friends. Nancy having a tryst with Jackson could've been all the motivation Richard needed to get rid of Jackson. Or maybe not. I hoped meeting with Richard would give me a feel for how, or if, he was involved.

I tapped my thumbs on the steering wheel. Any minute now, Richard would turn the corner with the boys from their after-school pick up. I only had a short window of time to talk to him alone before Nancy came home from work.

What if he had killed Jackson in a fit of jealous rage, and planting the tree had been a random act? My pulse pounded in my neck. Any whiff of danger and I'd high-tail it out of there. Then, I'd go to the police.

Maybe.

A white van turned onto the street. Blood pumped through my veins as I watched a Good

Guys Heating and Air Conditioning van roll into Richard and Nancy's driveway. Brandon and Clay, their two prepubescent boys, hopped out and ran to the front door. I was familiar with the hectic after-school routine and gave Richard a few minutes to get inside and the boys settled.

I drove forward and parked directly across the street. I ambled up to the single-story ranch home. A Halloween welcome mat with a jack-o-lantern imprint greeted me. I rang the doorbell.

The inside door whished open and Richard's mouth slackened, a puzzled look on his face. "Yeah," he said.

A dark-screened security door separated us. "Sorry to drop by unannounced, but my phone went flat, or else I would've called." I held up my turned-off phone. I kept my tone friendly. "Do you have a few minutes to talk?"

Richard crossed his arms. "Talk about what?"

Behind him, the boys craned their necks to see who was at the door. I waved and used a chirpy tone. "Hi, guys." They both looked at me with deadbeat expressions.

"Go on, now." Richard shooed them away. "Go to your rooms and do your homework."

The younger boy gave me a quick smile as the older one pulled him toward the back of the house.

Richard leaned his squirrelly face closer to the screen. "What d'ya want?" He sucked on a tooth.

I swallowed dry air. For a flicker of a second, I considered ending this now. *No. Do it.* I'd come this far; I couldn't back out now. I spoke in a whisper so his sons wouldn't hear me, "I want to ask what you know about Jackson's murder."

He opened the screened door and stepped out onto the front porch. "I don't want the neighbors to see us, and we can't talk in the house with the boys around," he said. He nudged his chin toward the side of the house. "We'll use the side gate and talk in the backyard."

Following his directions, I opened the latch on the gate of the high privacy fence. A small greenhouse was at the corner of the yard. Richard moved to the front of the greenhouse and lit a cigarette.

Unease rolled through my stomach, and I stumbled on my feet. *Maybe this wasn't a good idea. What if he's the murderer?* Richard had a sour face, but I needed to stay focused and friendly.

He flicked his cigarette ashes on the ground. "So, what d'ya want?"

The greenhouse door was wide open, and two bags of organic soil slumped on the countertop. The pungent smell of compost crept into my nostrils and down my throat. "How's Nancy doing?"

A slow sneer crossed his lips. "I thought you came to talk about Jackson."

I dug my feet into the ground. "Nancy and I are both suspects. I'm well aware of that." *And so are you, you little weasel.* "But I didn't kill Jackson."

He narrowed his eyes. "You were at his house around the time he was killed."

"The police have the autopsy report. They know he was killed *after* the time I left his place."

Richard snorted and his mouth twisted into a

snarl. "What were you doing at his house anyway?"

Irritating prickles covered my skin like an itchy wool sweater. I straightened my stance. "Watching a movie. We were friends."

"Dude had lots of friends. Especially lady friends." He squinted one eye, took another drag, and exhaled smoke through the side of his mouth.

Keep cool. "Yeah. He was the kind of guy people liked. That's why I don't understand. This is so weird—"

"What's weird is how Jackson got murdered when Psycho Girl moved back to this part of town." He sniffed. "You ain't changed a bit. Always keeping to yourself. Doin' wacky shit."

His words cut deep. He'd been one of the school bullies who'd hurled cruel names at me after I'd been released from the psychiatric hospital. I swallowed my pride and let his comment slide. "Look, I wanted to talk to you because I'm worried about Nancy. I want to make sure things are okay. I mean—the police see us both as suspects, and I know neither one of us did it."

"Well, I know Nancy didn't." Richard scrutinized me.

I crossed my arms and fixed my stare into his dark eyes. The silence between us stretched taut and tense as a rubber band pulled to its limit. I wouldn't snap. "I believe she's innocent, too. But since neither Nancy nor I killed him, who did? Do you have any ideas? Have the police told you anything?"

"You're assuming I don't think it was you. I

mean, you and Jackson was close, right?"

"Look, I don't know what you're getting at, but I've lived on the bay side of town for the past fifteen years. I hadn't seen Jackson in—"

"Well, whoo-whee. Ain't you special?" Richard spat on the ground.

My jaw ached. This wasn't going as I'd planned. "I think we've gotten off on a bad start here—"

A door slammed.

"Ahh shit." Richard looked over my shoulder. His mouth slackened.

I followed his startled gaze to the back of the house. Nancy stomped through the backyard toward us, her hair so stiff and spikey that she could have used her head as a medieval battering ram.

Fuck. My stomach hardened. I'd thought there'd be at least another forty-five minutes before she came home. I put on a warm smile, hoping it might buffer her temper. "Hi, Nancy."

She stepped within inches of me, and I swore I saw steam rising off of her red-hot face. "I thought that was your car out front." Her tone wasn't friendly. "What the fuck are you doing here?"

I backed up, the pounding in my chest growing stronger and louder. I couldn't let her see my fear, but all I could offer was a weak smile. "I-I wanted to see how you're doing."

Her jaw muscles flexed. "Next time send a text."

"Nancy, I'm on your side." I threw a glance at Richard, his arms crossed as he aimed a death glare straight at me. I had no back-up here.

"We're not friends." Nancy's expression shifted from hate to disgust. "And the police are asking me all kinds of questions about you."

My breath hitched. "What kind of questions?"

Nancy inched forward and closed the gap between us. "I have a lawyer, and he advised me against talking to you. So, get the fuck off my property."

Richard picked up a shovel off the ground and held it out like a baseball bat. "Go on, now. Get."

I held up both hands and walked backwards, my heart racing. This crazy couple was capable of anything. "Fine. I'm leaving."

Adrenaline sent me racing out the gate with Richard yelling loud enough to rattle the neighbor's windows. "And don't you ever harass anyone in my family again, ya hear?"

Back in the safety of my car, I locked the door and released a breath. What a fucking disaster. I'd only stirred up Nancy and Richard and made myself look desperate. But I was desperate. Desperate for answers.

Driving away, my mind whirled with unanswered questions. I still had no clue if Richard had killed Jackson, but the visit had made me realize one thing: if Nancy had hired an attorney, I was right to think I needed one too.

After I'd left the psychic that morning, I done a search for the top criminal attorneys in the area and narrowed it down to a couple of options. Either of which could wipe out my entire bank savings. But I had no choice. Unless the police found the killer soon, I'd have to fork out the cash. I needed someone on my side. I also needed a friend. A good friend. The obvious person was Melissa. She'd understand why I'd talked to Nancy and Richard.

I'd kept my worries and secrets so close I'd forgotten how to share deep feelings and fears with a friend. It shouldn't be hard, though. Melissa never backed away from a chin wag, and with any luck, she'd help me see how I could clear myself of being a suspect in Jackson's murder. I had to allow myself to become vulnerable. I had to open up.

Melissa had proven to be my most supportive friend. She understood how much I'd lost recently, and how the suspicion the police have toward me regarding Jackson's murder was unnecessary stress. How I needed answers.

She worked until late tonight, but I'd agreed to look at apartments with her in the morning. That would be my chance.

CHAPTER EIGHTEEN

"GOING TO NANCY'S house wasn't the smartest thing to do," Melissa said, clenching both hands on the steering wheel of her Volvo and driving along Crab Creek Road toward home.

I sat in the passenger seat, frustrated. I'd spent the whole morning with Melissa, looking all over town at apartments while she rambled on about how furious Nancy was that I'd gone to her house and talked to Richard about Jackson.

Nancy had gotten to Melissa before I'd had a chance to explain. Now, I was in the position of defending what I'd done. "But I need to know what the police are asking them. I'm a suspect in this too."

"She wanted to call the police and say you were harassing her—"

"That's bullshit, and she knows it."

"I talked her out of it, don't worry. But Nancy has always been fickle. Her mood is more unpredictable than the weather."

"But why won't she talk to me? Does she seriously believe there was something romantic going on between me and Jackson, or that I would have killed him?"

"She doesn't trust people so easily, that's just who she is." Melissa exhaled a long breath. "Look, being a suspect in Jackson's murder is bullshit, I get that. The detectives are just doing their job, though. I don't think you killed Jackson. And I don't think Nancy did, either. And Richard? Ha! He's more cowardly than Scooby Doo."

I picked at my fingernails. Melissa didn't understand the full scope of what I was up against. "He knew Nancy and Jackson were having an affair. Isn't that at least motivation? Crimes of passion happen all the time."

"Seriously, look at yourself. You're a nervous wreck. You need to relax and let the police do their jobs. They'll investigate everyone. They'll find Jackson's killer."

The knot in my chest tightened. This wasn't nerves. This was obsession. "Do you think the killer is someone we know?"

Deep lines formed on Melissa's forehead. "I sure as hell hope not."

"What about the band? Did he have a beef with any of the guys?"

"Nooo, Jolene." Melissa rolled her eyes. "They all loved Jackson."

Releasing a breath, I looked out the window as we passed open farmland with neat rows of green lettuce shoots. "What am I going to tell Aaron?" I asked. "He comes home with the kids in six days. I don't even want to think about how he's going to react once he hears I'm a suspect in a murder investigation."

"Get real." She turned left onto Willow Road. "Aaron won't believe you killed Jackson. He'll understand that it's all just police procedure."

"Let's hope so. But he certainly won't want the kids staying with me while all this is going down."

"You're overthinking again. It may never get to that point. The police could be arresting Jackson's murderer at this very moment."

My shoulders relaxed. Melissa was right. Overthinking was a killer of time and focus. "That's what I hope."

Ahead, a police car was parked across from my house. My heart pounded. A forensics van was parked on the vacant McDougal property, too, and about a dozen people in teal- colored T-shirts were congregated in a circle. My eyes stayed glued to the commotion. Cadaver dogs sniffed the dirt. "What the hell are they doing over there?"

"Digging up dead bodies." Melissa giggled and turned into my driveway.

Acid rolled up my throat. Burying a body in the woods was something other people did. Sick people. Psycho people. Evil people. "You're being ridiculous."

"I'm not. The McDougal family sold the property to a developer, you know. And I'll bet the developer found something while clearing the land. And the people are probably volunteer archeologists sifting through soil for a colonial burial site or remnants of an Indian village."

The torn skin under my fingernails throbbed, and I pressed the sore tips into my thigh. "Something tells me the forensics van isn't there to assist with an archeological dig."

Melissa glanced in her rearview mirror. "Who knows, but I'm curious what they're up to." She parked the car in front of the garage. "Come on. Let's go and ask."

"I'd rather not." The less I knew, the better.

"Fine. I need to get ready for work this afternoon, anyway."

I hurried along the brick footpath to the front door, afraid to glance across the road. I wanted Melissa to be right about the volunteers working on an archeological dig. My gut knew otherwise.

"Thanks for looking at apartments with me," Melissa said, trailing behind.

"No problem." I unlocked the front door and went inside. "You've helped me so much these past few months... I just hope you find a place to settle into soon."

"I should know within the next week or so. Either I move to Richmond to live with my aunt or stay here in Lighthouse Beach." She sighed. "I'd rather stay at the beach."

"I hope you stay, too." I set my purse on the armchair. "But I guess it's time I got used to living here on my own."

Melissa patted my back. "Seriously, you have too much time on your hands. You overthink situations. Why not come out to Ocean Joe's later, and have a beer and eat crab cakes instead of sitting here alone? You can hang out at the bar and chat it up with us bartenders and waitresses."

Not a bad idea, but I was too concerned about planning my next move to commit to anything.

"Yeah, I might see you there."

"Great. I'm going upstairs to get ready for work. Let me know if you see anything interesting happening across the road."

"Will do." I cracked open the shutters on the living room window and watched the activity across the street. Maybe they'd found the bones of another body. I shivered and went into the kitchen. My fingers twitched for a double dose of Xanax, but instead I set the kettle on the stove and grabbed a green tea teabag. I needed all the clarity I could get. I'd been good at sticking to my OCD medication on its own.

I sat at the kitchen table and relaxed as my breaths slowed. Melissa was right. I needed to stop overreacting. I needed to just let the police do their work.

Ding dong.

The doorbell jolted me from the stillness. I wasn't expecting anyone.

Wheeeee. The whistling kettle on the stove, steaming.

Ding dong.

Wheeeee.

I rubbed my forehead then hauled myself off the chair, turned off the kettle, and begrudgingly made my way to the front door. A middle-aged couple in matching teal T-shirts stood on the verandah. "Good afternoon," I said through the screen door.

The man held up a flyer. "Good afternoon, ma'am. We're volunteering on behalf of the family of Mike Morton."

My knees weakened and neurons scrambled to organize in my brain. The word 'MISSING' screamed out in bold text from the flyer. Mike's smiling face looked back at me. It was the same photo used in the news reports. "Oh yeah?"

The sour-faced woman slipped in front of the man. "You might have heard on the news that police believe Mike Morton may have met with foul play somewhere on Willow Road. Our team is combing the area today. We're asking land-owners to allow our volunteers to walk their property." She narrowed her eyes. "Didn't you receive the notification in the mail?"

"Notification? No, when—"

The woman puffed. "All residents were mailed a notification two weeks ago and were given a chance to us deny us access in advance. No one protested."

"What's going on?" Melissa came to my side in her robe, drying her wet hair with a towel.

"It's a search party for Mike Morton," I said.

The man lifted the flyer to the screened door and Melissa looked closer, her eyes widening. "Mike Morton?" She looked at the volunteers. "Is that why you guys are looking around across the street? Did you find something over there?"

"We're looking for any evidence," the man chimed in. "A gravesite. His watch. His phone. Clothing. Bones."

Melissa put a hand to her chest. "Good Lord."

Being informed about today's search would've been nice. I looked at Melissa. "Apparently, a notification was sent in the mail. Did you see it?"

Melissa shook her head. "I never even look in the mailbox. All my mail's being diverted to my post office box until I find a permanent residence."

The woman pointed her thumb to the yard. "We all set to go, miss?"

I wanted to say, 'hell no' and slam the door in her self-righteous face. I didn't need a mob scouring my property and searching for evidence of Mike's disappearance. But I took a deep breath and let it out slowly. *They'll never find his grave.* I painted on a fake smile. "Of course. I have twenty-three wooded acres back here. Knock yourself out."

The man tipped the rim of his baseball cap. "Thank you, ma'am. We'll start with the front lawn and go from there."

The couple walked off, and I watched as teal-topped volunteers crossed the road from the McDougal property onto mine.

"Damn." Melissa stood next to me watching the activity. "I wish I didn't have to get dressed and go to work. You'll have to fill me in on if they find anything later."

I envied Melissa's innocence. "I'll do that."

Melissa went back upstairs, and I stepped out onto the verandah. Nerves rattled my bones while volunteers assembled on my lawn. What were they looking for? Clothing? Wallet? Footprints? All of that was long gone. I shoved my hands into the front pockets of my loose jeans.

They won't find him. He's buried too deep. Deep under the trunk of the tree.

A car engine rumbled and a white sedan pulled up in front of my house. Noah climbed out of the driver's side and met my gaze. My knees weakened and I grabbed hold of the post. I hadn't talked to him since the day I'd taken ownership of the house and he'd stopped by, questioning me about the family tree. That was two months ago.

He waved and headed across my lawn, straight toward me.

The pounding in my chest grew quicker, sharper, pushing my ability to breathe to the limit. I didn't have to wonder why he was here. He'd come to find Mike.

CHAPTER NINETEEN

SWEAT DRIBBLED DOWN my spine as Noah approached the front of the house. I couldn't let him see my fear, so I put on a smile of an average homeowner who was curious about the progress of the search.

"Good afternoon, Jolene." Noah's voice was as bouncy as his steps up the verandah.

Too enthusiastic. Immediately, I didn't trust him. "Well, hello there."

He smiled like a kid on a treasure hunt. "Think they'll find anything out there?"

"Probably the old baseball Annette lost twenty years ago." I elbowed his arm. "Or that painted bong you and your idiot friends kept hidden."

His neck turned pink. "I'm talking about Mike Morton."

I turned my eyes to the volunteers combing the lawn. "What makes police think he's out there somewhere?"

"The last time Mike was seen he was on foot only 400 yards from this house." He pointed toward Crab Creek Road. "A driver that night saw a man matching Mike's description make a turn onto Willow Road."

My nose twitched. This was new to me. I'd known a few drivers had witnessed Mike hitch-hiking on Crab Creek Road, but had someone really seen him turn onto this road? "Oh…?"

"And the only people he knew on this street were Patsy and Annette. I even remember seeing him at Patsy's Fourth of July party only a month before he was reported missing."

The memory flooded in—Mike staggering around the backyard party. Patsy's annual neighborhood barbeque had grown into a town tradition on the scale of a festival. She'd relished the holiday, and always had an ice-cold keg of beer and hot dogs on offer to whoever wanted to stop by and play croquet or cornhole.

My lips pressed together, hot hair blowing out my nose. It infuriated me how Mike had taken Patsy's kind nature for granted. Drunk her beer, eaten from her table, then raped and tried to kill her daughter. Now, I hated the scumbag even more.

I coughed back the acid in my throat and spoke like I had some input. "I remember. He looked pretty drunk that day. Didn't stay long."

"Uh-huh." Noah looked away. "Well, we're determined to dig up every lead."

My shoulders tensed. *Leads.* What fucking leads? Certainly, he wouldn't take Madame Celeste seriously. A graveled voice interrupted my thoughts.

"I'm ready to go, boss." A hunched older man in a plaid shirt tipped his red baseball cap at Noah. One hand clasped the push bar on a light cart holding a ground-penetrating radar device.

Noah turned to me. "We'll talk about this some more later." He stepped off the verandah and greeted the man.

I crossed my arms over my chest. Noah's evasiveness troubled me, but it was the equipment the old man had on his cart that rattled my nerves. I was familiar with GPR from field study work in college. Back then, radar had only been able to penetrate three feet into the ground. But technology had changed over the years.

For the next ten minutes, the volunteers walked side-by-side across the front lawn. The GRP operator followed the group with Noah sniffing up his ass like a dog in heat.

I stepped off the verandah and trailed behind the group. Picking at the dirty grime under my nails. My heart tripped a beat with each step the volunteers and GPR took toward the backyard.

Noah nudged the operator and pointed to the family tree. "I need you to scan around this tree before you move on to other parts of the property."

The operator tipped the rim of his baseball cap. "No worries, boss."

Strength left my knees and I staggered to the picnic table next to the tree, where I sat on the bench. I crossed and uncrossed my legs, unable to stop them from shaking. Noah had to know Mike was under the tree. How?

This is it. My life is over.

The operator whistled a chirpy tune and slowly pushed the bleeping cart around the full perimeter of the sprawling roots.

Noah hovered over the screen on the radar. "Make sure to get right up to the trunk," he said.

"Getting there, boss." The operator resumed his whistling and spiraling, slowly inching closer to the trunk.

My eyes stayed glued to the snail-paced operator. He hesitated only inches from the trunk and let out a high-pitched whistle. I sucked in a breath, held it in my lungs.

Noah rushed to the monitor. "What is it?"

The operator pursed his lips and shook his head. "We've got no anomalies here, boss. Just a bunch of roots."

I released a one-ton breath and my chest collapsed. *Nothing?* My hands gripped the edge of the hard seat. Annette's voice echoed in my head. *Pretend it never happened.*

It never happened. It never happened. It never happened.

Noah rubbed the back of his neck. The lines in his forehead grew deeper. "Are you sure? Maybe you need to run over it again—"

The operator shook his head. "Nope. If something is buried under this tree, it's either obscured by all the roots or too deep for this equipment to detect it."

Closing my eyes, I sank into the darkness. A rotted body shrouded under a lace canopy of roots flashed behind my eyelids and I opened my eyes to Noah staring at me. We were only ten feet apart, but the silence between us stretched for miles.

"We finished here?" The operator looked

between me and Noah. "I've got a lot more ground to cover."

Noah's face soured, but he didn't take his eyes off me. "Yeah. We're finished."

"Baker!" A man called out.

I turned to the familiar voice. Detective Larson waved to Noah and walked toward him. Larson was involved in Jackson's murder investigation, but what the hell was he doing here? My body shivered, though it wasn't cold. The detectives shook hands and turned their backs to me. They huddled close, speaking too low for me to hear from my perch on the picnic bench.

The volunteers dispersed into the woods. They'd find nothing out there. It was Noah and Larson deep in discussion under the tree that had me concerned. I had an itching feeling something bad was going to happen.

I wanted to fade away. Disappear. My pulse raced like I'd jogged a marathon, but I slid off the picnic bench and meandered toward the house like I had no cares in the world.

"Jolene. Wait."

Noah's voice. I stopped at the bottom of the deck steps. *Shit.* I slowed my breath and turned my head, doing my best to act nonchalant. "Yeah?"

Detective Larson acknowledged me with a wave. "Hello, Miss Parker. Sorry to intrude."

Too late for that, asshole. I slid my hands into the pockets of my dress. "What's up?"

Noah walked toward me. "Can we talk to you inside for a few minutes?"

Did I have a choice? "Uh, sure. Come on in."

They followed me up the deck and into the kitchen. Noah pointed to the round kitchen table. "Can we sit here?"

I nodded and everyone sat.

Noah gave me a best-friend smile. "I'm going to be up front with you, Jolene." His tone was businesslike. "The department has been receiving anonymous phone calls about Mike's disappearance for the past five months."

Blood drained from my head and pooled in my gut like cement. I glanced between the solemn-faced detectives who waited for my response. Hesitation was my enemy. Straightening my spine, I tried to keep my voice from shaking. "W-what has the caller said?"

Noah spun a pen on the tabletop but kept his eyes on me. "The first call came through back in July, the caller only said that Mike Morton's body was buried on a property on Willow Road."

My throat ran dry, and I couldn't swallow. I'd been right all along. There had been someone on the lawn. Someone had seen. Or had Annette told someone? No. She'd promised. "That sounds awful."

"Yeah, well—we debated whether to inform the Morton family because we wanted to make sure it wasn't a hoax." Noah leaned back. "But Mrs. Morton calls our office every year, desperate for any new information. We felt we had to tell them about the caller when she called this year. That's when the family decided to put up the reward."

I pressed my arms to my side to still myself. *This*

is nothing. Don't panic. "A fifty-thousand-dollar reward because of one anonymous phone call?"

Noah's lip twitched. "They had other reasons to believe the caller."

This is nothing. Don't panic. "Are you referring to the psychic Mrs. Morton hired?"

"You know about that?" He flashed a sardonic smile.

"I've heard gossip."

Noah sighed. "The psychic aside, two weeks after the Morton family put up the reward, we got a second anonymous call. This time, the caller said he'd seen what happened to Mike and knew where he was buried."

His words hit my head and spun everything around. *Someone saw what happened.* I rubbed my fingertips over my dry lips, wanting to run off and comprehend what I'd just heard, but Noah watched my every move. "So, the caller," I said, "he's looking for the reward, right?"

"He didn't mention it." Noah kept his gaze on me.

Cold tingles spread over my scalp. *Who saw us?* I looked at Noah. "He... the caller is a man?"

"We're not sure. The caller uses a voice synthesizer."

I hugged myself, rocked a few times, then stopped. "What else did he say?"

"He ended the call."

"He's probably a kook," I said, sitting up straight. "He's sending you on a wild goose chase."

Noah snorted. "He's certainly taunting us. But he called a third time. This time, he said Mike is buried behind a house on Willow Road, and that the clues were right under our noses."

The moment got stuck in a freeze-frame as Noah's words echoed in my mind. *Mike is buried behind a house on Willow Road.* I wanted to say something clever, but the circuits in my brain crossed and all I could do was mutter. "Oh, really?"

"That's when we had a closer look and reinterviewed everyone who lived on this street or was in the vicinity at the time Mike went missing." He used his fingertip to draw a long line on the tabletop.

I licked my dry lips. "Why the game-playing? Anyone who really knows where Mike is would want to collect the reward."

"Not this person," Larson said. "When he called the third time, he insisted he wasn't interested in the reward. Only wants justice for Mike."

Noah shot Larson a quick glance, then leaned closer to me. "Jolene." His tone had shifted from informative to somber. "We got a fourth phone call a couple of weeks ago. This time, the caller was more specific." He paused and his gaze intensified. Sweat dripped down my neck, and I suffocated in the thick air.

"The caller said Mike Morton is buried under the oak tree behind Patsy's old house," Larson said, breaking the silence.

Ringing exploded in my ears. I needed to stay calm when everything inside told me to scream. *The anonymous caller. The leaves. The stalker.* It had to be connected. I turned to Noah; his expression twisted from eager to sad to grim, distorting his features. How well did I really know him? "It's a prank."

Noah brushed imaginary dust from the table. "Could be. But we have to explore all leads."

I hugged myself to calm my shaking body. The person dressed in all black who Mrs. Nichols and I had seen was the anonymous caller. Had to be. And the caller was also Jackson's killer. I had so many questions, but my lips couldn't move. Bringing up Jackson's name while I was a suspect in his murder wasn't smart. How could I be sure if what Noah had just told me was true, or if he was rattling my cage? "Can't you trace the call… find out who the caller is?"

Noah groaned. "He uses a non-traceable cell phone."

Another explosion rattled my head, pounded in my ears. I grabbed hold of my throat and hoped to keep fear out of my voice. "But the GPR would have found something."

"Not necessarily," Larson said.

Larson's buoyant tone sank my confidence. The room spun and a wave of nausea washed through my stomach. *Keep your head clear.* "What do you mean?"

Noah glowered at Larson, but then turned to me with a straight face. "I need to ask you something, and I'm going to be blunt. Is Mike buried under the oak tree?"

My legs couldn't stop shaking. If I confessed right now, I'd be hauled off to jail. And with the way Larson was scrutinizing me, I had a bad feeling it could also make me look like Jackson's killer. Maybe it was time to confess, but I knew to keep my mouth shut until I talked to an attorney. I narrowed my eyes and my throat squeezed so tight that my voice came out a whisper, "Of course not."

Noah looked at me with sympathy. "You know... you don't have to protect Patsy and Annette anymore."

I tilted my head. *Where is he taking this?* "Protect them from what?"

He released a breath. "We know Mike Morton raped Annette two weeks before he disappeared."

Every follicle on my scalp tingled a warning. "W-who told you this?"

"During our investigation, we looked back at the notebooks from other cops working around the time Mike went missing. We found that Annette came to the station one night but would only speak with a woman officer. Retiring officer Carol Bellford was the only woman at the station that night, and she was due to retire in two days. So, when Officer Bellford told Annette the report would be passed on to another officer, she quickly retracted her statement. The officer noted that Annette became paranoid and was concerned that people in town would find out. She insisted on retracting her statement and then fled the station. The officer never filed a report but kept all her notes on file."

My cheeks warmed and I looked away. Annette had been ashamed of how easily she'd put herself in that situation with Mike. So mad at herself for reporting it to police and then retracting her charges. So afraid people would find out. Now this. "Yes, that's true. She never wanted her mother to find out. Not anyone, for that matter."

Detective Larson broke in. "You and Annette were quite close. Did Annette and you lure Mike to this house on the night of August 3rd?"

I jerked backwards. "What? No! Why the hell would we do that?"

"A chance at revenge." Detective Larson shrugged, like it was a normal assumption.

Rage burned under my skin. Mike had been a monster, and I'd kill him again if I had to. The detective's too-friendly faces told me something was up—something I wasn't privy to. My eyes shifted between Larson and Noah. "You're crazy. He was the last person either one of us wanted to see. What are you two getting at anyway?"

Noah leaned back. "Do you know anything about what happened to Mike Morton?"

"No."

Larson grumbled something incoherent.

Noah glanced at him and then back at me. "There's something else I need to ask you." He paused a moment. "The Morton family. They have a special request—a favor you might say."

I wiped my palms on my jittery thighs. "What kind of favor?"

"They want your permission to dig under the oak tree," Larson said. "Perhaps even cut it down."

I stiffened my muscles to control the shaking. "No. I can't—" My voice didn't hold, and it cracked like an ice cube in hot water.

"The Mortons are counting on your compassion to help them find their son," Noah said.

I'm not compassionate. I'm a killer. It was time to call an attorney. "I'm sorry." I pressed a hand to my chest. "I have to say 'no.' I'm sorry for the Morton family, but I've been entrusted to keep the property intact. I know Patsy would not have wanted her tree damaged in any way."

Detective Larson leaned forward. "The Morton family wants to put this to rest. That's why they're willing to replace any damage done to your property. They can generously compensate you for damages."

Larson's cigarette breath was too close for my comfort, and I scooted my chair back. Patsy had specifically stated in her will that I should take care of the tree but saying that to the detectives would only add suspicion. "It's Patsy's tree. I can't cut it down. If anyone can understand, Noah, it should be you. Think about all the memories you made at Patsy's parties around the tree."

Noah's face screwed tight. "That's not the point—"

"But it is. The tree is part of Patsy's legacy. A legacy she entrusted me to keep."

"Come on, Jolene." Noah's brows wrinkled. "We're trying to make this easy. We have enough evidence to warrant probable cause so, let me lay it out for you." He cleared his throat like he was preparing to give a speech. "One, Annette and Patsy had motivation to kill Mike Morton. Two, Mike was last seen only 400 yards from this house. Three, he was reported missing two days after last seen near your home. Four, a hole deep enough to bury a man was filled and a tree planted on top it—at the same time Mike was reportedly missing. Five, my father has detailed notes about you and Annette having cuts and bruises and acting strange when coming home with the tree." He put his hand up. "Oh, and then there's the tipster calls that line up too conveniently with what we know."

Too stunned to speak, I slowly shook my head in denial, but deep inside my voice spoke the truth: *Someone knows. Someone wants to hurt me.*

"This order comes from high up," Larson said. "If you won't willingly agree to let us cut down the tree, then we'll have no choice but to come back in the morning with a warrant and an excavator."

My eyes darted between the two detectives staring at me. "I'll have my attorney put a stop to this."

"I'm sorry it came to this." Noah pushed the chair out from under him and stood. "But we'll be here tomorrow morning at nine a.m. sharp." He stormed out the back door.

Larson stood and squinted one eye like he was examining me under a microscope. "We're not giving up until we find out if Mike Morton is buried under that tree." He grunted and followed Noah outside.

Tears burned in the backs of my eyes. I shut the back door. There was nothing I could do.

Fuck. Fuck. Fuck.

The anonymous caller. Who the hell was it?

I went to the kitchen sink and gripped the edge like a lifeline as I watched Noah and Detective Larson through the window. They were back at the family tree, pointing to the length of its roots. *They think Patsy and Annette killed and buried Mike.*

My hope sank like a deflated dingy. I wasn't sure what scared me most: that the police knew Mike was buried under the tree, or the anonymous caller who had told them.

I had no choice but to come clean about what I'd done, but not to the police.

Not yet.

Since the police eyed me as a suspect in Jackson's murder, I had to approach this with strategy. Someone was setting me up, and I needed legal protection. My hands trembled as I picked up my cell phone and called one of the criminal attorneys I'd researched.

This was going to cost in more ways than one.

CHAPTER TWENTY

A STOCKY RECEPTIONIST IN a red suit led me into Riley Baxter's wood-paneled office. "Please have a seat, Miss Parker." She placed a file folder on top of Riley's desk.

I slid into the bucket seat facing the attorney's desk. The leather beneath my hands was soft as silk, but the lead ball in my stomach reminded me that nothing about this meeting was soothing.

"Mr. Baxter will only be a moment." The receptionist poured a cold bottle of Fiji water in a crystal glass on top of the side table next to me and then walked out.

I'd spoken with Riley on the phone only a couple hours ago. When I'd explained I needed a criminal defense attorney because I'd killed someone in self-defense, and confirmed I could afford the hefty retainer, he'd agreed to meet with me immediately. I was finally doing the one thing I'd wanted to do for seventeen years: tell my story. Confessing all of it. Then, I'd take charge of the next step—staying out of jail.

"Hello, Jolene. Sorry to keep you waiting." Riley rocked into his office like a young hot-shot criminal attorney off a slick television law series.

Expensive suit, buffed nails, and a face shaved so close that his skin shined.

We shook hands and he took a seat behind his desk and glanced at the file folder. He looked at me with a face of concern. "Go ahead, Jolene. Start from the beginning."

I picked at the tender skin under my nails. This wasn't easy, but I was being billed by the quarter hour and I couldn't afford to waste a breath.

The words streamed from my mouth like water from a running tap—one long, endless flow. Each sentence emptied the well of pent-up guilt and remorse I'd stored deep in my bones. I explained everything—from the moment I'd met Annette and Patsy to the time Annette and I'd taken the acid and Mike had invaded the house and threatened to kill us. It was here that my voice cracked, and tears broke loose. "I killed him. We buried him in a pit and planted the tree on top of him the next morning."

I wiped my cheeks. Sniffled. What a fool I'd been.

"Why didn't you call the police to begin with?" Riley asked, sliding a box of tissues to me. "If it was self-defense; you two would have gotten off."

The room faded. I was nineteen again—standing over Mike's lifeless body—alone and afraid, so needy of Annette's acceptance and Patsy's love. Could I have done anything differently? Pressure built in my sinus and pounded across my cheeks. They'd been my world, but now they were gone, and none of it mattered to anyone but me. Tears rolled down my face, unabashed. I ripped out a few tissues and pressed them against my wet eyes.

"Take your time, Jolene," Riley said.

My shoulders dropped an inch. Riley's kind voice and patience worked like an elixir to my anguish. Part of his gig I was sure, but it felt good enough for me to carry on. I grabbed more tissues, blotted my eyes and blew my nose. If only getting the story off my chest could take away the nightmare.

I balled the tissues in my hand. "We were young and stupid. See… Mike had raped Annette and she'd reported it to police, but then withdrawn the charges because she didn't want her mom to find out. After we killed Mike, she was afraid it would've looked like a revenge killing. W-we were terrified. Certain we'd go to jail. Our parents couldn't afford expensive lawyers. I was naïve, impressionable, immature—"

Riley interrupted, "I understand. I really do. Go ahead and relax. Have a drink of water."

I drank half the glass of water and sat back in my chair, holding the tumbler with both hands. *Breathe. Breathe. Breathe.* I had to stay in charge of each move. "I want to make a plea deal with the prosecutor. I'll tell every detail of my story, but I won't plead guilty in Mike's death. I killed him in self-defense. Period."

"Here's the thing." Riley sat back and spoke in a casual manner. "You hired me to give you the best defense, but you haven't even been charged with a crime. I can't give you proper legal advice until you've been charged with something. And it sounds like we won't know if, or what, you'll be charged with until after the results of the dig tomorrow."

"Trust me. When the police dig under the tree in the morning, Mike Morton will be found. That's why I'm here to see you." I sat up and put the glass back on the side table. "The thing is, I don't want the tree to get destroyed. Patsy Farr entrusted me with the care of the property, and that includes the tree. It states so in her will."

"I'll have to see the grounds for the warrant before I can advise you," Riley said.

I hung my head in defeat. Trying to fight the warrant would only draw more interest in what's under the tree. This would never go away. "So, tomorrow they find Mike. What next?"

"I've successfully represented several self-defense cases. But we do have the matter of withholding evidence in an ongoing investigation. How many times have the police asked you about Mike's whereabouts?"

I ran my hands down my face. All the times I'd lied to Old Man Baker and Noah played in my head. "Several times. And I know that's a problem. But how serious?"

"Well, it's not good. The penalties for obstruction of justice in an ongoing investigation can be heavy."

A dense weight of regret balled in my chest. Many people had been affected by what I'd done—and hadn't done. People would want justice. "What about community service… anything but jail?"

"That's what I'm aiming for. Happens that I'm

on good terms with the prosecutor, but I can't make any promises and we'll have to take this one step at a time." He clasped his hands and rested his elbows on the desk. "But I'm curious. Tell me more about the anonymous tipster who told the police where Mike is buried. Why do you think the caller waited seventeen years?"

"That's a mystery I'd love to solve. According to what the detectives said, the caller only wants justice for Mike. But I never told anyone. Annette never told anyone."

"Hmm." Riley paused and aimed a gaze that went through me like a ghost. He looked at me from all angles—inside and out—and then sat upright in his chair. "Jolene, excuse me if it seems I'm going off-track here, but do you see a psychiatrist?"

Katie. I shifted in my chair. I'd been so preoccupied, that I'd missed my last couple of appointments. "I see a therapist from time-to-time."

"Then it won't be a problem having a professional validate your mental condition?"

My fingers curled. I didn't like what he'd implied. Katie always tried to assure me the anxiety and OCD flare-ups weren't akin to insanity, and I'd just started believing her. She'd called my dissociative episode, which had caused me to stop talking when I was ten, an isolated occurrence. She didn't know about what I'd done to Mike, though. I straightened my spine. "I see her for anxiety and OCD. Not because I'm crazy."

"Uh-huh." Riley clasped his hands together

then steepled his pointer fingers.

His doubtful expression was too familiar for my comfort. My throat grumbled and I gripped the arms of the chair. "My common condition is controlled with medication."

"Okay. Let's set that aside for now." He steepled his hands. "Back to Mike Morton. The next morning, when you planted a tree on top of him… you knew what you were doing at that time."

I looked down at the deep blue carpet. "Yes. The trauma caused me to detach from all emotion, though. It was the only way I could cope with the shock."

"I understand. And Annette was okay with having the man you'd killed buried in her backyard."

Annette's young face flashed in my mind, back to the time when I'd asked her the same question. She'd answered with a controlled, robotic voice and expression. *Nothing happened.* "She didn't act like it was a problem."

"And you felt the same?"

"How could I feel bad about something I'd convinced myself never happened?"

Riley leaned forward on his squeaky chair. "Other than the time you killed and buried Mike, had this ever happened to you before? The blocking out of time?"

Pain gripped my chest, stealing my breath and dragging me back to the day my mother had died. The shock. The emptiness. The blank face of my drunk father who never spoke to me. My silence had become my protection, blocking out the loneliness. "Yes. And I was put into a hospital for it."

Riley looked closer at my face. "A psychiatric hospital?"

My lungs collapsed into a rock-hard ache. The memory of my father's withdrawal and indifference flooded my brain, taking me back to the time I'd wanted to scream, to grab onto something solid, but I'd had no voice, nothing stable, only silence. A hollow body with no voice. "Yes. When I was ten. The doctors thought I'd blocked out the trauma of losing my mother."

Riley picked up a pen and wrote on a yellow notepad. "And which hospital were you committed to?"

My body numbed. Insane people got committed. "Lighthouse Beach Psychiatric. But that was so long ago—"

"I may need you to authorize release of medical records."

I forced a laugh. "Why? I'm not insane."

"Of course not." He dropped his pen on the notepad. "Just gathering information." He sat back into a relaxed position, an ankle on his knee. "Let's move on. Tell me about the Jackson Howell murder. Why are you a suspect?"

A cold sweat broke out on my palms. His interest in my psychiatric history made me uneasy but this meeting needed to move on. I locked my knees together and hugged myself. All my layers of lies had been stripped away, and I sat naked in front of a stranger with no way to cover up. "The police believe I was the last person to see him alive. Apparently, that's enough to keep me under their radar." I then gave him the lowdown—including the oak sapling planted over his body. "I believe the police are making a connection between Mike Morton under the family tree and the tree planted on top of Jackson."

He expression softened. "Is there? I mean, you did blank out parts of your memory after the attack on Mike. Is it possible you blanked out again, killed Jackson and planted the tree?"

Anger rolled up my throat. "No. Absolutely not. I did not kill Jackson. I've been set up. I've come to you for help—"

"It's fine, Jolene." His tone was calm, soothing. "I only ask because I'm familiar with trauma-induced blackouts. It's not unheard of. But let's move on. Tell me… who do you think set you up?"

Saying these things aloud, it suddenly sounded convoluted. But I was already in deep and found no reason to stop now. "I don't know who exactly, but probably the same person who's stalking me." I went on and told him about the person dressed in all black that Mrs. Nichols and I had seen. "He's been stalking me at random times ever since that night."

"Have you reported this stalking to police?"

"No. He's never approached me. He just slips in and out of my sight."

"Do you know him?"

"Of course not. I'm not even sure it's a man, to be honest. The person wears all black and a hoodie. I can never get a look at the face."

"Any threats?"

I hugged myself. "No. Just follows me."

"Hmm. Unfortunately, unless someone threatens you, there is nothing the police can do."

"But there's something more. A few months ago, I was at a teacher's assembly and I saw him outside the school. He'd left an oak leaf on my car windshield."

Riley narrowed his eyes. "You saw him do this?"

"No. But I saw him running away through the parking lot. No one else was around."

"Okay." He ran his hand over his mouth. "But putting a leaf on your windshield is not a crime."

"But it's not the first leaf." I pulled the anonymous letters bound with a rubber band from my purse. "For the past four years, someone has been randomly sending me a leaf in the mail. I have a total of nine letters." I handed him the bundle.

Riley removed the rubber band, shuffled through the envelopes, and then opened one. His eyes narrowed as he unfolded the waxed paper. "A leaf."

"All the letters are the same. The first one came to my house about three years ago when I was still married." I exhaled a breath. All this talking had knocked the wind from me. "After the divorce, they kept coming, but to my townhouse by the bay. Then to my home on Willow Road."

"You checked out the return address?"

"A fake one. It doesn't exist."

"Uh-huh." He opened another envelope, then another. "Just a leaf? Never a note?"

"Just what you see. Nothing else. And the

leaves started showing up more frequently a few months ago. Right at the time police received the first anonymous call." I watched him, waiting for a reaction.

Riley stayed tight-lipped as he opened the file folder on his desk. He slid an envelope next to the file then pressed a finger against his lips. A spark flickered in his eyes. "Hmm."

I fiddled with my chain bracelet. "What are you thinking?"

"I'm not certain." He traced his fingertips down the file page.

I leaned forward to catch a glimpse of what had him so absorbed. The application I'd filled out at the reception desk. A vein pulsed on my wrist. I'd only given basic information, so why his sudden twisted face? "Something wrong?"

"Did you fill this out yourself?"

"Of course. When I arrived at your office."

Riley placed a few of the envelopes side by side with my application and then stood. "Come… look close at the handwriting on both your application and the handwriting on the letters. Compare the two."

Standing next to him behind the desk, I looked at my own handwriting. I'd written in print. A simple style I'd picked up as a kid after a teacher had praised my neatness. I'd pretty much stuck with it.

I studied the handwriting on the envelopes. They were also written in print. A similar block-style print. I snorted. *He thinks I did this.* Determined to keep control, I crossed my arms.

"Okay. The handwriting is similar. Military style. A lot of people write like this."

"No, Jolene." His tone softened. "Look closer. The handwriting on the envelopes looks *exactly* like your writing on the application."

I snapped up the envelope and application and held them next to each other as I searched for a difference. "Look." I pointed to the letter 'R' on the envelope. "This 'R' is squared." I held up my application. "Mine is rounder."

Riley looked closer. He sniffed and jutted out his chin. "Perhaps."

Heat flared up my neck. He was wrong. Wrong as the conspiracy theorists who believed man had never landed on the moon. Did he believe anything I'd said to him today? "Are you implying I sent these leaves to myself?"

He put his hands on his hips. "I'm not implying anything, really. It's just an observation."

"Why would I send leaves to myself? It makes no sense."

"No. It doesn't. But you do have a history of blocking out memories." He shrugged. "Then again… the similarity in the handwriting could be a complete coincidence."

"That's all it is—a coincidence." I plopped the file back on the desk and took my letters back with me to my seat.

"Getting back to Mike Morton." His tone picked up and he sat. "I need to ask you something, Jolene."

My mouth dried. I nodded. "Yes?"

"Is it possible that Mike Morton is not buried

under the tree?"

"What do you mean?"

"Is it possible he wasn't dead when you buried him?"

My eyes shifted to the ground. *Had we buried him alive?* I'd asked myself that question several times. I had no answer—only shocking thoughts of Mike's gaping mouth full of dirt. *Dirt. Dirt. Dirt.* I looked at Riley. "He wasn't breathing. He was dead."

"You said you didn't plant the tree until the next morning." He paused, waiting for confirmation.

My fingers found a spot on my palm stained with dirt. I scraped the skin to feel the warmth. "Yes. Early."

"Maybe he dug himself out of that hole during the night. Maybe he disappeared for another reason, and now he's come back to stalk you."

I pressed my fingernail into the sore I'm made on my hand. My heart raced. The urban legend of the man in the pine barren. Self-doubt seeped into my thoughts. *Was he alive when we buried him? Did he crawl out of the hole?*

No. I remembered seeing the imprint of my sneaker on top of the soil the next morning. I jabbed my finger into the broken skin. I looked at Riley. "You think I'm insane?"

"I didn't say that. I'm just looking at all angles. From what you've told me, there may not be a body."

I looked out the tinted glass window overlooking the parking lot. Riley wanted to give me the best defense. I knew he did. But he also thought I was crazy... and maybe I was, but sometimes insanity was truth. I turned to him. "There is a body. I know because Annette and I buried him."

"We'll take this one step at time." He stood. "In the meantime, Jolene, go home and try to get some sleep."

Resigned to Mike being found and my secret exposed, my next problem was how to explain all of this to Aaron and the twins. They were all I had left of family. Would they still love me once they learned what I'd done?

I lifted my weary body from the chair. "I'll see you tomorrow."

CHAPTER TWENTY-ONE

THE NEXT MORNING, I stood on the back deck as a roaring excavator ripped across my green lawn, its tracks tearing through the turf like an army tank. I pressed a fist to my mouth to hold back a scream.

"The court order is clear." Riley folded the warrant Noah had handed me only moments earlier. "The police have enough evidence for probable cause. And you can forget fighting this. Apparently, the Morton family have friends in high places. It's signed by the governor."

I stuffed the warrant in the back pocket of my jeans and watched Noah and Detective Larson on the lawn near the family tree. Two men wearing dark blue jumpsuits with 'Forensics' emblazoned in white letters across their backs approached and shook hands with the detectives.

Noah waved the excavator to move closer to the tree, and then held up his hand to halt.

The claw fell to the ground and an orange-vested driver jumped out of the cab of the machine. Forensics and the detectives greeted the driver and started a demonstrative conversation while pointing at different parts of the tree.

I couldn't hear a word but smelled and tasted my defeat. Sweat. Bile. Nothing could stop this from happening.

Riley patted my back. "Wait here. I want to get closer to what they're doing." He made his way to the team of people surrounding the tree.

The back door squeaked. Melissa came out onto the deck wearing grey sweats and tan Ugg boots. She scratched the side of her head and narrowed her eyes toward the commotion at the tree. "I heard all the noise. What's going on?"

My chin trembled and heat spread across my cheeks. We hadn't spoken since she'd left for work yesterday afternoon. So much had happened since then. If she'd been home when I'd returned from Riley's office last night, I might have broken down and told her everything. But after half a bottle of wine and a Xanax, I'd drifted into a deep sleep and hadn't woken up until my alarm had gone off an hour ago.

I shoved the warrant deeper into my back pocket and kept my attention on the activity. "The police have a warrant to dig under the tree."

She came to my side and clutched my arm like a scared child. "A warrant... why? Does this have something to do with the search for Mike Morton?"

Nausea turned in my stomach. I needed to spew out the poison of my secret and tell Melissa everything. She was my friend. She'd understand once I explained, wouldn't she? I glanced at Riley standing near the excavator along with Noah and Detective Larson and the forensics team. Riley was right—until the body was found, I needed to keep my mouth shut. "I–I think so."

"I don't get it. What's the deal with the tree?"

I shook my head like I was just as confused. And I was. *Who the hell told the police where Mike was buried?*

She jiggled my arm and tilted her head like a curious puppy. "Well… what does the warrant say? Tell me."

Fuck. Hiding the truth for all these years had suddenly seemed easy. Now, I couldn't even look my friend in the eye. I kept my focus on the police and wondered how they planned to treat the tree.

"Joleeene." Melissa dropped my arm. "What's going on?"

I understood her interest. Any normal person would act just as inquisitive, but I needed to stay calm and quiet. "Something about evidence about what happened to Mike."

The forensics team, Riley, and the detectives all stood in a semi-circle talking as two more men approached the tree. They wore jeans and green polo shirts with a tree logo on their front pockets. They each carried a chainsaw. Noah caught my eye, and then turned away.

My breaths came fast and hard. I didn't like standing helplessly on the deck. I wished Melissa wasn't there to watch this unfold, but I couldn't stand by while this team of workers destroyed my tree. "I need to get closer and see what's happening."

Melissa was on my heels—nothing I could do

about that. She lived here, too. I slipped into the space between Riley and a forensics officer, and edged closer to Riley. "What's going on?"

"They're going to start removing limbs from the tree. We all have to back up."

Everyone backed up as the two workers from Greenview Arborists approached the tree and pulled on a chainsaw. *Vroom vroom vrooooom.*

My body tensed as I pressed my hands to my ears, blocking out the dreadful noise slicing through my brain. "One, two, three, four, five. One, two, three, four, five. One, two, three—"

The noise had drilled into my head, breaking my perfect sequence. I ran my hands through my hair, scraping into my scalp and suffering every brutal slice cut from the tree.

Vroom vroom vrooooom. The arborists hacked off the lower limbs.

"One, two, three, four, five. One, two—" Hot blood thrummed through my veins. I couldn't focus and started again.

"One, two, three, four—"

A cherry picker moved in and the arborists started work by chopping off the scarlet crown. *Vroom vroom vrooooom.* As the branches and boughs toppled, red leaves fell like teardrops to the ground.

This is happening so fast. I had to start over. I had to stop this from getting worse. It didn't have to happen this way. The tree could be saved. I ran to the workers. "Stop! You're destroying Patsy's tree."

Riley pulled me back. "There's nothing we can do, Jolene."

My knees buckled, and Riley looped his arm into mine for support. The chainsaw restarted, sending branches crashing to the ground. A large dump truck backed onto my lawn and the arborists tossed the branches and debris into the back.

In less than an hour, the tree was stripped down and looked like a naked totem pole.

Melissa looked at me with droopy worried eyes. "What the fuck, Jolene… what's under the tree?"

"Excuse me." Riley smoothed a hand over his paisley silk tie. "I'm Jolene's attorney, and I've instructed her not to speak with anyone until this search is complete."

"This is a bunch of crap." Melissa puffed and walked away toward the detectives.

Riley pulled me closer. "You doing okay?"

"Not really." I didn't bother telling him that no matter how much I didn't like snubbing Melissa, it had been the agony of watching the tree get destroyed that was killing me inside. It felt like someone had torn into my chest and ripped out my beating heart. I was alive, but empty.

The roar of the cherry picker broke my thoughts. It was roping the top of the naked tree. I stood frozen as three chunks were roped, sawed off, and tossed aside until all that remained of the majestic tree was a three-foot tall stump.

"Let's start digging!" Noah called out.

I paced the yard, watching from a distance. My legs grew tired, but I couldn't rest until this was over.

The excavator dug a wide, one-foot-deep circle around the tree, like a moat. It kept digging round and round in the circle, making it deeper with each turn. The noise screeched against my eardrums and hurt my teeth. I put my hands over my ears.

Two feet. Three feet.

The bearded forensics officer held up his hand, and the excavator stopped. "Let's get to work."

The two-man forensic team stepped into the hole with hatchets in their hands. I clutched my stomach. The frisky cadaver dog sniffed and scratched around the trunk too much for my liking.

The men whacked at the thick roots, but the stump held strong, determined to keep its position in the ground.

Whack. Whack. Whack.

I flinched with each bruising blow at its tender, fibrous roots. Each hit chipped closer to my painful secret. This was the end. The end of an era. The end of the memories of Patsy's love of the tree and her love for me.

The forensics team crouched to their hands and knees, reached past the roots, and sifted the earth with their gloved hands.

The bearded forensics officer climbed out of the hole and approached Noah. I drew closer to hear what was happening.

Rubbing and swiping dirt off his hands, the forensic officer spoke to Noah and Larson. "The root system under this tree is massive. Oak roots in this area don't normally go deeper than two, maybe three feet deep. These roots are at least five feet deep."

A shrill, nails-on-chalkboard noise sliced through my brain, shutting out all my senses. I cupped my ears to shut out the sound, then Annette's voice came through loud and clear. *The hole is at least five feet deep.*

"Damn tree must've been fertilized with steroids," the younger forensics officer said, wiping his forehead on his shirt sleeve. "We'll need to pull back the stump so we can get deeper."

Noah turned to the orange-vested excavator driver. "You heard the man. Let's rip out the stump."

"You got it, boss." The driver saluted and took off.

Riley came to my side with a concerned expression. "Hey, maybe you want to come back to the deck and sit down."

"No, I can't sit." I walked away, shaking off the noise in my head. Wandering along the tree line surrounding the house, I paced closer and then further away from the nightmare, unable to decide if I wanted to watch or not. I picked at the raw skin on my thumb where I'd peeled off my cuticle. Nerves burned under my skin.

When I reached the side of the house, I looked to the road. My heart chugged a ragged beat. People. I counted six. Mrs. Nichols was one of them. They stopped talking and looked at me—the deer in the headlights. From where they stood, they couldn't see what was going on in the backyard with the tree. But the police, forensics, and K-9 vehicles parked on the road were enough to make them assume a crime was being investigated.

The excavator roared back to life, and I dashed back to the work at the tree. The claw had grabbed hold of the stump and was now wrenching, jerking, and tugging it out of its earthly foundation like it was a wisdom tooth being pulled from a jawbone. Moments later, the stump lay on its side.

My feet melded to the ground, and everything moved around me in slow motion. Then the engine stopped, and every nerve in my body sizzled like a frayed electrical wire.

Noah moved in closer to the hole and stump then crouched to his haunches.

The cadaver dog sniffed around the ripped roots, pawed the earth, and sat. "I think we have a body here, men," the K9 officer said, slipping the hound a treat.

The forensic team hopped into the hole and hacked away at the roots still clinging to the tree. On their hands and knees, they sifted through soil.

Minutes passed until the younger forensic officer spoke. He pulled aside some roots. "Hey, Roger. Looks like human bones."

My vision blurred and my knees wavered.

The bearded one I now knew as Roger took a closer look. "Holy shit, man. That's incredible. The taproot grew straight through the torso."

Dark spots appeared, and my eyes couldn't focus, but I dared a glance in the hole.

White bones. A tuft of hair. My legs collapsed, and all I heard was my pent-up scream.

CHAPTER TWENTY-TWO

I SAT AT THE kitchen table and Riley handed me a glass of water. My hands shook so hard that I could barely lift the drink to my lips. "Thanks."

I'd momentarily blacked out, and Riley had helped me back inside the house. My vision was blurred—everything except the white bones entangled in tree roots. My stomach turned, but I'd already vomited its contents on the lawn. The image was forever imprinted in my brain.

Riley sat in the chair next to me. "Detectives Baker and Larson want to interview you. But remember, they have nothing to charge you with. I told them you were feeling traumatized by all of this and would go to the station for an interview later."

"What if they come knocking at my door?"

"Say nothing. They can't arrest you. They have no charges against you. But they will expect you to cooperate in the investigation soon. In the meantime, you have nothing to say."

My breaths came hard and fast, straining my chest. It was time to face my truth and confess my crime. Picking at my cuticles, I spotted a thumb-tack on the table. My fingers twitched. The pin tip could pick out the dirt accumulating under my nails.

The nightmare over the past few days had had me so preoccupied, I'd completely forgotten to take my meds. The Anafranil helped control my obsessions. Now, persistent thoughts and sensations of greasy dirt were making my insides twitch and squirm.

The anonymous caller. The leaves. My stalker.

I picked up the tack, put both my hands under the table, and pressed the sharp tip under my thumbnail. I dug deeper and deeper to catch all the filth and scrape it away. A puncture tore my flesh with excruciating pain. I winced. Still, nothing matched the pain of my guilt and remorse. "I won't talk with anyone. You have my word on that."

"I did some research last night. Seems this Mike Morton guy was known to police as a violent criminal."

"That's true." I squeezed the tack in my hand.

"Then finding you innocent of any wrongdoing in Mike's death shouldn't be hard to prove. But obstruction of justice during an ongoing investigation is more serious."

My head dropped, and I saw my inflamed thumb where I'd scraped a layer of skin away. Felt nothing. "How much more?"

"That, I need to work out with Madeline, the county prosecutor. You have no criminal record, so it'll be easier to make a deal."

I pressed harder on the painful wound. "But I won't spend time in jail, right?"

"Take a deep breath." Riley looked at me with pity. "Has your doctor prescribed anything to calm your nerves?"

My eyes turned to the purple stain pooling under my thumbnail. Blood mixing with dirt. Impossible to clean. I gripped the tack tighter. The Anafranil didn't always curb my anxiety. "There's a bottle of Xanax on my nightstand upstairs. First room on the left."

"I'll run up and get it. You need to relax. I'll talk to the prosecutor about this immediately." Riley went upstairs.

I tossed the tack back on top of the table and wiped the blood on my jeans. The back-door's handle jiggled, and Melissa walked inside. I jumped up for a hug, but her frosty face put a freeze on my tracks. Our eyes locked for one awkward moment. What did she see: a friend or a double murderer?

Melissa closed the door. Her face was dead white. "I overheard the detectives saying the body under the tree is Mike Morton... that they found his wallet."

My heart thudded against my eardrums, muffling Melissa's words, but I clearly understood their meaning. I grabbed the hem of my T-shirt and twisted the fabric. *Wallet. Bones. DNA.* Wouldn't take long to confirm his identity.

Melissa glared at me as she slid into a chair. "Tell me what's going on, Jolene… because this is freaky."

Slipping back into my chair, I pointed upstairs and spoke softly. "My attorney told me not to discuss this with anyone."

"What do you need an attorney for?" Her head jerked back. Did you know Mike was buried there?"

My eyes shot toward the opening into the living room for signs of Riley. In seconds he'd come down the stairs. I wanted to tell her what I'd done, to tell someone other than Riley. I wanted to shout it from the rooftops. But it would all be out in the open soon enough. "I...I can't say anymore. Not now."

Her eyes turned wide and wild. "Did Patsy know? Did she do this?"

"I'm going to talk to the police soon. Then, you'll know everything"

Melissa sat back. Her hands shook as she stared into my face for a long second. "You're scaring me, Jolene. Tell me what you know."

Footsteps pounded down the staircase. My eyes shifted toward the kitchen opening where I could see Riley coming down the stairs. I turned to Melissa and her wide eyes scrutinizing my every move. She wouldn't back off until she got an answer. I kept my voice low. "I'll tell you later."

Riley walked into the kitchen and glared at Melissa with an expression as hard as his tone. "Jolene is under counsel not to discuss this matter with anyone."

Melissa's face shifted from pity to confusion. "Honestly, Jolene... this is too weird. I'm going to grab a few of my things from upstairs and stay with Nancy tonight."

My chest cramped, twisting and squeezing until

the tightness reached my throat and made it hard to breathe. How had it come to this? My plan to start my life afresh and reestablish old friendships had disappeared in a flash. I imagined the talk around the dinner table at the Miller house this evening. Nancy, Richard, and Melissa, all speculating about Jolene the Psycho Girl. I was an outsider again. "Do what you must."

Melissa bolted out of the kitchen.

Riley looked at me in silence as Melissa's feet tapped the staircase. "Do you have anyone who can come stay with you?"

I hugged myself. False bravado wouldn't work with Riley. He knew my darkest secrets and was seeing firsthand their effects on my life. I had no one. I was losing everything, and I had no friends. Riley was my only ally, but his support could bleed me dry financially. I certainly didn't expect his sympathy.

Riley shook out a Xanax and handed it to me. "Here, take this."

I needed two. "Thanks."

He set the medicine bottle on the kitchen table. "Make sure not to discuss the details of the case with anyone. Not the media, your neighbors, or your roommate."

I twirled the pill between my fingers, wondering how I would explain this to Aaron. "I'll need to tell my story to the police soon."

Footsteps came down the stairs. I left the pill on the table and went into the living room, where Melissa stood at the bottom of the stairs with a duffle bag over her shoulder. I opened my mouth to ask when she planned on coming back, but then realized how pathetic that sounded. "I'll catch up with you later."

"Sure." She gave me a that's-not-likely smile and was out the door in two seconds.

Tears welled and I blotted the corners of my eyes with the back of my hand. I had no delusions of our friendship continuing. Who wanted to hang around a killer?

Riley wrapped an arm around my shoulder and led me to the couch. "Sit down and try to relax, Jolene."

Taking a deep breath, I realized that what Melissa thought of me was the least of my worries. I sat in the armchair and pressed my palms on my thighs to stop the bouncing. "How can I relax when someone out there knows what I've done? What other crazy thing is the caller going to tell the police? I mean, the caller was right about Mike being under the tree, so that makes him credible to the police. Right?"

"I suppose."

"What if he calls and tells the police I killed Jackson? Why wouldn't they think that was also credible?"

"You're making a lot of assumptions, Jolene. Let's stick with the situation at hand." He went to the front window and cracked open the shutters. "I hate to break this to you, but now there's a news van outside talking to police."

I shriveled like an ant on a hotplate. As if having my neighbors watch this day unfold wasn't embarrassing and dreadful enough, tonight it would be all over the news. At least Aaron and the twins were still in London.

"There's also a few gawkers lingering on the street." He closed the shutters. "The good news is that the medical examiner is removing the body now. Once the police leave, everyone'll disperse."

A dull weight pulled me down as I sank deeper into the sofa, wishing it could swallow me up.

Riley sat next to me. "I need to get back to the office and talk to Madeline immediately. But you should know that even though I've advised the police that I have to be present for any interview with you, they may still knock on your door and want to ask you some questions."

"I'm not saying a damn thing! I'll give them your card, right?"

"Exactly." Riley stood. "I'll call you later today or tonight with how we can proceed. But in the meantime, you need to stay put at home. The cops will find any reason to haul a person to the station. You know, an unpaid parking ticket, expired registration."

"I'm an expert at laying low."

Riley's lips quirked into a smile. "Before I head out, do you need anything from the grocery store? A pizza delivered?"

The growls in my stomach and loose jeans around my waist reminded me that I needed to eat. I had enough food in the refrigerator and pantry to source a few meals. "I don't need any-thing."

"Then, I suggest you take your medication and relax until you hear from me. I promise, Jolene, this will soon be over."

Squeezing my sore thumb, I appreciated Riley looking out for my best interest, but he couldn't understand. My nightmare was long from over.

CHAPTER TWENTY-THREE

SECONDS AFTER RILEY left the house, I went into the kitchen for the Xanax I'd left on the table. I snatched up the orange bottle, grabbed a second pill, and swallowed both with one gulp of water. Soon, my heart rate would slow to a pace where I could breathe, relax, and disappear into a deep sleep that was far away from this nightmare.

But, right now, my body popped with adrenaline. Sparks of fear burned under my skin. I splashed cold water on my face to cool the heat.

Wiping my face with the dishtowel, I dared a peek out the kitchen window. A lump grew in my chest, squeezing my lungs. Patsy's beautiful family tree. Gone. Decapitated and ripped out limb from limb. No amount of professional restorative garden work would repair this damage.

My breaths quickened. I had to see what was left of the tree. I whipped out the back door. Twigs snapped beneath my feet as I circled the tree's remains. The smell of yeast mixed with upturned soil slammed into my face, but I couldn't let that stop me from looking at the damage.

Yellow crime scene tape cordoned off the hole

where Mike had been dug out. The arborist had removed the trunk and large branches from the property. Only the torn-out stump remained, dangling on its side next to tangled roots.

A breeze rustled through dry autumn leaves. A flock of black crows crossed the sky, landing on the barest branches in the forest. The late October sun dipped low along the treetops, casting a golden glow in the sky. I shivered underneath my long-sleeved T-shirt. Patsy would have made a celebration of the cool autumn day—she'd have thrown an impromptu oyster roast and invited friends to drink wine and share laughter outside near the tree.

Drawn by the colored rings on the stump, I dropped to my knees for a closer look. I'd studied dendrochronology, the science of tree-ring dating, in college. Each of my past seventeen years were mapped out in the varying colors of the wide and narrow cellular rings.

Resting on my heels, I put my hand on the dark and rough outer bark—the skin of the tree, a collection of the dead cells of the tree's growth. The next few rings were the inner bark which provided support to the skin and carried sugars from the leaves down to the roots. The newer, water-carrying sapwood rings followed; they were a tawny color, like the delicate skin of a baby. Moving deeper toward the center was a wide band of brownish heartwood rings, and finally the chocolate pith in the center.

My fingertips traced over the years from the outer bark to the pith and then back again. Segments of my past unfolded in my mind like a time-lapsed video.

College graduation.

The drought.

The flood.

My wedding.

Annette's death.

I pressed my sore thumb on the spongy pith—the oldest part, which had formed when the tree had first been born. The part which had carried life-giving nutrients from the ground.

Squeee. My heart rate jumped, and I pulled back my hand. The high-pitched sound had come from the stump like an anguished last breath.

The taproot went straight through his torso.

Chills scrambled up my spine and shot to every follicle on my head. Rusty red sap oozed and bubbled from a dark sapwood ring. It dripped over the rings like thick and sticky blood. *Mike.* This tree held more than a record of seasons. It held the DNA of a human.

Trees communicated with other trees. What a story this oak could tell.

It would tell of its birth in a faraway forest. How it had been dug up as a tender sapling and nursed in a pot of organic soil. How it had made its way to the garden center and been bought by two college girls. How it had been planted close to the edge of a forest over a man's dead body. How the trees in the forest had befriended the oak so it wouldn't feel alone. How the oak had helped support the whole network of trees yearning to edge closer to the manicured lawn. The tree had been part of this land. It had had a story. A life. Now, it lay slaughtered on the lawn.

My battered and bruised heart ached, but I had no tears left behind my puffy eyes.

I'd grown to love this tree, this ground, this place where the blood of my secret ran deep into the soil, spreading like tentacles through the cracks in the earth to the groundwater, only to evaporate into the atmosphere, into every breath I took.

A shadow moved across my vision and the hair on my neck rose. I turned my head; a dark figure appeared in the corner of my eye. I jumped to my feet. My breaths grew sharper, quicker.

I twirled around, surveying the backyard.

The forest.

The lawn.

The gazebo.

Vacant. Quiet. Only me. A gust of cool air swept across my face. The rustle of dry leaves falling from the trees in the forest filled the long silence.

Neighbors and reporters had been here earlier. Was someone still lurking on the property? I looked around again. No one.

I ran into the house, bolted the doors shut, and set the alarm. Pacing the living room floor, I tried to steady my nerves.

Breathe. Breathe. Breathe.

It had been nothing, I rationalized. The shadow of a hawk overhead. A nosy neighbor or reporter spying on me. Nothing threatening.

My heartrate slowed, and using ERPT therapy, I envisioned my muscles turning as supple as a warm candle. I fell back into the armchair, closed my eyes, and focused on my breathing. Slow and steady, I calmed with each intake of air.

Lulled by the quiet of the house, my mind cleared of thoughts, and my body floated weight-lessly as I drifted into a soothing sleep.

Ring, ring. Ring, ring.

Adrenaline bolted through my limbs, and I jumped up, blurry-eyed.

Ring, ring. Ring, ring.

The landline in the kitchen. My head was cloudy, fuzzy, and I didn't want to pick up the call. The only phone calls which ever came through were from the creepy heavy breather and moaner.

Ring, ring. Ring, ring.

Panic rolled up my spine and I clomped into the kitchen with the thought to yank the line from the wall, then smash the phone to smith-ereens.

Ring, ring. Ring, ring.

A fiery rage burned in my throat. I grabbed the handset and lashed out at the caller. "Who is this?"

"Jolene?"

Aaron. My heart jumped to my throat and I smoothed my hair, as if he could see I was a ship-wreck. "Aaron, I-I—how are the kids?"

"We're fine. You don't sound too good though. I've been calling your cell phone for almost two days. Haven't you seen my messages?"

My cell phone. *Shit.* It had gone flat while I'd been dealing with this disaster. And now I couldn't construct a coherent sentence. The heavy dose of Xanax I'd taken thirty minutes ago had slowed my responses, and the fog wasn't leaving my head fast enough.

"Jolene?"

"Sure, I-I'm fine." I cleared my throat. "I had a killer migraine… it kind of knocked me out. I must've forgotten to plug my phone into the charger."

"I got concerned when I didn't hear back from you."

I pressed my lips together and looked out the kitchen window, to the empty space where the family tree once stood. Should I tell him now? He'd hear it soon enough, and wasn't it best if he heard it from me first? Joyous laughter and screeches from the twins broke that thought. "There's been a lot going on over here," I said, making sure to sound perky, "but it'll wait until later. Everything okay with the twins?"

"They're doing great. We took them all over London today and texted you some pictures. The kids have been chomping at the bit to tell you about it."

Tears came to my eyes, and I tried to push them back, but that only made my throat constrict. I realized this was the last time I would have a light-hearted talk with my children. Once they learned about what I had done, would they still see me as worthy mother? It was unlikely they'd move into the house with me anytime soon. I ripped a paper towel off the roller on the counter and blotted my eyes. "I'm here now," I said. "Put them on."

"Sure," Aaron said. "Here's Eric."

"Hey, Mom!" Eric squealed. "It's been so cool. We saw where they chopped off people's heads."

Clutching my chest, I fought back the ache straining my throat, threatening my ability to speak in a normal voice. "That sounds like the Tower of London."

"Yeah, that's it… wait a minute." A muffled swishing sound. "Mom, Jennifer wants to talk to you."

"We went inside a big castle," Jennifer belted out, breathless. "And we saw all these beautiful clothes that belonged to the kings and queens."

I kept my sadness clamped. "Oh, tell me about that." I sat at the kitchen table and listened as Jennifer gushed about the great time they were all having. How India's family was soooo nice to them and had bought them English lollies and fish n' chips.

"I'll take a look at the pictures you sent to me as soon as my phone is charged," I said. "I can't wait to see your pictures."

After ten minutes of the twins swapping the phone and telling me about their adventures, Eric said, "Mom? Dad wants to talk to you again. I love you."

My body slumped as Eric's voice faded away.

"Hey, sorry to interrupt," Aaron said, "but it's getting close to midnight here, and the kids really need to get some sleep. We have another early day tomorrow."

"I'm glad the kids are having a good time," I said, my voice cracking.

"It's been great." He sighed. "Only two more

days, and then it's back to reality."

The ground shifted beneath my feet. Reality was worse than he knew.

Let them enjoy their good time. They'd find out soon enough that Mommy had done a bad thing.

CHAPTER TWENTY-FOUR

RAIN PELTED AGAINST the tinted windows of Riley's office as I sat numbly and registered what he'd just said. He'd spoken with the prosecutor, Madeline Cannon, and she'd assured him I'd be cleared of any wrongdoing in the death of Mike Morton.

"Mike had a record dating back to when he was eight years old and smashed a cat's head to a pulp," Riley said. "He was a thug in middle school—well-known for starting fights and breaking into houses and stealing. Then, he graduated to assault and was arrested a couple of times. Somehow, he slipped through the cracks and made it back into society. Then, of course, he raped Annette." He sighed. "You can forgive yourself, Jolene. You killed in self-defense."

I clasped my hands together like a sinner praying for redemption. Remorse still flowed through my veins, though, and I doubted the feeling would disappear. Even if I forgave myself for killing Mike, my act had forever changed my DNA. I tightened my core and prepared for the blow. "What about my lying to the police?"

"You'll be charged with obstruction of justice,

that's certain."

Nerves rolled through my empty stomach. "But I'll avoid jail, right?"

"I'm sorry, Jolene." Riley's expression turned sympathetic. "The prosecutor feels your actions have caused the Morton family eighteen years of anguish which they can never reclaim, and they want, and deserve, justice for that."

My heart thumped hard against my chest. I looked to the ground and focused on my breathing. I'd caused the Morton family too much unnecessary pain. Although Mike had been a despicable loser, his family shouldn't have had to suffer for so many years. That was all my fault. "They probably want to see me hang from the gallows."

"This is about the law, Jolene. Not vigilante justice. And it helps that you've been a model citizen and will have character references from the school staff at Bayview Middle School."

"What happens to a model citizens like me who get arrested for obstruction of justice?"

"First, you'll plead guilty to the charges. The prosecutor will recommend a reasonable plea bargain sentence to the judge: three months in the low security county jail."

I pressed my clasped hands against my pounding chest. I'd known this was coming, but it suddenly felt unexpected. "Three months? Are you fucking serious? What about community service?"

"It's not an option. The prosecutor wants justice for the family. This is a good deal, Jolene. Take it."

A painful lump formed in my throat. I was

guilty and had to take my licks. "I'll take the offer. What happens now?"

"Tomorrow morning we'll go to the police station. Madeline will meet us there and you'll tell your story to the investigators."

My senses dulled, and I slipped into a suspended moment. Rain popped against the window and I looked outside. A woman with a red umbrella jogged through the parking lot to her car, free as a bird. I envied her. Envied a woman I'd never met. I thought I might laugh. I turned to Riley. "When do I go to jail?"

"That'll be up to the judge, but I expect it will be immediate. The prosecutor is working on expediting the hearing and the sentencing. The court wants this matter dealt with immediately." Riley went silent for a moment. "Go home and rest, Jolene. We'll know more tomorrow, and soon, this will all be over."

I bolted out of the offices of Baxter and Simpson and into the elevator along with a Fed-Ex delivery man and an old couple wearing clear plastic rain ponchos. Panic pounded in my chest. *How the hell am I going to cope with being imprisoned?*

The doors closed, and the elevator slowly rolled downward.

The air grew heavy and hot. I took in short breaths as sweat beaded along my hairline. If I thought this elevator was cramped, how would I cope with being in a crowded jail? I was used to seeing the sky and breathing fresh air.

No fresh air. No fresh air. Just a box.

Stop thinking. Heat spread across my back and my heart drummed faster. I looked to the ceiling for signs of ventilation. *Where the hell is the vent?* A stream of thoughts ran through my mind. *What if it's hot in jail? Or cold? Will I have a blanket or a fan?*

I just wanted fresh air.

Ping. The elevator stopped on the tenth floor, and two chatty young women stepped inside, followed by a rush of cool air. The doors closed, and the women's backs pushed me against the old couple in plastic. Someone coughed and the temperature in the claustrophobic space increased to oven-roasting mode.

The elevator stopped with a bump, and a man with a suit and briefcase walked in.

"Pardon me," I whispered as I pushed closer to the crammed couple behind me. With nowhere to move, I closed my eyes.

Chatter. Hushed voices.

Ping.

The doors opened again, and I rushed out to the cool air of the glass atrium lobby. The rain thrashed against the glass roof and the sound echoed through the open space. The lobby was set up like a garden with tall palms and exotic plants and welcoming tables comfortably spaced about for relaxing or having a casual meeting. A coffee shop and a bank. People milled around talking and texting on cell phones while others waited at the entrance doors for the rain to slow.

I'd left my umbrella in the car and wasn't in any hurry to get drenched. The aroma of freshly brewed coffee gave me an excuse to just sit still for a moment.

I grabbed a hot chia latte and had just sat down on a comfortable sofa when my cell phone rang. *Aaron. Damn it.* I cleared my throat and answered with an all-is-cool voice. "Hey."

"Jolene. Listen. We're at Heathrow getting ready to board our flight back." His tone was rushed, sharp. "My mom just called and said she saw on the news that a man's body was dug up. Under the oak tree in your yard. What the hell is going on over there?"

My vision blurred. "It's true. I wanted to tell you the other day… I want to tell you every-thing, but I-I can't talk about it right now."

"So, you've known this… about this body bur-ied in Patsy's backyard?"

I turned away from the Goth couple sitting in the module next to me. "Yes. But—" I lowered my voice, "I'm in a public place and can't talk about it right now."

"Did Patsy kill the man?"

"Aaron, honestly—"

"Holy shit. Are you involved?"

"I'll tell you everything when you get back."

"What am I supposed to tell the twins?" He lowered his voice again. "Mom said it's all over the news, so they're going to hear about it from the kids at school."

"Tell them I'll explain everything when I see them." I had no idea how.

Aaron's breaths deepened, like he was cupping his mouth over the phone. "Just answer one ques-tion. It's a 'yes' or 'no' question."

"Okay."

"Are you involved in what happened?"

I hesitated, but only because I wanted to savor this moment where Aaron knew nothing about what I'd done. "Yes."

CHAPTER TWENTY-FIVE

THE TEMPERATURE IN the meeting room at the police station dropped a few degrees when Madeline Cannon marched in. She looked around fifty, with a slender figure, long nose, and joyless face. She was all business.

Riley introduced us, and she looked at her watch. "Where the hell are the detectives?"

Nerves carved a pit in my stomach, and I shivered in the cool room. Madeline took the empty seat next to Riley.

Noah walked into the room with Detective Larson trailing behind him. Noah offered his hand to Madeline. "Sorry to keep you waiting. I'm Detective Baker and this is Detective Larson."

After introductions, all eyes were on me as I once again told my story by rote. Home invasion. Self-defense. Burying the body. Lying to police. During my confession, I watched Noah's expression shift from hurt to confusion, and then to anger. "Why didn't you report this sooner?" he asked. "Why wait all this time?"

I fell into a numb state of guilt and remorse. Because I was insane? Because I'd made a promise to forget it ever happened? What was my crazy reason? If I had reported this sooner, I'd have damaged the loyalty Annette and I had shared. Our sisterly bond had been far too much to risk.

Another reason was that, for so long, I'd believed Annette was right—the police would have thought we'd killed Mike in revenge for the rape. And Patsy. Sweet, loving Patsy. The truth would have dimmed the light of her bright spirit. We'd never have done that on purpose. We hadn't wanted our idyllic lives changed. Living with the secret had seemed easier, and I'd found no reason to change the status quo. But it was too late for what-ifs.

I exhaled. "Because I was traumatized...and misguided. Annette kept repeating the lie—that we'd never killed Mike. Never buried him under the tree. Over time, it became believable."

Noah's face paled. "You're telling me Patsy never knew Mike was buried under the tree?"

"She would've had a heart attack long ago if she'd known the truth. She definitely would have convinced us to call the police. It was Annette who was adamant about keeping this a secret. I was just naïve and afraid."

"Tell us, Jolene," Detective Larson said. "Who do you think made the anonymous calls leading us to the tree?"

I looked at Detective Larson and Noah. "I really don't know. I hoped you could tell me."

Detective Larson's eyes zeroed in on me. "Do you have any idea how much time and resources we've put into this case? All wasted because of your lies?"

My cheeks burned. I had no excuses left. "I'm sorry—"

Madeline slid her thin leather briefcase on the table. "Gentlemen," she said, "the state is charging Miss Parker with obstruction of justice, to which she already pleads guilty. She is set to appear before a judge in two days for a sentence hearing."

I looked to the ground. *This is really happening.* Muffled words flowed between Madeline and the investigators but all I could hear was the pounding of my heart.

I was going to jail.

After the meeting, Noah came to my side and spoke quietly into my ear. "Too bad it went on for this long."

An emotion marked his face—something I couldn't define. Not shock, not disgust, but… empathy. No, that made no sense. "I agree."

Noah left the room with Larson, and the rest of us followed.

The confession at the police station had left me drained, and I was glad to finally get back home. The house was quiet, and I roamed from room to room. Melissa had been sleeping in Patsy's old room. The door was closed, as it had stayed since she'd gone to Nancy's house three days ago. I knew she wasn't home because her car wasn't in the garage.

I didn't like intruding in her space but wondered if she'd come back to the house when I was at the police station. I opened the door and gulped.

Melissa's things were gone. Her bedding. Her clothes. Her shoes. I checked the bathroom—all drawers were emptied, cleared of toiletries. She'd left completely without a goodbye.

I sat on the mattress and looked out the window, to the bare spot where the family tree had once stood. The emptiness in my chest pushed against my ribs. I'd lost so much, and now Melissa was gone. The damaged friendship was all my fault. The stress of holding my secret had made it impossible for anyone to really know me. Only my mother, Annette, and Patsy had really ever understood me, and loved me regardless of my flaws.

My ringtone on my cell tinkled. Aaron. I couldn't put off this conversation. Inhaling deep, I answered the call. "Hey."

"What the fuck, Jolene? Why the hell didn't you ever tell me you killed a man?"

My stomach turned. I'd told the story so many times now that I'd become desensitized to the shock. But Aaron deserved to know everything. "It was in self-defense… and so long ago… so traumatic. I blocked it from my memory. It's hard to explain—"

"I'm coming to your house right now—"

"No." I kept my tone firm. "Not today. I have some other obligations." The meeting with Riley had left me drained.

"I need to know what's going on." A growl edged his voice. "What do I tell the twins?"

"I'm going to explain everything to you. Then, we can figure that out."

"I sort of prepared them, based on what I know." He sighed. "We got in late last night, but they were both still wound up this morning and insisted on going to school to see their friends. If I was going to send them to school, I had to tell them something. They needed to be prepared for what kids might say."

"What did you say to them?"

"I told them you were on the news because of something you did a long time ago, and that you'd explain it all to them later."

"And they didn't ask questions?"

"Honestly, I don't think it fully registered. They were still tired from the trip and excited about seeing friends."

"I want to see them."

"They looked tired when I dropped them off at school. No doubt they'll crash after they come home. Maybe it's best if you come over here to see them this afternoon."

"Will India be there?"

"Of course."

No. No. No. I didn't want to have this conversation around his live-in girlfriend. "Let the kids rest tonight. I'll tell you the whole story right now, and we can discuss how to explain everything to the children without causing any more trauma."

"Okay. So, tell me everything."

He'd already heard the recent news, so I caught him up on what Annette and I had done all those years ago. "The sentence for obstructing justice is three months in jail. My hearing is in two days, and my attorney said I can expect the judge to approve the sentence."

"Whew. That's a lot to take in." He paused for a beat. "Maybe it's best if I break the situation to the twins slowly. You know, let them rest tonight. Play it by ear tomorrow."

I agreed. Learning that their mother was also a killer would take some time to comprehend. "Call me after they come home from school. I want to know if you find out if anything was said to them during the day."

"I'll do that."

"And I'll set everything right when I see them."

———◆———

Two weeks later, I sat with Riley and Madeline in a pin-drop quiet courtroom, waiting for the judge. Shame and remorse kept me from making eye-contact with anyone in the gallery, so I stared straight ahead. The bronze seal of the court hung on the wall behind the judge's bench, flanked by the American flag and the Commonwealth of Virginia flag.

My eyes focused on the scale of justice symbol on the state flag. *Sic semper tyrannis*—thus always to tyrants. Here I was, the tyrant on the ground with the foot of justice pressed firmly on my chest. I exhaled a tired breath, resigned to the loss.

The shuffling of feet and whispers of people gathering in the seats behind us let me know the courtroom was filling fast. I dared a quick glance backward at Aaron who gave me a reassuring smile. Turned out, a couple of the kids at school had teased the twins about their mom killing a man and going to jail. That had broken my heart, so Aaron had brought them by the house so I could tell them the truth. "I killed the man in self-defense. He was a violent criminal who was trying to kill me and Annette. If I hadn't killed him, he would have killed us."

When I'd explained that I was going to jail for lying to the police, and not for killing the man, the twins had understood. The details hadn't mattered to them. They loved me just the same.

A few others were seated in the courtroom. Noah. Detective Larson. A younger man and woman who I didn't recognize and assumed were reporters. Then, my heart stopped. Solemn-faced Mr. and Mrs. Morton sat at a table next to us, whispering and holding hands. Guilt squeezed my windpipe, and I choked on strangled breath.

Riley leaned close. "You okay there?"

I nodded, dabbing the corner of my eyes with my finger.

The bailiff stepped in front of the bench. "All rise."

Judge Freemantle came out from her chamber wearing a black robe, small round glasses, and more wrinkles on her face than a grumpy Shar-pei. She sat behind the judge's bench and started the hearing.

After proceedings, Judge Freemantle turned her attention to me. "Jolene Parker," she said, "you are charged with obstruction of justice for knowingly lying to police investigators about the whereabouts of Mike Morton during an ongoing investigation. Your lack of cooperation has caused enormous grief to the Morton family, not to mention lost police resources. You are fined $10,000 dollars and sentenced to three months in the county jail. You are to report to jail one week from today to begin your sentence."

This was no surprise to me. Riley had explained exactly how the hearing would unfold, but it was almost November, and if I was going away in two weeks, I'd be in jail over Thanksgiving, Christmas and New Year's.

At the pound of the gavel, the court adjourned.

Riley whisked me past the handful of reporters and parking lot gawkers, and into his luxury BMW with tinted windows. He threw me worried looks as he drove toward my house. "Are you going to be okay?"

"I hadn't anticipated being in jail over the holidays. That's going to be hard."

"Yeah. That's tough." Riley kept his eyes on the road, a frown falling on his face. "I honestly didn't know if the judge was going to put off the sentencing until the New Year, but Madeline was right, the State wants this matter put to rest." He threw me a glance. "How do you think you'll cope in jail?"

"I've been living in a mental prison for over seventeen years. I can handle three months in a physical one." That was a lie. No normal person believed they could handle prison.

"All right." He paused for a moment. "And what about Jackson Maloney's investigation.

Have the police contacted you again?"

"No."

Riley nodded. "That's good."

Nothing about this was good, or would be, until I found the anonymous caller. I hadn't received any leaves or creepy calls since I met with Riley. Maybe the anonymous caller to police was satisfied that justice had been served. Maybe now that I'd been sentenced, I'd never get another letter and never see the stalker again. But I found no reason to discuss that with Riley. I stayed quiet and stared out the window for the remaining fifteen-minute drive to my house.

Riley pulled into my driveway and put the car in park. "Good luck, Jolene. If you need me for anything else, you know how to reach me."

"Don't take this personally, but I hope this relationship is over and I never have to see you again."

"No hard feelings." Riley winked.

I hopped out and waved goodbye as Riley backed out of the driveway. He honked the car horn and took off. His job was done, but my nightmare was just beginning.

Resigned to my fate, I went inside, poured a large glass of wine, and drank it down in three gulps. It was only two in the afternoon, but I'd craved the warm rush I got from the first shots of alcohol.

I took the bottle with me to the other side of the kitchen where I'd set up a cozy corner, like Patsy had done to make the large kitchen the hive of the home. I plopped into the two-seater sofa facing the small flat-screen television.

This was where I wanted to stay. Huddled in a corner.

CHAPTER TWENTY-SIX

*D*ING DONG. DING *dong.*
     Bells rung in my head and my mouth was dry as desert dust. I opened my eyes and found myself lying in a fetal position on the small sofa in the kitchen's cozy corner. An empty bottle of wine was on the coffee table and the television had shut down to sleep mode.

Ding dong. Ding dong.

I sat up and squinted into the sun-lit room. The orange bottle of Xanax was on the floor. Then, I remembered. I'd double-dosed myself again last night. Shouldn't have, but I'd needed to keep away the obsessive thoughts of being boxed into a jail cell playing over and over in my head.

Ding dong. Ding dong.

Rubbing the sleep from my eyes, I shuffled toward the living room and looked out the peep-hole. It was Aaron. Damn it. I still wore my clothes from the hearing yesterday, with the added touch of my hair being matted flat to my head.

I brushed out my hair with my fingers, then pinched my cheeks, and opened the door. "Hey, you. Come on in."

A trail of expensive cologne followed him

inside, making me more aware of my ruffled appearance.

Concern lined his face. "How've you been holding up since yesterday's hearing?"

I straightened my shoulders and pulled on the hem of my blouse. "I knew I'd get three months and a fine, but I hadn't expected to be in jail over the holidays."

"Hmm. That does suck. But I've given this whole situation some thought." He pointed to the sofa. "Is it okay if we sit down and talk?"

I pressed my lips together. In all the time I'd known Aaron, he'd never requested we sit and talk. "Uh, sure."

He sat at the end of the sofa and I took the armchair next to him.

"I understand a lot more now," Aaron said. "The neurosis, the OCD, the drinking—all that suffering was due to this secret eating away at you."

"I'm not looking for pity."

"You never did. That wasn't your style."

"Thanks, Aaron." I hugged myself. "How are the twins?"

"Things have calmed down at school with the bullying. In fact, they're going to a Halloween party at a friend's house tomorrow afternoon. Jennifer has a princess costume and Eric is going as Spiderman."

Tears welled in my eyes. I should have been the one taking the twins to the party. But it was best for them if I stayed low on the radar. At least for now. "I'm so, so sorry about all this. I never wanted to hurt you or the twins—"

He leaned closer and put his hand on my thigh. "I know. I believe you. And the kids understand you killed that man in self-defense. I just wish I'd known what you were going through. Things could have turned out different."

My muscles relaxed with his warm touch. Would things have been so different? Aaron had always been an excellent father and all-around good guy. But he also had a wandering eye, and that would never change. I took his hand and squeezed firmly. "Maybe. Or maybe things turned out exactly as they should have."

Aaron leaned back into the sofa. "What's important is that now you can let go of the past and move forward."

Not really. There was still the anonymous caller. The leaves. Jackson's murder. So much hung over my head. And even though Aaron was being supportive, I didn't want to get into the details with him. Learning what I'd done to Mike Morton was enough for him to absorb. "Moving on is exactly what I have planned. And the twins... I'm going to miss them terribly, but I don't want them to visit me in jail."

"I agree. But I also feel it's important the twins stay close to you, so while you're away, we'll arrange for a weekly call. You won't go through the holidays without seeing their faces on Skype or whatever it is they let you use."

My sinus swelled with tears I didn't want to cry. Separated from my babies. Again. I dabbed my runny nose with the back of my hand. "That'll work. And you'll bring them here today after school, right?"

"I'll make sure you see them every day until you have to go." He looked at his phone. "Right now, I need to get back to the office."

I waved goodbye from the verandah as Aaron backed out of the driveway. Desperate for caffeine, I went to the kitchen and popped a capsule into the coffee machine. Having Aaron's support gave me a needed boost. At least I'd stay connected to my children.

Three months. I only had to last three months.

Ding dong. Ding dong.

My first instinct was to ignore the doorbell but hiding from my life never did me any good.

I looked through the peephole. *Shit.* Nosy Mrs. Nichols. I'd seen her on the street with the other spectators when Mike's body had been found. By now, she'd seen the news and knew what I'd done. Another person I couldn't put off talking to. I opened the heavy inner door and acted surprised. "Mrs. Nichols. How are you?"

"Oh, Jolene. I-I hope I'm not disturbing you. I just wanted to check in... make sure you're doing okay." She smiled, but the lines around her wide eyes showed pity.

"I'm doing just fine." I opened the screened door. "Please come in."

She gave me a warm hug. "When I heard all the details about what happened...." She sighed and shook her head. "It's not a nice thing to say, but that boy got what he deserved."

"I know a lot of people feel that way. But I

hurt the Morton family, and I feel horribly guilty about that. I don't know if that feeling will ever go away."

She patted my hand. "You're not a bad person. I've known you for most of your life. Since you were a wee one. I even remember when your father sent you to that ridiculous psychiatric hospital."

My stomach tightened. Mrs. Nichols was well-intentioned, but I didn't like being reminded of my 'Psycho Girl' days. "What do you know about that?"

"Only what Patsy told me. But don't worry, dear. I don't share what people tell me in confidence. My point is that Patsy loved you like a daughter. I know that. And I loved Patsy. And for that reason, I want to be a support to you. You're a good-hearted soul who would never hurt another person on purpose."

"But the anonymous calls to police… someone knew what I did and waited all this time to report it to police. It… it's doing my head in."

"It is odd. If what I hear on the news is right, the informant never requested the reward."

"For all we know, the police really do know who the caller is, but are keeping it confidential."

"Hmm." Mrs. Nichols tapped a finger on her lips. "That's possible. But you must wonder why this person took so long to report what they saw you and Annette do."

"I think about it every day. What if the anonymous tipster is the same person you saw running along Willow Road that night Mike was last seen?"

Mrs. Nichols slowly shook her head, her eyes showing the pity I'd become too familiar with seeing on people's faces. "I really don't know, dear. I suppose it could be the same person. But it's all in the hands of the police. I'm so, so sorry. I wish I could help."

My heart warmed with gratitude for having Mrs. Nichols as a long-time friend. That she also loved Patsy and Annette had bonded me to her like family. Maybe things weren't as bad as I thought. Today, I realized that at least I had the support of Mrs. Nichols and Aaron. "I was just getting ready to have a cup of coffee. Would you join me?"

"No thank you, dear. I've had my one cup I allow myself every day. Besides, I can't stay. Mr. Nichols needs me back at the house. I just wanted to check in and let you know that, if you need a friend, I'm right down the road."

I remembered all the times Mrs. Nichols had kept an eye on the house for Patsy if she was out of town for a long period. True-blue, Patsy had called her. "May I ask a favor?"

"Anything, dear."

"As you know, I'm going to jail for three months."

Her shoulders dropped. "I do. And I'm so sorry—"

"It's okay." I took her hand. "I'm concerned about the house while I'm away. I'd like to have someone I trust check on it periodically. Turn different lights on and off to make it look lived-in."

"Say no more. I have plenty of time on my hands these days." She turned and pointed her chin to the security panel near the door. "Just give me your new code and I'll be happy to check in as often as you need me to."

If only I could trust her with my theory about the leaves, the stalker, and the anonymous caller. She'd definitely ask me a lot more questions. Or maybe she'd think I was bat-shit crazy. As well-meaning as she was, I couldn't trust that she wouldn't tell someone else. Better to stay quiet. "I'll need you to check the mailbox, too. I've already pre-paid my utilities and other bills for the next three months, so I don't expect anything that can't wait until I return."

"You won't have to worry about anything. I'll leave all your mail on the kitchen table. I can call you with updates if that makes you feel better."

"It does."

Mrs. Nichols looked at her tiny oval wrist-watch. "I can't stay any longer, dear. And I'm sure you have plenty on your mind and business to sort out. I'll come by again in the next few days and you can give me the security code and keys with any special instructions."

I hugged her one more time and closed the door as soon as she stepped off the verandah. After drinking the coffee I'd let go cold, I ran upstairs and jumped into a long, hot shower. Aaron was coming by later with the twins, and I was ready to finally hold them in my arms again.

While towel drying my hair, I heard my phone ping and I looked at the screen. A text from

Melissa. Adrenaline rushed to my limbs and I swiped open the message.

Hey Jolene, I'm sorry for not staying in touch, but I've quit Ocean Joe's and moved to Richmond to take care of my aunt full-time. I feel awful for running out on you the way I did. I was shocked and confused by everything that was going on. But now that I know the full story, I just want to wish you the best of luck.

My shoulders straightened. Maybe Melissa did care about our friendship. But it still hurt that she hadn't said all this to me face-to-face. I texted her back.

Thanks for reaching out to me. I'm sure your aunt appreciates having you around full-time and I hope it's all working out well for you. Let's get together for drinks the next time you visit Lighthouse Beach. Stay in touch!

Melissa never responded. No thumbs-up or smiley face emoji. Nothing. I guessed she'd moved on.

The days passed with no more letters with leaves. I hoped the informant was satisfied now that I was sentenced. He had his justice. What drained my brain was the feeling that he was planning another move.

And I was certain there was another move. That scared me, too, because how could I protect myself from a danger I'd never see coming?

But I couldn't let the obsessive thoughts ruin the whole week.

Aaron kept his promise. He and the twins came over every night for dinner, homework, board games, and movies. Turned out, the twins were proud of me for protecting myself and understood how I'd been afraid.

I only wished telling the truth had set me free.

The night before I reported to the county jail to serve my sentence, I dropped to my knees and huddled the twins together in my arms. My throat constricted, and I hid my face so that they wouldn't see my eyes mist. It was only three months, but I'd miss their warm embraces and heartbeats thumping next to mine. "I'm going to miss you more than you can know."

Jennifer stroked my hair. "It's okay, Mommy. We'll be fine."

"Come on, guys," Aaron said, tugging on the twin's shirts. "Your mom will be back home before you know it."

I stood and hugged Aaron, grateful for his support. He wasted no more time and swiftly left the house with the twins. With my back pressed against the door, releasing the tears I'd held back all night.

My children would survive this—I knew that. But would I?

Dragging my feet into the kitchen, I wiped away my tears and emptied the dishwasher. It was best if I didn't think too much about missing the children. It wouldn't help.

Ring, ring. Ring, ring.

The landline. I hadn't heard from the creepy caller for a couple of months. The last call had been legit, from Aaron when he couldn't reach my cell phone.

Ring, ring. Ring, ring.

I picked up the handset, held it to my ear. "Hello?"

"Gotcha," a synthesized voice said.

Air rushed into my lungs, and I scrambled to find words. "Who the fuck are you? What do you want?"

"Gotcha," the voice repeated.

"Fuck off!" I slammed the handset to the ground then ripped the phone connection from the wall. My heart pounding and pounding. Even though I was going to jail, someone wasn't satisfied. Someone was determined to continue to torment me. But to what end?

I double checked the locks on all the doors as questions pounded in my head. Was my life at stake? My sanity? Who could I trust?

Could I tell the police about the synthesized call? Riley probably wouldn't buy it since I had no evidence. No return number or recording.

A dull thud landed in my chest, and my weak legs carried me to the sofa where I collapsed into a ball, cornered and defeated.

CHAPTER TWENTY-SEVEN

WEEK AFTER WEEK, for eight full weeks, clanking doors and random screams became the background noise of my day-to-day existence in my windowless room. I had a bunk, three square meals of tasteless food, and a grumpy roommate named Sally who spent most of the day sucking on her teeth.

The holidays had come and gone, and I'd manage to convince Aaron and the twins that jail was no big deal and time was going fast. What a liar I'd become.

Books and magazines held little interest because I found it too hard to focus. The jail psychiatrist had said no to Xanax and instead increased my Anafranil to curb my anxiety and prevent obsessive thoughts and compulsions. Dazed and complacent was how I felt. My days were spent half-asleep—that soft place where my heavy body sank into cushy and comfy clouds. I'd always feared being alone, not belonging anywhere. Now, I floated untethered in a foggy world, unworthy.

I longed for someone like Patsy and Annette, who had loved me with all of my flaws and had my back in every situation. I could have used that right now. An ally. Because I was certain someone was setting me up for Jackson's murder, and damn if I didn't need a friend who I could tell all of this to.

Keys jingled. "Hey, Parker."

Rolling my head, I saw it was Beth. The middle-aged security guard stood at my door. "You have a visitor," she said.

My ears pricked. I turned to my side and lifted my heavy head. I still had hopes that Aaron would surprise me with a visit from the children, even though we'd both agreed to keep the kids away from this environment. I dreamed of holding them again. "Who?"

"Noah Baker."

With a groan, I flopped my arm over my head and closed my eyes. Not again. This was his second attempt at stopping by to visit me since I'd been in here. He wasn't on my visitor list, so he'd obviously used his police authority to get access. The guards had told me he'd left quietly last time. Unusual for a cop, I thought. The question was chiseled into my brain—what did he want? A sour taste came to the back of my throat. I already knew the answer. He was a Lighthouse Beach homicide detective with Jackson's murder to solve.

I was an obvious and convenient suspect. Noah had heard my story about Mike and knew firsthand how I'd lied to police. Why wouldn't he assume I'd lied about not killing Jackson?

"I don't want to see any visitors today," I told

Beth, and rolled onto my stomach, turning my head to face the concrete wall.

"Suit yourself." Beth's keys faded away into the ambient sound of chaos.

I stared at the cracks on the beige painted wall. *No police.* Talking to Noah would only trigger bad thoughts, and I was too tired to fight the demons. I'd become content in my clouded world, separated from what was happening on the outside. To avoid triggers, I avoided newspapers and television. No one visited me, and that was exactly what I wanted.

Pulling my pillow closer to my cheek, I closed my eyes. For now, I would doze back into that hazy world between wakefulness and sleep.

CHAPTER TWENTY-EIGHT

I LEANED MY DROWSY head against the metal cubicle and held the phone to my ear. Mrs. Nichols was rattling on in detail about her three-times-a-week visits to my house. I was grateful for her help, and I had nothing else to do, so I let her ramble about how she'd switched on lights in different rooms and pulled weeds from the garden. How she'd driven to the house instead of walked, so it looked like the resident had visitors.

"I owe you and Mr. Nichols a lot for your help," I said, putting as much cheerfulness in my voice as my lagging brain could manage.

"We're your friends, dear. It's what we do."

"I don't have many friends these days."

"Well… I did run into a couple of your *friends* at the mall the other day."

"Oh? Who's that?"

"The one with the dark spiky hair and the other one—the tall one with blonde hair."

"Nancy and Denise?"

"Yes. I think so. Well, they recognized me first and were anxious to know if I'd heard anything from you."

A layer of fog lifted from my head. "What did

you tell them?"

"Pfft. I told them we stay in touch. But I didn't want to go into any detail with them. I know they're your friends, but, to be honest, they seemed like a couple of snooty women to me. I didn't like the way they were asking so many questions about you."

A jolt shot up my back. I sat up straight and switched the handset to the other ear. "What kind of questions?"

"Let's see—asking if you'd been charged in Jackson's murder... if you're going into a psychiatric hospital... if you're going to move back into the house... that kind of thing. But I didn't like the tone of their questions."

My chest deflated. They didn't care how I was doing. They thought I was Jackson's killer. Why wouldn't they? Even though I'd killed Mike in self-defense, I'd kept it secret for years. *Who did that kind of shit?* To them, I was a sideshow freak. "What did you tell them?"

"Simply that you're getting along just fine. I didn't like the tone of their questions, so I cut the conversation short."

I imagined Nancy, Denise, and even Melissa hanging out at Ocean Joe's, laughing and reminiscing over beer and fried oysters as waves crashed along the shoreline. A scene I'd never be part of again. At least not with them. "Well, it's true. I'm getting along fine." I took control of my shaky voice. "Any news about the anonymous caller?"

"None that I've heard, dear."

The call soon ended, but the conversation with Mrs. Nichols played over in my head. Nancy and Denise were talking about me behind my back while I was stuck behind bars, helpless to defend my character and innocence. My name was being tarnished.

Hot blood surged to my head with so much pressure that I thought steam might shoot out of my nostrils. I released a breath. It pissed me off that Nancy and Denise were sniggering behind my back, but what could I do? As long as I was locked up in this jail, I was helpless. How could I fight back?

The murder investigation could go on for years, and I'd still remain under an umbrella of suspicion until they found the killer. I had to clear my name as a suspect in Jackson's murder.

The anonymous caller and Jackson's murderer are the same person.

To find the anonymous caller, I had to start thinking straight. The high dosage of meds I was being fed every day clouded my thinking, but I could do something about that.

When the nurse dispensed my pill every morning, I wouldn't swallow it whole. I'd wait until I was alone and bite off half, tossing the other half. Going completely off the meds cold-turkey wasn't going to help. Lowering the dose would clear the fog in my head and put my thinking in balance. Fuck the obsessive thoughts. I had to a bigger battle to fight.

After five days of secretly halving my dose, my mind started clearing. My children were at the

forefront of my mind and with all the drama happening in my life, I wanted to give them stability.

I called Aaron's house. It wasn't my weekly
scheduled call to the twins, but I longed to hear
their voices. I also had a wonderful idea.

"Hello?" Aaron's voice was unnaturally tinny.

"Hey. It's me."

"Jolene." He coughed, sniffled. "Is everything
all right?"

"I'm okay, but you sound like crap."

He made a grumbling noise, then said, "India
and I just split up."

"What—oh, I'm sorry to hear that." I was sin-
cere, too. India had been kind and caring toward
my children. She'd never interfered with discus-
sions Aaron and I had regarding the twins.

He sighed deeply. "Yeah, well. She just told me
last night. It came from left field. I'm still a bit
shocked."

"I'm sorry about that. Really. How are the
twins handling it?"

"They're not here." He groaned. "They heard
India and I argue, and we needed some privacy.
I didn't want them listening, so I took them to
Mom's place for a couple of nights. I haven't told
them she's moved out yet."

"How do you think they'll take it?"

"They'll be hurt at first. But they'll get over
it. You're their mother. And they know you love
them and would never abandon them."

A rope twisted around my chest, squeezing out
my breath. "I miss them so much."

"They're anxious for you to come home."

"I have a plan for my homecoming. Instead of dropping the twins off at the house when I get released, I was thinking you could drop them off at the new oceanfront resort hotel. The one with the huge pool and lazy river. I'm going to book two nights there."

"That's extravagant. Are you sure you can afford that?"

Aaron didn't know that, thanks to the investments I'd made with the inheritance from my father, I could definitely afford it. I also wasn't ready to go back to the empty house yet.

Plus, I deserved some quality time with my children. Time to make joyous memories.

I didn't want to spend that precious time at the house with the damage in the backyard staring the twins in the face as a reminder of what their mom had done. I needed to get the debris cleared away and move on. I'd take care of that right after my reunion with the twins. "It's only for two nights. I want to make our reunion a fun occasion."

"I guess I can't blame you."

"You sound mopey. You don't have to stay at home and mourn India. Your college buddies in New York are always begging you to go up and visit. After you drop the twins off at the hotel, why not head up there? It'll be good for you to get some support."

"That's not a bad idea." He paused. "You're sounding cheerful. What's been going on?"

It was times like this, when I felt close to Aaron again, that I wanted to open up and tell him all of the paranoid theories I had swimming in my head. But history told me to back off. He'd accepted the secret about Mike and the tree. He'd accepted me coming back as a loving mother to our children and sharing split custody. I wanted things to stay exactly as they were.

"I'm getting closer to release, so yeah, my spirits have lifted." I switched the handset to the other ear. "Look, I've got people behind me waiting for the phone, so I should say goodbye now. Tell the twins I called and that I love them, all right?"

"Oh." His voice sank. "Will do."

I went back to my cell and fell onto my bunk, feeling a tinge of pity for Aaron. Not because India walked out on him—hell, he'd bailed on me when I'd needed his support the most—but because he seemed like a lost soul.

On the other hand, my head was lighter, clearer. The support from Aaron and the love of my children gave me all the strength I needed. I had a solid foundation for moving forward. For the first time in months, I was experiencing something unusual: hope.

CHAPTER TWENTY-NINE

THE WHITE ENVELOPE arrived at mail call. The same fake Lighthouse Beach return address. The folded piece of waxed paper. The distinctive shape of an oak leaf. Bright red bleeding through its veins.

A scream caught in my throat. Every follicle on my head tingled and set my scalp on fire. I pressed the letter to my chest and all of my angst came out in a moan.

Sally rolled over and looked at me. "What's up, bitch?"

"Nothing. Nothing." I gave a shaky smile. I didn't want to draw attention to myself, but I needed to show someone I trusted what was happening. Sally just wasn't that person.

"Try doing nothin' more quiet." Sally rolled back to her side.

I slipped the letter between the pages of the worn copy of *War and Peace* I'd been trying to read and put it under my pillow. Sitting on the edge of my bunk, I closed my eyes and took deep breaths.

Relax. Relax. Relax.

A vision of a creek gently flowing through

a green forest came to mind and my heartbeat slowed to the lulling rhythm, but the water then turned red, flooding my eyes. I jumped to my feet with a gasp.

Sally shot me a killer's glare and groaned.

I ran out into the common area. It was free time on our cell block, and inmates roamed the four corridors surrounding the reinforced glass recreation area.

Scraping at the dirt beneath my nails, I stepped into the noisy rec room—a sea of khaki jumpsuits yapping and napping over the loud game show on the television. There was no one in this place who I could talk to about my situation. I went back into the corridor and strolled the square around the rec room, avoiding eye contact with other inmates. Nobody here was trustworthy.

Well-intentioned-but-gossipy Mrs. Nichols was out of the question. And when I had tried to bring up the leaves in the mail with Riley again, he'd reminded me of the handwriting coincidence and suggested I discuss the matter with a psychologist.

I'd considered hiring a private investigator, but I'd already paid a shitload in attorney fees. While I still had a healthy bank account, once I got out of jail, I'd need the money I had left in savings to help me get by until I started working again.

I looked down at my fingernails, ripped so short they looked like part of a Lego log. There was no visible dirt, but I felt it. Dirt. Grit and grime so deep under my nails that I'd need to scrape the flesh to truly get clean.

With no one watching, I snuck into the cleaning supply room and grabbed a bristled scrub brush from the sink and turned on the hot water. I'd thought about doing this a few times while I'd been here. Times when the pain of what I'd done seeped into my thoughts and *pounded, pounded, pounded* on the guilt and remorse. Today, I wouldn't hesitate. I needed to relieve the anxiety and there was only one way.

I scrubbed the bristled brush against my palms and fingers. Using the sharp bristles, I jabbed and scraped at the grime beneath my nails.

Scrub, scrub, scrub.

Watery blood swirled in the drain, taking away the pain.

"Come out, damned spot. Out, I command you!" I channeled Lady Macbeth, but quoting Shakespeare wasn't going to cleanse my fear, guilt, and remorse. For that, I needed to bleed. And I could never bleed enough.

Scrub, scrub, scrub.

Someone wanted to make sure I never forgot what I'd done. Why?

"Jolene?" A woman's voice.

I dropped the brush in the sink and turned around. It was Candy, another inmate in my cell block. A real loudmouth. She stood at the door with a sideways grin. "I thought I heard someone in here. You okay, girl?"

"Doing fine." I turned off the tap and pulled a handful of white paper towels from the wall dispenser, and I wrapped them around my raw hands. "Just getting some paper towels."

Candy stepped inside the small cleaning closet and looked at my hands. "You sure? 'Cuz I sees blood."

A spot of red bloomed through the white paper. I cupped my hand over the blood. My pounding heart reverberated through my body. *Calm down.* I forced a laugh. "A scab fell off and it started bleeding. It's all good."

Candy moved in close and arched a brow. "You trying to hurt yourself?"

My throat tightened. If Candy told people I was trying to hurt myself, the nurse would examine my hands. No one could know that I was still plagued by random thoughts, or how much relief I felt with the completion of a ritual. "Oh, hell no. I don't do that kind of shit. I have a whole life waiting for me outside of this dungeon."

"Hmph. Lucky you." She shrugged and walked out.

I leaned my back against the cold tile wall. Tension pulled across my shoulders, and I pinched the bridge of my nose with my good hand. This mind fuckery had to end right now. It was time to stop the obsessive thoughts and rituals. Nothing could prevent bad things from happening. Logically, I'd always known that—but the voices and the urges wouldn't let me rest.

Regain control. I'd done it before. Even after we'd buried Mike, I'd managed to move forward with my life. I'd graduated from college, started teaching, bought my own apartment, gotten married, had children. I'd managed to control the triggers. It was the letters with the leaves which had set my demons free.

I tossed the paper towels in the trash and left the cleaning closet for my cell. My fingertips throbbed where I'd gouged my skin. I needed Band-Aids, but the nurse would want to know why, so I crossed my arms, hiding my hands.

Grateful Sally wasn't in our cell, I sat on my bunk with my back to the wall and my knees to my chest, trying to figure out how the fuck I was going to fight back against this anonymous tormenter. Being stuck in this hellhole for another few weeks wasn't going to help. If I had any hope of finding out who was sending me the leaves, I needed an ally. A strong ally. As much as I hated asking for help, I had no choice.

Aaron was out of the question. I didn't want him that close to my personal life. Keeping our relationship cordial and focused on the children was exactly how I liked it.

I thought about calling Kate, but I didn't need therapy. Not yet.

Only one person in my orbit could help, and his name rang over and over in my head.

Noah. Noah. Noah.

Putting aside that I was a suspect in Jackson's murder, and he was the homicide detective on the case, only he could answer the questions swirling in my head. Answers which could get me closer to finding who was tormenting me with the leaves and why. Who were the other suspects in Jackson's murder, and who'd made the anonymous calls leading the police to the family tree?

Though I was wary of his intentions for wanting

to visit, I had little to lose. Noah had information
I needed. I only had to meet with him and ask.

CHAPTER THIRTY

THE VISITING ROOM was set up with grey round tables and hard plastic chairs. A family of three occupied a corner table. A young couple held hands across another table. Next to them, what looked like a distraught mother was visiting her tattooed son. I almost didn't recognize Noah. He wore a trendy, button-down shirt over black jeans and sneakers that screamed I'm-a-cool-dad. His walnut-brown hair wasn't combed and slicked as usual. It hung loose and wavy at the top, cut short around his ears and hairline on the back of his neck. No suit and tie.

He caught my eye and stood as I walked toward the table. His smile matched the warmth in his eyes. "Thanks for seeing me, Jolene."

Handshakes and hugs were permitted, but his best-friend demeanor made me wary, so I sat. "You're persistent. I figure it must be import-ant." I tried to read his intentions in his face. All I noticed were dark circles under his eyes and a greying hairline.

He slid into the chair across from mine. "How are you doing?"

"Hanging in there. But that's not why you're

here."

"Actually, it is." He exhaled. "I never wanted things to happen like this. I'd hoped all along that nothing was under that tree but roots."

"Me, too." I cracked a smile and leaned back in the seat. "And, what? You wanted to tell me that? I'd rather know more about the anonymous caller. Who is it?"

"We don't know."

"You're lying." I crossed my arms. "You must have some idea."

"I'm telling you the truth. We haven't received any more calls at the station."

I leaned forward and rested my elbows on the table. "I find that hard to believe. Why would someone lead police to Mike's body, but never try to collect the reward?"

"Justice. That was all he claimed to want."

My teeth grinded together. It wasn't true. If the caller was satisfied with justice, why would this person send me another leaf? The words almost slipped from my mouth. "I think the caller has other motives."

Noah tilted his head. "Like what?"

"I'm not sure. Call it intuition."

"If you have a clue, please share."

Leaning back in the seat, I looked up to the paint-chipped ceiling. Oh, how I wanted to share. Share my entire twisted theory.

"Jolene," Noah said. "Let's talk about Jackson's murder—"

"Ahhh, here we go." I dropped my chin, pointed at his face, and spoke through my gritted teeth.

"That's why you're here. Another interrogation."

"Not at all," he said. "In fact, I've been taken off Jackson's murder investigation."

Adrenaline shot up my spine and I sat as straight as a soldier. "What? Why's that?"

"Because I don't believe you killed Jackson." Noah kept his voice low. "Some people in the department didn't like my opinion, so—"

"Wait. Back up." My neck grew an inch, and my voice almost squeaked. "You believe me— that I didn't kill Jackson?"

Noah examined my face. "Yes. One-hundred percent. Problem is, I got vocal about my views at the station a couple of times. The chief didn't like that I was getting too emotional—as he put it—about the case. He believes I can't remain impartial."

It took a few moments for his words to make sense. *Is Noah on my side?* "I don't get it. Why do you believe me?"

"While I always suspected you knew something about Mike Morton's disappearance, I was sure you didn't kill Jackson. It didn't make sense. You kept Mike's whereabouts a secret for years. And when his missing person investigation opened, you became even more protective of your secret." He scooted his chair closer to the table and leaned in. "You're a smart woman. Too smart to do something which could draw attention to you during Mike's investigation."

I slumped back in the chair, taking a moment to enjoy the light sense of relief. I had a cop on my side. "What other suspects do they have?"

"There are some crazy theories, but I'm sorry, even though I'm not directly involved, I'm not at liberty to discuss an open investigation with you." He smiled. "I really came here as your friend."

A niggle in my gut said to believe him, even trust him. "My friend. Okay. It's nice to know not every cop thinks I killed Jackson."

"I certainly don't." He clasped his hands and rested them on the table. "And as your friend, I don't want you to feel you have to suffer any-more. You can always talk to me."

There was that expression again. *Empathy.* "Why?"

"I-I know…." His gaze shifted to the table, he exhaled, and then looked up at me with the twisted face of anguish. "I know what it's like to have a painful secret," he whispered.

Hairs prickled on my arm, and I wasn't sure if it was from fear or concern. I wasn't used to see-ing Noah this vulnerable. I sat straight and leaned forward. "Tell me."

He glanced at the guard and then back to me, keeping his voice low as he went on, "I shot a man… killed him. He was a criminal, but it shouldn't have happened."

Were we friends now? I reached out for his hand then retracted. "When… how?"

"About four years ago, I was on duty, and we entered a house knowing there was an armed man inside who'd just killed his wife. I was the first in—I shot him. Killed him. He had a gun in his hand, but I should've told him to drop it. I didn't. I got scared. I broke protocol." He let out a deep breath. "During the investigation, I lied. I knew there were no witnesses, and I could get away with it and no one could find out. I just plain lied."

I held back my gasp and it stuck in my throat. He'd shot someone and covered it up. *He'd lied to the police.* I'd always thought Noah was a by-the-book cop, like his father. "You've never mentioned this to anyone? Not your dad or Catherine?"

"No. I'm telling you this because, well—I understand how the burden of a secret can grow heavier each year. How it can negatively impact every area of a person's life. Coming to terms with one's past isn't always easy."

"I'm at a loss for words."

"Good. Because it's not really something I want to talk about. It's something I never wanted anyone else to know."

"You can trust me. I'm good at keeping secrets." I smiled at the irony.

He laughed so hard that his shoulders shook. "Good one, Parker."

A warm tingle spread from the crown of my head to the tips of my toes. "It's been a long time since I've seen someone laugh. I like it."

"That's good. Because there's another reason I've come."

His tone had stayed casual, but tension returned to my neck. "Oh?"

"I've known you for a long time. And that's a hard thing to say in this town. The area's become more and more transient. And to be honest, I could use a friend too."

Unease sent my stomach into knots. "What about your wife?"

"Not these days." His lip twitched.

"Sorry—I didn't mean to pry."

"You're not. My relationship with Catherine has been strained for a while."

I wondered if his secret had destroyed his marriage the same as my secret killed mine. I didn't want to ask. "Ups and downs. That's the nature of relationships."

"Our relationship's been down for so long that we've ended up on opposite poles," he said.

My muscles relaxed then, and over an hour flew by as we talked and bonded over our lost-at-sea outlooks. His vulnerability had made it easier for me to open up. I finally told him, "The problem in my marriage was that I liked wine and pills and Aaron liked pretty twenty-year-old girls."

The lines on Noah's face deepened. "As long as we're commiserating, the problem in my marriage is that I spend too much time at work. And when I am home, my head is still on the job. I can't stop thinking about my cases." He ran a hand over his mouth. "I didn't intend for it to happen, but I guess I fell in love with my job and neglected my wife."

An ache pressed against my chest. Seeing Noah downtrodden bothered me on a level I hadn't experienced in a long time. It was like watching a dear friend suffer. "That's repairable. You and Catherine have Alex. Isn't that enough to build on?"

"Maybe." He rubbed his nose. "We're organizing our schedules so we can get away for a short vacation. Just the two of us. We'll leave Alex with my mom."

"That's exactly what you and Catherine need. Time to reconnect."

He half-shrugged. "Maybe. Problem is, even though I'm not working directly on Jackson's murder investigation, it's going to be tough not being close to it." He exhaled a breath. "Jackson's parents call almost every day, you know. It's hard telling them we have nothing."

Regret wrapped around my chest, constricting my breaths. The Howell's lives had been torn apart by one person. I'd done the same to the Morton family, but as much as I liked to think my time in jail offered redemption, I'd never feel okay about what I'd done. I needed to do more. And Noah and I both wanted the same thing— justice for Jackson. "Does his family think I killed Jackson?"

"That, I don't know. But they most likely know you are a suspect."

A fire burned in my belly. The Morton family had suffered a long time because I'd never spoken out. They'd found their justice. Now, I wanted justice for Jackson's family. It wasn't a matter of should I tell Noah about the ominous creepy caller, stalker, and leaves—I had to tell him.

"I feel terrible for Jackson's family," I said. "I'd do anything to help find the killer and give them some sense of closure."

Noah placed his hand on mine. "I know you would."

Something in my core softened, and I exhaled a breath. *The letter with the leaf.* Could I tell him? We were both looking for a clue to the caller and Jackson's killer. Or would he react like Riley and think I was crazy?

No. Noah treated me like a normal person, like a friend, and I wanted to take a chance and trust him. Adrenaline charged through my veins and shot a random thought into my head: What if Noah was the sender of the leaves. The stalker. Then I'd be handing him my proof.

A quiver rippled from within, and I shook the theory from my head before it had a chance to grow legs. It was an unjustified and meaningless thought. I had control over that shit.

Trust your instincts.

If ever I'd needed my instincts to be right, this was it. This wasn't just about me anymore. It was about Jackson too. Justice for Jackson.

My fear of not being believed, of being looked at as crazy, it had slowed my ability to find my tormentor. No more. I was being released in less than two weeks. If I was going to tell Noah everything, I had to do it now. "I want to show you something. A letter."

"From who?"

"It's anonymous. And I'm certain the sender is also the anonymous caller and Jackson's murderer."

"Whoa." Noah pulled back. "You mean the caller who reported where Mike was buried?"

"I think the same person who called the station has been calling me."

Noah scooted his chair closer and rested his arms on the table. "Go ahead."

"It started with heavy breathing calls on Patsy's old landline. I figured it was kids playing pranks. But on the night before I left for jail, I received another call." Goosebumps covered my skin. I rubbed my arms and continued. "This time the caller spoke through a voice synthesizer. He said only one word, 'gotcha.'"

"No kidding." Noah's eyebrows drew together into a V.

"This is what I don't understand," I said, "if the anonymous caller who reported Mike being buried under the tree only wanted justice, why am I still getting letters and freaky calls? I think someone is carrying a grudge or has a vendetta. I don't know. But I have no proof of anyone threatening me or causing me harm, so I can't exactly report this to the police. I exhaled a puff of air and dropped my shoulders. "I just need someone to believe me. Someone to help me figure out why this is happening to me."

"I believe you, Jolene." Noah turned his head and stared out the barred window for a moment. "What's the letter say?"

"It's easier to explain if I show you, but it's in my cell, and if I leave—"

"Don't worry." Noah pointed his chin to the guard. "I can let administration know you need to retrieve paperwork for me. I know the warden here."

I pressed my lips together. It was time to take a leap of faith.

CHAPTER THIRTY-ONE

I FOLLOWED THE GUARD back to the visiting area carrying the envelope in my hand. Earlier today, I wouldn't have expected that I'd team up with Noah to find answers. I squared my shoulders, bracing myself for what I was about to do. Would Noah believe me?

Noah rose from his chair when I walked into the room. "You look like you've seen a ghost."

"Something like that." I looked around the visitor room. I wasn't sure how to start because the whole scenario was jumbled in my head; it was only a theory, not completely woven into reality. I sat and kept my voice just above a whisper. "Someone's been following me, stalking me for years."

Noah sat and leaned close with his arms crossed. His expression flitted from shock to concern.

"Don't look at me like I'm a delusional nutcase," I said.

"I don't think you're delusional or a nutcase." He pointed to the envelope in my hand. "Is that the letter you think has something to do with your stalker and anonymous caller?"

I handed him the envelope. "I think it does."

He scanned the front and back of the envelope, and then pulled out the folded waxed paper. His face scrunched as he unfolded the wrap. "A leaf?"

"An American Red Oak leaf."

"Hmm." Pinching the stem, he held it to the ceiling light and looked closer. "Same as the family tree?"

"It appears so."

"Why would someone send you a leaf?" He put it back inside the folded waxed paper.

"To scare me. To taunt me. To remind me that someone else saw what I'd done. I... I really don't know."

Noah examined the front and back of the envelope again. "The return address?"

"Fake. I've been getting the envelopes with a leaf in the mail for the past four years. The first one came when Aaron and I were still married. They're always postmarked from the main post office at Lighthouse Beach."

He sat back. "Do you have any idea who would do this?"

"Not a clue."

"Have you told anyone else about the leaves?"

I blew out a hot breath, frustrated at how Riley had suggested I'd been sending the letters to myself. Noah didn't need to know about that. "I told my attorney."

Noah tilted his head. "Riley Baxter didn't see a connection between the oak tree on top of Jackson, the oak tree you planted over Mike, the anonymous calls, and these letters?"

"I haven't been charged in Jackson's murder, so

he didn't seem interested since he wasn't defending me for any crime there."

"But you could have reported your suspicions
earlier—back when you made your confession at
the station."

"Are you kidding? I already have enough suspicion hanging over my head as it is. And I'm
fully aware that just because I have a feeling these
leaves are connected to Jackson and the anonymous caller at the station and my house, there's
no proof of any crime."

"But what does this have to do with the
stalker?"

A cold shiver crept over my skin, and I shuddered. It still unnerved me to recall details of that
night, but it was getting easier. "On the night we
buried Mike… I saw someone run across the
lawn."

Noah hesitated. "Okay…"

"Mrs. Nichols… she didn't see Annette and me,
but she told me she'd seen someone dressed in
all black running along Willow Road that night.
You should know about that. She reported it to
police."

Noah scratched his chin. "I remember reading
her interview, and I did talk to my dad about the
report. He said the police at the time checked
out the area for footprints or any other evidence.
Came up with nothing."

Tired of not being believed, I glared at Noah
and pounded my fist on the table. "Someone was
on the lawn that night," I said, loud enough for
the visitors at the next table to give me the side-

eye.

The guard turned his gaze to us, and I clasped my hands on the table. *Don't make a scene.*

"It's okay, Jolene." Noah put his hand over mine. "Tell me more about this stalker."

Noah's dulcet tone and solid touch calmed my nerves, and I continued, "The anonymous caller... it has to be the person I saw on the lawn that night. Someone who saw Annette and I bury Mike. Someone who's sending me leaves now. Someone with motives I can't begin to imagine.

"He shows up at random places, like the grocery store, school, or even near my house. Always dressed in black pants. Sweats, maybe jeans. But always with a black hoodie over his head. As soon as I notice him, he disappears."

"You know it's a man?"

"Not certain. But I can't help but think it's the same person who's sending me the leaves and making the calls. What I can't figure out is who would want to torment me this way? What would they have to gain?"

"Think hard. Would someone from your past have a grudge against you?"

One person came to mind. "Nancy Miller. But I don't remember her resenting me in the past. Only recently...when she thought Jackson was flirting with me. She was obsessed with Jackson. Could that be motivation?"

"Maybe. The detectives know a lot about Nancy and Richard. But I'm going to investigate this further. I promise." Noah glanced back at the bored guard staring at the floor, then squeezed my hand. "I'll personally look into this. And I'm glad you confided in me."

A warm flutter rippled through my abdomen. For a moment, I dared to imagine being closer to Noah. He knew me better than most people. But it could never happen. Noah the honorable man with me, the dishonorable woman. I valued our friendship too much.

He pulled his hand back. "I'd like to see if we can get fingerprints. You mentioned other envelopes—"

"Ten in total. I have them hidden away at the house."

"How can I get them?"

My leg jiggled, and I wiped my sweaty palms on my thighs. I was doing this. Handing him all of my evidence. "I'll give you the access code to the security system, but you'll need a key for the locks. Mrs. Nichols, my neighbor down the street, she's watching over my house while I'm gone. I'll have to call her and let her know it's okay to give you the key."

"Great. Tell her I'll come by to pick up the key in the next couple of days."

"You'll find the letters in the wall cabinet in the garage. Top shelf behind the cans of paint. Look for a brown envelope." I paused. Noah was sincerely interested in what I was telling him. I felt vindicated, like someone was really paying attention to what I had to say. It was a strange and uplifting sensation, but I knew better than to get my hopes up too high. "You're seriously going to look into this? You don't think I'm being paranoid?"

"Yes, I'm seriously looking into this. And no, I don't think you're being paranoid. Relax. We're in this thing together, remember?"

"Thanks for being on my side."

"Hang in there. You're almost out of here. Unfortunately, I'll still be out of town when you're released—on that holiday with Catherine—so I won't be checking into work until I get back."

"Sounds romantic."

He snickered. "More like a last-ditch effort to save the marriage."

"Good luck with that."

"Yeah." He half-smiled, a flicker of sadness crossing his face. "At what point do you throw in the towel? No, never mind, please don't answer that."

I didn't like seeing Noah downtrodden. As much as I'd like a chance to get closer to him, I hoped he and Catherine patched things up on their get-away.

"Ten minutes to wrap it up," the guard called out to the room.

My shoulders dropped, and it was hard not to frown. Talking to Noah had given me new hope, and I wasn't ready for him to leave. "How's your father?" I asked, hoping to extend our conversation. "I suppose he's satisfied the case is solved."

"Oh, yeah. He's happy. He was relieved to hear Patsy wasn't involved. The old man actually has more energy these days."

"That's good." I meant it and held no grudge.

Solving the mystery had brought closure for many people. I should have done this years ago.

Noah tapped his finger on the envelope with the leaf on the table. "I'll make this a priority check at the station and get back to you when I return from Florida. Next time we talk, it'll be outside of this place."

We fist-bumped our goodbye and I let out a sigh of relief. I was going to get some answers. But as Noah walked away, carrying the only evidence I had which could point to Jackson's killer and my stalker, the old sense of unease weighed me down.

I hoped I'd made the right decision to trust him.

CHAPTER THIRTY-TWO

I HOPPED OUT OF the back seat of the taxi and onto the end of my driveway. Free at last. The old country house stood before me like a loving mother with outstretched arms welcoming me home. I breathed in the fresh March air, savoring the gift of free will.

The rhythmic hammering of nails broke my tranquility. Construction across the street. Another ginormous house in the new neighborhood of cul-de-sacs and McMansions. An ache of nostalgia pressed on my chest. Patsy would have cried over watching the land on this street get over-developed. Good thing she'd never suffer the changes.

But another change was coming. My change. Someone had set me up in Jackson's murder, and Noah was going to help me prove it. He didn't believe I was insane, and in time, everyone else would see that too. I hoped the vacation in Florida with Catherine was what they needed. I cared for Noah in that way. He'd become a true friend.

I'd been tempted to call him for the past week, but after his story about how his work interfered with his marriage, I'd backed off on the impulse.

I looked at my letterbox, reluctant to open it. Mrs. Nichols had said she was leaving my mail on the kitchen table, so I wasn't expecting anything. *Perhaps another leaf.*

My neck tensed. Anxiety itched under my skin.

I opened the letterbox. Empty.

I exhaled a sigh of partial relief. I couldn't rest until I knew who'd been sending the leaves. But Noah wouldn't return for a few more days, so I had to be patient. For all I knew, he was already working on a lead.

I hurried up the driveway. I'd only stay a minute. My suite at the oceanfront awaited. All I needed was to grab some clothes and a few necessities.

I entered the house. *Beep, beep, beep,* the security alarm gave the thirty-second warning. I entered the code and shut the door behind me. My shoulders relaxed and I leaned my back against the door, grateful for home.

Then I flinched; an odd odor had filled my nostrils. A thick, sweet smell. Not a pleasant sweet. A sickly metallic sweet. I set my purse on the floor. The shutters were closed, but a light was coming from the hallway upstairs.

I switched on the floor lamp next to the sofa and looked around for the source of the smell. Besides being dusty, the room was exactly how I'd left it before going to jail. I headed to the kitchen, but something next to the armchair on my right caught my eye. Clothing.

A pair of dark jeans lay crumpled on the floor. My heart jumped into my throat.

Someone is in the house.

The air stilled, and tiny hairs rose on my neck.
Mrs. Nichols had been taking care of the house,
but this didn't look like something that belonged
to her.

Thump.

A noise from upstairs. Icy tendrils of fear coiled
up my body and froze my lungs. Was that a foot-
step, or a groan from the old house? I turned
toward the door on my toes, careful not to make
a sound.

Creeeak.

The floorboards. Someone was upstairs. Mrs.
Nichols? Blood rushed to my eardrums, pounding. What would she be doing here?

She wouldn't be here.

I dashed toward the door and reached for the
knob.

"Jolene?" Melissa's gentle voice called out. "Is
that you?"

My breath hitched and I turned. What was she
doing here? She'd returned her house keys and
moved to Richmond months ago.

"Hey," Melissa called out from the top of the
staircase. "You're home."

I patted my chest, relieved but unnerved. She
wore a black wig in a cropped Dutch boy style.
"You scared me. What are you doing here?"

"Oh, I came to welcome you home."

"What's with the wig? Going to a costume
party?"

She took a few slow steps down the stairs. "Oh,
I'm going to a party all right."

Something wasn't right. Besides the strange

wig, Melissa's normally clear eyes were inky blue, almost black. She was also disheveled, like she'd worn the same denim shorts and dirty brown tank top for days. "Are you okay? I thought you were in Richmond."

Melissa dragged her fingertip down the railing, a half-smile contorting her mouth. "Richmond one day. Your house the next. Who knows where you might find me tomorrow?"

The air chilled, and I rubbed my goose-bumped arms. Her cheery voice had never sounded more fake. This wasn't the Melissa I knew. She stepped off the staircase and I instinctively hugged her, hoping to clear the awkwardness. But her body was rigid, uptight in my arms. I put some space between us. "You want to tell me what's going on? We're friends, you know."

Melissa made a face of disgust. "No. We're not friends."

Her words stung like a slap across the face. "Why are you acting like this? Did I do something to upset—"

"Oh, you did a lot of somethings."

Looking away, I tried to make sense of this. Our nights drinking wine and watching trash TV. Laughing and reminiscing about our early years. All the kindness she'd shown me. Now, a hard-edged face stared at me. "How'd you get into the house?"

"I made an extra copy of the key to hold onto. You know, in case of an emergency."

Her calculated tone set me off kilter and I zeroed in on her eyes. "But I changed the alarm code—"

"And I deactivated the alarm to the back door to the garage before I moved to Richmond. It's not hard to do if you read the operator's manual." Melissa's eyes turned dark and menacing. "We don't have much time, so I'll make this real quick."

My head spun with confusion, and I wanted to believe this was a prank. That any moment all the friends I never thought I'd had would soon pop up and scream, 'welcome home.' But the rancid air signaled something sinister. I backed away from Melissa and asked, "Much time for what?"

"Time for me to finish my job." She rubbed her hands together. "Time for me to take from you something cherished and precious."

The hairs on my scalp rose, sending icy tingles down my neck, but I squared my shoulders against the fear. "What's this about?"

"Annette. That's what I'm talking about."

I twitched. This didn't make sense. "What about Annette?"

"She was my dearest friend, and you stole her from me. You stole a life that should've been mine."

"Annette was friends with everyone. That was her personality."

"Bullshit." The word shot out like a cannon ball. "Annette had only one best friend. Me." She pounded her chest then continued, "Until you and your mother pranced your asses into our lives all la-de-dah like you were the most important people in the world."

An ache sprang up in my chest. Patsy and my mother had been closest of friends since their own childhoods. I could almost hear their laughter from the verandah where they'd drink pink wine spritzers while Annette and I played in the yard. But this moment wasn't a walk down memory lane. "I was eight years old. Why are you bringing this up now?"

"Because Annette and Patsy were my family, and you stole a life that should've been mine. I want you to understand what that feels like."

"I miss Annette and Patsy, too. We all do."

"Like I care how you feel." Melissa stepped close to my face and her jaw muscle twitched. "I want you to know how much you've hurt me. I want you to suffer the agony of having what you love ripped away and being left with nothing."

My chest collapsed into a tight knot of resentment. *Nothing?* As if I didn't know what having nothing meant. Having my mother ripped away, my children ripped away, my dignity ripped away, my sanity ripped away—a big part of my life ripped away because of one foolish choice. A choice I'd been coerced into by the same person Melissa was so obsessed with right now.

But I'd never seen her this volatile and irrational. "We've both lost a lot. When my mother died—"

Melissa jabbed her finger close to my face and bared her teeth as she spoke. "You lost nothing. You had a father. You had a home. You went to college. You found a good husband. You had two healthy kids. You had Annette, Patsy. A big happy family." Her mouth twisted. "You. Had. Everything."

I moved away to put a greater distance between us. "It might have looked that way from the outside, but honestly—"

Melissa lunged forward with a wildcat's glare. "Ha! Looked that way? It *was* that way. My parents were crack heads scraping by on welfare who hardly knew I existed. It was Annette and Patsy who gave me a safe and loving place where I belonged."

Melissa was dangerous and deranged. I couldn't make sense of her behavior, but I knew it wasn't good. I fanned my face with my hand. The sickly smell lingered and turned in my stomach. "This is a lot to take in. After being cooped up for three months, I could use some fresh air." I edged past her, toward the front door. "Let's sit out on the verandah. We can talk about this—"

Melissa grabbed my arm and yanked me back hard. "You're not going anywhere."

I jerked my arm out of her grip. Heat rose from my abdomen, burning my throat and putting fire in my voice. "I'm going outside, Melissa."

Melissa pushed my shoulder back toward the living room and got inches from my face. "Oh, no, you're not. Not until you hear everything I have to say."

I put up my hands, ready to shove her away. "Hey, no need to get physical." I sidestepped, making sure not to turn my back to her. She was ready for a fight, but the last fight I'd been in hadn't had a good outcome. My muscles tensed.

How could I make her see this was a nonsensical argument? "You're talking about things that happened when we were kids. Surely, it's something we can sort out as adults."

Melissa stepped closer. Her throaty voice filled the space between us. "Shut the fuck up."

I stepped back until my back touched the wooden staircase rail. "I never knew you had all these feelings pent up inside."

Her face twisted. "How could you know? You were too busy having the time of your life with *my* best friend."

"Things are different now."

Flames of red shot up Melissa's neck and face. "No. They're not. Everything is still the same. You're a taker. Always taking and taking. Now, it's my turn to take."

The wooden staircase rail pressed into my back. "What do you want, Melissa?"

"Humph. You'll know everything soon enough. The first thing you should know is… I saw you and Annette kill Mike. I saw everything." She pointed to the ground. "Right there. In front of the fireplace."

Tingles of fear ran up my spine as details of that hot summer night flashed into my mind. The rustling outside the living room window. "Were you on the verandah?"

"Watched the whole scene." Her voice turned eerie calm. "Remember the trailer I used to rent over on Holly Road?"

That was a few streets away from here. I didn't remember her living there but nodded like I had.

"Sure."

"That night, Mike showed up at my place, high on meth and rearing for a fight. We argued and I kicked him out. He rambled about how he was going to hitch a ride to the beach and grab some ass. Except he turned right instead of left, and I wondered where he was going. I threw on a black hoodie." A glint of fire flashed in her dark eyes. "I followed him down to Willow Road, hiding in shadows."

Blood thrummed through me, pounding in my head as images bombarded me from all directions. The dark figure running across the lawn. The years of random sightings of a man in a black hoodie.

It was Melissa.

I put both hands to my temples. This made no sense. "If you saw us kill Mike, why didn't you call the police?"

"I did." A spark flashed in her eyes. "You're talking to the anonymous tipster right now."

My mouth dried as my flight or fight instincts got stuck in debate. I had too many questions to run. "If you saw everything, why didn't you report it right away?"

"Ohhh, this is where it gets interesting. I thought it would be poetic if I waited until the return of the cicadas."

"What the hell—"

"Remember the hissing of cicadas that night? So loud it filled the air with electricity?"

I'd never forget that deafening sound. "So what?"

Her eyes lit up and she waved her hand like an orchestra conductor. "I wanted to build this to a crescendo. I wanted to see Mike's body dug up with the cicadas in the midst of cicada song." She dropped her hand. Her face twisted into a ghoulish grin. "But Annette's death was premature, and I made a modification to the plan."

"That's why you waited? For the cicadas?"

"I had other reasons. At first, I just wanted to see what you and Annette were going to do. Then I couldn't believe it when I came by a few days later and found Patsy in the backyard watering a tree planted over the spot you two buried Mike." She shook her head. "A story like this couldn't be made up."

"I still don't understand why you waited."

"I'm telling you. I liked watching you and Annette live with the tree. I waited for the moment one of you would crack. Especially since Patsy fawned over that damned tree like it was one of her own children." Her tone turned borderline nice. "But you and Annette drifted through life like sweet angels. I mean, let's face it, you got married right next to Mike's gravesite. Anyway, I decided it might be fun to hold out for seventeen years."

Ice ran through my blood. Her twisted vengeance showed no end. "What do you want, Melissa? Why are you telling me all of this now? And don't give me that bullshit about cicadas."

"Because I've been waiting for the perfect time to take what always should've been mine."

This didn't make sense. "But the reward... you

never asked for the reward."

"Pffft. Like fifty grand could change the rest of my life. I got something better. Something price-less. Since you're neurotic anyway, I got to have some fun and trigger your paranoia." She snorted. "It's fun watching you suffer. The drinking, the drugs, the OCD. You give me a lot to work with."

"You need help, Melissa," I said in a gentler tone which I hoped left room for reason. "You're not thinking straight"

"Ohhh, no. My mind has never been clearer. And now I'm ready to move forward with my plan."

"What fucking plan are you talking about?"

"You need to understand… one thing which really bothered me about you all these years is how well you've lived with the secret, keeping it all together." Melissa's face contorted into sharp angles. "I couldn't stand watching you live the high life in Bay Shores with a successful husband and two happy kids. It wasn't supposed to turn out that way. You weren't supposed to be happy.

"On the other hand, we had Annette." Melissa's face softened into an expression of sorrow. "Poor girl couldn't even get pregnant. And everyone knew Tristan was a womanizer before she even married him."

It was true. Annette had never found the true love she'd dreamed about. Tristan had wined and dined her all the way to the altar, and then cheated on her when she hadn't been able to conceive. None of that was my fault, but that wasn't a point worth arguing. "You cared for Annette. We all did."

"I cared for her more than I care for you. See, I wasn't going to just sit back and let you carry on with your happy life. No. No, instead, I came up with an ingenious way of reminding you that someone else knew your secret. I wanted to put a thorn in your happy life. That's when I started mailing you the leaves."

Every follicle on my body prickled. Nothing prepared me for this, for Melissa. "You're the sender."

"Yeah. Remember, I don't like seeing your life run smooth. I mean, here you were with an adoring husband and healthy three-year-old twins. I had to shake things up for you."

Heat rose on my neck. It had been the leaves in the mail which had first heightened my OCD and paranoia. The leaves which had torn apart my mind and my marriage. Melissa had been provoking me the whole time. She'd been orchestrating my destruction this whole time. "You're crazy."

"Oak trees and oak leaves. Fun times, huh?"

Cold fingers of fear climbed up my skin. She was the informant. Melissa had sent all the leaves. That meant she'd killed Jackson. My eyes darted between the door and Melissa's dark eyes. Her face distorted into features I didn't recognize as human. Savage. Beast. Monster. Every impulse screamed for me to get the hell out of this house.

I bolted for the door, but Melissa blocked me and pushed me backward. "Don't go yet. We have so much more to talk about." Her sadistic smile was punctuated by a twinkle in her eye.

Danger. Danger. Danger.

Every cell in my body snapped to high alert. *One, two, three, four, five. One, two…*

Stop. Counting wouldn't help. I had to fight my tormentor.

CHAPTER THIRTY-THREE

I LOOKED AROUND THE living room for a weapon—the candlesticks were long gone, but an iron poker stood ready next to the fireplace. The thrum of my heartbeat played in my ears. I'd done this before, and Melissa was as wild as Mike had been when I'd smashed in his head.

You can do it.

I inched closer the fireplace tools. As long as she was engrossed in telling me all the reasons she hated me, I could keep her distracted. "Tell me, Melissa. Have you been stalking me all these years?"

A flicker of confusion crossed her face, like she'd been thrown off her focus. She squared her shoulders and snarled. "What the fuck are you talking about, you crazy bitch?"

"You've been following me. Stalking me."

She laughed. Not a funny ha-ha laugh. A cruel you're-fucked-up laugh. She walked a slow circle around me. "I only followed you one time. Back in July when you were at your last teacher's assembly. When I put that leaf on your windshield."

I turned, careful not to have my back to her.

"You followed me other times, too. Admit it."

"You really are a 'Psycho Girl', aren't you?" She circled closer.

I backed up toward the fireplace poker as Melissa glared at me with mascara-rubbed eyes. Her overdone red lips against her white teeth made her look like an evil circus clown. The depth of her wickedness had no end, and I only had one chance. *Just like I did with Mike.* "Yes. Maybe I am a little psycho," I said in a placating tone.

"Shut. The fuck. Up." She stood in front of me like a defensive linebacker. "I'm doing the talking here."

We stood face-to-face in front of the fireplace. The poker was behind me within reach. But my attention stayed on Melissa's every move. I didn't dare speak a word. Her reactions bounced like a ball on a Roulette table. Where they would land was anyone's guess. I wasn't taking chances.

Melissa reached her hand behind her back and into the back pocket of her denim cut-offs. "I've spent years hating you, Jolene Parker. It has been a pleasure making you suffer."

My legs shook, but I wouldn't show Melissa my fear. *Go, go, go.* I turned sideways and reached for the poker.

A sharp jab pierced my hip, and my hand went to the stinging pain. *Oh, shit.* Melissa held up an empty syringe, wearing a grin of satisfaction so evil that I swore I saw red in her eyes. "What the hell was that?"

Melissa cackled. "A little SUX. Succinylcholine, if you want to get medical."

Anger rose from my core and I lunged for her throat, but my adrenaline hit the floor and my arms flopped about like a rag doll with no stuffing. My breathing slowed as my throat constricted tighter and tighter until only a slit of air entered my lungs. Everything blurred.

Melissa took hold of my shoulders. "Let's not fall over," she said in a voice as gentle as that of a mother soothing a worried child. "Getting bruised isn't part of the plan."

She slumped my limp, heavy body into the armchair. My heart raced faster, but I couldn't move a muscle.

"Try not to panic when you realize you're paralyzed."

A fiery blast of burning chemicals flushed through my veins. My pulse slowed and strength flowed out of my body, but I was fully alert.

"In a minute, you'll feel like you're choking. Just like Mike would have felt when blood came out of his mouth. And just like Patsy felt as I watched her take her last breath."

My head fell back. Hot tears filled my eyes. I didn't want to believe what I'd heard.

Melissa killed Patsy.

My brain told me to move, but my legs grew heavy and strength left my muscles.

Melissa leaned over me, smirking. Terror raced up my spine. She'd killed Patsy. Now she was intent on killing me. "W-why?" My coarse voice scratched against my raw throat.

My eyelids grew heavy as I gasped for air. I

willed my mouth to move, to scream for help, but my lips were rubber. Intense pressure squeezed my neck, slowly strangling me, and I was helpless to fight back.

Melissa's hot breath touched my face. "I kept waiting for you to break down again, like you did when your mother died and went crazy."

Heat rushed to my skull. Hot tears streamed down my cheeks. My mother. I wanted her with me now. I wanted the people who'd loved me the most. Annette, my dearest friend. And my sweet Patsy, her kind spirit taken from all who loved her. Melissa was the antithesis of all that was good in this world.

"After you killed Mike, I thought you might go crazy and get put away where you belong. But you always stay in control, don't you? No matter what happens, Jolene always manages to stay in control and come out on top." She let out a cackling laugh, then suddenly stopped. "Not anymore."

I tried to move. *Fingers. Toes. Arms. Legs.*

Nothing worked.

Lead weights pulled my eyelids down. Shut.

Melissa's voice echoed in my mind. *Just like Patsy when she took her last breath.* She'd killed Patsy, and now she wanted to kill me.

Everything went black.

CHAPTER THIRTY-FOUR

THE COOL, TILED floor against my cheek let me know I was lying on the kitchen floor. My head pounded and my tongue stuck to the roof of my mouth. My arms and legs were bound in what felt like a straitjacket. It didn't matter what instruction my mind gave my body—nothing moved.

I cracked open my iron-heavy eyelids and realized my body was wrapped snug inside a paint-speckled canvas sheet. The kind used at construction sites as drop-cloths. Daylight streamed through the closed slats on the blinds over the kitchen window. How long had I been unconscious? An hour? A day? Confusion fogged my thoughts.

Melissa stood at the counter next to the sink. She wore latex gloves and seemed engrossed with writing in a notebook. My notebook. The one I used for jotting lists and reminders.

Rage burned under my skin. She'd killed Patsy. If she'd been capable of murdering a woman who'd shown her nothing but kindness, then she was capable of anything. What kind of evil was she planning next? I tried to move, but whatever drug Melissa had injected in me had depleted all use of my muscles.

I scanned the room through my droopy eyelids, and then spotted an outline of someone lying on the floor near the back door. My vision slowly came into focus, and I saw it was Mrs. Nichols. Her back was to me, her legs askew and one ankle twisted. Blood pooled on the floor like a halo around her head.

The smell. It was the blood. Butcher-shop sharp with a tang which stuck in my nose hair. My stomach churned shooting a surge of reflux up my esophagus. An involuntary moan escaped my throat.

Melissa turned from her writing then fell to her knees and crawled to me, licking her lips like a rabid dog. "Good. You're awake." She rolled me onto my back. "Stupid Mrs. Nichols. The old biddy just couldn't mind her own business. She came by about twenty minutes before you did— probably intended to welcome you home. But I couldn't let her get in the way of my plan. She was at the wrong place at the wrong time. I had to kill her."

Saliva and bile trickled down my chin. I looked up at her round face framed in the cheap black wig. She held my notebook and what looked like a man's brown toiletry bag. "But Patsy… why?" I managed to whisper.

She sat back on her haunches. "Because I'd reached my breaking point. See, after Annette died, I came by to visit Patsy almost every day. Do you remember that?"

I bent my elbows and realized that, when Melissa had rolled me onto my back, the wrap had loosened, giving me room to move my arms. I spoke through my scratchy throat, "Patsy loved your visits."

She grunted. "I visited her more than you did. Did you know that? It was me. Me who sat with her while she cried and reminisced about Annette." She shook her head. "But no matter how much love I gave her, she always loved her Joley more." Her mouth tightened and her nostrils flared. "I couldn't bear it any longer. You and Patsy together like mother and daughter. You didn't deserve her."

I pressed my back flat to the ground as I inched my hands up my stomach, loosening the binding wrap even more. "But Patsy loved everyone. She loved you."

"Stop with the bullshit. Things only got better for you after she died." She grunted and rolled onto her knees. "She gave you this fucking house."

"I didn't know she was going to do that."

"I didn't know she was going to do that," Melissa mocked in a baby voice. Then her expression shifted into a nasty grin. "Your privileged life is that way. You never know what next good thing will fall in your lap. You just know something will."

Her evil had no limits. "You killed Jackson."

"Oh, aren't you the genius? Yes. I killed Jackson."

"He was your friend."

"Yes, we *were* friends. But see, here you were

again, getting it all. Inheriting Patsy's house and land, traipsing back into the neighborhood like it was a normal thing to have the good things in life handed to you on a platter."

"What did Jackson do to you?"

"He got close to you, and I didn't like it. You didn't deserve to have him. You don't deserve anyone."

"It wasn't like that—" My fingers curled and sensation was returning to my limbs.

"Shut the fuck up. Did I ask you to speak?"

Even if I could reach my arms out, my legs were still hindered by the wrap. I was as helpless as a wiggling worm on hot concrete and had no chance of getting past Melissa. I couldn't fight if I wanted to.

"Remember the night you came home after visiting Jackson? It made me sick listening to you. Even worse was listening to Jackson talk about you *ad nauseam* when he was as Ocean Joe's a couple of nights earlier. You were all he could talk about. How pretty you are, how classy you are, how smart you are. I vomited in my mouth just listening to him. I wanted to kill him that night."

Hot tears ran down my cheeks. He hadn't deserved to die.

"So, when you came back from his house on Saturday night, I saw an opportunity to kill the motherfucker and set you up as a suspect." Melissa laughed, sitting back on her butt with her legs bent. "I grounded an Ambien and put it in your wine. It didn't take long for you to plonk out. I practically had to walk you up the stairs."

That night flashed in my mind—how I'd felt so woozy and dizzy and how Melissa had teased me about drinking too much. The combination of Xanax and Ambien had been the real culprit. I groaned, the sound rumbling in my throat.

"As soon as you were in bed, I put on the sneakers you were wearing," she said. "Then I stole the keys to your Jeep and drove to Jackson's house. He was more than happy to invite me inside."

My urge to scream strained my vocal cords, but I let her talk while I worked at loosening the wrap.

"When I told Jackson I wanted to sit outside and light a fire in the firepit, he didn't complain. Once we were outside, a jab of SUX and a whack to the head with the shovel was all it took. I just dragged his ass to the shallow fire pit and covered him with leaves."

"What about the tree?"

"A stroke of genius, right? Jackson had oak saplings all around his house. I figured you'd appreciate that touch. Shiiit. I remember the expression on your face when Nancy told you she'd found Jackson with a tree on top of his buried body." She rolled her head back and laughed. "I wish I could've taken a picture."

Melissa's twisted mind held no logic, and I grasped at any hope of sympathy. "I want to change things. I didn't know what I was doing back then. I'm a different person now." My voice cracked through my raw throat.

"I don't want to hear your fucking excuses. You've never ever been my real friend. Back in the days when you were in college and married, when your life was so perfect, if I had called you in need of girlfriend support, you would have been polite, but you wouldn't have spent your time with a beach rat like me." She snorted. "Not like you did after you moved into this house after Patsy died and you had no one. After your brain hit rock bottom."

"That's not true."

"Shut up. I have a plan to make a good life for myself." A malicious grin underscored her dark eyes. "And I'm going to use your children to help me get what I want."

Blood rushed to my head and pounded, pounded, pounded. "What do my children have to do with us?"

Melissa opened the brown bag and pulled out a syringe and a vial. "Let me explain how this is going to work. Each vial is one hundred and fifty mils of SUX. It's the dose I gave you. The maximum safe dose. The reaction is immediate, and as you've experienced, it causes temporary paralysis, but keeps you alert—well, that is until you lose the ability to breath for yourself, and you pass out due to lack of oxygen to the brain."

My body floated, and this didn't feel real, like I wasn't in the room with a killer.

This isn't happening.

I gulped a breath and came back to my senses, because this *was* happening, I wouldn't dissociate. Not now.

Melissa grabbed another vial. "Two vials will kill you." She put the second vial back into the bag.

Her lips curled into a devilish grin. "It wasn't easy getting my hands on this drug, but it's amazing what risks starving medical students are willing to take for a fresh benjamin in their hand." She uncapped the needle and popped it into the vial.

"You can't actually believe you'll get away with this."

"I do. And I will. I figure Aaron will come looking for you later on when you don't show up at the hotel. That's when he'll find you." She glanced at Mrs. Nichols. "Unless Mr. Nichols gets here first. But that old man is like a koala—he sleeps ninety percent of the time." She shrugged. "Either way, I'll be long gone. But enough of all this talking. Time is of the essence here."

Melissa stuffed a cotton dishtowel in my mouth, leaving me to breathe only through my nose.

"I'll tell you exactly what's going to happen from this moment forward." She held up the spiral notebook she'd been writing in earlier. My notebook, full of notes to myself. Grocery lists, appointment times, miscellaneous notes. "I've already written your suicide note." She chuckled. "As you know, I'm an expert forger."

Suicide? I squirmed on the hard ground, my feet and elbows pushing against the too-tight wrap. No, no, no.

She snickered at my effort. "Give it up. Besides, we don't have much time, and don't you want to hear what's in your note?"

Tears filled my eyes and sinuses. How could I have missed the signs that Melissa was a monster? How could I have been so naïve?

"Good. Because it's time to get down to business." She held the notebook in front of her and read aloud.

"To Aaron, Jennifer and Eric,

I love you all very much and want you to know that my decision to leave this life had nothing to do with my love for you. I simply feel I have nothing left to give and everyone would be better off without me."

Melissa hesitated and grinned at me, then she continued in her an angel-soft voice.

"Unfortunately, Mrs. Nichols came by the house and tried to stop me. She was just in the wrong the place at the wrong time. I had no choice but to kill her. The courts were wrong to conclude I'm not a risk to society. Not only that, but I managed to fool everyone into believing I wasn't a risk to myself. I fooled them all.

"The only thing that was true for me in this world was my love for you. Unfortunately, that wasn't enough to kill the demons battling in my mind.

"Yours forever, Mommy."

Melissa stood and placed the notebook on the kitchen dining table. "Short and simple." Her voice returned to being guttural. "That's how I like to keep things."

Overwhelming strain pulled on the muscles in my chest. Hot tears ran down my face. I couldn't bear knowing my children would face the agony of such a grief at their tender ages. A parent's death by suicide would forever haunt them. Melissa wasn't only killing me but killing the happiness of my children by filling them with this lie.

Fear clambered up my spine as Melissa propped

the notebook on the kitchen table so it was visible. Using every ounce of strength, I tried to spread my legs apart by pushing against the canvas wrap. Sweat trickled down my neck.

Melissa came back to my side, standing over me with the full syringe in her hand. "I'm going to drag you to your car and give you a three-hundred-mil dose of SUX," she said. "Then, I'll start the engine and let the carbon monoxide do the rest. This time, you won't wake up."

My cries were useless against the thick towel, and my struggle only put more glee in Melissa's eyes, so I settled. I could barely get a drift of oxygen through my snot-blocked nose.

"Your life will be over, but I'll get to start on my new life." A devious grin crossed her face. "Once you're gone, I'll be in the perfect position to console Aaron and the twins."

Rage burst through my skin, and I squirmed again—harder than before, lifting my butt off the ground and loosening the wrap's grip even further. Hope surged through my veins. I had a fighting chance.

Melissa paced the floor beside me. "Oh, didn't you hear? Aaron has hired me as a nanny to the twins."

The ground dropped beneath me, and I was falling into a dark hole where all I could see was Melissa's face. I moaned into the dishtowel as hot tears blurred my eyes.

"That's right," Melissa said. "He hasn't said anything to you because we both decided it was best to wait until you got home. But… since Aaron and India are no longer together, I figured he'd need a nanny." She burst out laughing. "A friend in need is a friend, indeed."

I closed my eyes, afraid to foresee the unimaginable. *Melissa in my children's lives.*

"And since the children will inherit this house and it can't be sold or rented… well, who knows what options will open up once the twins become attached to me?"

Melissa stooped and held up the needle, like a viper ready to strike, then she rolled me to my side and stuck the needle in my hip. I winced at the pinch. The surge of heat, stinging, wavering in me until I was enveloped in warmth. My eyelids drooped and I sucked air through my stuffed nose, but oxygen wasn't reaching my brain.

My eyelids grew heavy as my body fell, helpless against the encroaching paralysis. Jennifer and Eric's newborn faces looked back at me. I felt the unbearable pain of knowing I'd never see my children again as it gripped my insides, squeezing so tight that each gasp of oxygen burned my lungs.

Melissa kicked me in the back. "I hope you die."

Searing pain ran up my spine. I wasn't ready to die, but that wasn't my choice to make.

I prayed for a quick death.

Chapter Thirty-Five

I WAS ON MY back with my eyes shut, sliding backwards across the kitchen floor. An incessant sound reverberated in my cloud-stuffed head.

Ding dong, ding dong, ding dong.

The sliding stopped and the back of my head dropped to the cold tile. I caught the clean floral scent of the Tide laundry detergent I kept on the floor next to the washing machine. Melissa had pulled me into the narrow, windowless laundry room off the kitchen which led into the garage. I tried to get more air into my lungs, but the towel in my mouth was jammed in tight.

Ding dong, ding dong, ding dong.

My heartbeat banged against my chest like it was trying to wake me from a year-long sleep. The doorbell. Someone was at the front door.

"Shit," Melissa half-whispered.

My eyes were soiled with tears and gunk, but I split them open and made out a watery image of Melissa crouching on the floor near my feet. She'd changed into the dark pants and hoodie, and her wig was askew. Her back was to me, and she looked ahead toward the kitchen. She held another full syringe in her hand.

The canvas wrap had loosened even more, but my muscles were still limp. The silence lasted minutes, and I could hear her breaths growing loud and rapid. She glanced back at me but didn't seem to notice I was awake. I didn't have to play dead, though. I could barely breathe, and my heart chugged like a clogged ketchup bottle.

My cell phone vibrated next to my head. My neck stiffened. I turned my head a micro-inch. She'd set her duffle bag and my purse on the laundry room floor. I squeezed my eyes shut, holding back tears. She'd been dragging me to the garage to carry out her plan.

My muscles tensed, but not because of the drug. This was rage. A primordial rage.

A murderous rage.

This evil woman didn't care that her plan would destroy the hearts of my children. In her demonic mind, their suffering was her opportunity.

I had to kill her. Adrenaline rushed through my veins, and I used all of my will to squirm out of the loose wrap.

Knock, knock, knock, knock.

Melissa gasped, crouching herself further to the ground.

"Jolene?" A familiar man's voice came from the outside the kitchen door, on the deck.

Melissa turned to me, and our eyes met for a tense second. We each had the same question— *who's here?*—but for different reasons.

Another knock, and then: "Jolene? You in there?"

My body twitched. *Noah.* But no. He was still

in Florida with his Catherine, right?

"Jolene!" This time the voice was more insistent.

Melissa whispered, "What the fuck is he doing here?"

If I could have answered, I'd have told her to get the fuck out of here while she still had a chance. Anything to save my own ass.

Footsteps on the deck. Was he peering through the front window? A sharp pain twisted in my chest. All I wanted was to hold my children again.

My brain sent a signal to my hands to stop convulsing. It worked. The drug was slowly wearing off, and I pressed my elbows into the wrap and loosened it enough so I could move my hands out. But I didn't want to attract Melissa's attention, so I stayed as still as a corpse.

If I moved, she'd shoot me up again. I needed to reserve every ounce of strength to fight my way out.

From her squatted position, she turned on her toes, so alert that I saw the fine hairs on the side of her face stand on end. With her ear to the kitchen, she mindlessly placed the full syringe on top of the washing machine.

A flush of adrenaline rolled through my blood as I glared at the tip of the needle sticking out over the edge of the washing machine. If I could grab a hold of the syringe and jab Melissa, I could escape.

I had to act fast, and that wasn't easy when my body felt as limp as a sock. Yet I twisted and turned my hands and elbows, willing every part of me to gain strength enough to reach up and follow-through. All I needed was one deep jab at a fleshy part of her body for this to work. Her hip would work best, but I'd settle on the muscled part of her calf or thigh.

I thought of Jennifer and Eric, and like a woman finding the strength to lift a car off her child, I knew I'd find the strength to reach up and grab the syringe. This was my one and only chance to escape. I refused to die under the terms of Melissa's suicide plan.

With my eyes barely open, I watched Melissa. She sat next to me with her back against the wall and her full attention on the kitchen windows. She was so close to me that I wouldn't need to stand to jab her. I had just enough strength to jab the needle and press the syringe. If it worked as fast on her as it had on me, she'd be paralyzed within seconds. I only had to get my arm out of the wrap. Then, I'd have enough time to unbind the wrap and get out of the house before she regained consciousness.

Nerves and uncertainty sent my pulse racing. I'd hesitated earlier when I'd had the chance to grab the fireplace poker. Not this time.

I could do it. I'd been decisive and precise when I'd had to kill Mike. What I lacked in physical strength, I made up for in focus and determination.

Knock. Knock. Knock.

Melissa pressed the back of her head against the wall. She stayed silent, but her face gleamed with sweat, and a vein throbbed on her throat.

Not a sound.

Then, I heard the clumping of heavy footsteps coming from the deck outside the kitchen door.

Melissa didn't move. All of the window blinds were down, so no one could see in.

The back doorknob jiggled.

I wanted to kick the washing machine, to make any kind of noise. I took in as much oxygen as possible through my nose and let out a hoarse cry. "Ahhhh!" My vocal chords weren't working, and my scream was barely a whimper against the dishtowel in my mouth.

Melissa shot me a death glare, then turned her attention back to the door.

I bit down on the towel. The footsteps drifted away. Noah was leaving, siphoning away all of my hope. I had no one else to rely upon but myself. Melissa was right. Aaron wouldn't find me until tonight. He and the twins would soon be at the hotel ready to meet me in our suite. But I wouldn't be there. Aaron would come by and check on me once he realized I hadn't checked into the hotel and he couldn't reach me by phone. By then, I'd be dead.

Melissa tip-toed into the kitchen to check on what was happening outside. I wiggled myself loose enough from the wrap to reach up and grab the syringe, but it fumbled from my grasp and hit the floor.

Melissa came at me. "What the fuck—"

I snatched the needle and jabbed it into her calf, pressing hard on the nozzle and praying it would work.

Melissa yelped and pulled the needle out. "You fucking bitch!" She tossed the syringe aside.

Inching backwards on my butt, I managed to roll onto my knees then half-stand.

"You're going to die!" Melissa kicked me in the stomach.

The sharp pain took my breath, and I crumbled onto the floor.

Melissa grabbed onto the countertop and looked down at me. "You can't... I won't let you." Her knees wobbled before my eyes, and then she fell to the ground, quivering.

The drug was working, I'd heard it in her cracked voice. But she crawled and clawed her way into the kitchen then collapsed on the floor. She was slowly losing control as I regained mine. But I had only minutes to act.

Using the laundry room countertop for leverage, I pulled myself up to my feet and unwrapped the canvas wrap from around my legs. The brown bag on top of the washing machine caught my eye. The bag which held the vials. The vials she'd planned to use in my murder. If I gave her a second dose right now, she'd die.

Melissa groaned, her pupils growing larger.

Tingles of excitement ran up my neck, but I focused on my breathing, on thinking clearly.

I could get out right now. Run.

Melissa writhed on the kitchen floor, drool dripping down her chin. I felt no pity. My jaw clenched, and hatred ran through my blood like a roaring river, pounding against my ears. Killing Melissa was about justice. My justice. I had the power to kill her the way she'd killed Patsy. The way she'd killed Jackson. The way she'd wanted to kill me.

I'd only jabbed her moments ago. One more dose was all she needed.

CHAPTER THIRTY-SIX

ISTARED AT THE unwrapped syringe and three remaining vials of SUX in the brown bag. A growl rumbled in my throat. An animalistic sound so deep it reverberated through my skin. Melissa was harder to kill than a city cockroach, but I would never give her the chance to take my life and children.

She had to die.

I peeled open the new syringe, popped the needle into a vial, and refilled the syringe with the killer dose. My jelly legs carried me the few short steps into the kitchen where Melissa laid on floor, convulsing and gasping for breaths. A flash of terror burst in her dark eyes. I felt no pity.

Holding onto the edge of the kitchen counter-top with one hand for balance, I bent my knees and aimed the needle at her hip.

Police sirens. Blaring louder and louder.

Turning my head, I listened as the sirens came closer.

Kill her.

The needle was only an inch from her flesh.

Don't stop.

The back door opened with a kick and Detective Warren charged into the kitchen. I tossed the needle onto the ground, and he aimed his gun at me. "Hands in the air!" His steely eyes zoned in on mine, then to the floor where Mrs. Nichols lay dead and Melissa dying.

I straightened my sore body and raised my arms, not sure if I was disappointed or relieved that I hadn't killed Melissa when I'd had the chance.

Footsteps stomped through the living room.

"They're back here!" Detective Warren yelled, "Someone call an ambulance. We have two down."

Noah bolted into the kitchen from the living room, looked around, then met my eyes. Deep lines etched his forehead. "Jolene, are you okay?"

I nodded, tears falling down my cheeks, because Noah's compassionate expression was one I hadn't seen in a long time. "Better than I probably look."

"Hey, Warren," Noah called out over his shoulder. "I'm taking the victim outside for questioning."

Detective Warren nodded at Noah, and I dropped my tired arms.

A uniformed police officer flew into the kitchen. "Ambulance is on the way—good God," he said, looking down at Mrs. Nichols in a pool of blood.

"Come on," Noah said, wrapping an arm around my shoulder. "Let's go outside."

My feet dragged and every muscle in my body screamed. "I thought you were out of town," I said.

"Let's just say it didn't go as planned. But I don't

want to talk about that right now. What's important is that you're safe." He sighed and pointed
his thumb toward Mrs. Nichols. "What happened
here?"

My heart ached. Mr. Nichols was going to be
devastated. "You'll have to ask Melissa."

"We have a hellava lot of questions for her."

"She was going to kill me... she forged a suicide note." My hand shook as I pointed to the
kitchen table.

Noah picked up the note and read, covering his
mouth and nose with his hand.

Still dizzy and weak, I stumbled to the back
door. "I need air." I made it to the deck and sat
on the top step. Shaking, I took in deep breaths.
Melissa had been planning to take over my life,
and I wouldn't have put it past her to succeed if
she'd killed me. Tears welled in my eyes. *My children. I want to see my children.*

Noah came out and handed me a glass of water.
"You look like you need this."

I gulped down every sweet drop then wiped my
mouth. "She wanted to kill me," I said, breathless
from chugging the water.

He placed his suit jacket over my shoulders and
sat next to me. "I read the note. Phew. I couldn't
have imagined Melissa was a murderer."

"What made you come by the house?"

"When I was in Florida, I found out it was
Melissa Harrington's fingerprints on the letters."
He sighed. "Things weren't going great between
Catherine and me anyway, so when I got the
news a few days ago, I decided to take the next

flight home and look into this some more."

"And Catherine?"

"She stayed on for the holiday. I'd say our marriage is over. But trust me, Jolene. Our problems have been brewing for a long time, and not because of this one case."

"Got it. So, what did you find out when you got back?"

"I learned through Detective Warren that Melissa had become a prime suspect because of story inconsistencies. They wanted to question her more but couldn't find her anywhere." He ran his fingers though his hair. "I knew you were coming home today, so I wanted to warn you about her. And I knew you were in trouble the moment I walked up the verandah and noticed all the shutters were closed.

"Mrs. Nichols didn't keep the house that way—she'd told me how she liked to keep the shutters and blinds open to let light into the house. When you didn't answer the door, my instincts kicked in and I called for back-up."

I shuddered beneath Noah's suit jacket. I'd come so close to killing Melissa. The rage still burned in my belly. "Melissa admitted to me that she set me up in Jackson's murder. She told me everything."

Noah nodded. "I wasn't sure how it all connected until you gave me the leaves. We found a clean fingerprint on one of the envelopes. It was run through IAFIS and, lo and behold, we had a bite."

"Melissa's prints were in the system?"

"Not for a crime. From a real estate salesperson application she submitted ten years ago. Standard stuff for agents to submit registered fingerprints with all applications. The fingerprints are passed onto authorities and become record."

"How did you connect this with Jackson's murder?"

"First, her aunt in Richmond? Yeah, she's been taking care of her all right. Taking care to steal her pension checks while she lay helpless and neglected in her bed."

"What?"

"A neighbor became suspicious when they noticed how Melissa wasn't around consistently, and she'd cut her aunt off from friends, claiming she was too sick for company.

"The neighbor called police, who then made a welfare check on the eighty-one-year-old disabled woman. Kelly Phillips was found locked inside an upstairs bedroom and chained to a bed. The window had been boarded shut. Melissa had left her a bed pan, some bottles of water, and a basket of non-perishable food stuffs to live on while she was away. Poor woman couldn't even call out for help because Melissa kept her drugged and helpless."

My chest seized, pulling down on my shoulders. Sweet Aunt Kelly, another victim of Melissa's cruelty. I'd felt sorry for Melissa when it had been her aunt who'd needed sympathy. "How long have you known all of this—that all this evidence and information pointed to Melissa?"

"The department investigated everyone close

to Jackson. Including Melissa. She wasn't an obvious suspect at first. First, she claimed to be at work the night you were at Jackson's house, which was backed up by her employer. You both claimed she was home around ten-thirty—which was the time you claimed to have left Jackson's house."

"Oh-kay."

"Like I said, we check every detail. Second, the receipt she'd given us from a service station outside of Richmond confirmed where she was around the time Jackson was killed. We backed it up by looking at the CCTV camera at the shop where she'd bought some snacks on her way to Richmond to see her aunt. Again, alibi confirmed."

"I'm not getting it—what made the investigators suspicious of her?"

"The hours between the time you fell asleep and the time you woke up. There are about six hours which were unaccounted for. I believed, like the medical examiner did, that Jackson was most likely killed sometime during those hours."

"Melissa… she told me she'd drugged me on that night I came home from Jackson's house. I was knocked out. That's why I never heard her leave the house." I winced at how I'd been duped into believing Melissa was my friend.

"While you were asleep, Melissa went to Jackson's house."

My chest grew heavy. Jackson had believed Melissa was a friend. "And he would have welcomed her inside with no problem. What about the oak tree? Where did—"

"Jackson had a few oak saplings growing in his backyard. Volunteers, my gardening wife calls them. You know, an acorn falls to the ground and takes root. In another year or two, there's a sapling. They're everywhere. It was most likely a last-minute thought for Melissa, but remember, it was that exact action which clued me into the belief that you didn't kill Jackson. But it was the letters you gave me which were the final clue."

"How?"

"When you gave me the letters with the leaves, I had every reason to believe something was amiss. All mail sent to patients and prisoners is reviewed by administration. Their duty is to review the origin and content of the mail. Under ordinary circumstances, the guard would have learned the return address on the letters were fake, and also questioned the intention of the leaf.

"That anomaly led me on the trail to Beth, the guard on the ward you were in. Beth buckled under pressure from police and admitted that Melissa had bribed her with a hundred dollars if she slipped the letter in. That's the moment I knew without a doubt that Melissa had killed Jackson and was framing you."

My eyes welled with tears because I'd never imagined a person could be filled with so much hate. Melissa was a master manipulator. She'd been the cat, and everyone else was a mouse. "Melissa killed Patsy, too."

"What the fuck?" Noah shook his head like a wet dog. "What are you saying?"

"Melissa told me. Patsy didn't die of heart failure, but of an overdose of SUX. And it's how she killed Jackson, too. The blow to his head was a decoy. It was the SUX which killed him. His body would have to be exhumed, but it would prove Melissa is a serial killer."

"Dear God." Noah ran his hand over his mouth. "We were having a tough enough time nailing a motive for her to kill Jackson—but Patsy? Why?"

I looked out beyond the spot where the tree once stood and stared into the beauty of the budding green forest. White and pink dogwood flowers dotted the woods like drops of spilled paint on a landscape painting. Patsy had loved the forest in spring, and because she couldn't be here, only I could be her voice. Just as she'd been my voice when I'd been left in a psych ward. "Melissa is evil. That's the reason she killed Patsy." Everything Melissa had told me about killing Patsy and Jackson spilled out. Including her vile hatred for me and her plan to take over my life.

At the end of my rant, Noah squeezed my hand and said, "You've done a great thing, Jolene. When you gave me the envelopes with leaves, you handed me the lead to Jackson's killer."

A heaviness lifted, and my body, though exhausted, felt lighter, free. This was vindication. I'd actually done something right. "But wait," I said. "What about my stalker? Melissa said she'd never stalked me, and strange as it sounds, I believe her. So, if she wasn't stalking me all these years, who was? Maybe she was in cahoots with someone else?"

Noah wrapped an arm around my shoulder. "You shouldn't believe a word she says. She's a psychopath. A liar."

Noah was right. Melissa had been lying to me almost my whole life. She had to have been the person who'd been stalking me. Who could ever really know her twisted mind?

None of that mattered anymore. Melissa would pay for her crime just like I'd paid for mine. At least I could now rebuild my life.

Chapter Thirty-Seven

Springtime, two years later

THE SUN HAD just set, and Noah threw another log into the backyard firepit. The fire crackled, and the sweet, smoky scent of pine-wood tinged my nostrils. Jennifer, Eric and our Golden Labrador, Benny, ran around playing catch on the lawn in the lingering daylight.

Noah sat back in the Adirondack chair next to me. "Another perfect day, eh?"

"I won't complain." I released a satisfied sigh as my shoulders slackened. We'd become friends, Noah and I, but nothing more. We were both too fucked up to make any promises. All that mattered was that I had never felt this content in my life. Perhaps when I'd been a child, before my mother had died, and when my future had been a bright and shiny fantasy.

I'd done things in my life I wasn't proud of, but I realized now that I was more—that people loved me regardless of my missteps, and because I brought joy and love to their lives. My children. My real friends, like Noah. I didn't spend any more time on regret. Everything that had happened had changed me for the better. I was enough.

Sometimes I still sensed the stalker nearby. A shadow or glimpse from the corner of my eye. But Melissa was in jail, and I easily brushed it off as lingering paranoia.

I still visited Katie from time to time. She'd explained how the dissociative episodes were provoked by trauma to protect myself. A defense mechanism. I had always thought the OCD had made me crazy. But no. I only had a mild case which could be managed with medication. My thinking had always been clear.

The obsessive thinking, the unwanted thoughts, the rituals which I'd believed warded off bad luck... all of that was normal for my condition.

Normal. Ephemeral. I'd never been crazy or insane to begin with.

Melissa, on the other hand, was a full-blown psychopath. An expert at manipulation and murder. She could easily adapt her personality to her needs at any moment to get exactly what she wanted.

If I hadn't been so desperate to be accepted, I would have figured out Melissa was my terrorizer. But I wouldn't waste my time ruminating over what-ifs. She'd been given a forty-year sentence for my attempted murder and two life-time sentences for the murders of Patsy and Jackson. She would rot in jail.

It had taken me a long time to learn that I'd been my own worst enemy. In my youth, I hadn't trusted my gut instincts. I'd looked to others for approval and validation. I'd wasted so much time not trusting myself to make good decisions. I could have lived a more authentic life if I hadn't been afraid to chase away my fears. Letting go of that need had given me the new life I'd always craved. Finally, I loved myself, too.

Noah pulled me close. "I have something for you." He handed me a brown envelope.

A log sizzled and popped in the firepit as I opened the envelope. Inside was a handful of dry oak leaves. My pulse quickened. "What's this about?"

"When I turned in the envelopes and waxed paper for fingerprints, I didn't include the leaves."

"Why not?"

"A voice inside told me to keep them. I didn't know why at the time. But I kept them." He took the envelope from me, pulled out the leaves, and placed the dry foliage in my hands. "I want you to burn these. Watch the last of that tree burn to ash. Disappear forever."

No emotion hit me—just a readiness to get rid of the leaves. Without ceremony, I stood and dropped the leaves into the fire. A whirl of smoke rose as I watched the leaves shrivel to ash.

Noah rested his arm around my shoulder. "Everything to do with that tree is now gone."

"No. That's not true. We can burn the leaves, but some things in this world refuse to die."

"What are you talking about?"

I took his hand. "Come with me. I want to show you something." I led him to the slump in the earth where the tree had been removed.

A green shoot sprouted from the ground like an arm reaching for the sky.

Noah's mouth gaped, and then he turned to me. "What the fuck is that?"

"When the forensics team removed Mike's body, they left the taproot untouched and refilled the hole with the soil they'd dug out. The taproot is the lifeblood of a tree. It will fight for survival."

He stared at the ground for a moment. "What are you going to do with it?"

Inhaling a deep breath, I let the warmth of satisfaction roll through me. Patsy had entrusted me to care for everything she'd loved about this property. "Let it grow," I finally answered.

I'd honored her wish because the family tree lived on.

EPILOGUE

July, thirty-four years later

IRELAXED MY OLD bones on a bench in the shade of the fifty-foot-high family tree. The cicadas in the forest rattled and hissed while I watched my grandsons take turns on the swing hanging from one of the tree's sturdy branches.

Several years earlier, a loophole had been found in Patsy's will, and I'd sold most of the twenty-five acres. I'd kept the two acres the house was on, and a quarter-acre-deep of forest surrounding the house so that I'd have plenty of privacy from the over-populated neighborhood. Sitting in the backyard, I could be proud that I'd kept Patsy's wish and lived in this house with my own family.

At the edge of the forest, I saw the shadow. I smiled at my friend. The darkness didn't come too close to me anymore, and the visits had become fewer and fewer over the years. When I did have a sighting, like now, it was away at a distance, watching me for a moment. Never for long.

Psychologists had explained how the hallucination had been imprinted on my mind. When I'd seen Melissa run across the lawn on that fateful night, I'd poured all my guilt, remorse, regret, pain, and anxiety into that image. The dark impression had become a stain on my brain.

After all the years which had passed, I still lived with the stalker—a remnant of the dark energy that had once kept me in a chokehold.

The image had embedded deep in my memory. So deep that it had become real. A shadow I'd now accepted. I had to; it always followed me. But now I could face the darkness, and the darkness would turn away.

Looking up to the blue sky, I saw everything clear now. Crystal clear.

Then, I narrowed my vision, blurred it all together. The top of the tree and the blue sky with clouds.

Children did this. Blurred their own vision. Crossed their eyes and skewed the world. It separated one from the present. It had taken a long time for me to admit that, after I killed and buried Mike, I'd skewed my own vision. For years, I'd wavered between the hazy, cross-eyed world of forgetting, and the absolute present. The two forces in constant opposition.

Laughter from my grandsons broke my introspection. My focus returned, and I looked ahead. The shadow was still at the tree line, but when I smiled, it turned and disappeared into the forest.

Gone.

At least for now.

DEAR READER,
Thank you so much for taking the time to read my debut thriller, The Family Tree: a psychological thriller. I can't express how much it means to me. This story was inspired by a recurring dream which triggered a question—what if I killed someone to save my life, panicked, and hid the body, could I live with the secret? Unlikely. But Jolene is a different person, and I do hope you enjoyed her story.

Reviews are like gold for authors. May I kindly ask you to leave a review on Amazon, Goodreads, or wherever you hang out socially? Your support is greatly appreciated.

Peace and love,

Sheila Koerner Grice

About the Author

S.K. Grice, aka Sheila Koerner Grice, is an American author living in Australia with her husband, daughter, three demanding dogs, and a backyard full of noisy birds and frogs.

When she's not in her writing cave or reading a book, she likes to spend time in nature and with family and friends laughing, drinking good wine, and being goofy.

Contact S.K. Grice

S.K. Grice loves to hear from readers. You may contact her at *skgrice@outlook.com*
To receive a FREE short story prequel of The Family Tree: a psychological thriller and news of her upcoming books, visit her website and join her Thriller Reader Group.
Website: *www.skgrice.com*
Follow S.K. Grice on social media

skgricebooks

sheila_grice
To learn more about the contemporary romance novels by Sheila Grice visit *www.sheilagrice.com*